MORE PRAISE FOR JUDITH E. FRENCH!

THE BARBARIAN

"Combining strong, fully developed characters, colorful descriptive locales, and a beautifully haunting romance, *The Barbarian* is a must-read."

—*The Midwest Book Review*

"*The Barbarian* is an exhilarating ride through the deserts of Egypt as a woman and a man fight for all they believe in against the might of a king."

—A Romance Review

"This sequel to *The Conqueror* is packed full of vivid historical details that will transport the reader back to mystical Egypt. A great read!"

—The Best Reviews

THE CONQUEROR

"Historical fiction fans will have a feast!"

—*Romantic Times*

"Judith E. French has skillfully crafted not only a top-notch romance but an excellent work of historical fiction."

—A Romance Review

"Don't miss *The Conqueror*."

—*Romance Reviews Today*

"Extremely compelling…[this book is] a difficult one to put down."

—LikesBooks.com

"*The Conqueror* is a strong historical tale…action packed."

—*The Midwest Book Review*

MIDNIGHT RAIN

"I heard it again—I mean I saw someone. Outside. In the rain, under the big oak. He was whistling. I thought…"

"It was me?" He gave a snort of amusement as he stripped off his wet denim jacket. His black Jimmy Buffet T-shirt was as soaked as his jeans. "Do you mind?" He motioned to his shirt. "Emma will kill me if I leave a trail of water from here to the laundry room."

It wasn't the first time she'd seen Daniel without a shirt, but tonight his hard-muscled chest and the thin scar that ran from one nipple down across his ribs seemed more ominous. "No." Bailey tried to make a joke of it as she attempted to slide the pepper spray into her pocket without being seen.

She failed.

"Were you planning to use that on me?"

Other books by Judith E. French:

THE WARRIOR
AT RISK
THE BARBARIAN
THE CONQUEROR

BLOOD KIN

JUDITH E. FRENCH

LOVE SPELL   NEW YORK CITY

*For Sorcha Gobnait Ni Scanaill,
with all my love.* Erin go braugh!

LOVE SPELL®

September 2006

Published by

Dorchester Publishing Co., Inc.
200 Madison Avenue
New York, NY 10016

ISBN 0-505-52685-9

The name "Love Spell" and its logo are trademarks of Dorchester
Publishing Co., Inc.

Printed in the United States of America.

Visit us on the web at www.dorchesterpub.com.

BLOOD KIN

PROLOGUE

Tawes Island, Valentine's Day

Frowning at the slash of orange that had caught his attention, Daniel eased off the marshy bank and out onto the surface of the frozen gut. Ice splintered ominously under his right boot, and he swore. The water here was at least chest-deep, with a good yard or two of black silt beneath—not a spot he wanted to claw his way out of in twenty-degree weather with a fifteen-knot wind. The Chesapeake Bay country was beautiful, but it could kill a man if he wasn't careful.

Like the senator . . . ?

Senator Joseph Marshall's disappearance while duck hunting on New Year's Day had launched a three-week rescue attempt that had drawn worldwide media attention. The coast guard, volunteer fire companies, and the national guard from three states had unsuccessfully searched the bay and every square inch of shoreline of the island and neighboring mainland, to no avail.

Daniel took another step toward the flash of color beneath the ice. Nausea rose in his throat. He exhaled slowly through clenched teeth and swallowed. Joseph Marshall's face was pressed grotesquely against the underside of two inches of ice. Those shrewd blue eyes were open wide; his mouth gaped in a silent scream. The thick, dark hair he'd worn so fashionably cut and styled streamed out on both sides of flaccid, fish-belly-white cheeks and a ragged protruding tongue.

Daniel let his gaze travel down the senator's submerged body. His guess was that Joe Marshall's political ambitions had been cut short by a single blast from a twelve-gauge shotgun.

Some might call it island justice.

CHAPTER ONE

June

Bailey clutched at the side of the boat and watched as the dark line on the horizon grew to a vivid patchwork of green and brown. "Is that Tawes?" She raised her voice to be heard above the *chug-chug-chug* of the smoking motor.

"That's her." The only other occupant of the shabby wooden skiff squinted into the sunshine from the shelter of a worn baseball cap, tucked a dab of snuff under his lip, and nodded. "Tawes Island. No other."

The stubble-chinned skipper's reply came out as "Nother," but Bailey was beginning to understand his quaint speech patterns. He'd identified himself as "Cap'n Creed Somers, but Creed'll do," back at the Crisfield Dock where she'd left her car.

"Not what she was," the garrulous waterman continued. "Ursters and cray'abs about played out. Not like the old days, when my daddy could make a decent living fer his family. You shoulda seen Tawes then. Real

3

ferryboat run ever' day but the Sabbath, hauling groceries, tray'ctor parts . . ."

Bailey nodded noncommittally as Creed rattled on,
his words nearly drowned by the slap of waves and
the chug of the noisy motor. She thought she'd
smelled alcohol on Creed's breath and never would
have boarded his boat if she'd known that she'd be the
only passenger. The trip from Crisfield had taken the
better part of an hour, but the aging skiff, which had
seemed disreputable back at the dock, had per-
formed faultlessly.

Being out on the water was a novelty for Bailey, and
she'd been captivated by the feel of the salt breeze on
her face and the haunting cries of laughing gulls. Of all
she'd expected to do on summer break, spending a
few days on an isolated island in the Chesapeake was
definitely at the bottom of the list; but now that Tawes
was a reality and not just a name on the evening news,
she felt her excitement rising.

Was it possible that she had been born and put up
for adoption here on this tiny island? After years of intense curiosity about her birth family, receiving the letter from Attorney Forest McCready informing her of an
inheritance seemed like the plot of a made-for-TV
movie. Was it going to be this easy to find the answers
she'd been seeking all her life? And how had Mc-
Cready located her if her adoption records were
sealed?

Bailey hoped this wouldn't prove a case of mistaken
identity. She wasn't getting her hopes up. If the house
this unknown great-aunt had supposedly left her was a
falling-down shack in a disreputable part of town,
she'd simply refuse the bequest, have a good laugh,
and go home with a great story to tell Elliott.

"I expect you heard about the excitement here last February," Creed said, breaking into her thoughts. "That hunting accident? The senator that got shot?"

Bailey nodded. "Yes. I did. On the evening news. And the papers." How could she not have seen it? When the senior senator from Maryland and the chair of House Appropriations went missing for weeks and then turned up riddled with bullet holes, the media had a field day. "A real tragedy," she said. "Senator Marshall was a native of Tawes, wasn't he?"

"Born and bred. Knew old Joe pretty well, I did. Should know him. He's a second cousin on my mama's side. Course, that was long afore he went off to Harvard and made himself a big name in politics." Creed spit over the side of the boat. "Ain't buried here, though. Missus had what was left of him cremated. Set him on her chimney mantel in a fancy jar, I suppose."

"I'm sorry," she said. "For your loss."

Creed shrugged. "No need. Joe and me wasn't what you'd call friends. Like they say, you can't pick your kin."

"No, I suppose not." A buoy bobbed just ahead. Two gulls balanced on the top while a third circled overhead.

"Never voted for him." Creed slowed the boat to half speed. "Don't want to throw up a wake coming into the docks."

Bailey turned her attention to the houses, docks, and boats directly ahead of them. The picturesque harbor looked like a painted scene on a calendar, too pretty to be real. She wished she'd thought to bring her camera. If she'd gotten some good shots, she could have had them blown up and framed to give Elliott for Christmas. The white walls in his Rehoboth Beach apartment were in desperate need of something besides the faded Parrothead poster and the menu of the nearest Chinese takeout restaurant.

"Pretty, ain't she?" Creed asked. "Gives me the chills ever' time I come in."

Two little boys crabbing off the first dock looked up and waved.

Creed waved back. "Make sure them jimmies is legal size!" he shouted. "Don't want the law on you."

The smallest child, a freckled redhead, reached into a bushel basket and held up a huge wiggling blue claw. "Got half a basket already, Cap'n Creed!"

Creed grinned and touched the bill of his cap in mock salute. "Time was only poor folks bothered with hard crabs," he said. "Soft crabs, now, there's a different story. Finest eatin' to be had. Dust your crab in flour, fry it up golden brown . . ." He rubbed his thumb and forefinger together. "Add some salt and pepper, a little 'mater and lettuce if you got it, and slap it between two pieces of homemade bread."

"Oh, look," Bailey exclaimed. A brown duck paddled out from under a dock with a string of fuzzy yellow and brown babies in her wake. "There must be a dozen of them."

"Hey!" A barefoot girl in denim cutoffs and a green John Deere T-shirt lowered her net and waved from the shallows.

"Hey, yourself, Maggie!" Creed replied.

She laughed, revealing a missing front tooth. Water dripped from her net, and Bailey could see a mass of wiggling creatures inside.

"Grass shrimp," Creed said. "Maggie's planning on going fishing."

Bailey glanced around for an adult but saw no one except a man unloading crab pots from a boat a few hundred feet away. "Those children really should be wearing life vests," she said. "This water looks deep."

"Deep enough," Creed agreed, "but they're island young'uns. Swim afore they can walk, most of'm. They look out for one another." He cut his engine and let the boat drift slowly against a weathered post. "This is it, far as I can take you."

Pigtails flying behind her, Maggie ran out on the dock to catch Creed's bowline, pulled it taut, and wrapped it around a cleat.

"Obliged," the skipper said. "Tell your mama I said thanks for that mess of green beans she sent over." He set Bailey's overnight bag on the dock. "Be a good girl and show the lady where Miss Emma's house is."

"That's her, ain't it?" The laughing innocence vanished, replaced by a hostile wariness.

"Mind your manners," Creed admonished. "Ma'am, she'll show you to the boardinghouse." He stepped up onto the dock and offered Bailey a calloused hand. "I usually make a run two, three times a week to Crisfield, but if you need a ride sooner, get Miss Emma to let me know."

Bailey thanked him and smiled at the frowning child. "I'm Miss Bailey Elliott. I'm pleased to meet you, Maggie."

Silence.

Bailey tried again. Nine years of teaching fourth grade had taught her how to break the ice with shy children. "Are you having fun on your summer vacation?"

Maggie spun and retreated down the dock. Bailey glanced over her shoulder at Creed, but his back was to them, so she picked up her case and followed her reluctant guide. Maggie trotted down three steps to a grassy path between two crumbling frame structures with boarded-up windows. Behind the buildings, a wider path led across an open lot to a narrow oyster-shell street lined with trees and modest Victorian-style homes. Clapboard two-storied farmhouses with wide porches, white picket fences, and yards bursting with flowers, small garden plots, and grapevine trellises added to the picturesque charm and atmosphere of the village.

Bailey stopped and stared in astonishment at a brown-and-white Shetland pony and yellow, two-wheeled cart standing in front of a tiny brick house with a steep roof and smoke drifting from a wide chimney. Horse-drawn wagons? Was this a town or a movie set?

In her brief telephone conversation with Attorney McCready, he'd warned her that Tawes had no automobiles, no hotels, restaurants, not even a police force, but what that meant really hadn't sunk in. How was it possible that such isolation existed so close to Baltimore, Washington, and the increasingly populated Eastern Shore? "Do people really use horses to get around on the island?" Bailey asked.

Maggie pouted and marched on. A flop-eared hound, tail wagging, materialized from a boxwood hedge and barked at them.

A front door opened and a shrill voice called, "Belle! Come back here!" Obediently, the dog turned back toward the house. Bailey smiled and waved, but the gray-haired woman in the flowered housedress and apron only stared, folded her arms over her ample bosom, and slammed the door.

"You must not have a lot of tourists here," Bailey said.

Maggie kept walking without saying a word.

The yards grew wider, and the simple homes gave way to more substantial ones of brick. One eighteenth-century house with shutters, a sweeping lawn, and massive oak trees was surrounded by a wrought-iron fence. A small bronze nameplate on the gate read, FOREST MCCREADY, ESQUIRE. The only sign of life was a boy cutting the side lawn with an old-fashioned push mower.

Bailey glanced curiously at the elegant stone steps and white pillared porch. She was tempted to go up and knock at the door, but her appointment with the lawyer wasn't until three o'clock. He might be with another client or still at lunch, and besides, she really needed to freshen up after her boat ride. She didn't want to appear rude by arriving an hour and a half early.

The thought of lunch made her realize how empty she felt. She hadn't had anything to eat since she'd grabbed a cup of coffee and a muffin at the Wawa in Dover, and she was starving. "I've come to see Mr. McCready," she said. Maggie might have been deaf for all the reaction she offered.

They passed several more homes that could easily have been on the National Register of Historic Places, one that had obviously been uninhabited for years. Another, a Greek Revival, had a large sailboat on blocks in the backyard.

The street meandered along the shoreline so that the homes on Bailey's right now faced the water. A wide side street opened on the left, but the houses along that way were smaller, less imposing, and set back from the road. They hurried past a lovely old red-brick church and enclosed cemetery, another row of frame houses, and a grove of cedars that ran down to the beach. The street forked, with one branch narrowing and spanning a wooden bridge over a creek on her left, while the main thoroughfare continued on past a hard-packed dirt parking lot and a square two-story brick building with a weathered sign that proclaimed:

> *Dori's Market*
> *Groceries, kerosene, tobacco and feed*
> *Fishing tackle, jeans, boat parts, and seed*
> *Bait, crab nets, shells, and whatever you need!*
> *Authorized John Deere dealer*
> *And if you bellyache my price is too high,*
> *Do your dealing in Crisfield, like my brother Ty!*

Two middle-aged men in worn ball caps stood on the wide concrete stoop outside the general store. Both turned to stare pointedly and whisper to each other before touching the bills of their hats and hurrying inside. Bailey felt her cheeks grow warm. She could have sworn they were talking about her. This odd behavior was making her uncomfortable, and she wondered if she should have insisted Elliott come along with her. Even if she had been born here, she didn't know a soul on the island, and they certainly couldn't all know why she was here. Could they?

"Bailey Elliott?" The screen door opened and a stocky woman stepped out. Her graying hair was twisted into a no-nonsense bun, and she wore a gingham apron over a blue checked housedress and knee-high rubber boots. "God a'mighty, Creed's getting slower and slower. I expected you here for dinner, girl!"

"That's Miss Emma," Maggie said before dashing back the way they'd come.

"Emma Parks?" Bailey asked. "Yes, yes, I'm Bailey Elliott."

"About time you got here." Emma's doughy face was

lined and weathered, her whiskey voice as husky as a man's, but Bailey was instantly charmed by the older woman's warm smile and the mischievous sparkle in her guileless blue eyes. "Need help with your suitcase?" Emma shifted a bulging grocery bag from one arm to the other and extended her free hand. "I'll be glad to carry it for—"

"No. No." Bailey laughed. "I'm fine. Do we have far to—"

"Just down a piece." She hurried down the steps, wiped her hand on her apron, and offered it. "Pleased to make your acquaintance, Bailey."

She murmured something in reply as Emma's calloused hand closed on hers in a visegrip.

"I hope you're hungry. I've got fried chicken, biscuits, green beans, and red potatoes keeping warm on the back of the stove. And a fresh-baked blueberry pie. I didn't make it, mind you. I'm not the pie baker my mama is—Mama does all the baking—but I'm not a bad cook. Not a soul on Tawes can match my crab cakes, but my pie crust . . ." Emma shook her head. "Not fit for pigs. I hope you like fried chicken."

"I love chicken," Bailey assured her. "But I didn't expect you to serve me lunch. I thought . . ." She glanced at the store. "Perhaps the grocery has sandwiches."

"Nonsense. Can't have it said my guests go hungry. Mary Wright opened a bed-and-breakfast two years back, but she never did get any guests. Mary can't cook worth a darn. Not that I get many myself. Just you and Daniel this month, and you can't count Daniel as a regular paying guest." Emma chuckled heartily as she led the way down the unpaved street, past a young man painting a boat and a fenced pasture where a boy and a black-and-white dog herded a flock of sheep toward a red barn that seemed like the backdrop in a Norman Rockwell illustration.

"Daniel's doing some carpentry work for me in trade for his lodging until he gets his cabin finished," Emma continued. "He's got property out on the point, his mama's family's old farm. Daniel's a Catlin, but his mother was born a Tilghman. The old Tilghman homeplace burned years back. Hit by lightning. All gone but the original summer kitchen. That was brick. It would have gone too, but the rain put the fire out before it got that far."

Bailey switched her overnight bag to her other shoulder and hurried to keep up with Emma's determined stride.

"Daniel cleared the site and built over the old half cellar, adding three new rooms and a porch to the old kitchen," Emma said. "Pretty as you ever seen. Daniel's a real craftsman." She stopped to wait for Bailey to catch up. "Pay no attention to these nasty boots. I was tending crabs in my shedding house. I sell soft-shells on the side. Anyway, the time got away from me, like it does, and I just headed down to Doris's for bread crumbs. I wanted to make crab cakes for supper. You like crab cakes?"

Bailey nodded. "I like almost anything but sushi. I prefer my seafood cooked."

"So do I, girl. So do I. I hear sushi's all the fashion in Baltimore."

The way Emma said it, it sounded like *Balt-mer*, and it was all Bailey could do to suppress a giggle.

"Not on Tawes. Course, most islanders love raw oysters and clams, but with all the pollution in the bay, they're not safe to eat anymore. Why take the chance, I say."

Emma stopped for breath. "That's it." She pointed to a white two-story house with blue shutters and a wraparound porch. A painted sign on a lamppost read simply, MISS EMMA'S B AND B. "I thought 'B and B' sounded better than 'boardinghouse,' more welcoming, but nobody's ever called it anything but Emma's Boardinghouse, so . . ."

"I'm surprised that there isn't more commercial development," Bailey said. "You're so close to the metropolitan areas."

"Oh, people get offers. But money isn't everything. Folks that do sell generally sell to other islanders. We like things the way they are." Emma motioned to the wide front door with the etched-glass panes and the pretty grapevine wreath. "Go right on in. Make yourself at home. I'm going around to the back door and get rid of these muddy boots before I track up my clean floors."

"Thank you," Bailey managed before Emma chattered on.

"If you want to freshen up before you sit down to the table, there's a private bath off your room. Upstairs. The Robin's Nest. I like to name all my rooms. Can't miss it. Down the hall. Last room on the right."

Emma was still talking when Bailey pushed open the front door and stepped into the foyer. The interior of the house was cool, bright, and spotless, with gleaming antique furniture, starched white curtains, and a faint scent of cinnamon and nutmeg. She stood still and listened, soaking in the peaceful atmosphere. For a moment there was no sound but the faint tick of a mantel clock.

"Ouch! Son of a . . ." A male voice broke the silence. "Damn it to hell!"

Bailey looked into the living room. Beyond, in the

connecting archway, a lean figure stood on the fourth step of a ladder.

"Don't laugh," he said. "It hurts." He shook one hand in the air. "Fetch me that bag of finishing nails, will you? On the floor there, beside the drill." The voice was deep, clear, and slightly tinged with the island flavor.

Amused, Bailey set down her overnight case and crossed the living room. She couldn't tell whether the carpenter was young or old, but from the way his long legs filled the worn blue jeans and his shoulders stretched against the green plaid shirt, she assumed he hadn't reached his dotage. The workman's hair, clean, and dark brown with a slight curl, was snugged back into a short ponytail and secured with a rough leather tie.

"Do you mind passing me the nails?" he asked impatiently. "Before I bleed to death?"

"Not at all." Bailey picked up the small paper bag of nails and handed them to him.

"I just have the . . ." He glanced down. Dark brows, straight nose, nice chin, in the tanned face of an outdoorsman. For a split second, surprise registered in his dark eyes, and then white, even teeth flashed, the charm in that boyish grin making his face intriguing. "Ouch again. You must be Miss Emma's guest, the one with the name like the drink." He took the nails, removed three, and handed the bag back before tucking two between his lips.

Turning back to his project, he hammered two nails expertly into the section of trim, and then descended the ladder. Blood stained his left index finger and the palm and wrist of his left hand. "Pardon me, Ms. Bailey," he said, cupping the offending digit. "But if I drip blood on Miss Emma's Aubusson carpet, there'll be hell to pay."

"Daniel Catlin!" Emma appeared at the far end of the dining room. "What kind of talk is that? I'll thank you to keep a decent tongue in your head in front of my guests."

"Yes, ma'am." Daniel glanced back at Bailey. "I think I've been put in my place. Excuse me."

She chuckled. "It's all right. I hear worse in my classroom every day."

"Is that blood?" Emma demanded. She snatched off her apron and wrapped it around Daniel's hand. "How did you do that? Never mind. Come into the kitchen. It needs peroxide and a Band-Aid. Let me see. Stop your fussing. You'd think you'd cut the thing off." She looked at Bailey. "Please come and have your dinner. This won't take a minute."

"I'd like to take my bag upstairs first," Bailey said. "And I really should call my . . . my friend—to let him know I've arrived safely. I promised him I would."

"Have you got a cell?" Emma asked. "You do? Well, good luck, girl. Our reception on Tawes is terrible. No towers nearby."

"Oh," Bailey said. "Is there a house phone I could—"

"Sorry. That's out too. Happens all the time."

Promptly at three, Bailey stood on Forest McCready's front porch and rang the bell for the third time. There was no answer, no sound from within, and no sign that anyone was in the house. Frustrated, she pulled the attorney's latest letter from her purse and read it for the fourth time today. She wasn't mistaken about the time or the date. What could be wrong?

What could go right? As Emma had predicted, she hadn't been able to get a signal on her cell. Not at the B and B, not on the street, and not here at the lawyer's office. The same message kept popping up: NO SIGNAL. She'd had a few minutes to spare, so she'd stopped at Dori's Market and asked to use a pay phone.

"Sorry, can't help you, miss," the clerk had said. "Phone's out. Haven't had a dial tone since last night."

Despite Emma's warning, Bailey was surprised that her cell wouldn't work. She'd never had problems with the service before, not even when she was on vacation at a friend's in Nags Head last summer. With a sigh, she tucked the phone back into her bag and tried the doorbell again.

"You looking for the squire, lady?"

Bailey turned to see the burly teenager who been cutting the grass earlier standing at the foot of the porch steps, a large pair of hedge clippers in his hand. "I have an appointment with Attorney Forest McCready."

"Squire McCready's not to home." The boy gestured toward the bay. "He's likely in Annapolis today. Or Baltmer."

"But I had a three o'clock—"

"You must be wrong about the day. He's not here. Miss Maude cooks for him, and she went to Crisfield on the mailboat this morning. If Miss Maude's not here, the squire ain't either."

CHAPTER TWO

"But I had an appointment. . . ." Bailey took a deep breath and lowered her voice. "I'm sorry; this isn't your fault. I'm certain it's just a mix-up in the dates."

"Must be. *Gone Fishin*'s not in the squire's slip." The boy pointed toward the back of the house. "No way off here but by water."

"I'll just leave Mr. McCready a note confirming that I was here at three." She fumbled in her purse. "If you do see him, please tell him that he can reach me at Emma's B and B."

He flushed and stared at his shoes. "No need for that, ma'am. No place else you could be staying." He tugged the brim of his ball cap and returned to his hedge clipping.

Bailey wedged the folded message in the outer door and retraced her path down the front walk. Halfway to the street she hesitated, experiencing the oddest sensation that someone was watching her. Turning back, she studied the draped windows. There was no sign of the young man she'd spoken with and nothing unusual about the house, so why was she feeling a prickling sensation at the nape of her neck? She shivered, suddenly cold, despite the warmth of the afternoon.

She glanced around, seeing no one, not the slightest movement on the street or from the adjoining yards or homes, other than a slight stirring of leaves on the massive oak trees and the flutter of a blue jay's wings as the bird landed on a nearby branch.

Her imagination was getting the best of her. What she needed was a good run. Ever since she was a child, whenever she'd been stressed, running had calmed her. She glanced down ruefully at her bone-colored Italian heels and her straight linen skirt, neither conducive to jogging. Maybe a walk through Tawes would ease some of her annoyance at being stood up by the estate attorney.

Twenty minutes later, although the day was a near perfect one, and the homes, outbuildings, and oyster-shell streets exuded a nineteenth-century charm that would have been the highlight of any house-and-garden tour, her mood hadn't lightened one iota.

She'd seen very few of the residents as she explored the town, but she had passed a middle-aged woman hanging clothes in a backyard, a man planting annuals around his front steps, and a teenage girl on horseback. All of them had reacted as though she were a hooded leper carrying the black plague. The housewife had abruptly picked up her half-full basket of wet laundry and hurried into her house. The gardener had answered Bailey's cheery "Good afternoon!" with an aggrieved grunt, and the rider had glared at her suspiciously, kicked her palomino in the ribs, and galloped away down the center of the street without uttering a word.

"This must be a movie set," Bailey muttered as she approached the old church and surrounding cemetery from a side street. "Either that or this town is a treatment center for the socially challenged."

A wrought-iron gate stood open, and Bailey couldn't resist having a look around. Inside the churchyard, she noticed many raised brick graves and headstones dating to the eighteenth century. Drawn by her fascination with the past, she wandered along the worn oyster-shell path, examining the names and dates until she came to a section sheltered by a gnarled cedar tree.

All of the graves in this area bore the surname Tawes, and one—obviously a recent burial—was adorned with a container of honeysuckle and wildflowers. The polished marble headstone was etched with the silhouette of a running horse and the legend ELIZABETH TAWES SOMERS, BELOVED DAUGHTER, WIFE, AND SISTER.

Certain that this must be the great-aunt who'd remembered her in her will, Bailey paused to run her fingertips over the name on the face of the memorial. Elizabeth Somers had been only sixty-three at the time she died on March 16 of this year. Not old at all. Sixty-three was far too young. So much for Bailey's conjecture about a white-haired old lady in her dotage. Maybe the house she'd been left wasn't the Munster family's summer cottage, after all.

Close by, deeper in the shadows of the cedar, lay another grave covered with thick green moss and decorated with a similar floral bouquet. Bailey's throat tightened as she leaned to examine the inscription etched into the stone: ELIZABETH "BETH" TAWES, GONE BUT NOT FORGOTTEN.

Lichen grew over the dates, and Bailey scraped it

carefully away. Sixteen years. This Beth had lived only sixteen years, and she had died on . . .

Suddenly light-headed, Bailey snatched her hand away from the cold marble. Her birthday. It couldn't be a coincidence, could it? Was this young Beth her birth mother? Had she spent a lifetime steeling herself to confront a teenager who was already dead?

"Tragic, isn't it?"

Startled by the voice behind her, Bailey turned to face a tall, horse-faced woman dressed in an immaculate beige suit and pearls. "I . . . I didn't . . ."

"Did I give you a fright?" She smiled, revealing too-white teeth. "I'm so sorry."

Bailey's heartbeat slowed to near normal. "No, really. I was just looking at . . . The gate was open."

"There's no need to apologize. The church and cemetery are always open. I'm Grace Catlin, the pastor's wife." She extended a plump, manicured hand. "And you must be Miss Bailey Elliott?"

"Yes, I am. But we've never met. How did you—"

Grace chuckled primly. "Tawes is a very small island, my dear. Everyone knows everyone else's business."

Bailey returned the smile. "So I'm beginning to learn." She enfolded Grace's thick fingers in her own. The woman's handshake was quick, cool, and practiced. As a minister's wife Grace Catlin likely had a great deal of experience in greeting parishioners at endless church functions. "Although I must admit, the island doesn't feel particularly friendly," Bailey said. "I was beginning to think that I'd forgotten to wear my deodorant."

"Yes. Well . . . no." Grace gave a small sniff. "You must excuse them, my dear. Tawes sees few mainlanders.

20

For the most part, our parishioners are suspicious of strangers."

"I can believe it. But I won't be here long. I came to—"

"To see Mr. McCready about your inheritance, I suppose. Poor Elizabeth caused something of a scandal, her leaving her earthly goods to a mainlander." Grace brushed an invisible speck from the front of her suit jacket. "Afraid you'll sell the property to developers. No one wants to see Tawes become another St. Michaels. All Washington weekenders and million-dollar sailboats."

"I didn't come here to cause anyone problems." Bailey brushed the dirt off her hands.

"Of course you didn't. We're really quite endearing, once you come to know us." She smiled again. "Old-fashioned. Salt of the earth, as the saying goes. I was born here, you know. My family was one of the first to settle in the colony. Several noted Revolutionary War heroes. Are you interested in the island's history?"

"Yes." Bailey picked up her purse from the grass. "My fourth-grade classes are doing a unit on colonial history this fall."

"Then you must come over to the parsonage and meet my husband, Matthew. The reverend is our local historian. He knows simply everything about the history of Tawes, and he always keeps a fresh pot of coffee brewing."

"That's kind of you, but—"

"Nonsense. Matthew will be so disappointed if you rush off without coffee and a slice of my famous apple cake. Please come. It will make his day, really."

Bailey hesitated. The offer of coffee sounded good, but she wasn't certain she wanted to make small talk

with the minister and his wife. Grace might be friend-
lier than the other islanders, but she seemed rather eccentric. Bailey guessed Grace to be in her mid-fifties,
but her speech and mannerisms made her appear a
generation older. And for all her pretense of gentility,
Grace's speech was stilted, her carefully coiffured hair
a little too dark, and her rouged cheeks a little too pink
to be natural. "I'm certain Pastor Catlin must—"

"Please. It's so seldom we have guests. You'll never
have a better opportunity to learn firsthand about the
island's history."

Against her better judgment, Bailey allowed Grace
to usher her into the two-story brick Federal-style
house on the far side of the cemetery.

"Matthew! We have company," Grace called as they
entered the cluttered foyer.

Somewhere in the rear of the house a dog barked.
Piles of books were stacked six deep on the bottom
steps of the staircase and on the seat of a spindle-back
chair that stood next to a marble-topped Victorian
table. "Excuse the mess, dear." Grace stooped to pick up
a squeaky dog toy shaped like a rolled-up newspaper.

Bailey hesitated. "You have a dog?" She knew it was
silly, but dogs always made her uneasy.

"Just a tiny one. And he's as sweet as can be." She
waved her hand toward the hall and adjoining rooms.
"The parsonage is charming, but keeping up with a
house this size when you have a pack rat for a husband
is a daunting task."

Bailey could smell the aroma of dark roast drifting
from the back of the house. Coffee was one of her
weaknesses, and she'd had only one cup today. "I can
imagine."

"Through here to the parlor. Everything is a mess.

My last cleaning woman didn't work out, and I haven't had time to replace her." The pastor's wife led the way briskly through the living room to a formal dining room. "The house hasn't had much done to it since we had to replace the roof after Hurricane Hazel. I'm afraid we have no air-conditioning, but there's usually a breeze off the bay, and this side of the house is shaded by the two big oaks. Matthew, where are you?"

A small terrier dashed through the doorway and hurled itself at Grace. Bailey moved to the far side of the dining table.

Laughing, Grace scooped up the small buff-and-white animal and cradled it against her ample breasts. "This is Precious," she said between wet, exuberant dog kisses. "I'm afraid we spoil her terribly. Matthew says I treat her like a child."

Bailey began to wish she'd never accepted the invitation for coffee.

Grace waved toward a chair. "Perhaps I do spoil Precious. We were never blessed with children. Sit down. I'll get the coffee. I won't be a moment." Still carrying the squirming animal, she hurried away.

Relieved that the dog was gone, Bailey glanced around the dining room. China figurines of gold-and-white shepherdesses and gaudy bric-a-brac covered the dark Victorian tables and the fireplace mantel. Two large windows were covered with heavy floral drapes that matched the fading wallpaper and the flowered carpet.

Bailey stifled a sneeze, thinking that the maid must have given notice quite a while ago. The room could have done with a thorough cleaning. The elaborate arrangement of plastic flowers that took up much of the table was as dusty as the multicolored crystals on the chandelier overheard.

The high-ceilinged room was large enough for the massive china cupboard and server, but four other pieces of furniture, two more side chairs, more artificial flowers, and two gaudy *Gone with the Wind* lamps made Bailey claustrophobic. Maybe she should abandon the dark roast and make a run for it, she thought.

Footsteps behind her registered just before a male voice proclaimed, "Welcome to Tawes, Miss Elliott."

Bailey turned to see a tall, lean man with wire-framed glasses and a thin, graying mustache stroll through the doorway that led to the front entrance hall. "Pastor Catlin?" She half rose from her chair, but he waved her to stay put.

"I am, yes, I am." He fumbled with the knot on his crooked tie. "At least, I was this morning." Chuckling at his own joke, he tucked a pipe into his pants pocket and extended a bony hand. "Call me Matthew. Everyone but Grace does. When I hear anyone address me as Pastor Catlin, I think they're speaking to my father. He was pastor here for nearly sixty years."

Bailey nodded. "I see."

"It's a pleasure to meet you," he said. "A real pleasure. I hope Grace has been treating you well."

"Well, well," his wife echoed as she swept in from the kitchen, carrying a silver tray with steaming cups of coffee and a plate of what Bailey guessed must be the promised apple cake. "Matthew, dear?"

The pastor withdrew his hand before Bailey could shake it, and took the tray from his wife. "This is heavy. You should have called me."

"I did. Several times." Grace sniffed. "Is that pipe tobacco I smell, Matthew? You know it sets a bad example for your congregation."

"The church is for sinners. What use is a pastor

parishioners can't feel superior to?" He handed Bailey a cup and saucer. "Cream?"

"Pay no attention to him." Grace sat across from Bailey. "Matthew fancies himself a comedian. Sugar? I'm afraid I have none of the pink stuff left. I took what I had to the committee meeting this afternoon."

Bailey shook her head, stirred cream into her coffee, and took a sip. "This is delicious. Thank you."

"Our guest was wandering through the graveyard. She says she's interested in the history of the island," Grace said. "I told her that you knew all there was to know about Tawes."

"Not everything," he corrected. "A little. This was a wild and woolly place in the early days. Pirates. Deserters from one army or another. Indians. Fascinating stuff. You know, Southerners are devoted to their ancestors, and it seems that the more wicked they were, the more interesting they are. I've always had a passion for history, and growing up here . . ."

"Don't be modest, dear. You have all those photographs and maps. And the church records go back, oh, as far as Reverend Thomas. You've heard of him, haven't you? The parson of the islands? An ancestor of Matthew's, and quite a legend in these parts. The Chesapeake was a sinful place before Reverend Thomas."

"I understand that there was some mix-up about your appointment with Forest McCready." Matthew reached for a slice of apple cake.

"One slice only, dear," Grace chided. "I don't want to have to send your trousers out for alterations again."

Bailey wondered how the news had traveled so fast, but she didn't attempt an answer. And as she suspected, Grace took up the slack.

"Probably Ida's fault. She's always messing up Forest's schedules. Why he keeps her on, I'll never know." She pursed her lips and mimicked sipping from a bottle. "Ida's worked for him twenty years, but she's not dependable, if you catch my meaning."

"That's unkind, Grace. We don't know that Ida did anything wrong. There isn't a lot of legal work here on Tawes, and it may have slipped Forest's mind. I'm certain it will be all cleared up tomorrow."

Two hours later, after escaping from the parsonage and walking back to the B and B, Bailey sat across from Emma at an oilcloth-covered, round oak table and told her about her meeting with Grace in the cemetery.

"More coffee?" Emma didn't wait for an answer, but refilled Bailey's white china mug to the brim.

She nodded. Emma's coffee was strong enough to dissolve a spoon, but it was good and hot, and Bailey savored every drop. Despite the apple cake she'd eaten earlier, she'd just taken a bite of homemade blueberry pie, a dessert that completed one of the best meals she'd enjoyed in months.

"They're a pair of odd ducks, those two," Emma said. "Did Matthew talk your ears off? He's all right, as ministers go. His sermons are short enough, but that Grace . . . Don't tell her anything you don't want spread all over Tawes in ten minutes."

"Grace insisted that I borrow her bicycle while I'm on Tawes. I tried to refuse, but—"

"But it was easier to take the damn bike than argue with her." Emma added a heaping spoonful of sugar to her coffee. "Grace has that way about her. She just wears you down. Don't worry about it. You won't put her out any. She rarely rides the thing. I think Matthew bought it for her two Christmases ago. Either she walks when she wants to go someplace or she takes her boat."

"It was nice of her. I would like to see something of the island while I'm here, but I'd hoped to finish my business with—"

"Forest," Emma supplied. She rose and gathered the dirty dishes. "Well, he's not as young as he used to be, but he's as shrewd as they come. Forest is a crackerjack lawyer. If he'd left Tawes and concentrated on his practice in Annapolis, he'd probably be a millionaire, but he's like the rest of us. We like the way we do things here—the way we've done them for hundreds of years."

"Your other guest, Daniel? Isn't his last name Catlin? Are he and the pastor related?"

"Honey, everybody on Tawes is related."

"Other than the color of their eyes, they don't look much alike, but—"

Emma scraped scraps off the plates into a pot. "For my chickens," she explained. "I can't abide a store egg. Thin shells and no color to the yolk at all."

"You keep chickens, too?"

"Sure do. Believe in doin' as much for myself as I can. Always have a few dozen eggs to sell at Doris's. Those ones she brings over from the mainland are storage age, old, no taste."

"Mmm, I suppose," Bailey agreed, amused. "Did you know Elizabeth Somers? Grace said that some people were unhappy that Elizabeth left me an inheritance. I was wondering if—"

"Lots of folks get their dander up about stuff that ain't none of their business." She placed a dishpan in the sink and turned on the water. "What did you think of my crab cakes?"

"Delicious," Bailey said. "And the pie was fabulous." She rose. "Let me help you with those dishes."

"Fair enough." Emma stepped back from the sink. "You can wash and I'll dry."

Later, when Bailey retired to her cozy bedroom, she realized that although she and Emma had chatted for an hour, the older woman had answered none of her questions. In fact, the entire day had been pretty much a loss, and she was beginning to feel like Alice down the rabbit hole. She'd never gotten enough signal on her cell to call Elliott; Emma's house phone still wasn't working; and she had been unable to get in contact with Forest McCready. The only thing she had done was to stuff herself with Emma's cooking. She'd be surprised if she could pour her butt into her new jeans in the morning.

She showered, pulled on a soft T-shirt and a pair of athletic shorts, and tried to read another chapter of the historical romance she'd brought with her. The story was a good one, but her eyes wouldn't cooperate. They kept drifting shut. Finally she gave up, yawned, switched out the light, and lay in the dark listening to the waves lapping against the shore, the rustle of leaves, and the occasional hoot of an owl.

Bailey dropped off to sleep almost immediately, waking sometime in the night wondering where she was. The sheets were clean and soft; the mattress was comfortable; she didn't need to use the bathroom; and she wasn't thirsty. What had roused her? She rarely had problems with insomnia, even when she traveled. So why . . . ?

The sound of whistling came from outside, a nursery rhyme that she hadn't heard in years. Bailey's mouth went dry as she slipped from the crisp sheets and went to the window without bothering to turn on a light. Wisps of fog enveloped the house, making it impossible to tell the exact source of the tune.

Her windows, she remembered, faced the bay, but there were trees between the house and the beach. The water was so black as to be almost Stygian; the trees were smudges of dark against a darker background, but patches of sand along the shore glowed with a dull iridescence in the night.

Goose bumps rose on her bare arms. She was on the second floor, her door securely locked with a dead bolt. Whoever it was outside—probably some kid or a drunk trying to find his way home—she was in no possible danger. So why did the old refrain unnerve her so?

The whistler was definitely there in the yard, between the lapping waves and the porch. He must be. If she looked hard enough, Bailey could almost fancy she saw his outline in the shadows of the walnut tree. She shut the window and locked it, but still the sound filtered through the glass into her room. Unbidden, the words of the old refrain rose in her mind.

> *Papa's gonna buy you a diamond ring,*
> *And if that diamond ring don't shine,*
> *Papa's going to buy you a coach and nine,*
> *And if that coach and nine won't pull,*
> *Papa's going to buy you . . .*

What? What was the rest of the song? Why did she care? Annoyed, she climbed back into bed and buried her head under a pillow. If she didn't get a decent night's sleep, she'd look like hell for her meeting with

McCready in the morning. And she would locate him tomorrow. It was ridiculous to think otherwise. She'd sign whatever papers she had to sign, inspect her inheritance, and take the first boat back to civilization.

Elliott had been right. He'd never been particularly sympathetic about her desire to know more about her birth family, but he'd always said that if she had to know, the thing to do was to hire a professional to investigate. Maybe this attorney, Forest McCready. If he lived here, he must know something about her birth mother. Or he would be able to find someone who did.

The cost of a private detective had always been out of the question on a teacher's salary, especially with Elliott's credit card debts, which she'd had to make good on. But perhaps if she got some money out of the property her great aunt Elizabeth had left her, she could hire this McCready to find answers to the questions that had troubled her for so long. And if she was lucky, she might even have enough left to pay off the loan on her car. She smiled, imagining what it would be like to be debt free. "Just dreams," she murmured, and giggled aloud. She'd probably end up with a fallen-down house that no one would want, and she'd have to pay to have it bulldozed before she could place the lot with a Realtor. Could you refuse a bequest? That was one more question to add to her growing list.

This time she lay awake for what seemed like hours, and when she finally drifted off, it was to disturbing dreams of being trapped in a spooky graveyard of crumbling tombstones made of crab cakes, and ringing cell phones that she was never able to reach before the caller hung up.

CHAPTER THREE

"Somebody whistling, you say?" Emma slid a plate of scrambled eggs, home fries, sausage, and toast in front of Bailey. Although it was just the two of them for breakfast, the kitchen table seemed crowded with a crockery bowl of fresh strawberries, another of hot muffins, a plate of pancakes, a pitcher of orange juice, as well as smaller containers of syrup, various kinds of jam, honey, cream, and sugar.

"Please, I can't eat all this," Bailey protested.

"Nonsense. Breakfast is the most important meal of the day. I'm used to cooking for Daniel. Let me tell you, that man can stow away the vittles." She slid into the chair across from Bailey, slipped hotcakes onto her already loaded plate, and slathered the pancakes with butter and strawberry jam. "Daniel's a tea drinker, though. Not much for coffee. Said he picked up the habit and can't shake it."

"I thought I saw someone under the trees last night." Emma averted her gaze, took a sip of her coffee, grimaced, and made a show of adding several spoonfuls of sugar. "He likes his tea with clover honey."

"You didn't hear anything?"

The older woman thoughtfully chewed her mouthful of pancakes before saying, "Can't say as I did. But your aunt, Elizabeth Somers, was born a Tawes. Old-time people used to say that the Tawes family had a lot of Injun blood. Claimed they had the 'sight.'"

"The sight?"

"Most folks got hearing, smell, taste, sight, touch. The Tawes women, they said, could see things and hear things other people didn't."

"What kind of things, exactly?"

Emma wiped her wide mouth with a napkin and lowered her voice to a whisper. "Ghosts."

"Ghosts?" Bailey couldn't suppress a chuckle. "You're serious?"

Emma's faded blue eyes narrowed. "Didn't say they did see ghosts. Just telling you what old-time people claimed. Probably just superstitious nonsense."

"You don't believe it, do you?"

"Can't say what I believe. I'm a Parks. So far as I know, no Parks ever heard the whistler, no, nor saw him neither. But I like to keep an open mind. You're the one with the Tawes blood, if Elizabeth was right about that. So you could have the Tawes sight."

Bailey shook her head. "What I heard was real. It could have been a radio or—"

"Or it could have been Benjamin Ridgely. He's been said to wander around this house on a foggy night."

"And where does he live—this Benjamin Ridgely?"

The homely face crinkled into a mischievous grin. "Somewhere between heaven and hell, I suppose. Benjamin died of the cholera at Fort Delaware during the War Between the States. His body was laid in a common pit. Neither his mother nor his intended ever saw him again—not alive, anyway. But some say he comes to this house still, whistling for his sweetheart to come out and walk with him, like he did before he got caught up in the foolishness and marched away to fight for Robert E. Lee."

Bailey pushed back her coffee cup. "It's a good story, Emma, but I don't believe a word of it. I told you, I don't believe in ghosts. Now, if you'll excuse me, I think I'll walk back to Mr. McCready's and see if—"

"He's still not here. Somebody would have come by to let you know. It's common knowledge that you're waiting to meet with him."

"All the same, I'll go into the village. I still haven't been able to call my friend. Maybe I can get a signal on my cell from the dock area."

"Suit yourself." Emma broke open a blueberry muffin and spread butter on it. "My phone's not working yet either. It'll come back sooner or later. I've known it to be out for a week or more."

"And nobody complains to the phone company?"

"Oh, lots complain, but nothing comes of it. Change doesn't come easy out here. If your call's important, I can round up Creed to take you back to Crisfield."

"No, no, that won't be necessary. I was just touching base with a friend—actually my ex-husband—to let him know that I'm all right."

Emma arched a thick eyebrow disbelievingly. "You're divorced and still friends?"

"Best friends, actually. I suppose I'll always love the bastard." She shrugged. "The thing is, I'm not 'in love' with him anymore. No dramatic tale of woe. My mother was sick for years and died halfway through my senior year of college. My father mourned her two full months before he remarried. He moved her best friend's daughter and her kids into our house and turned my bedroom into a playroom. My solution was to elope with Peter Pan during winter break."

"Peter? I thought you said his name was—"

"Elliott. Ainsley Elliott the third. He's a sweet guy. You'd like him. Everybody does." She stood up and began to clear away her unfinished plate. "The problem was that eventually I grew up and he never did."

By midafternoon, as she paced Forest McCready's porch for close to an hour without any sign of him, Bailey's last shred of faith in the attorney faded away. Thoroughly disgusted and unwilling to sit and wait another day without results, she decided to inspect her great-aunt's property on her own. Leaving McCready's home and walking back to Emma's once more, she found her hostess coming from her shedding house with several soft-shell crabs in a wicker basket.

"Mr. McCready still didn't show up. I've had it with him," Bailey said. "Could you give me directions to Elizabeth's place?"

"I don't know." Emma set her basket on the sand. "It's a ways out of town. You could get lost. There aren't any signs, and all the dirt roads tend to look pretty much alike. If you got turned around in the marsh, you could fall into a sinkhole. It's not quicksand, but just as dangerous. I've known of farmers losing hogs, even cows and horses."

"I'm not going to wander off into any marsh. I just want to look at Elizabeth Somers's property."

"Elizabeth *Tawes* Somers," Emma corrected. "Elizabeth was widowed at eighteen, six months after she was married, hardly long enough for the Somers name to matter. Elizabeth was a Tawes, no matter what she went by." She frowned. "The farm's a long walk. It's going to be a hot one."

"I'll take the bike."

"Don't suppose it would do any harm for you to take a look-see. I can draw you a map . . . if you're certain—"

"I'm certain," Bailey insisted. "And if Mr. McCready shows up, he can damn well wait for me for a change."

Half an hour's ride by bike through farm fields and old timber forests brought Bailey to a narrow oyster-shell lane lined with cedar trees. She'd seen only one other person since she'd left the outskirts of Tawes, a farmer repairing an old-fashioned split-rail fence. The man had been on the far side of a meadow, but she'd waved. It hadn't surprised her when he ignored her gesture. So much for country hospitality.

Pleased that she'd been able to find the property, she turned onto the lane. The shade was cool after the bright sunshine, but riding on the packed oyster-shell surface was easier. The driveway was longer than she'd expected, and she wondered if she'd misunderstood Emma's directions.

"Follow the lane. You can't miss the brick house," Emma had assured her. "If you pass it, you'll ride smack into the Chesapeake."

Bailey knew she was close to the water, because she could hear the shrill cries of gulls. And only a few minutes ago a big black-and-white bird that she was certain was an osprey had flown over the road with a fish in its beak. She could smell the bay. Was it possible that Elizabeth had left her waterfront property? That seemed too good to be true. No matter what the house looked like, if the lot had a view of the water, it must be worth something.

The crushed oystershells crunched under her bike tires, and birds called and flitted from the trees on either side of the lane. The path curved and ran downhill. This was turning out to be a real adventure, but where was the house? Had she missed it in the trees?

Abruptly, the cedar tunnel opened into a meadow of yellow-and-brown daisies. The lane continued on past a freshwater pond, through an old apple orchard, and alongside a pasture where two horses grazed. One of them, a long-legged chestnut with a white blaze on its face, trotted to the fence and whinnied a greeting. The other horse, silky-maned and black, raised its head and watched her with great, liquid eyes. Bailey was tempted to try to pet the chestnut, but when she approached the railing, the animal snorted, twitched its ears, and backed away.

"You're no different from anyone else on this—" She broke off as she caught sight of the blue-green bay stretching as far as she could see at the bottom of the hill. "Oh," she exclaimed. Laying the bike beside the drive, she hurried on past a high boxwood hedge and stopped short. Her breath caught in her throat.

The lane turned in toward a sprawling eighteenth-century brick house. Bailey's heart began to race. "No," she muttered. "It can't be. . . ." She looked around, but there was no other structure that could have been a house. There was a dormered stable with a sharply peaked roof, several old brick outbuildings, gardens, and newer farm buildings, but not a single cottage. A sweeping lawn in need of mowing ran down to a sparkling stretch of pristine sand beach. Below and to the right of the house, a creek opened into the bay, and several hundred feet from its mouth a solid wooden dock extended into the wide waterway.

"It's not possible. All this couldn't be mine." Mouth dry, Bailey approached the back of the house, where a frame addition led to a wide porch and a covered well. The house seemed quiet, deserted. A birdbath was empty; grass grew around the back step and between the bricks in the curving walk.

Nervously, she crossed the porch to a Dutch door and knocked.

No one answered. Bailey listened. Nothing. On a whim she tried the doorknob, and it turned in her hand. She pushed open the door. "Hello!" she called. "Hello! Is anyone here?" The only answer was the buzz of a bee from the yard behind her.

She took a deep breath and stepped into a kitchen. The air was stale and slightly musty. "Hello?"

Had she lost her mind? Two days in Sleepy Hollow and she—a Girl Scout who'd won three honor badges in two years—had become a criminal, breaking into strangers' houses. She'd end up shot or locked up, and she'd have to call Elliott to come and bail her out. But with her luck, even the phone at the jail wouldn't work, and she'd end up planting corn on a chain gang.

Then she remembered that there were no police on Tawes, and she moved into the center of the room. The shadowy kitchen was large, a comfortable blend of modern appliances and lovely colonial furnishings. A wide brick fireplace, large enough to roast a whole pig, dominated one end, a handcrafted cupboard the other. There was a plank table, backless benches, and a dry sink under double windows with checked yellow curtains. A thin layer of dust coated the table and the maple cupboard with the lovely set of blue-and-white dishes, a piece that appeared to be as old and well preserved as the house.

She ventured up a step and through an open doorway into what was obviously a dining room. The table and chairs in there were cherry, Queen Anne, and either genuine antiques or the finest replicas Bailey had ever seen. In the corner stood a tall case clock in maple, its hands stopped at ten o'clock, the pendulum still. The initials J.T. and the date 1784 were carved into a decorative panel near the base. Bailey gazed at an oil painting of a mischievous young girl wearing a robin's-egg-blue antebellum dress and broad-brimmed hat, and holding a white kitten. She was studying the portrait for the artist's signature when she heard a door open and footsteps directly overhead.

She froze, uncertain as to what to do. Through another doorway she could see a wide hall and a staircase. The footsteps became louder. It wasn't her imagination. Someone else was in the house.

Panic made her knees weak. She wanted to run back into the kitchen and out the door, but if she did, whoever it was would take her for a thief or . . . After all, if she had inherited this property, it was legally hers, wasn't it?

You idiot, she thought. *What if it's a burglar?* She hadn't seen another soul for miles, so she could hardly scream for help. Deciding that she'd been reading too many suspense novels, she drew herself up to her full five feet, one inch and called out, "Who's there?"

"Bailey?"

Her eyes widened in surprise. Wasn't there anyone on this godforsaken island who didn't know who she was? Before she could think of what to say next, a middle-aged man with a weathered face half-hidden by a baseball cap appeared in the hallway.

"Mr. McCready?"

"Do I look like Forest McCready? What are you doing here by yourself? It's not safe."

"Is this or is it not Elizabeth Somers's house?"

"It is."

"Well, I've been told that she left it to me in her will. So I'm not a trespasser."

"Didn't say you were, girl. What I said was that you're in danger here. You never should have set foot on Tawes."

Bailey stepped back. "You haven't told me who you are and what you're doing in Elizabeth's—"

"She was my sister. I'm looking for something that belongs to me."

"I think that you should take that up with Attorney—" She broke off in midsentence as the sound of a gasoline engine roared outside. She went to the nearest window, parted a curtain, and looked out as a man halted a four-wheeler in the side yard. "It's Daniel Catlin from . . ." She trailed off as she realized that the stranger was no longer there.

"Bailey?" Daniel shouted.

"Here!" She hurried out the way she'd come, taking care to close the kitchen door tightly behind her.

He met her halfway around the house. "I found your bike back in the lane, but I didn't see—"

"I was inside." She drew in a quick breath.

"What's wrong?"

"Nothing. It's just that . . . there was someone else in the house." She could feel a blush rising to her cheeks. "The back door was open, and I wanted to see . . ." She shrugged. "I know I shouldn't have, but I went in. I was looking around when I heard . . . There was an older man upstairs. He claimed to be Elizabeth's brother and . . ."

Daniel's eyes looked worried. "Will Tawes. Did he threaten you?"

"Not exactly. He did tell me that I shouldn't be here . . . on the island—that it wasn't safe."

"Wait here. I'll go in and take a look around."

"There's no need to make a fuss. If he really is who he says he is, my great-aunt's brother, then he probably has as much right to be in the house as I do. Maybe more, since nothing is official yet."

Daniel had already started up the porch steps. "Stay out here."

She followed him. "Is he dangerous?"

"Most people think so. Elizabeth did. She hadn't spoken to him in over thirty years."

"But if he's dangerous, aren't you—"

"Just wait here."

Uncertainly, she retreated to the edge of the oyster-shell lane and watched the house for any sign of movement. Minutes passed, and she'd almost decided to go in and look for Daniel when she heard the back door open and the soft tread of his athletic shoes on the porch.

"There's nobody in there now," he said. "I went all the way up to the attic. The door was latched from the outside, so he couldn't be up there. Chances are he slipped out through a side door or through the cellar."

"But I didn't see him come out."

"Lots of Indian blood in the Tawes family, and old Will is as quiet as any Iroquois when he wants to be. He comes and goes on this part of the island without anyone catching sight of him for months at a time."

"Is he mentally unbalanced?"

Daniel laughed. "No more than any of us. No, Will is just ornery. Some say downright mean. He's tough as smoked eel and twice as slippery."

"You said that he and Elizabeth—"

"Bad blood between them. Real bad. People on Tawes tend to see the world as black-and-white, no gray to it when it comes to the codes they live by. Elizabeth thought that her brother did something so unforgivable that she never could get past it."

"Too bad. But why would he take such a dislike to me when he's never met me before today? He could be the only living relative I have. He could fill in a lot of blanks about my birth family . . . about my mother." She hesitated. "Is it the property? Does he resent me because she left—"

"Hell, no. One thing Will isn't is greedy. He's got three, four hundred acres of his own. This farm came down from their mother. It was always meant to be Elizabeth's. He wouldn't want to leave his own place and live here, and he'd never sell to outsiders for a profit. Whatever grudge Will holds against you, it has nothing to do with money."

"It's probably difficult for you to understand, but . . ." She hesitated, unwilling to discuss her personal life with a virtual stranger. "I have a right to know about my mother."

He shook his head. "Sometimes it's better to let the past go. A person who asks too many questions may get answers she doesn't want to hear."

"I don't believe that. My parents were educators, but they believed that adoptions should be kept secret. They wouldn't tell me anything about my birth parents. The more they refused to discuss the matter, the more important it became for me to know. I wasn't even aware that I was born on Tawes until a few weeks ago."

"Elizabeth stirred up a hornet's nest when she left her farm to you; that's certain." He grinned. "Speaking of Forest McCready, he's looking for you."

"It's about time. But it was kind of you to take the time to come all the way out here."

"It was Emma who insisted I find you. She's not easy to say no to."

"That's what she said about the pastor's wife."

Daniel looked amused. "Those two don't always see eye-to-eye."

"I assumed that."

"Can I give you a ride?" He indicated the four-wheeler. "You'll have to sit on my lap, but I'm a gentleman. I don't bite."

Bailey shook her head and laughed. "A tempting offer, but no, thanks. I can get back to the village the way I came." She looked back at the house. "You're a carpenter. What's your opinion of the condition of the house? It's lovely, but it probably needs repairs. I noticed that there were some rotting boards on the back porch and a loose shutter on the end of the house."

"You're right. It does need restoration. Not a great deal, but some basic work. Have it done before you put the place up for sale and you'll get a lot more for it."

"I've seen the quality of the work you're doing for Emma. Would you be interested in the job?"

Daniel shook his head. "Nope. Too busy with my own place. And I don't know of anybody else on Tawes you could hire either. The best thing for you is to find a contractor in Crisfield."

"Oh, I'm sorry." Disappointment made her words crisp. "I suppose I can't persuade you to reconsider?"

"Nope. The best thing for you to do is finish up your paperwork with Forest and go home. You may have been born here, but Tawes is no place for you. And the sooner you leave, the better."

CHAPTER FOUR

"I can't tell you how sorry I am for the confusion," Forest said as he ushered Bailey into his office. "You must think the worst of me."

The attorney, near sixty and dressed in khakis, a navy three-button knit shirt, and docksiders, was tall with a pleasant, open face, rosy cheeks, warm brown eyes, and graying hair styled in a short military cut. His handshake was firm but gentle, and she liked him immediately in spite of all the delay.

"I've treated you abominably, and you have my word that it won't happen again."

Office didn't accurately describe the elegant room that opened off the wide entrance hall in Forest McCready's home. Two comfortable leather chairs, a couch, and a mahogany tea table were grouped at one end of what he explained had once been the location of dances, weddings, and holiday parties for the elite of the island. Floor-to-ceiling bookshelves lined the walls on either side of the marble Greek Revival fireplace. The remainder of the room was tastefully furnished with authentic hunting prints and antique furniture, mostly Sheridan. The only items that might have fit the description of office necessities were a walnut desk with an old-fashioned black phone in the front corner. Forest McCready might be a simple country lawyer, but he wasn't a poor one.

Two Irish setters, tails wagging and tongues lolling, rose from a magnificent blue-and-cream rug in front of the fireplace. "Down," Forest said. "Miss Elliott hasn't come to see you." He dug into a pocket of his khakis, produced two dog biscuits, and tossed one to each animal.

"They're beautiful," Bailey said. "And the rug too. Unusual, with the indigo-and-navy coloring. I've never seen one like it. It must be old."

"Yes, it is. My grandfather bought it in China. It's Tibetan, early nineteenth century. I've tried to convince Fee and Ryan that it's not exclusively theirs, but I'm outnumbered." He waved her to a high-backed chair and lifted a silver teapot. "Tea? Or would you prefer coffee?"

"Tea is fine." Delicious scents rose from a basket of scones, a flowered plate of tiny crescent sandwiches, and a crystal bowl of strawberries dipped in chocolate.

"Sugar?" the attorney asked. "Please. Help yourself. I'm famished. Didn't have time for lunch before I left the mainland. My sister Maude had these waiting for me when I got here." He arched a graying eyebrow mischievously. "That and a tongue-lashing for keeping you waiting. She won't let me forget it anytime soon."

Bailey took a deep breath and plunged in. "I went out to Elizabeth Somers's farmhouse today. Tell me that that splendid old house isn't what she left to me."

Forest shrugged. "I'm afraid it is. The farm is the only

property she owned, two hundred and forty acres, a twenty-two-foot skiff, and the household furnishings. Savings aren't much, somewhere in the neighborhood of a hundred and sixty-seven thousand, I believe, mostly in CDs. Elizabeth wasn't into taking chances in the stock market." He took a sandwich. "Try them, please. She-crab with just a hint of chives. And Margaret makes her own bread. Wonderful."

Her hands began to tremble so that the thin porcelain cup and saucer began to rattle. Bailey set them down on the table, opened her mouth to make a reply, and came up blank. "I'm sorry," she stammered when she could finally speak. "Did I hear you correctly? The bequest to me is a hundred and sixty-seven thousand dollars, that house, and over two hundred acres of waterfront property?" When Forest nodded, smiled, and took a bite of his sandwich, she continued. "An aunt that I never knew existed left all that to me?"

Forest finished the sandwich, wiped his mouth with a napkin, and met her disbelieving gaze. "All of the land isn't waterfront. Much is marshland, woods, and upland pasture. It's in the form of a trust, so some, but not all, of the bequest is sheltered from taxes, but you will owe quite a bit to federal and state agencies. With the price of land today, you should have no problem covering those expenses."

"But why me?"

"Simple. Elizabeth was a childless widow, your grandfather Owen Tawes's only sister. Owen had a twin brother. There was just the three of them: Elizabeth, Owen, and Will. Your grandfather died long before you were born. Other than her estranged brother, you're the closest relative Elizabeth had left alive. Real blood kin, as we like to say on the island. Elizabeth's always taken an interest in your welfare. She was instrumental in your private adoption. Actually, both of your adoptive parents have distant ties to family on Tawes, but that's going back generations."

Bailey couldn't feel her feet or her hands, and she had the distinct sensation that her brain was as numb as the rest of her. "I understood that adoptive children couldn't inherit from birth relatives. Isn't there a law—"

He chuckled. "Elizabeth could have left her worldly goods to the SPCA if she'd wanted to. She told me that if you turned out to be responsible, she'd always intended that you should have her home."

"I don't even know . . ." She tried to organize her thoughts. "The church cemetery. I was . . . rather . . . Yesterday I was looking around. I found Elizabeth's . . . *Aunt* Elizabeth's grave, and . . ." She balled her hands into fists on either side of her lap. "Elizabeth—Beth Tawes, the sixteen-year-old. Was she my birth mother?"

"Yes, she was." Compassion swirled in his brown eyes. "She was a sweet girl, very bright. Everyone loved her. Except for hair color, you're her spitting image. Beth was blond, like her mother. You have the Tawes look about you. Elizabeth's hair was a dark auburn. Will's too, when he was younger."

"How did she die? My mother. Complications of childbirth?"

"She'd suffered some injuries in an accident. I believe the cause of death was listed as blood loss, but I suspect it was a combination of factors."

"What about the father? My father? Surely—"

Forest shook his head. "Beth never said. There were speculations, of course, but no one came forward to claim paternity. You might check the church records. You were christened here at Thomas's Chapel when you were several weeks old. There might be information there."

"I wasn't placed for adoption immediately?"

Forest shook his head. "No, if I recall correctly, you were closer to three months of age when you left the island."

"But why? Who took care of me? And why—"

"Your great-uncle, Will Tawes, Owen's twin. He assumed custody at the time of your mother's death. Elizabeth wanted you, but Will was always stubborn. He felt you were his responsibility."

"But why did he give me up a few months later? And why didn't Aunt Elizabeth step in then? Why place me for adoption if—"

"I'm afraid I can't answer those questions." He looked uncomfortable.

"So the only one who can is Will Tawes himself?"

Forest set down his cup and saucer, folded his arms over his three-button sport shirt, and leaned back in his chair. "He could give you the details if he wanted to, but he may not. Will's not an easy nut to crack."

"He could at least tell me about my mother's death. And he could identify my birth father."

"Maybe, but I'm not sure how much he knows. Most people on Tawes think that if he did know who your father was, he'd have shot the man years ago."

A shiver flashed under Bailey's skin. "He's a violent person, then."

"I don't know if *violent* is the right label for Will Tawes. In my opinion, he's a tortured soul who's suffered great personal loss and may have been wronged by the justice system. He is a hard man, but fair. Will lives by the code of simpler times. He may have been a

48

hell-raiser in his youth, but to my knowledge, he hasn't been in any real trouble for a quarter of a century."

"He was at Elizabeth's today. Upstairs. He said he was looking for something that belonged to him."

"He spoke to you?" Forest looked surprised.

"He told me that I shouldn't have come to Tawes, that it wasn't safe for me here." She edged forward in the seat. "Should I be afraid of him?"

"No, I highly doubt that. He'd have no reason to—"

"What if he's angry that his sister left her estate to me?"

Forest shook his head. "Will wouldn't have expected anything. He's not avaricious, and he's no thief. If he told you that he was hunting for something of his, believe him. Will is somewhat of an eccentric. He keeps to himself, and when he does show his face, people stay clear of him."

Forest offered her a scone, but as appetizing as they looked, she was no longer hungry. "I'm sorry. I wanted . . . That is, I'd hoped . . ." She exhaled softly. "I'm not usually at a loss for words. I teach fourth grade, and I'm used to keeping my students' attention for hours at a time."

"You were naturally curious about your birth family."

"Exactly. My parents—my adoptive parents—were very good to me. I never wanted for anything. But they were older when I came to live with them. I spent a lot of time in day care, and they were never . . ." She forced a smile. "I don't mean to whine. I loved both my mother and father, and I had great respect for them. But I always felt that I was an afterthought. That perhaps they would have been happier with a miniature poodle."

"They were dog people?" He glanced at the retrievers and smiled. "At times, I can see how someone could prefer dogs to—"

"No. We never had any pets. Mother said she didn't care for dog hair or the mess. Both of them were conscientious, active in community affairs—simply not very affectionate. I always knew that I was adopted, but it wasn't a subject that was discussed in our home."

"So you knew nothing of your background?"

"Nothing. I had a lively imagination, and I came up with all sorts of scenarios. My favorite was that I was a princess stolen by kidnappers and sold on the black market when it became too dangerous to collect the ransom."

"Sorry. No royalty. The closest the Tawes family can claim to royalty is the daughter of a Nanticoke sachem back in the early seventeen hundreds. Her name was Leaf . . . Leaf something. Matthew would probably know. You've met our pastor, I understand."

"Everything I've done since I've set foot on this island seems to be common knowledge."

Forest laughed. "You think it's bad for you? I was born here. Matthew's wife, Grace, can probably tell you every misdeed my father ever committed in the first grade. We like to think of Grace as our community conscience. She hears, she remembers, and she records for posterity. She's younger than I am, but she seems to have mind-melded with some higher source that all ministers' wives have access to."

"I suspected that when I met her, but she was pleasant to me, invited me in for coffee. She loaned me her bike to use while I was on Tawes."

"Good. I'm glad you have transportation, because things may take a little longer to resolve than I first thought."

"How so?"

"Yesterday, when I was going over old deeds in the courthouse, I came upon a little snag, a minor conflict about property lines going back to the mid-eighteen fifties. Nothing to trouble yourself about. It all goes to you, but I need to clear this up so that there will be no problems if you decide to sell the property."

"How long are we talking about? Should I go home and—"

"No, no need to do that. A few days, perhaps a week. Certainly no longer. I think you should stay on at Emma's, take the opportunity to see something of the island. I understand the school where you teach doesn't open until September."

"Yes, after Labor Day. But I didn't plan on staying so long."

"Sometimes, Miss Elliott, the best things in life come to us through serendipity. You really should know something of your heritage. Tawes is quite an amazing place, unmatched anywhere in the world. The islanders, for all their quaint ways, possess an amazing strength, sustained by their faith in God and the bounty of the earth and the tides."

"You sound more like a poet than a lawyer."

"You've caught me out. I'm a secret romantic." He chuckled. "Seriously, Miss Elliott—"

"Please, call me Bailey."

"Bailey. You should take time to get to know us, to find pride in your heritage. Matthew can give you all sorts of information about the Tawes family and the island's turbulent past. Our men and women have fought in every war since the French and Indian, including the War on Terror. We lost relatives in the World Trade Center attack and in the terrible disaster in New

Orleans and the Gulf Coast. And if you aren't personally interested, it's a legacy you should have, to pass on to your children and grandchildren, if you ever—"

"I've never had a child. I'd like to, but . . ." She spread her hands. "Who knows? Perhaps one day . . ."

"Don't wait too long," he advised. "Find a good man and take the leap. I once thought that Elizabeth would be my wife." He smiled regretfully. "We were engaged to be married, but we argued, and we were both too stubborn to realize that giving in would have been better than ruining what we might have had together. Enough of that. There never was a finer woman than Elizabeth Tawes. Her death was a great shock to me and to a lot of us. You would have liked her."

Bailey felt a great sense of loss for this aunt she would never know. "Why didn't she ever contact me?"

Forest resumed his professional countenance. "She felt it was best for you." He rose. "You are more than welcome to have another cup of tea." He glanced at his watch. "I don't want to rush you, but I'd like to return to the mainland. The sooner I can begin work on that snag in the deed . . ."

"Of course." Bailey knew a polite dismissal when she heard one. Forest McCready was clearly embarrassed that he'd allowed personal feelings to intrude on what should have been a business discussion, but she was glad he'd spoken out. If Aunt Elizabeth had had to die young, it was nice that someone mourned her.

"You'll stay on a few days, then?" Emma asked. "God knows I'd appreciate the extra income. Folks aren't exactly lined up to take your room."

"They would be if you'd advertise," Bailey said. The two were seated on the back porch. Emma was peeling potatoes for supper, and she'd given Bailey a dish-pan full of green beans and instructions to snap them.

The backyard was enclosed with a white picket fence. To the right, on the far side of the grass, in a large wire run, chickens scratched in the dirt, chased one another, and clucked softly. Beyond that, perhaps two hundred feet from the house, was the Chesapeake. The tide was low, and gentle waves slapped against the foundation of Emma's shedding house, the dock, and a wide stretch of sand. Emma's boat was snugged against a tarred post with enough line to allow for the rise and fall of the tide.

"Advertise?" Emma grimaced. "And put up with God knows who tramping through my house and insulting my cooking? I do well enough with visiting relatives and such as you." Her gaze became intense. "It won't put you out any, leaving your own place empty? You won't come home to find you've been robbed, will you?"

Bailey laughed. "I hope not. But I have good neighbors on both sides. One is a Newark policeman. Mine's a town house, two stories, but small. Just the right size for me. No pets, although I've been thinking of getting a cat."

"Cats are good company." Emma reached down to pet the scarred tabby curled around her ankles. "Cats are independent. You never own one, and sometimes you think they own you. But you'll never have mice in the—" A phone rang from inside the house. "Wait until I answer that." Emma hurried inside and a minute later called through the dining room window, "It's for you, Bailey. No, just take it from there." She pushed open the screen and handed her the receiver.

"Bailey?"

"Elliott. I've been trying to reach you."

"I've had my cell on. I've been trying yours, but no luck. All I get is, 'Service not available.' Where are you? The dark side of the moon?"

Bailey laughed. "You'd probably think so. No problems. Well, actually, a little one. But nothing's wrong. Phone signals out here are spotty."

"Nonexistent, if you ask me. When are you coming home?"

"I'm not certain. A few more days. Wait until you hear my awesome news."

"Your aunt left you a crab trap and two stray cats?"

"Nooo. Be serious. Better than that. You aren't going to believe this. . . ."

"Get out!" Elliott shouted when she filled him in on what she'd learned from Forest McCready. "Waterfront property? All the more reason to come home. Better yet, come to Rehoboth. I have to tend bar at the Driftwood tonight, but I have the next three days off. We'll celebrate big-time. I've got a buddy who works for Seaside Realtors. He can probably give you an idea what the place is worth."

"I'm not sure I want business advice from any friend of yours."

"Why not?"

"Because he can't be too bright, or he wouldn't be a friend of—"

"Low blow, Bails. Very low. But I'm in a forgiving mood. I get off at two. Could you—"

"Not coming home tonight. Not coming to Rehoboth tonight. But I'll do you one better. You say you have time off. Why don't you come to Tawes? See the house for yourself? Bring your bike. There are lots of dirt roads we can—"

"Dirt roads." He groaned. "Can't do, kid. I bent a front

wheel last week. Betsy's in the shop. You know Voladya, a genius at fixing bikes, but slower than hell. Sure I can't persuade you to cut your little jaunt short and come down here?"

"Next week, maybe. My attorney is working out some little deed problem here. I'll call you as soon as I get back."

"All right. You're a hard woman, Bails."

"Not hard enough." After they'd exchanged a few more friendly insults, they said their good-byes and she handed the phone back to Emma.

"The ex?" she asked when she returned to the porch.

Bailey nodded. "Elliott. He was worried. I gave him this number before I left. He said he kept trying that and my cell but—"

"Couldn't get through." Emma returned to her potatoes. "Sounds like you're more than friends."

"No. Just friends."

"You've got to work at holding a marriage together. Certain it can't be mended?"

"No." Bailey sighed. "He loves me, but his first love is gambling."

"Ah, enough said."

Bailey concentrated on the snap beans, carefully removing the pointed tips and depositing them into a bucket at her feet. "Forest McCready knew my birth mother, Beth Tawes. Did you know her?"

"A little." Emma's sunburned face reddened. "She was a pretty girl, always had a book in her hand. She sang in the church choir."

"Do you remember if she had any special talents? Did she draw or paint?"

Emma rose abruptly, spilling potato peelings onto the worn cedar floorboards. "No, I don't recall that. It was a long time ago. A pity she died so young. Nobody knew how it came to happen. Course, nobody knew she was in the family way, either."

"Do you have any idea who my birth father was?"

The gray-haired woman stiffened. "Nope. Can't say as I do." Her round face creased into a scowl. "Best let that old dog lie. No good can come of stirrin' up what's long past. No good at all."

CHAPTER FIVE

The scents of frying bacon, coffee, and hot cinnamon buns lured Bailey from her bed early the following morning. Daniel, looking like a country version of Keanu Reeves and smelling faintly of shaving lotion and new denim, was already at the dining room table. His hair was still damp from the shower, and Bailey had an almost irresistible urge to push back the single wayward lock that had fallen across his forehead.

"Are those new Levi's you're wearing?" Emma teased. "Wasn't certain I could pry you out of the old ones."

Daniel grinned good-naturedly. His teeth were white and even, making his slightly crooked smile a killer. "The ones with holes in both knees are in the washer, Miss Emma. I'll wear them tomorrow just for you." He glanced across the table at Bailey. "I hear that you'll be spending a few more days on Tawes. Any chance I could enlist your help in repairing the grape arbor today?"

"I'd appreciate it," Emma said. "I've got to check my

crab traps this morning. And if I let him slip away, Lord knows when he'll get back to mending it. It looks like a good year for the Concords, and I don't want them spilling all over the ground."

Bailey had the feeling that she'd been set up, but she couldn't think of a good excuse not to help. It wasn't as though she was on a schedule. She wasn't certain she wanted to spend time in close proximity to Daniel Catlin, and she wasn't sure she didn't. He was a damned attractive man, and she'd been living like a cloistered nun far too long. Sometimes, when she listened to the exploits of her fellow unattached teachers after a holiday weekend, she felt as though she'd been raised in a different century.

It wasn't that she didn't enjoy sex. Hell, sex had always been the best thing she and Elliott had going for them, and the pleasure had lasted long after the flames of infatuation had died out. The fact was, except for one night on a forgettable cruise to the Bahamas, her ex was the only man she'd ever slept with. And the way her life had been going, that wasn't about to change anytime soon.

So what harm would it do to flirt a little with the resident carpenter? It wasn't as though she was about to take up residence on the island. A few days, a week, and she'd never see Tawes or Daniel again. What did she have to lose? She was already divorced and in her mid-thirties. Her biological clock wasn't simply ticking; the hour hand had already slipped past eight. If she didn't allow herself a little fun, pretty soon she'd be one of those bloodless, schoolmarm stereotypes.

"All right," she agreed, "but I warn you: My fence-mending skills are right up there with my cow milking. Pretty nonexistent."

"All I need is a pair of hands and a strong back."

She glanced down at her hands, noticing that her nail polish could use a touchup. "Two hands, present and accounted for. I won't vouch for the strength of the back."

"That's settled," Emma said. "Now, eat up, so I can clear away these dishes and get to my day's work."

And thus, quite easily, Bailey found herself drafted into the project and holding a cedar crosspiece in place while Daniel drove nails into the spot where the wood intersected with the post. He worked in silence, giving simple instructions with a minimal amount of words.

The sun was bright and drops of dew still sparkled on the grape leaves. Between the strikes of the hammer and the rasp of Daniel's handsaw, Bailey was captivated by the beauty of the early morning. To her left a panorama of bay stretched from horizon to horizon, the blue-gray water as smooth as a mirror, crowned by a cloudless robin's-egg-blue sky. Directly over her head, gnarled grapevines arched on a frame so seasoned by weather and time that it seemed almost part of the living branches. The salt breeze that blew off the water smelled as sweet and invigorating as fresh dark roast, and the drone of bees and the occasional *rat-tat-tat* of a woodpecker eased the tension in the back of her neck and lifted her spirits.

She felt sixteen again, full of giddy anticipation without knowing why. "Tawes really is a magical place, isn't it?"

"Mmm." Daniel pulled a nail from the half dozen held between his lips, set it, and drove it home with sure, powerful strokes.

God, but he had nice shoulders. He didn't have the

bulky muscles of a gym jock, but his Hard Rock Café T-shirt left little to her imagination. It wasn't such a leap to consider what it might feel like to be held in those strong arms. "You were born here?" she asked in an attempt to divert her thoughts from damp sheets and heavy breathing.

He nodded. "Born and bred, as Tawes folk say."

"So you know my great uncle?"

He removed the nails. "I suppose. As well as anybody."

"Could you take me to meet him?"

"Nope." Daniel tucked the nails back into his mouth.

It was the second time he'd turned her down, and the rejection stung. "I know I've already met him, but it wasn't under the best of circumstances. I really think I need to ask him some questions."

Daniel turned away, sorted through several cedar lengths, and lifted one into place. He eyed it for length, then took it down and began to saw off about three inches.

Determined not to be put off, Bailey laid a hand on the handle of the saw. "Why not?"

His dark eyes hardened. "Because he's as apt to take a shot at you as not. He doesn't like visitors. Guards his property lines like a pit bull."

"I'm not trying to offend anyone. I think I have a right to know the facts about my mother—about who my father was."

He stood up. "You know who they are. They raised you."

"It's not the same," she protested. "You can't understand what it's like to grow up without knowing anything about your grandparents—aunts and uncles, cousins. I don't even know what my heritage is. Am I German? Dutch?"

"English. Maybe some Welsh. A little Nanticoke. The Taweses came from Cornwall, same as the Catlins."

"No one will tell me anything. I warn you, I'm going to talk to my uncle Will, with or without your help."

Daniel shrugged. "Suit yourself, but don't ask me to be part of your getting your head shot off. Will's a hot-head, and stubborn. He's not about to change for a woman—even if she can claim Tawes blood."

"Maybe." She rose to her feet and tried to keep from showing the anger she felt at his indifference. "But I won't know until I make an attempt, will I?"

Bailey found Matthew Catlin on his knees weeding around the tombstones in the far corner of the church cemetery. "It used to be that each family kept up its own plots," he explained. "But lots of our younger genera-tion have left to work on the mainland now. They find Tawes too . . . What is that expression? Laid low? Laid-back? Too slow and old-fashioned. Fishing and crab-bing have fallen off. Some say the bay is dying, killed off by pollution and overfishing. I can show you first-person accounts from the seventeenth century, in which men claimed they'd found oysters the size of din-ner plates, and fish were so thick you could walk from island to island without ever getting your feet wet."

"So caring for the cemetery falls to you?"

"No, no, I wouldn't say that. No need to worry about the Tawes family, or the Parks, the McCreadys or a half dozen other families. Just some, and it wouldn't do to let those forgotten folks be neglected."

"Your grandfather was a pastor as well, wasn't he?"

"Father, grandfather, and great-grandfather, not to mention the uncles, cousins, and even a great aunt—although she went over to the Quakers when she married a Dickerson from the Eastern Shore. Mother had hopes that Daniel would study for the church as well, but . . ." Matthew sighed. "He wasn't cut out for it. Nor for being a farmer or a waterman. Smart. Did well in college, but he always had a restless air about him. Had a high-paying job with the government for years." He shook his head. "Gave it all up last fall. Quit and came back here to pound nails. Lots of people thought Daniel was crazy to give up the pension. Not much money in being a carpenter."

"I was hoping that I might have a look at some of the church baptismal records this morning. Mr. McCready said that I was christened here as an infant."

Matthew yanked out a dandelion and added it to the growing pile of wilting weeds. "Hmm. What would that be? Thirty? Thirty-odd years ago?"

"Thirty-five."

He looked thoughtful. "My father was pastor here then. He would have been the one to officiate. Trouble is, Father was better at delivering fire-and-brimstone sermons than keeping his records in order. I have a meeting after lunch, and tomorrow is full. Give me a few days and I'll take a look and see if I can locate the book for that year. But don't get your hopes up—the seventies are pretty sketchy."

"Oh." She'd hoped to get a chance to read them today, but it sounded as though Matthew was going to be as pleasantly unhelpful as the rest of them. She forced a smile. "There is another idea I had. I'd like to go and talk to my great-uncle Will. Could you give me directions to his home?"

"Will Tawes?" The pastor frowned, and for just an instant Bailey thought she read panic in his eyes. "Mr. Tawes has a bad reputation on the island," he said stiffly. "Not mentally stable. He isn't a member of our congregation. Hasn't attended church in . . ." He scoffed. "Not since his brother's wedding, as far as I know."

"Mr. McCready says that Will—"

"You can't accept Forest's opinion. He defended Will at the trial. One of his first cases. They lost, and Forest has always felt as though it might have been his fault—that if he'd had more experience, he could have kept Will from going to jail."

"How long did he serve?"

"Nine years. Went to prison a bitter man and came back worse. No." He shook his head. "He's not someone you want to associate with. He's dangerous."

"That's what your brother said."

"Is it?" Matthew looked slightly puzzled. "Daniel should know. Sometimes I think they're a lot alike." He gathered the weeds into a basket. "I hope those baptismal records still exist. Unfortunately, we had a fire a few years back, and . . ."

"I hope they aren't lost."

"We'll remain optimistic." Matthew rubbed his back. "Tomorrow I have church business, and there's Birdy Parks's birthday on Friday. I might get to those records Friday morning, but the following day, Saturday, is our archeological group's monthly dig day. Five, six of us—four ladies and two men—go with me to our new site in Creed's skiff."

"What kind of site?"

"Quite exciting. An Indian fishing camp, at least we think it is. We've found some Woodland-era pottery and some points and fishhooks. If you're interested?"

"Yes. I'd love to come. If I wouldn't be—"

"Always room for one more enthusiastic digger.

Dave's visiting his son in Oxford, but his wife will be there. Alice. You'll like her."

"And you go by boat?"

"Too much marsh to reach the site by land. I depend on Creed to get our group safely to our digs." He chuckled. "We—that is, Grace and I—own a twenty-foot Boston Whaler. My Grace is quite competent at the tiller, a regular Captain Ahab, but she hates the marsh and she hates mosquitoes. I, on the other hand, am hopeless when it comes to tides and engines. My parents nearly disowned me. I've lived on an island my entire life, and I can't even swim. I thank the good Lord for Creed Somers and his trusty skiff."

"He brought me over to the island. Quite a colorful man, Captain Somers."

"Yes, colorful. Unfortunately, poor Creed is a soul possessed by the curse of alcohol. But when he hasn't been at the bottle with his drinking companion—that wayward Baptist woman, Ida Love—he's a decent man and a fine sailor. Creed Somers will take anyone anywhere in his skiff for hardly more than the price of gas."

"Will he?"

"Yes, indeed. You might think of hiring him to give you a tour of the island. There are some lovely coves, even some uninhabited islands that are a haven for waterfowl. You should see as much of Tawes as you can. It won't be here forever, you know. Every year we lose land to erosion. It just washes away into the bay. That's what happened to our old cemetery. The water came in and claimed it. Lots of old Tawes families' graves claimed by the bay."

"I'll keep that in mind. I brought my sketchbook and pencils. I may find time to attempt to some sketches."

She smiled at him. "I was wondering, did you know my mother, Beth? Do you remember her?"

"Matthew was away at college." Grace walked toward them briskly. "He wouldn't have known her. She was much younger, and her uncle kept her secluded. Few people knew her well." She fixed her husband with an amused stare. "I saw the opening of your next sermon on the table. It needs work. It's not like you to use clichés, dear."

"Perhaps I'd best give it a little more thought. You're usually right about my sermons."

"It's just that I know how eloquent you can be. If you'll excuse us, dear, I have cookies in the oven. And Matthew has spent far too much time this morning playing gardener."

He held up his hands in surrender. "Duty calls. Don't forget the dig. Saturday. Nine o'clock sharp at the dock."

"Should I bring anything?"

"Insect repellent. Buy some from Doris. And get Emma to pack you a lunch. We usually come back about four."

"You haven't bullied Bailey into accompanying you to that marsh, have you? Matthew is certain he's going to find an intact Indian dugout. He's been searching for fifteen years."

"This is a good spot, the best."

"I've heard that before. I warn you, there are mosquitoes the size of seagulls. It's dirty and hot. Not exactly—"

"It sounds like fun," Bailey said. "I'd love to see it, as long as we aren't breaking any state laws about disturbing historical—"

"Not a problem," Matthew assured her. "Mildred Bullin is a retired archeologist. Our dig is fully sanctioned. We record our finds properly and turn everything over to the state for preservation. We—"

"Yes, yes, dear. Go along, now." Grace made shooing motions. "Matthew has no sense of time. And if I don't shepherd him, he'll be late for his finance meeting."

"Thank you for your help," Bailey said. "And if you could look for those records, I'd appreciate it."

"What records?" Grace asked.

"My christening. I'd hoped to find—"

Grace pursed her lips. "You must remember that Tawes is a conservative community. I don't mean to dash your hopes, but it's possible, even likely, that my father-in-law didn't record the ceremony in his official records. You were, after all, born—there's no gentle way to put it—out of wedlock. You're the innocent party, but it's traditionally been the custom to seal adoption records to protect all concerned, especially the adoptee. You've obviously had a good life with loving parents. Perhaps that's where you should leave the matter."

"Both my birth mother and the mother who raised me are dead. My adoptive father has a new life on the West Coast. Who could possibly be hurt by my knowing something about my roots?"

"You could. More than you seem to realize." Grace brightened. "Since you're staying awhile longer, please join us for Sunday services. And don't forget my invitation to lunch afterward. I won't take no for an answer. Now, if you'll excuse us."

Grace's voice took on a nagging tone as she caught up with her husband, but they were too far away for Bailey to catch what she was saying.

"Don't bother to set a place for me," Bailey muttered under her breath. She'd been thinking of taking them up on their offer to go to church, but Grace's overbearing manner set her teeth on edge. Although her parents hadn't been religious, Bailey had often found herself drawn to the quiet and peace of old houses of worship. She might or might not attend Sunday services, but she had no intention of sharing Grace's table anytime in the foreseeable future.

Leaving the cemetery, Bailey walked to the harbor to see if Creed's boat was there. When she didn't see it, she sat for a while with her knees drawn up, watching the ducks and the seagulls. The scene was so lovely she itched to draw it, and wished she'd brought her sketchbook and charcoal instead of leaving them in her suitcase.

A pregnant woman in her late twenties wearing yellow shorts, sandals, and a green maternity top that read BABY ON BOARD came down the dock carrying a brown paper bag. "You must be Elizabeth Tawes's niece, the one everyone is talking about." She offered her hand. "I'm Cathy Tilghman. I teach at the elementary school here in town."

Bailey shook her hand. "Bailey Elliott. I teach fourth grade in Newark."

"I knew it," Cathy said. "You have the look."

"Really?" Bailey laughed. "Is *teacher* stamped on my forehead?"

"No, and the Tawes gossip neglected to say what you did for a living, but I thought, If she's watching ducks, she's interested in the world around her. I'll bet she's a teacher."

"Guilty. I love kids and any animal that won't bite or kick me."

"Well, let me introduce you to Molly Mallard. Mike is around here somewhere. He's the proud daddy, but I have a suspicion that he may be a bigamist. There's another hot babe sitting on eggs under the dock."

Bailey laughed. "The nerve of him."

"I was going to name the ducklings," Cathy continued, "but Jim—that's my husband—Jim warned me that I'd be brokenhearted if any of the diddles didn't make it. And it's rare for a duck to raise all of her brood."

"Hey, Molly," Bailey said. "Glad to make the acquaintance of you and your children."

"Aren't they cute? I love coming down to the dock to watch them. I beg leftovers from my neighbors." She opened the bag to reveal bread crusts and cornflakes. "I love feeding them. The ducks, not the neighbors. Jim says I'll make welfare birds out of them, but . . ." She laughed. "You can see how much attention I pay to what he says."

Bailey took a handful of the offered feed and the two sat side by side, tossing bits to the mother duck and her ducklings and chatting as though they'd been friends for years.

"So, what do you think of Tawes?" Cathy asked after a few minutes.

"Beautiful. Different. Some of the people . . ."

Cathy laughed. "That's what I thought when I first came here. I'm from Princess Anne, on the Eastern Shore. Jim and I met at Salisbury State. He warned me what I was in for. It took a little getting used to, but I love it here. I really do. I want to raise kids here—three, at least. Jim's mom and I get along great, and she offered us her house rent free when she moved in with her sister across the street."

"How long did it take before your neighbors stopped watching you from behind the curtains?"

"Two, maybe three years. It helped that I was a Smith. There have always been Smiths in Crisfield, and then there's Smith Island. The general feeling was that although I was a mainlander, I came from good stock."

"What does your husband do? Is he a fisherman?"

"No, Jim is a conservation officer. Not a fabulous salary, but he loves it. Can't imagine doing anything else. We do a little farming on the side, mostly organic vegetables for the Baltimore market."

When the bread was gone, Cathy issued an invitation for her to come and see the Tawes Elementary School any weekday. "It's small, not many students, but we're proud of it. We have computers and a great library. Your great-aunt was instrumental in that. She found a government site where we could get free books from the Library of Congress, and she convinced some of the major computer companies to donate rebuilt ones."

"Maybe I should try the same tactic. Our library books are old, and there aren't enough computers to go around. Some of the kids have them at home, but others don't. And they're going to need that knowledge in the future."

"I agree," Cathy said enthusiastically. "I really love what I do, and we think Tawes is special. I teach a combined second and third grade." She balled up the empty paper bag. "Some of our kids didn't do as well as we hoped in the state testing, so I and a retired teacher volunteer hold summer catch-up classes to bring them up to speed."

"What about high school? Creed Summers said that they go to Crisfield by boat every day?"

"Yes. They've done that for, I don't know, maybe twenty years. A few kids are homeschooled, and some go away to boarding school, but most don't mind the commute."

"I can't imagine going to school by boat instead of bus, but I suppose somewhere in the world, kids go by plane."

"Please come and visit the school. We only have class until twelve; then you can come back to my house and have lunch with me. It won't be fancy, but I think we'd have lots to talk about."

"I'd like that," Bailey admitted. "I came down to the dock looking for Creed. Is this a day he's making the ferry run?"

"Yes, it is, but—" Cathy rubbed her belly. "I think this one has three feet. She kicks like a mule." She giggled. "What was I saying? Oh, yes, Creed. He doesn't tie up here. He has a dock behind his place. It's about a mile and half out of town. Turn left when you leave Emma's; then go about a mile on the main road."

"I love the way you say that. Main road."

Cathy laughed again. "Wait until you take Hessian's Redoubt. That's Creed's road. It makes the dirt road look like an interstate. Take a left at the fork in the main road. There's no sign, but there's a big walnut tree with a lightning-scarred limb. Out past the old cemetery. Stay clear of that. Some of the graves have sunken in and . . ." She shivered. "I wouldn't want to have to dig you out of what's left of a two-hundred-year-old pine coffin."

"Me either."

"Take the left onto Hessian's Redoubt and follow the ruts along the water's edge. You pass two farms, then go through a wood, and Creed's house is on your left. It has a red roof and a barn that leans hard to starboard." She glanced at her watch. "Uh-oh. I'd better run home and get dinner started."

The most normal person I've met on this island, Bailey thought as she turned toward Emma's. She really liked Cathy. The young teacher seemed smart, dedicated, and full of fun, someone that she'd have enjoyed getting to know anywhere. She'd make certain she stopped by the school before she went home. Perhaps she and Cathy could exchange e-mail addresses.

As she passed the parsonage, Bailey glanced toward the house. There was no sign of Grace or Matthew, but as she walked by, she caught a hint of movement at a window in the living room. Imagination, or was Grace Catlin spying on her? It must be her imagination. Any moment now she'd hear spooky music coming from the attic. Chuckling at her own foolishness, she hurried on, wondering what fattening marvel Emma would put on the table tonight.

"Will you get away from that window?" Matthew admonished. "Do you want her to think the worst of us?"

"Me? What were you thinking to invite her to go on your dig?" Grace asked. "She's an attractive young woman, a stranger, and a Tawes. I don't need to remind you that a minister of the gospel must be above reproach. Some of our parishioners will remember Beth's disgrace."

"Old gossip. And you know Bailey isn't responsible for what happened thirty-five years ago."

"I didn't say she was. She's seems like a sweet girl. But why start people talking again? Let it lie, I say. It's a tragedy, certainly, but it's done with."

"Will Tawes paid for his crime."

"Did he? He's out, isn't he? And he's still carrying a grudge. You know that it wouldn't take much to set him off. Some people have been talking about the senator's death, saying it was no accident."

"The police said it was. A hunting accident."

"Think that if it gives you solace, Matthew. But the sooner she leaves Tawes, the better it will be for all of us. And encouraging her to stay only tempts that devil Will to kill someone else."

"You have no proof he killed Joe Marshall."

"Maybe not, but I'm not the only one to suspect it. Emma told me that Bailey heard the whistler two nights ago."

"Emma's always been a worrier. She was probably dreaming."

"And if she wasn't? If I'm right, Joe's won't be the only blood to spill on this island. Mark my words, Will is dangerous. And so is Beth's girl."

CHAPTER SIX

"Daniel!" Emma called from the foot of her stairs.

He'd spent all Thursday afternoon installing the down-stairs toilet in the cabin, had returned to the boarding-house, and was about to jump into the shower before supper. Barefooted and shirt half-unbuttoned, he retraced his steps to the top of the stairs. "What is it?"

"I have to go out. There's a pork roast, a peach pie, and baked potatoes in the oven. Could you do salad? I need you to take care of supper. And remind Bailey about Mama's birthday party tomorrow."

Daniel scowled. "If you're trying to play matchmaker, forget it. It's better if she leaves before things get out of hand."

Emma shook her head. "It's already out of hand. You heard him two nights ago, didn't you?"

"I didn't hear anything," he lied. He'd talk to him, try to reason with him. He'd done it a dozen times, but maybe this time . . .

Emma scoffed. "Right. Tell that to Joe Marshall. I'm

scared, Daniel." She stared up at him. "Do I have to shout up the stairs so half the town can hear?"

He grimaced, lifted a palm in mock surrender, and descended halfway down the steps.

Emma lowered her voice. "I want you to take over here for the evening. That's all there is to it."

"Why don't I believe you?" He knew this was about Mallalai, and Emma's determination to get him to move on with his life.

"She's dead, son. It's a hard fact, but that doesn't mean you need to go in the ground with her. It's only right to mourn—"

"Leave it. I'll deal with it in my own time." He turned to go back upstairs and muttered, "In my own way."

"Daniel."

He stopped two steps from the top landing.

"You're not dealing with it; that's the problem. Hell-fire and damnation! I'm not asking you to sire her babies, just serve supper and make a damn salad. She barely ate a bite at lunch today."

Daniel scowled over his shoulder at her. "You're an interfering—"

"Busybody? I thought that was Grace's job. I care about you, boy. Maybe I'm one of the few who does." She raised one beefy shoulder and rested a foot on the bottom step. "Not hard on the eyes, though, is she? Never saw a Tawes girl who was."

He wouldn't give Emma the satisfaction of knowing just how attractive he found Bailey. She was a beautiful woman, petite, with a waist a man could span with his hands. She had nice legs, and a man couldn't be shot for looking—at least, not in the Western world. And he'd always favored small women with nicely shaped, firm breasts. . . .

Emma snickered. "You do think she's cute."

"You won't leave it alone, will you?"

"Just supper. That's all I'm asking of you. Anything else is on your own conscience."

Memories of Mallalai washed over him as he tore butter lettuce and chopped scallions for the salad. There was a jar of sun-dried tomatoes and another of black olives, and he absently added some of each. Letting his thoughts drift back to Afghanistan was as agonizing as probing an abscessed tooth with an ice pick. What happened there . . . His feelings about Mallalai were hard to forget.

Logically, Daniel knew that Emma was right. He couldn't go on living like a monk or he'd end up as bitter as Will Tawes, but fifteen months wasn't long enough to get over it. Maybe fifteen years wouldn't be either.

Her eyes had been what had drawn him, large, dark, almond-shaped eyes . . . eyes fringed with thick, long lashes, eyes that spoke volumes without her uttering a sound.

She'd been bundled up with layers of clothing from the crown of her head to the toes of her soft leather boots the first time he'd met her. She'd wound a scarf around her head to protect her face from the snow, and only those mysterious eyes showed. Later, when she removed her outer clothing, when he could see her features, he thought her the most beautiful woman he'd ever seen.

She'd come to his tent with one of his most trusted informants, Daoud, and her brother Zahir. The two men carried Russian Kalashnikovs; the weapon slung over Mallalai's shoulder was a shiny, American-made

M16. The three had come from a valley controlled by Taliban sympathizers, over a pass that had been blocked with snow for three weeks—a pass that the village elders had sworn was impossible to traverse at this time of year.

Daoud had sobbed when he related how two mules and his cousin, seventeen-year-old Osman, had been swept away in a snowslide the night before. Mallalai stood silently behind him, her gaze darting around the tent, and didn't shed a tear. The three of them were hungry, half-frozen, and weary beyond belief, but refused food and rest until they passed on the message Osman had died to deliver.

"You're making dinner?"

Bailey's voice cut the frigid mountain air, tearing away the fabric of the past, so that Daniel's senses returned one by one. The odors of wet wool, mule shit, and onions frying in mutton fat gave way to spicy peach pie and roast chicken. The lump in his throat dissolved, and he let out the breath he'd been unconsciously holding as Mallalai's image wavered and then faded. In her place stood an auburn-haired woman in khaki shorts and a sleeveless summer blouse.

"Is there anything I can do to help?"

"Set the table." He motioned to the wall cupboard. He dumped radishes and celery into the salad bowl and carried it to the kitchen table. "Emma had to go out. No reason why we can't eat here."

"Dinner wasn't necessary."

"Emma thought it was." Memories of the first meal he'd shared with Mallalai lingered. Yogurt. Naan made with coarsely ground grain and baked in a mud oven. Raisins. Roasted goat so stringy that muscle fibers kept getting stuck between his teeth. She'd devoured her meager portion ravenously and licked her fingers. Later he'd learned that she, Daoud, and Zahir had eaten nothing but snow for three days.

"Look," Bailey said. "I'm sorry for what happened— when you were working on the grape arbor. I overreacted. If I was rude, I—"

"No, you weren't rude." He sliced the steaming chicken. "I was." She held out a serving platter and he forked a mixture of light and dark meat onto it. "And for the record, this is supper. Dinner is the meal served midday on Tawes."

She smiled. "I stand corrected. Supper. And will you join me, or am I to dine alone?"

"I'll eat. Emma has a special way with roast chicken. Some kind of seasoning she rubs into the skin before she puts it in the oven." He removed the potatoes and put them in a bowl.

"We'll need butter and—"

"Sour cream."

They both reached for the refrigerator door at the same time, and their hands brushed. He jerked back and she gave an embarrassed chuckle. "Sorry."

"My fault." She passed him the butter and sour cream. He put them on the table and took a chair opposite Bailey as she began to relate her chance meeting with Cathy at the dock.

One small hand rested on the oilcloth, and he wanted to cover it with his own. Instead he busied himself with his napkin and tried not to stare at the hollow of her slender throat or the smattering of freckles on her nose and cheeks.

She'd obviously showered before coming down to the kitchen. Her damp hair was twisted up on the back of her head so that tendrils curled at the nape of her neck. She smelled good enough to eat. Her perfume scent was light and spicy, almost like green apples.

Mallalai had worn jasmine.

"So tell me," Bailey urged. "How is it that a bright young government employee with an important career and a good retirement check on the horizon throws it all away to come back to Brigadoon and become the village handyman?"

"Who said it was an important career?"

"Your brother."

"Matt's easily impressed." His voice grated. He found himself thinking about the shape of her mouth and what it would taste like if he kissed her.

She laughed. "I'm all ears."

"It's a long story, and most of it not for mixed company. It was probably inevitable. We're an inbred lot here on Tawes, and despite the obvious brain damage, we're independent as hell. The government career sounded good to begin with, but when push came to shove, I wasn't cut out to be a regimented, nine-to-five bureaucrat."

"Why do I think there's a lot more to it than that?"

She had a really nice smile that went all the way to her eyes, blue eyes that reminded him of Elizabeth's and Will's. When she smiled, Bailey Elliott went from cute to knockout, and the temperature in the kitchen rose noticeably.

She was damned attractive, and he found himself responding to her in ways he hadn't done since . . .

Whoa, boy, back off, he thought. *This is definitely not a woman you want to get messed up with.* For a lot of reasons . . . her connection to Will Tawes number one on the list.

"Why weren't you drawn to the church?" Bailey teased. "Matthew told me that your father, grandfather, and great-grandfather were all ministers."

"I always was the odd man out in the family." He concentrated on his salad, stabbing at an olive, missing, and pinning it against the side of the bowl. *Hell*, he thought. He hadn't been this nervous around a pretty girl since he was fifteen. "My arrival was something of an embarrassment to my parents. Matt is more than twenty years older than I am, and my mother assumed she was past childbearing."

"Mother and Dad were in their forties when they adopted me. Everyone always asked me if they were my grandparents." She took a bite of the chicken. "Delicious. But then, everything Emma cooks is terrific."

"It's why I haven't moved out to the cabin," he admitted. "I can cook well enough to keep body and soul together, but Emma is a master chef."

"Ah," she teased. "So you admit you have a soul?"

"It's an old saying. Tawes is full of clichés."

"You wiggled out of that nicely. I can believe you worked for the government. Never giving a straight answer must be a requirement for the job." She dabbed at her lower lip with her napkin.

Apparently she wasn't wearing lipstick, because none came off on the cloth. That peach color must be natural, he thought.

"Part of the reason I changed careers."

Bailey was sharp, with a mischievous sense of humor and a lively curiosity. In spite of himself, he was intrigued. If she were anyone else he would have been interested . . . more than interested. He would have suggested they dig out a bottle of Emma's best wine and take it upstairs, where they could be more comfortable. But this wasn't any woman . . . this was Beth Tawes's daughter.

As they shared the meal, he found himself talking much more than he normally did, telling her stories about his childhood on the island and her great-aunt Elizabeth. "She was a teacher too. We knocked heads more times than I can count." He grimaced. "I was a handful, but she didn't give an inch. She wouldn't let me get away without doing my best. For all her toughness, the kids loved her. I usually had the job of unsaddling her horse before school and—"

"Her horse? She rode? I love horses. I used to beg for one every birthday and Christmas, but the closest I ever got was riding lessons one summer at camp."

"Elizabeth was a fantastic rider. She rode to school every day from the farm, snow, rain, or sun. And when she decided that her horses needed more than a lean-to shelter here in town, she threatened to quit if the board didn't build her a proper stable."

"Did they?"

He nodded. "They did. A nice box stall and an enclosed area where the horse could graze. I think they have sheep in the pasture now."

Daniel had meant to minimize the contact between them, see that she had a decent meal, and make himself scarce, but it didn't turn out that way. After supper they shared the chores, cleaning up the kitchen, and doing the dishes. And somehow he found himself sharing the front porch swing with Bailey as the long summer evening slowly slipped into purple dusk.

"I'm surprised," Bailey said softly as they watched the first lightning bugs of the season blink on and off in the yard. "Somehow I'd thought of Elizabeth Tawes as a sick old lady."

"Elizabeth? Hardly." He laughed. "She rode into town to pick up her groceries the day before the accident. As far as I know, she was never sick a day in her life."

"I'm sorry I didn't get to meet her."

"Me too. She was one of a kind."

"Obviously much more pleasant than her brother."

Daniel pushed off with his foot and set the porch swing rocking. Bailey was sitting close enough that he could slip his arm around her shoulders, but instead he held tight to the back rail. "Will's had a lot to make him what he is."

"He's an aging man who served time in prison. That doesn't make him Blackbeard the pirate. I don't know why everyone's afraid of him."

"Will's a hard man. Some have reason to fear him." He paused. "Still, if you decide to sell Elizabeth's farm, you might ask Forest, to give him first chance to make an offer."

"A recluse who lives out in the woods? You think he'd have the kind of money the land is worth?"

"If not Will, some other people on the island. Nothing's ever been sold to mainlanders, as far as I know. Emma said you didn't feel very welcome here. Some are bound to think you'd bring developers in, tear down the old homestead, and put up condos."

"It's not mine yet," she said. "I can hardly decide what I want to do with property I don't own. But one way or another, I will certainly be selling. What would I do with a farm?"

Bailey wished she'd been a little more discreet about her intentions of selling the farm, she thought later as she made ready for bed. Alone. Daniel's demeanor had turned cooler after that statement. Before that, she'd thought he was going to kiss her . . . hoped he was going to kiss her. Hell, she'd almost made the first move and kissed him. But obviously she'd either mis-read his body language or offended him.

For a few seconds she wondered if she'd been way off. She'd thought the air between them had sizzled. He'd been a perfect gentleman, but her intuition told her that beneath that country-boy charm and easy smile lurked a rascal with a dangerous streak more in common with an eighteenth-century highwayman than a simple country carpenter. Something elusive and almost scary.

Damn, but she'd been reading too many historical romances. She tossed the paperback she'd brought with her onto the nightstand. No more Scottish lairds and kidnapped lasses for her tonight.

She woke once in the middle of the night and sat bolt upright, breathing hard, certain that she'd heard the eerie whistling outside her window again. But as she lay there, heart racing, fingers gripping the cotton coverlet, only the rustle of the wind in the trees dis-turbed the deep quiet. "A dream," she muttered, "only a dream." She covered her head with her pillow and didn't open her eyes again until morning.

By nine thirty Friday morning, after sharing break-fast with a cheerful Emma, Bailey struck a deal with a sober but unshaven and obviously hungover Creed Somers to take her sightseeing around the perimeter of the island in his boat.

"Have to have cash up front," the waterman warned her. "Gas costs money, and they won't give me credit at the dock. Tight as washed-wool trousers, the lot of them.

Lived here all my life. Never stole a cent from nobody, and I can't get gas for my boat without hard money."

Murmuring sympathetically, Bailey had handed over fifty dollars in cash, Creed had gassed up his boat, and they'd set out. The weather was cooler than the day before, cloudy with the threat of rain and with a slight chop to the waves, but Bailey was determined. If she waited, she might chicken out, and if she did that, she knew she'd always regret not trying.

Even if she hadn't had ulterior motives, she would have enjoyed the morning on the water. Although they passed a few crabbing boats and a larger vessel that Creed said belonged to State Fish and Wildlife, most of the time they were alone with stunning views of woods, stretches of beach, and pastureland. Now and then Bailey spied farmhouses or smaller cottages nestled into the forest or sheltered by rolling terrain.

"The far side of the island's mostly marsh and wetland," Creed said, "good duck and goose hunting. That's where Daniel discovered the senator's body."

She didn't answer. She'd almost but not quite forgotten the news stories about the gruesome find. Apparently Joseph Marshall, the senior senator from Maryland and the chair of House Appropriations, one of the most powerful committees in Congress, had been frozen faceup in the ice. The image that rose in her mind gave her goose bumps. She swallowed, trying to ease the constriction in her throat. She remembered that Joseph Marshall had been suggested by some as strong vice presidential material. So powerful and wealthy a man with so much ambition cut down in his prime. She hadn't realized that Daniel was the one who'd found him.

"Nobody knows exactly what happened." Creed leaned over the side and spit a wad of tobacco. "Went out by hisself duck hunting and never come back alive. Found his dogs, though. Safe and sound. They wandered up to Allan Goldsborough's farm. Nice Labs they were. Golden. Don't know what happened to the dogs after that. I suppose the family sent somebody for them." He pointed. "There's your aunt Elizabeth's place. See it, through the trees there?"

"Yes, yes, I do. Where's Uncle Will's home? Is it nearby?"

"Near enough." Creed turned the bow of the skiff out away from the shoreline.

"I want to talk to him. Can you take me there? To his house?"

"Nope. Not goin' anywhere near'm." Creed's accent seemed to thicken, and she thought she read something like fear in his eyes.

"I'll give you twenty dollars more. Just let me off on the beach."

"Not for two hundred greenbacks. Not for a thousand."

"Wait, please. Can you let me get off on Aunt Elizabeth's dock? Just tell me what direction his house is in, and I'll find it myself."

Creed shook his head.

Bailey fished in her wallet and came out with a new fifty-dollar bill. "No one will know. Just pull up to Elizabeth's dock. You don't have to wait for me."

"Are you out of your head, girl? You don't know what you're messin' with. Will Tawes is meaner than a constipated snake—beggin' your pardon."

"I've already met him—talked to him. He isn't going to hurt me. I'm his great-niece. Either let me off, or . . . or I'll jump off."

"Damn fool woman," he muttered, but he turned the bow back toward the creek mouth. "Serves you right if he does shoot you. Damned mainlanders. Think we're stupid."

Bailey didn't hand over the fifty-dollar bill until the bow of the skiff nudged against the dock. "Which way to his house?"

Creed scowled and pointed. "It's not far. Just follow the shoreline. Call out before you come up on him. He carries a rifle wherever he goes, and people say it don't take much to set him off."

As Creed's boat pulled away, Bailey wondered if she'd made a mistake. If her great-uncle's behavior in the house had been any indication of his temperament, he might take a shot at her. But she didn't think so. Forest McCready had vouched for him. And Will Tawes was her relative. They shared Tawes blood, if what everyone said was true. She couldn't miss this chance to question him about her mother. If she went back to Newark without knowing the answers to her questions, she might never find out.

From the dock, Elizabeth's farmhouse looked even bigger and grander than it had from the land. There was a whole brick story-and-a-half wing on this side that she hadn't noticed before. Surely somebody would pay a fortune for this view.

Walking along the beach, she found an overgrown lane through the woods that led in the direction Creed had pointed. She followed it, dodging briars and what looked like poison ivy for several hundred yards. Then through the thick foliage she smelled wood smoke and spotted one corner of the roof of a house.

Ahead, a dog's warning bark brought Bailey to an abrupt, heart-pounding halt. Immediately from the shoreline on her right came a guttural baying. Then a third dog sounded in the underbrush to her left. Bailey's knees turned to water. Dogs were her greatest weakness. Since kindergarten, when she'd been attacked and severely bitten by a stray on her way home, she'd suffered a deep and persistent fear of dogs. Frantically she grabbed a fallen branch to defend herself and backed against the nearest tree.

A massive red dog burst from the underbrush. Bailey raised the stick over her head.

"Hold it right there!" Ax in hand, Will Tawes stepped out of the trees and onto the path directly in front of her. "You're trespassing."

CHAPTER SEVEN

Bailey's gaze flicked from the man with the ax to the enormous Chesapeake Bay retriever that materialized out of the thick cedars. It padded forward, hackles raised, teeth bared, and yellow-golden eyes locked on her.

Beads of sweat ran down the outside of Bailey's throat to trickle between her breasts. *Dogs. Why did there have to be dogs?*

The first animal, the one that had startled her by leaping out of the undergrowth, moved to stand between her and Will. The dog's lips were drawn back over ivory fangs, ears pressed tight to the head. Both dogs had ceased barking, but their unnatural silence seemed even more lethal.

Black specks danced before Bailey's eyes, and an odd buzzing sounded in her head. She opened her mouth to speak, but all that came out was a small gasp.

"Hell and damnation. Put down that branch. You're scaring my dogs."

Scaring his dogs? Her stomach clenched as it had

the morning after she and Elliott had finished a bottle of cheap tequila. Her vision blurred as she lowered the stick, swallowed, and managed, "Call them off. Please."

Will made a slight gesture with his right hand. Instantly both dogs dropped onto their bellies. The fiercest-looking one, a male with a huge head and a scar across his muzzle, emitted a deep rumble low in his throat.

"Hush, now."

The animal lowered his head to rest his muzzle on paws half the size of Bailey's hands, but continued to stare at her. She suspected that if she made a move toward his master, those gleaming teeth would find her . . . would clamp and tear through flesh and bone. People said that animals could smell fear, but she didn't possess the strength to control hers or to keep from trembling.

She wanted to run, to put distance between her, the dogs, and Will Tawes with his big ax, but she couldn't. She'd started this, and she had to finish it. "If you're Elizabeth's brother, you're my uncle." Her voice sounded feeble, even childish, but it was the best she could summon.

For what seemed forever he said nothing, merely studied her with an unwavering gaze. She'd been told that he was older than his sister, but he didn't appear to be a man in his mid-sixties. Despite the graying hair, he was lean and muscular, and he moved with the ease of a man in his prime.

"Leave the past be. Get off my land. Go home, and don't come back."

She glanced at the dogs to make certain they hadn't moved closer. "You're the only relative . . . the only blood relative I have," she managed. "I have the right to know what happened to my mother. Why, after three months, you decided to put me up for adoption."

He shook his head. "You'll get nothing from me but heartache. Get out of here while you can." He rested the blade of his ax beside the toe of his heavy work boot and leaned on the handle.

"My mother was your niece. You must have cared something for her. And if Aunt Elizabeth left me her farm, that makes us neighbors. All I want—"

"Are you deaf, girl, or just stupid?"

"I'm not stupid! And I suspect that you aren't either. Why won't you have the decency to answer a few questions about my family?"

A third dog, a tricolored mongrel with long hair and one pale blue eye ringed in black, crept out of the tall grass and sidled up to push his nose into the back of Will's knee.

Eyeing the dog, Bailey said, "Don't I have the right to know about my family? About how my mother—"

"Let her rest." The blue eyes that glared out of her uncle's rough-hewn face were hard.

"I can't."

He shrugged. "Suit yourself." Turning, he strode away down the path toward his house.

"Wait! Uncle Will."

The three dogs trotted after him.

"Uncle Will!" She ran after him into the yard, but before she could catch up, man and animals crossed the wraparound porch and entered the house. "Please!" The oak door slammed shut, and she heard the solid click of a metal bolt.

Bailey banged on the door with her fist. "All I want is to know how she died."

Silence.

She pounded again. "I'm not going away. You might as well open up, or I'll stay here all day!"

Minutes passed. She knocked again without results.

Frustrated, she sat down on the top step. "I can be just as stubborn as you can!"

A dog woofed.

Her heart skipped a beat, and she summoned her courage to shout, "I mean it!"

In the distance, a boat motor coughed, caught, and roared.

Bailey ran around the corner of the house in time to see a skiff leaving the dock with her great-uncle and the three dogs on board. "Damn it! Coward! Come back here!"

She kicked at the oyster-shell path. "Double damn it!" It wasn't fair. First she had no one of her own, and then she had a great-aunt and -uncle and the possibility of answers. And now she was as clueless as she'd ever been.

No, she told herself. That wasn't true. She'd discovered where she was born, who her mother was, and where she'd been christened. Or had she? Was it all some perverse game?

She sat on the edge of the porch and looked around. She was hot, thirsty, and a long way from town. She scoffed. Town? Tawes wasn't a town; it hardly qualified as a village. More like an asylum. No wonder she was such a basket case. With so much in-breeding on the island, she was fortunate she hadn't been born with two heads.

Grudgingly, she had to admit that this wasn't what she'd expected. The outbuildings and yard were well kept, the house trim, and the barn freshly painted. In an open area, trees had been cleared for a garden.

Neat rows of vegetables mulched with straw radiated from a scarecrow in a red hunter's vest and cap. Hummingbird feeders hung from the porch rafters; there was even a birdbath under a peach tree.

It seemed that Will Tawes was an enigma.

Now what? She felt foolish, but not foolish enough to give up.

On a whim, she rose, went to the nearest window, and peered in. The shadowy room was orderly, with comfortable furniture, floor-to-ceiling bookshelves, and paintings on the wall. No stacks of old newspapers or bales of discarded clothes. No giant balls of string. It was becoming very clear that her uncle Will was not the backwoods crackpot she'd expected. She moved along the porch to look into the next room, but there inside shutters were closed, blocking her view.

At the end of the porch, a modern addition with floor-to-ceiling windows appeared to have been added on to the story-and-a-half brick residence. Here, a wide cedar deck looked out over the dock and bay. The first window was obscured by drawn blinds, but the second was unobstructed. Bailey shaded her eyes from the bright sunlight and gazed into a spacious room with a high cathedral ceiling and skylights.

"Ohhh," she gasped. Tables. Chairs. Easels with partially drawn sketches of birds of prey. Lifelike carvings of ducks and geese in various stages of completion. An otter that looked real enough to breathe lay on its back with a fish between its front paws, and just inside the window stood an exquisite replica of a raccoon with two babies, her paws against the glass, black nose pressed against the glass, staring out.

"You old scoundrel. I know an artist's studio when I see one."

Excitement made her giddy. This wasn't a case of mistaken identity. She'd found where her love of sketching and watercolor had come from. And crazy or not, she'd found her identity. She wasn't Bailey Elliott—she was Bailey Tawes of Tawes Island. For the first time in her life, she had roots and a family history.

The implications of what she'd seen made Bailey's walk back to the village seem insignificant. Far from discouraging her from attempting to talk with her uncle, the visit made her want to know him more. She wanted to inspect his work closely and find out if her mother had possessed a talent for drawing or sculpting. She was eager to question Emma about Will's skill at carving, but when she got back to the house, she found it overflowing with women.

"Don't tell me that I forgot to mention it this morning?" Emma hurried past with a basket of eggs, a box of tea bags, and two bottles of concentrated of lemon juice. "Today is Mama's eighty-fifth birthday party. Half the island will be here by evening."

"Please don't think you have to include me," Bailey began. "I can—"

"Nonsense, girl. Grab an apron and a knife and start peeling potatoes. Grace has it in her head that we'll need fifty pounds of potato salad."

"But I don't have anything for a birthday gift for—"

"No gifts. Cousin Harry Parks's youngest had to have heart surgery just after he was born. We're all chipping in what we can to help with what insurance didn't cover. Mama insisted on it. You can donate or not. No one will know or care a dot."

"I'll be glad to help out. If you'll just let me change my clothes—"

"Bailey! Out here!" Cathy, the young teacher she'd met at the dock, motioned to her from the open kitchen door. "I've got a dishpan full of steamed crabs to pick for crab cakes. Can you give us a hand? We're on the back porch."

Helping Cathy sounded better than being trapped in the hot kitchen on potato-salad detail with Grace Catlin and two gray-haired women in Mother Hubbard aprons. Bailey hurried upstairs, washed, and changed into a clean T-shirt and shorts. Taking the path of least resistance, she exited the B and B by the front door. Rounding the house, she joined her new friend, who immediately introduced her shy sister-in-law Maria, a chubby brunette in her early thirties, and a neighbor, Amy, who also taught at the school.

"Maria's my husband's sister," Cathy explained as she pointed out her nephew Eric, seven, wandering along the water's edge with a crab net, and her niece, Julie, a toddler who was being carried around the yard, being "spoiled rotten by Maggie and the other girls."

"And this is Joel." Amy shifted her newborn to her right shoulder and patted his back. "Come on, little man, I know you have a burp in that tummy somewhere."

Joel expelled a small burst of air, and Cathy laughed. "Isn't he precious? I can't wait for my baby to get here."

"When he starts crying in the middle of the night, you'll wish he was still inside," Amy teased, tucking Joel back into his infant seat and popping a pacifier in his mouth.

"Not a chance."

Bailey looked at the pile of steamed crabs heaped on the table. "I warn you, I'm a novice at this," she said as she accepted a tall glass of iced tea.

"You'll catch on fast enough," Amy assured her. "If you're a Tawes, it's born in you."

Cathy handed her a wooden mallet. "This is to crack the claws."

"Don't smash the crabs with it," Amy said.

"You break them apart like this," Cathy explained, demonstrating. "And don't break the claws until last, because they're better than a knife to extract the white meat, here and here."

Amy nodded. "Easy as catching frogs in a rain barrel."

"We don't eat these things." Maria indicated a yellowish glob. "They're eggs. And these are lungs," Maria said. "We throw them away."

"When we're finished picking these, we'll show you how Amy's mother makes crab cakes." Cathy put a finger to her lips. "And not a word to Emma."

Amy giggled. "She thinks we're using her recipe."

Within a few minutes Bailey not only felt at ease with the group but thought she had the knack of crab picking. And although she was a lot slower than the others, she soon was adding a respectable amount of crabmeat to the large mixing bowl.

Soon more women and children arrived, most carrying pitchers of tea or lemonade, platters of baked ham, roast turkey, salads, pies, biscuits, and cooked vegetables. Two teenagers staggered under the weight of a glorious four-layer cake crowned with a spray of yellow confectionary roses, a cake so large and professionally done that it could easily have served two hundred wedding guests.

"Inside with that cake," Emma ordered. "Put that on the dining room table. If we set it up on the outside table, we'll have more flies than roses."

"I don't know why that would bother you." Amy chuckled. "It's what happened to my anniversary cake."

"Yes, and who ate it?" Emma propped fisted hands on her hips and struck a pose. "My hens. We're not taking that chance with Mama's birthday cake. She'd have our heads in a bushel basket." She pointed toward the kitchen door, and the cake transporters cheerfully obeyed her instructions.

Children ran in and out of the house. The baby fussed; Amy fed him, and he dropped off to sleep amid all the chaos. Old men wandered by with frosty tall glasses. Women rescued toddlers from certain disaster, soothed them, and pushed them into waiting arms. And through it all, Emma remained calm and cheerful.

Bailey was both amazed and content. Here on Emma's porch, she found a completely different reception from the one she'd received earlier on Tawes. Cathy, Maria, Amy, and Emma's easy acceptance seemed to bridge the gap between her and the islanders. Soon she found herself laughing and talking as freely as if she'd known them all for months.

Once the crabs were picked, the women fashioned them into crab cakes, secretly adding spices other than the ones Emma had ordered. Then Maria and Amy took control of the kitchen range, heating cast-iron frying pans, adding oil, and frying half of the crab cakes while putting others in the oven to broil.

Cathy motioned Bailey toward the kitchen door, but Emma wasn't to be fooled a second time. "It doesn't take four of you to do up crab cakes," she pronounced, pressing both Cathy and Bailey into Grace's service. The pastor's wife gave them a huge bowl of macaroni salad to finish and containers of raw vegetables to be washed and cut for serving with dip.

By five o'clock the working men began to arrive: Matthew, Forest McCready, and Creed appeared first. Forest and Matthew brought extra chairs and tables from the church social hall, and Creed was weighed down with a violin and two buckets of oysters in their shells. Daniel appeared with Emma's mother, the guest of honor.

"Mama, I think you know everybody here but Bailey," Emma said as she settled the white-haired lady in the blue-striped cotton dress into a comfortable rocking chair on the porch. "Bailey, this is my mama. Her name is Maude Ellen McCready Parks, but most folks call her Aunt Birdy. She used to be the best fisherman on Tawes Island, but now she just tells other people how to fish."

"Somebody has to," Maude said. The elderly woman stood just under five feet tall in her black lace-up shoes and weighed no more than a ten-year-old girl. Her childish voice was high and sweetly thin, like a small bird, the exact opposite of Emma's low rasp.

"I'm pleased to meet you, Mrs. Parks," Bailey said.

Maude turned her head and Bailey saw that her eyes were white with cataracts. "Come here, child," she said. "Let me touch your face."

"Go on," Emma urged. "She won't rest until she sees what you look like."

Cathy gave Bailey a little push.

Feeling self-conscious, Bailey did as she was instructed. She took Maude's bony hand, closed her eyes, and brought the woman's fingertips to her cheek. "Ah," Maude crooned. "You're little but mighty. Pretty as your mother." Her touch was surprisingly light as she skimmed cheekbone, brow, the line of Bailey's nose, and her lips. "She's a Tawes, all right. No mistake. Got her aunt Elizabeth's stubborn mouth." She drew her hand back. "Welcome, child. Welcome home."

"Thank you," Bailey murmured. Oddly, the old woman's touch had been comforting, almost a caress. Satisfaction that she had been officially pronounced a Tawes gave her a curious but happy warm feeling in the pit of her stomach.

Some of the men set up long tables and benches in the yard, while others rolled a stump out from behind the house and placed it on end under an oak tree. Matthew and Daniel brought smaller stumps and set them around the larger one as stools. Creed drew a bow across his violin strings, and women and children stopped what they were doing and gathered near.

"Forest is the fastest oyster shucker on the island," Emma declared, settling on the largest of the stools. "Next to me." She whipped a small knife out of her apron pocket and wagged it back and forth in challenge.

"Don't fill her head with lies." The attorney grinned as he found a seat and took out his own oyster knife. "You were lucky last time. I wasn't in my best form last fall, but this time you'll see who the master shucker is."

"You tell her," Maude teased. "Success has gone to her head."

"Now, Mama, you're supposed to be on my side."

The violin sighed and Creed broke into an old tune, drawing the bow faster and faster until the strings seemed to take on life of their own as Emma and Forest began to open raw oysters. Each contestant had his or her own team, choosing bivalves from the bucket, washing them, and handing them one by one as the knives bit and twisted, releasing the succulent oysters into a common tub. Men began to whistle and cheer their favorites while the watching women clapped and taunted the two shuckers.

Bailey watched in fascination as the piles of shells and the laughter grew. From the fringes of the crowd came the notes of a harmonica and then another violin joined in. Then, abruptly, Emma gave a final flick of her knife and stood up.

"Finished!" she bellowed. "How about you, Forest?"

The attorney glanced down at the bucket at his feet. His shoulders slumped, and his smile faded. "All I can say is, I've been robbed!"

"Robbed, nothing!" Emma roared. "You been beat, fair and square."

"Well, then," Matthew said, "what are we waiting for, ladies? Let's eat."

Amid laughter and good-natured jibes between the rival teams, men, women, and children flowed toward the tables that the men had set up earlier in the yard. "What will they do with all the oysters?" Bailey asked Cathy as they joined the ranks of volunteers carrying bowls and plates of food and pitchers of iced tea, lemonade, and water outside.

"Oyster stew. It doesn't take long to cook, and Emma will slip inside and make a vat of it sometime after supper. That's what all those clean quart jars are for. Nobody will feel like cooking dinner tomorrow, so each family will take home a jar or two of stew. Along with all the leftovers." She laughed. "I won't have to make supper for three days, and that's fine with me."

"I see," Bailey said. She'd supposed that such a large group would eat off paper plates, but sometime during the oyster-shucking contest, teenage girls and boys had brought real dishes, silverware, and cloth napkins from the house. In less time than she'd imagined possible, order reigned out of chaos: Everyone found seats, Matthew offered a blessing, and the guests began to eat.

Later, after the main courses, and once Maude's birthday cake had been admired and cut, some of the older boys organized games for the young children, and groups of guests broke away to play horseshoes and darts. When Bailey began to gather dirty dishes, Cathy shook her head. "Not tonight," she said. "The rules here are that the ladies cook and the men do the cleanup. Besides, everyone will be back for seconds soon enough." She motioned. "Come here. I want you to meet my mother-in-law. You'll like her."

Creed began to play his violin again, and a middle-aged woman sang the words to an English ballad about a sailor who went away to sea and never returned to his waiting sweetheart. Her voice was sweet and clear, and when the final notes of the song faded, Bailey found that she had tears in her eyes.

"Don't have too much fun," Daniel said, coming up behind her in the purple dusk. "You're already an islander by blood. If you're not careful, you might find it hard to leave."

"You're a fine one to talk."

Daniel grinned and handed her another glass of iced tea. "Sorry I can't offer you something stronger. There are sodas cooling in ice on the porch, but we don't serve alcohol at gatherings. Too dangerous."

Bailey laughed. "The tea is fine. But your 'no alcohol' rule doesn't seem to have stopped Creed. I think I smelled something stronger than lemonade on his breath."

"I wouldn't doubt it." He caught her hand and pulled her away from the chattering group of younger women. "Come on."

"Aren't you supposed to be washing dishes?"

"Not this time. I put in five hours at Susan and Tom's wedding in April. I washed so many pots that my hands shriveled up. I couldn't drive a nail straight for a week."

They circled around a fire where children were toasting marshmallows on sticks and walked to the end of Emma's dock. The moon was up, full and pale, spilling a path of shimmering light across the dark waters of the bay.

"They say you can make a wish when the moon paints the waves," Daniel said. "If you don't tell, it will come true."

"Have you tried it?" She sat down on the end of the dock. The rough boards were still warm from the sun.

"I'm not much on wishes. I used to wish that I lived in the days of the pirates and that my father was a buccaneer instead of a pastor." He chuckled. "It never worked, but it's probably because my father wished I was a preacher's son instead of a pirate-in-training."

"You went to school here on the island?"

"Until the eighth grade. Then my mother home-schooled me until I was eighteen."

"College?"

"University of Delaware."

"You're kidding. Me too." He smelled faintly of after-shave. It was a good smell, not sickly sweet, but masculine. "I guess you've been to Deer Park?"

He groaned. "My buddies carried me out of there one night. They said I was singing. Loudly."

"What was wrong with that?"

"It was the Penn State fight song."

She laughed. "I don't believe a word of it."

"Cross my heart and hope to die. They threatened to drag me out and lay me on the train tracks if I didn't shut up. Three guys—"

"Enough. What was your major?"

"History. Until I switched to political science, and then philosophy. It took me five years to graduate."

"Welcome to the club."

They were still talking when Emma began to extinguish the lanterns and bid her guests a good night. "Hey, you two," she shouted from the porch. "Come on! I won't have you setting a bad example for the children."

"The children should be in bed," Daniel protested.

"And so should I," Bailey murmured, yawning.

"I agree."

"Alone, thank you."

"Yes, ma'am." He assumed a hurt tone. "I know when I've been put in my place." He bent his head and brushed her cheek with his lips. "Night."

"Night." She took a few steps across the lawn. "Thank you," she said. "It was fun."

"It was," Daniel agreed. "You're a nice lady. If things were . . ." He nodded. "It's been a pleasure to know you, but . . ."

"But?"

"Remember what I said, Bailey. Tawes isn't the place for you. Go home. If you don't, you'll regret it."

"Is that a threat?"

"No, it's not a threat. I'm the last person you need to be afraid of. Just take my advice and leave. Soon."

"I will," she replied. "After I get what I came here for."

"You might get more than you bargained for," he said. "I want you safely out of here. Before it's too late."

* * *

Midnight found Daniel not in his bed or Bailey's but on the site of his unfinished cabin. He lit a kerosene lantern and built a fire in the hearth to boil water in an old tin coffeepot for tea. He did his best thinking when he drank tea. He liked Assam, loose tea leaves, brewed in a proper pot. He liked his tea strong, without milk or sugar, but if he had clover honey to stir in, that was good too. Here, in the night, he had no honey so he drank it black. He was savoring the last sips in his cup when he heard the front door open.

"Evening," he said.

Hard footsteps. Quick. He rose to face a red-faced Will Tawes, anger radiating off him like heat from the hearth bricks.

"You're about early. Or late?"

"Who sent her to my house?"

"Sent who?"

"Beth's girl. Is it Emma's doing?"

Daniel motioned to the coffeepot. "Tea? We missed you at Aunt Birdy's birthday party."

Will shook his head. "Beth's girl had no business coming here."

"Her name is Bailey. Bailey Elliott. I tried to tell her to stay away, but she's stubborn. Like someone else I could mention."

"I want to know if this is Emma's meddling."

Daniel shrugged. "I doubt it. She's afraid that the old trouble will start up. That folks will talk. She likes Bailey. So do I. She deserves better."

"So did Beth."

"You should tell her. Tell her before someone else does."

"Stay out of this. You're the only Catlin worth your

102

salt, and we've been friends a long time, but this runs too deep."

"You're dragging me into it by coming here. People are scared. Not just Emma. Other people. Some think that Joe Marshall's death wasn't an accident . . . that you took justice into your own hands."

"If folks want to accuse me of killing him, they should say it to my face or keep their mouths shut."

"Did you do it, Will? Did you shoot him?"

"If I did, if I could murder a man in cold blood, would I be foolish enough to admit it?"

"Maybe."

"Lucky for you, you won't find out if I am that dumb. Because if I did kill him, and I told you I did, then I'd have to make certain you didn't live to tell the tale, wouldn't I?"

CHAPTER EIGHT

My belly burns with white-hot anger. Once again Beth's returned to shame me. I won't stand for it. I killed the sniveling little bitch, but I think now maybe she died too easily. I stand here, at the start of Hessian's Redoubt near the old settlers' cemetery, thinking longer than I should about the past. I know I shouldn't waste too much time on things that can't be changed.

The lane, what there is of it, peters out at Creed Somers's place. It never amounted to much more than hard-packed ruts, and last winter's storms washed out a whole section when the high tide rose up over the road.

Most islanders who want to visit Creed leave the main trail at McCready's old homeplace and follow the shoreline a half mile to Creed's dock. He never does, but he's nothing but a sorry excuse for a drunk who always was too stubborn for his own good. Just because his mother drowned herself on that stretch of beach is no reason for him not to take the shortcut forty years later. He claims her ghost walks there, but half the time he sees the world through a haze of cheap wine or homemade white lightning.

Earlier tonight, the moon was shining bright enough to crab by, but sometime after midnight the wind shifted and thick clouds moved in. Still, moonlight or not, I can find my way in the dark. I fear neither God nor the devil. A lantern would show where I was stepping, but you never know who's out, who might spot you. And after a lifetime on this island, if I can't find my way, day or night, fog or snow, then I deserve to sink in the marsh quicksand or trip over a beached log and break my neck.

Walking along the high-tide mark, I don't make much noise, but I can hear plenty. Owls, rails, cicadas, frogs, and the occasional nasal *ee-nt, ee-nt, ee-nt* cry of a nighthawk make such a ruckus that it's hard to keep your thinking straight. I don't carry a gun with me. I'd thought about bringing my rifle just to show Creed how serious I am about him staying clear of Beth's bastard, but I thought better of it. Most people on Tawes respect me—even fear me. I doubt that many can say they like me, but that doesn't matter. It wasn't always that way—there was a time when I never lacked for company—but it's true now, I'm not so heartless as some claim. I abhor violence. I'll avoid it if I can. If I can't, then heaven pity the poor misguided soul who stands in my way.

Some wrongs can't be tolerated, and Creed has tried my patience beyond all belief. He's putting us all in danger by showing that woman around, running his mouth off. I can't allow that. Creed was there and saw it all. He was as much a part of it as anybody. He knows too much, and drink always loosens his tongue.

A fool is a dangerous man, and whatever sense Creed was born with he's drowned long ago in alcohol.

I hear the shouting long before I make out the yellow flickering lamplight through Creed's kitchen windows. It seems he has company already, and I'm not pleased. What I have to say to him is best said in private. Annoyed, I leave the easy beach walking and circle through the woods, taking care where I step and ducking to avoid low-hanging limbs. The trees in this grove are old-growth, a mixture of oak, maple, and beech, with a few cedars thrown in for good measure. There are almost no greenbriers, and you can walk as easily as on the streets of Tawes, even in fog as thick as this.

As I draw closer to the house, I can make out some of the angry words being flung back and forth. Creed's voice I recognize by the whiskey slur. A fool could tell he's been sucking at the Jack Daniel's bottle, and his temper is up. He's mad, but he's scared too. And he should be.

"Get the hell off my property!"

"You know more than you're telling!"

"Shut up! Do you want to wake the dead?"

More curses. A door slams.

Banging—a fist against wood. "If there's more bloodshed, it'll fall on your head!"

A window opens and both barrels of a shotgun discharge, one after the other.

Silence. I hunker down and wait—wait for Creed to come out again, maybe reload and run the intruder off with a good charge of rock salt or even birdshot. Creed always wants to fight once he has the drink-courage in him, but he'll go for his shotgun rather than use his fists like a real man . . . especially if he's scared shitless.

Twigs snap. Loud muttering. What could have been

the shadow of a man moves away from the door as silently as a doe, past the woodpile. Creed cooks and heats the house with his woodstove, like his father before him. No electricity poles out this far on Hessian's Redoubt, and Creed's generator burned out years ago. Not that he could afford the gasoline to run it if it did still work. A drinking habit consumes all a man can scrape together.

I strain to see through the heavy layers of fog. Sound plays funny tricks on your ears on a night like this. You can't trust your senses. A cramp in my left calf makes me gasp with pain, but I grit my teeth and don't move. The shadow I'd seen could have been a deer.

I wait. The cramp passes. Farther off, leaves crackle and a screech owl hoots—a shrill whinny so much like a frightened horse that many a farmer who should know better has gone to see what's amiss in the barn. The owl's scream flushes a rabbit. Its agonized squeal breaks off in midcry. I can imagine the crunch of bone and tearing of flesh. I sniff the wind, trying to catch a scent. Fresh blood has a sweet odor, not foul, but fear gives off a smell all its own. A screech owl is a skilled night hunter, and any prey had best lay low if it doesn't want to be owl supper.

Creed doesn't show his face outside, but he isn't quiet either. He rants and shouts, using all manner of foul language. Then I hear the crack of breaking wood and crockery. "Son of a bitch!"

An empty fifth shatters a kitchen window. How sodden in drink does a man need to be to pitch a bottle through his own windowpane when the replacement costs an arm and a leg?

I wait another quarter of an hour to see if the troublemaker is still crouching in the dark, hoping Creed will be fool enough to step out of the house. When nothing bigger than a tree frog stirs, I cross the yard, past the stacks of winter cordwood and the chopping block, to knock on the back door.

No answer. Creed hasn't passed out. I hear him in there thrashing around, ranting, making threats he'll never follow through on. What respect I have for the man is fast evaporating. I knock harder.

Heavy footsteps. The door opens a crack. Creed sways like a mast in a gale. I smell the stink of kerosene from the smoky lamp behind him.

"Will you get off—"

I push past him into the kitchen and begin to cough. It's close in here, what with the lamp, the booze, and Creed sweating like a horse. The house is a mess. Chairs are overturned, shards of broken dishes litter the floor, and the place reeks of spilled whiskey and old cabbage.

"Leave me alone!" he says. "What do you want?"

"I want to shut that mouth of yours before—"

"Before what?" He thrusts his drink-distorted face into mine.

His whiskey breath makes me gag.

"Before people find out?" he asks. "Before the truth comes—"

I hit him. Blood flies, splattering my cheek. "It's over!" I say.

Coward that he is, he starts to blubber like a girl. I think of her and the rage boils up inside me.

"It's not over. I sleep . . . sleep with it . . . every night. Wake with it . . . every morning," he whines. "Her face is the first thing I see. Every day."

"You're weeping over a whore?"

"She wasn't."

"As much as her mother before her. Whore of Babylon! Slut."

"She was nice to me." Spittle flecks his unshaven chin.

"A bastard's bastard? She deserved what she got!" I hit him again. My fist strikes his chin and he staggers back.

"She didn't . . . didn't deserve to die."

"Didn't she? She wanted it! Flaunted her body. But you couldn't see it, could you? Couldn't see past—"

He swings at me. I duck, backing away from his flailing arms. I would never have lived to grow up if I hadn't learned to be quick, to hit before I was hit, and to run when I had to.

"You were jealous. You couldn't stand all that innocence!"

I dodge his clumsy blows and stumble against the open doorjamb. Creed lowers his head and charges like a drunken bull. I sidestep him and retreat into the yard. "You fool! You'll kill us all for something that's long done with. Joe's already dead. Who's next?"

Creed keeps coming. Keeps screaming his lies. "You!" he accused. "It was you! It was all your fault!"

The back of my leg strikes the stump he uses for a chopping block. I windmill my arms to keep my balance, and my fingers brush the handle of the ax he uses to split wood. I close my fist around it. I know now what I have to do . . . what Creed Somers has brought on himself. . . .

I wrench the ax loose from the stump and swing it in a wide arc. The blade catches his right thigh and slices through it like a cleaver through soft butter. His flesh opens like a ripe melon. A tide of blood wells up and overflows the gaping wound.

Creed howls. He falls back, clutching his wounded leg. I come after him into the kitchen with all the fervor of an avenging angel.

The pale circle of yellow light from the smoking lamp illuminates the beauty of the weapon in my hand. The blade glistens crimson . . . drips scarlet pools on the rug.

Creed grabs his shotgun off the table. "Get out! Get out or—"

I laugh. I am beyond stopping and he, above all, should know it. Common sense would tell me to cut my losses and flee, but he's gone too far. I can't allow this any more than I could allow Beth's whoring to go on unpunished. I go for his head with the ax.

He never has time to raise the gun to his shoulder, and tries to fire from his waist. But the hammers click on empty chambers. His eyes widen and he grabs for the shells on the table. I shriek with glee as I realize the stupid fool hasn't reloaded.

My blade cleaves skull and teeth with a hollow, sucking thud. Droplets of blood spray around me like warm rain, and Creed falls like a lightning-struck sapling. Blood gushes from his ruined skeleton of a face. He chokes twice and gives a garbled gasp.

I hit him again.

Oddly enough, my weapon seems to take on a mind of its own. I chop and chop until what lies on the floor no longer resembles a human head or neck. I don't stop until the gore begins to soak my hair and clothes, and my arms tire from the weight of the ax.

Panting from the exertion, I lean back against the table, somewhat amazed at the amount of blood that has drained from Creed's lifeless body. More blood than a deer or a hog, and thicker, it seems to me. The feeling of revenge is sweet, and the cloying scent fills my nostrils, tainted with the odor of Jack Daniel's. I wonder if his body will ever decay. Maybe the alcohol will preserve him for years.

Not years, surely. Rats and mice, perhaps even crows will find their way into the house and feast on the—

"What's going on? Creed? What's . . ."

A voice from the adjoining bedroom yanks me from my musing. A familiar woman's voice . . . her words as slurred and confused as Creed's had been before he began to gargle his own blood. I drop the ax, pick up the fallen shotgun, and crack it open. Shoving two shells into the double chamber, I ease back the hammers and turn expectantly toward the bedroom door.

Long seconds pass.

Retching.

"Creed? Creed, help me. I'm sick." The knob rattles.

I wait, barrels trained on the door. "Ida?"

She opens the door. The slut's hair hangs loose and tangled, her blouse open, one sagging tit bare. Her exposed nipple is long and brown, shriveled as a dried prune. She blinks, stares at the thing on the floor, and blinks again before opening her mouth to scream, a shrill, high-pitched shriek.

I pull both triggers. The buckshot catches her midsection, blowing her backward into the bedroom. Her bare heels thud against the floor. One arm flings out and thrashes like a chicken with its head cut off.

I reload the shotgun, follow her into the darkened room, shoot her once in the face, and a second time in the chest. The sound nearly deafens me, but I don't have to check to see if she is dead. I use a clean corner of a bedsheet to wipe down the weapon, then discard it on the floor beside her.

I never cared for Ida.

She pretended to be more than she was because she'd been a teacher. Once, when we were a lot younger, I offered her my friendship, but she thought she was too good for me, and turned up her nose at it. She deserves what she got. Actually, she deserves more, but I'm aware that time is passing. Soon it will be daybreak, and I have much to do.

Outside, in a lean-to shed behind the kitchen, Creed keeps two cans of spare kerosene. I use those liberally on the floor, the curtains, and the bodies. The last thing I do before smashing the lamp and leaving the house for good is to find Creed's violin and lay it next to his body. The flame flares and catches.

I don't bother to close the door. Fire needs air to breathe. The house is built on pilings, with space beneath for rising water. Between the broken window and the open door, there'll be draft enough. With the kerosene everywhere, Creed's old wooden house will go up like a torch.

He always said he wanted to know what hell was like. Now he'll get his wish.

Outside, I strip to my skin, hold my breath, and toss the blood-soaked garments through the open door. I don't want to leave any evidence that might lead suspicion to me. Who knows how many nosy outsiders might invade the island, asking questions?

Creed always kept a change of clothes on his boat. I walk down his dock, dive into the bay, and wash myself as best I can before retrieving clean pants and a shirt. I'm no thief, but it's hardly stealing. I doubt that Creed will have need of garments where he's going, and I'd hate to walk home naked in the damp air. I know I'll have to dispose of these clothes later, as well. It's a pity. There's a lot more wear left in the shirt.

Bailey awoke about eight thirty Saturday morning with an intense throbbing in the back of her head. She hadn't fallen asleep until sometime after two, thinking about her crazy uncle, the property she'd inherited, and Daniel . . . Daniel and his contradictory behavior most of all. And even after fatigue had gotten the best of her, her sleep had been disturbed by fitful dreams. Twice she'd gotten up and gone to the bedroom window, certain that she heard the whistler outside in the fog. Now she couldn't get the tune out of her head.

> *Hush little baby, don't say a word*
> *Papa's going to buy you a mockingbird. . . .*

Ten minutes in the shower and two aspirins later, she wandered downstairs in search of strong coffee and found Emma at the round kitchen table in tears.

"What's wrong?" Bailey asked.

The older woman raised her head from her folded arms and tried to speak. Her graying bun was coming undone from the bobbypins, her eyes were red and swollen, and her voice was a croak. "Creed," she managed. "He's dead."

"Dead?"

"Daniel saw the flames in the sky early this morning. By the time he got there the whole house was gone. It was too late to do anything."

Stunned, Bailey dropped into a chair across from Emma. "His house burned?" An image of the laughing waterman with the violin tucked under his chin surfaced in her mind. How could he be gone, and all that lively music with him? "Are you certain? Maybe he wasn't—"

"He was in there, all right. Daniel said he saw . . . part of a leg bone through what was left of the kitchen wall."

"How could . . ." Woodenly, Bailey rose and poured herself a cup of coffee. Her hands and fingers felt numb. The coffee was too hot, but she barely noticed as she took a sip and then hastily swallowed. "He . . . he was drinking last night."

Emma drew in a shuddering breath. "The damn fool drank most nights. And that house of his was a tinderbox, waiting to go up in flames. But that's a hell of a way to go."

"I'm so sorry."

"We've been friends since we were hanging onto our mother's apron strings." Emma wiped her running nose and her eyes with the back of a big hand. "Daniel's tore up bad. He said he saw a lot of death over there . . . where he was. . . . But it's different when it's a man you've known all your life."

"Over where?"

"Iraq. Iran. Somewhere where those terrorists make life impossible for decent folk. I never can keep the two countries straight. When he was with the government."

"Is he here? Daniel? He didn't spend the night here. . . ." It was a question, but Emma either didn't hear her or didn't want to answer.

"Creed sure was good with those kids last night, wasn't he?"

Bailey nodded. "And he played beautifully."

"Sorry old drunk. He was a fine-looking man in his youth. Had a lot going for him, but it all sort of fell

114

apart. Creed was married a couple of times. No kids. But it always ended bad. Jack Daniel's doesn't do much to hold a man and a woman together."

"Where's Daniel now? If there aren't any police here, who will do the investigation—take care of . . . of the remains?"

Emma sniffed, blew her nose loudly on a napkin, and poured herself another cup of coffee. "Oh, I expect we'll be overrun with fire marshals, state police. Coroner will pop up from someplace. Talbot, most likely." She shook her head. "Creed remembered more of those old songs and stories than anybody on Tawes. I expect a lot of it died with him."

"I only knew him a little while, but he seemed like a nice man."

"He was flawed, same as all of us. Never could keep a decent lamp burning. He never trimmed his wicks right. I tried to show him how, but Creed could be stubborn. He said he didn't care if his ceiling was smoke blackened."

"He had no electricity?"

Emma scoffed. "Shoot, most of us didn't have power until we were grown. Nothing wrong with old ways. Not that I don't like my television and running water, but we did without for years, like those before us. I can't see we turned out any worse than kids today."

"Did he have any family?"

"Cousins. Nephews and nieces. Aunts and uncles. I expect Forest will hold the wake, once the coroner is done with the body. Forest's a second cousin, but he and Creed were always close. Used to do a lot of duck hunting together, but Forest said he was through with it. Didn't want to end up like the senator."

"Senator Marshall?"

"Only senator I know that ever came off of Tawes. They didn't bury him here, though. His wife wanted him somewhere off island." Tears began to course down Emma's reddened and sunburned cheeks. "I just can't believe Creed's gone."

"I'm so sorry for your loss."

"It's not your fault. Creed brought this on himself, but it's hard to lose a friend like that. Awful hard."

Many of those who'd been at the birthday party the night before drifted into Emma's to talk about Creed's death. Emma and some of her friends brewed endless pots of coffee and brought out food left over from the celebration. After two hours of listening to villagers repeat stories about Creed and a rehash of his life, Bailey slipped outside, took the bike from the shed, and rode out into the country to get away from all the grieving.

At first she'd intended to go back to Elizabeth's house, but as she neared the lane, she kept thinking of her uncle Will and wondering if he'd heard of the tragedy. She rode back and forth on the road, looking for an entrance to his place. When she couldn't find one, she pushed the bike down Elizabeth's driveway toward the water. She still wasn't ready to give up hope of making some connection with her great-uncle, and she was prepared to risk being devoured by his dog pack to give it one last try.

The lane was noisy with birdsong and the buzz of bees, and the air smelled of honeysuckle and salt water. Her spirits lifted. She was so glad she'd gotten out of Emma's house. The two riding horses were grazing in the field where she'd seen them earlier, and they lifted their heads and whinnied a greeting as she passed. She'd have to ask Emma whom they belonged to. She never saw anyone caring for them, and though she was no expert on horses, the animals seemed in fine shape.

She left the bike at the edge of the woods and hurried down the shady trail toward Will's house. This time, no matter how hard she listened, she didn't hear the dogs. She hoped that was a good omen.

The yard, when she reached it, seemed as quiet as the woodland path. The house stood quiet, too. No smoke drifted from the chimney, and no sounds—human or animal—came from inside. She climbed the steps to the porch and knocked on the closed door.

No answer. She wondered if her uncle was inside and ignoring her, but when she followed the porch around, she saw that the dock was empty. His boat was gone; apparently she'd come out here for nothing. Reluctantly she started back down the steps, and then noticed an open sketchpad and charcoal pencil lying on the porch swing seat.

She picked up the pad and glanced through it. The first two pages were filled with line drawings of an owl. Wing, beak, talons. An owl in flight. A tiny owl ripping at a mouse. The third page contained sketches of mice, scampering up the same steps she'd just climbed, nestling in a hollow log, and one drawing of a mother mouse with four little ones nursing.

She flipped to the next page. Blank. She spent a few more minutes inspecting the owl and mouse drawings and then laid the sketchpad back on the seat as she'd found it. But as she stood to walk away, she had an idea.

Taking pad and charcoal, she sat on the step and began to sketch her great uncle's face. For more than an hour she worked at the drawing, smudging the charcoal, rubbing out lines, adding more. When she was finished, she was pleased. It wasn't her best work, but it was the best thing she'd ever done from memory without looking at her subject.

"See what you make of that, old man," she murmured, replacing the pad and charcoal, but leaving the page open to the portrait. If he was an artist, he must have an artist's curiosity. And if she proved to him that she possessed talent, maybe he would thaw enough to tell her something about her mother.

In any case, time was running out. Forest McCready would fix whatever had to be fixed with the inheritance, and she would be leaving Tawes, probably forever.

CHAPTER NINE

It was early afternoon before the police were through with their preliminary questions. Daniel had repeated his story of seeing the smoke at first light and going to investigate. He gave a written statement on his observations, detailing what he'd seen when he approached the smoldering ruins of Creed Somers's home. When he returned to Emma's at two, she was waiting for him on the porch swing. He knew by the expression on her face that there was trouble.

"What's wrong?" he asked as he opened the gate.

"You'd better go and try to talk to Matthew." She came down the steps to meet him. "I went by the parsonage to ask if there would be a prayer vigil for Creed at the church tonight, and I could hear Grace and him shouting at each other from the street. Your brother's in a bad way, and she isn't helping."

"Has she ever?"

"She was yelling that Will Tawes was a crazed killer." Emma took hold of his arm and looked directly into his eyes. "I'm worried about Matthew, Daniel. I don't think he's been taking his medication. He didn't seem himself the last few Sundays. It's not like him to be giving sermons about God's wrath and the end of the world."

Daniel stiffened. "I'll do what I can, but you know how it's always been with the two of them. All she has to say is, 'Jump,' and he asks, 'How high?' "

"He's scared, and Creed's death is bound to hit him hard. They've been friends for half a century."

Daniel knew Emma was right about that too. Despite the way Creed had lived his life, the two had grown up together. A blow like this could send his brother into a serious depression. "Is Bailey in the house?"

"No. She took the bike and rode out this morning." Her eyes widened. "You don't think she's in danger?"

"Not from Will, if that's what you're thinking. I'd better go and see how Matt is."

"You do that, and if there's anything I can do, you let me know."

When Daniel found neither Matthew nor Grace at the house, he crossed the cemetery through the rows of old gravestones and entered the church by the side entrance.

"Have you heard?" Grace asked as he closed the door behind him. "Creed's dead. Nobody listened when I said that Joe Marshall was murdered. Will got away with killing him, and now he's burned Creed alive in his house."

"You can't accuse Will without proof."

"Will hated him. You know he did."

"If Will wanted Creed dead, he would have been dead long before this. Nobody knows what happened.

Creed could have been drunk out of his head and knocked over the kerosene lamp."

"You know it was no accident," she insisted, clutching at his shirtsleeve. "You know as well as I do that Will's to blame."

Daniel resisted the urge to push her away and waited for his eyes to become accustomed to the semi-darkness. It was a cloudy day, and the only light was that which filtered through the stained-glass windows, windows shadowed by the sheltering oaks on either side of the church. From somewhere in the front of the sanctuary he heard sobbing.

"I told Matthew that he was dangerous. That it wouldn't be over as long as Will Tawes—"

"Grace, for the love of God, would you shut up?" He brushed past his sister-in-law and walked to the front pew. Matthew, sobbing, was on his knees at the railing, his hands locked around the upright supporting posts. "First Joe. Now Creed. Who's next?" He began to weep again.

"Matt, get hold of yourself." Daniel put his hand on his brother's shoulder. "Your parishioners need you now. They need you to be strong."

"Elizabeth brought this trouble down on us," Grace said as she came up behind him. "She started it all up again when she left her farm to an outsider."

Daniel whirled on her. "You're not helping. Has he been taking his medication? How long has he been like this?"

"Oh, so it's my fault? Who's stood by him all these years? Who sees that he goes to the doctor regularly? Orders his pills? Covers for him when he forgets to take them or just decides he doesn't need them and can't crawl out of bed in the morning?" She shook a finger in his face. "Don't you take that tone with me. You're his brother. Where were you when Matthew needed you?"

"Maybe living with you and listening to your mouth day after day makes him depressed."

"Don't," Matthew begged. He rose unsteadily to his feet and reached out for his wife. "Don't blame Grace. It's not her fault."

"If it's anyone's fault, it's Will's. His and that girl of Beth's."

Daniel glared at her. "Leave her out of this."

"First you defend a murderer and now—"

"Either shut up or get out of here so I can help him."

Grace clutched at her husband. "Are you going to stand there and let him talk to your wife like that? In a house of God? Where's your pride? How can you call yourself a man?"

"Enough!" Daniel had never laid a hand on a woman in his life, but it was all he could do not to pick her up bodily and toss her out of the church.

"Stop, please. I can't stand it when the two of you—"

"There, there, Matthew." Grace wrapped a protective arm around him. "You'll make yourself sick. Come home and let me make you a pot of coffee. People may be coming to the church to pray for Creed's soul. If they discover you here like this, they might talk."

"It's no disgrace to be ill," Matthew said. "No one would make me leave my church."

"No, of course not," she murmured. "It's the shock of Creed's death. You were always too sensitive. Your brother is a good man, Daniel. I wouldn't expect you to understand how tenderhearted he is."

"Please." Matthew straightened his shoulders. "We're

all distraught. Grace didn't mean to speak unkindly of Bailey."

"She never means to speak unkindly about anyone, does she?"

Matthew bristled. "I'll ask you to show respect for—"

"Just go," Grace said. "Go and leave us."

"Is that what you want?" Daniel studied his brother. "Maybe it's best, until you cool down."

"You heard him," Grace said. "The church is no place for threats."

"Forget it. You deserve each other." Daniel started toward the door, then stopped. "See that he gets his medication. Or I'll come by and force it down his throat."

An hour later, a white twenty-two-foot skiff with *Naughty Lady, Crisfield, Maryland,* painted in fluorescent red script across the stern, arrived at the Tawes dock. Immediately after the skipper cut his engines, a tall, lanky man with a blond ponytail, Oakley sunglasses, and a diamond stud earring got off the boat, paid the captain in crisp fifty-dollar bills, and pushed a Schwinn mountain bike down the dock. "You'll be back for me at three tomorrow?" The captain nodded, eased his Bradley center-console out into the current, and pulled away.

Bailey caught sight of the newcomer coasting down the street a few minutes later as she came out of Doris's Market. "Elliott? What are you doing here? And this isn't your bike, is it?"

"Loaner. And I could ask you the same thing." He circled back, stopped the bike, and gave her a hug. "Two days at most?" He peered at her over the top of his dark wraparound sunglasses. "Overstayed your time, haven't you?"

"I told you it was going to take a little longer than I'd thought."

"I know you did, but you said a minor problem."

"You didn't tell me you were coming."

"I didn't know it myself. I tried your cell this morning, got nothing, and decided to come over and see if you were okay. You didn't tell me these yokels spoke a foreign language."

"Oh, you get used to it after a few days. I hardly notice the accent anymore. But how did you get here?" In Rehoboth Elliott blended in with the crowd, but here on the island, his lemon yellow Ralph Lauren polo and Cole Haan loafers made him overdressed. "Creed Somers runs the ferry and . . ." She trailed off, deciding to broach the subject of the fire and Creed's death later, if at all.

"What's going on in town? Somebody rob a bank? I saw two, three state policeman and somebody wearing a jumpsuit that said 'Medical Examiner.' "

She handed him the bag of groceries and cleaning products she'd purchased from the market. "How did you know that the B and B was down this way?" She couldn't imagine that any of the villagers would be particularly helpful.

"Didn't. Been looking for it all around this 'picturesque town'—isn't that what you called it? I didn't see a single sign for a B and B." He grimaced. "Not much of a welcome. Aren't you glad to see me?"

"Yes, I am." She hugged him again. "But how did you get here?"

"Simple, my dear Watson. Drove to Crisfield. Your car still has four wheels and a battery, by the way. I parked next to it. Then I walked around the harbor until I found somebody who was willing to bring me over for a hundred dollars."

"Big spender," she teased. "And is your 'ride' waiting for you?"

"I'm all yours for twenty-four hours, babe. I had to promise the skipper a hundred and fifty to come back and get me tomorrow."

"Two-fifty? Where'd you get that kind of spare change?"

"That's for me to know and you to find out." He shrugged. "Just consider me a man of mystery."

"And where do you expect to sleep tonight? There aren't exactly any Holiday Inns on the island."

He flashed her a charming smile. "Is your bed a double?"

"Forget that."

He laughed. "It wouldn't be the first time. Remember New Year's Eve, when we got back from—"

"That night is something I prefer to forget. Lucky for you, Emma has an empty room. Sixty dollars." She held out her hand.

"Well, actually, babe, all I've got is what I need to pay Captain Kidd to take me back to civilization, and an extra ten bucks for gas. I sort of hit Crisfield on empty."

"Why does that sound familiar?" She'd have to pay Emma for his room, but she didn't really care. After what her ex had cost her, a night's lodging was peanuts. "I am glad you brought a bike, though. We can ride out to the farm in the morning. Wait until you see the view."

"You're right," Elliott said the following day after they'd explored the house, the beach, and the grounds on

Elizabeth's property. "This is worth a bundle. And I know just the guy who can help you get the most out of it. Why don't you come back with me this afternoon, and I'll set up a meeting with Steve? He handles big deals like this all the time."

"Thanks, but no, thanks. I think there's some kind of thing in the will where I have to offer the house and land for sale to the locals first."

"You can't do that," he said. "Not until you know what it's worth. You could be sitting on a couple million here. How many acres did you say went with the house?"

"It's really a special island," she said. "There's so much history. Even going to the churchyard gives me chills. All those ancestors buried there. It's like I have real roots, you know?"

Elliott plucked a blade of grass and bit it. "Dum-dum-dum-dum," he teased. "First the innocent girl is lured to the island by the promise of a fortune. And then the vampires come out of the graves at night to *suck her blood*."

"You're not funny. I've met some really nice people here."

"Sure, like Miss Emma. Where did she get those overalls and those rubber boots? She looks like she wandered in out of a cow barn."

"Emma's sweet. I like her. And I don't care what she wears."

"Right. That is one ugly old woman. Her nose looks like somebody broke it and stuck it on lopsided."

Bailey gave him a playful shove. "And yours is so perfect?"

"I like to think so." He caught her by the shoulders and pulled her toward him.

When he leaned to kiss her, Bailey turned her face so that his lips brushed her cheek. "Don't."

"Was it so bad?"

"Sometimes it was."

"Don't you believe in redemption? We could give it another try."

"I'll pass. I think I like having you for a friend better than a husband."

"You're cold, Bails. Icy cold."

"Actually," she said, trying to change the subject, "I was thinking I might keep a few acres for a summer cottage."

"It's the water. The water's drugged. Run! Run before the vampires get you. Isn't it a full moon tonight?"

"No." She laughed. "It isn't a full moon, and there aren't any more vampires on Tawes than on the mainland. Just people who don't like change."

"I worry about you."

"Don't," she said. "I'm doing fine. I've made friends here."

"And you're coming back to Delaware when, exactly?"

"As soon as the attorney settles the estate. Cross my heart and hope to die."

"Okay." He dug into his waist pack. "But I'd feel better if you'd carry this with you." He tossed her a key chain with a pepper spray container attached. "Just in case."

"I thought you needed a silver bullet to stop vampires."

"Nope. Pepper spray. It works every time."

Elliott made a final plea for her to leave with him before loading his bike onto the waiting *Naughty Lady* in the harbor a little after three that afternoon. "Call me," he insisted. "And don't listen to any scams about selling that property to locals. Promise me you won't do anything until you talk to Steve."

"Good-bye, Elliott. Hope you're not late for work. And next time, save more than ten dollars for gas. You'll be lucky if that gets you across the Maryland line."

Elliott waved and she waved back.

"Hey, there." Cathy called to her from the end of the dock. "I was afraid for a minute that you were leaving."

"Just a friend of mine," Bailey explained. "He thinks I'm going to be devoured by vampires."

"Yikes." Cathy laughed. "Should I be worried? Does he know something I don't?"

"I hope not."

"Isn't it awful about Creed Somers? I guess you heard right away. You'd have to, what with Emma and Daniel at the house. What's up with Daniel? This is getting to be a bad habit, his discovering bodies."

"I know," Bailey agreed, falling in step beside her as they walked toward the center of the village. "Creepy, isn't it? After the senator."

"Faceup under the ice. Yuck. Could it be any worse?" She grimaced. "It gives me nightmares just thinking about it."

"My nightmares are all about someone whistling nursery rhymes."

"What?"

"Nothing." Bailey shook her head.

"Have you got time for a cup of coffee? I just put a pot on. I'd like to ask a favor."

"Sure, if I can."

"We turn here. It's not far."

"Nothing in Tawes is far," Bailey replied.

"You've got that right." Then Cathy's mood grew serious. "I just heard from Margaret Thomas that the medical examiner found the remains of a second body in the ashes of Creed's house. They think it's a woman, but they can't be sure. There wasn't much left after the fire."

"A woman? How terrible. Bad enough that Creed—"

"It's probably Ida Love." Cathy waved at a boy sitting on the back step of a white clapboard two-story house with a picket fence around it. "Hi, Josh."

"Hi, Mrs. Tilghman."

"Tell your mom I said thanks for the baby clothes."

"I will."

Cathy lowered her voice as they walked past the far corner of Josh's yard. "I don't know if you could say that Ida was Creed's girlfriend, but they drank together a lot. And they were always getting into scraps. Afterward, one or the other would have a black eye or a fat lip."

Bailey stopped. "That's terrible. I didn't know Creed that well, but he didn't seem like a man who would abuse a woman."

Cathy shrugged. "It was probably mutual abuse. She wasn't particularly pleasant when she drank. Not that I condone such violence."

"Is it common on Tawes?"

"No, no more than anywhere else, I suppose. No, less, I'd say. People generally look out for their neighbors here. If a man hit his wife or if he abused his children, it wouldn't sit well with people. Forest McCready or Matthew Catlin would have a talk with him."

"But they didn't with Creed?"

"They tried. From what I hear, they tried more than once. But Ida was as bad as Creed. It was the drink.

When he wasn't drunk, you couldn't ask for a nicer man. He'd help anyone in trouble."

"But the body might not be Ida's," Bailey suggested.

"Maybe not, but it looks bad. Ida's been missing since yesterday. She went to Emma's for the birthday party, but never came home after. Amy heard Ida's cats meowing yesterday morning. Their food and water dishes were empty. And that's not like Ida."

"How awful, but I don't see what—"

"First coffee and then I'll beg," Cathy said. "It's complicated."

"First your problem and then coffee."

"All right, but I really wanted to soften you up first." She pointed to a Dutch gambrel with a basket of orange begonias on the doorstep. "Here we are. It's small, but it's all ours."

"It's charming. I love the blue door and shutters."

Cathy led the way through a sunny living room into a country kitchen. The table was already set with two cups, a cream pitcher, and a plate of cookies. "Party leftovers."

Over coffee, Cathy explained that it was Ida who'd assisted at the summer-school program. "If I can't find a replacement, I'll have to cancel classes, and some of these kids will be left high and dry. It's only a few weeks, and—"

"Aren't you rushing things?" Bailey asked. "You don't know for certain that Ida . . . that she was killed in the fire. She could be anywhere."

Cathy stirred cream into her coffee. "She could be, but she's never left her cats shut in the house without food before. She adores them. Calls them her babies. Usually, no matter how much she's had to drink, she comes staggering home, puts medicated powder on the tom's bald spot, and lets them out to potty. She's been gone a day and a half now. It doesn't look good."

"It just gets worse and worse, doesn't it?" Bailey toyed with the handle of her coffee mug. "I'd like to help you—if Ida doesn't show up, I mean. But I really wasn't planning on being on Tawes that long. Forest McCready said—"

"Don't say no yet. You're my only hope if we've lost Ida."

"But I'm not certified to teach in Maryland," Bailey protested, putting down the chocolate-chip cookie without tasting it. "I couldn't—"

"Ida wasn't either. She was officially my assistant, and there's no reason why you couldn't fill the bill." She rubbed her protruding belly. "Down, boys. He's so wiggly in there, it must be twins."

"Could be a girl."

"I doubt it. Not unless she's going to be a football player or a wrestler." Cathy leaned forward. "I know it's a lot to ask. The job doesn't pay at all."

"The money doesn't bother me. It's just that I—"

"Please, just consider what I have to say." She took a big breath and rushed on. "Listen, I know you need somebody to do the repairs on Elizabeth's house. And I know you asked Daniel and he turned you down."

"How . . ." Bailey began, and then she chuckled and shrugged her shoulders. "I know. Nothing on Tawes is a secret."

"Not for more than twenty minutes, anyway. But my point is, you need somebody on the island. If you hire a mainlander, you'll have to wait forever, and it'll cost you three times what the job is worth. You know Daniel is good at what he does, and he works cheap."

"You're forgetting that he's already said no."

"And you're forgetting that everybody on Tawes is kin. My husband happened to come home for a late lunch, and I happened to mention that Ida is missing."

"To make a long story short?"

"My Jim is Daniel's first cousin and best buddy. If you'll help me out with the kids, just for a few weeks, then he'll get Daniel to do your carpentry work at a reasonable price."

"You think?"

"Consider it a done deal," Cathy assured her. "Scout's honor. Daniel owes us a favor, and we'll call it in. Pretty please, Bailey. Just think about it. It's a great deal."

Bailey sighed. "I hope that Ida is fine and will show up with an explanation of where she's been, but if she doesn't . . ."

"If the worst has happened?"

"I'll consider it."

"Good. Be at the school tomorrow morning at eight."

"And if Ida's there?"

"If she is, we'll kiss her on both cheeks, and I'll find something to keep you busy for the day. I never let potential volunteers escape."

"Now you sound like Emma."

Cathy chuckled. "I couldn't find a better teacher, could I?"

CHAPTER TEN

My nerves were still on edge Monday morning after the authorities had verified that there had been a second fire victim. And I wasn't alone. Most people on Tawes were upset. I don't believe they'd been this fussed when the senator turned up dead.

When I become anxious, I need to be alone. I took the boat out two miles, cut the engine, and just let it drift. I do my best thinking out here with nothing but the sky and water and a few seabirds to distract me. Here, I can remember how things used to be, the wrongs that were done to me, and why I couldn't let it continue.

I'm assuming that the remains of the bodies were removed by the medical examiner for further study, but I doubt anything more will come of it. After all, how many accidental fires are there in Maryland in a year? And if there's enough bone left to show ax cuts, they might suppose that it was a murder-suicide. I can't imagine that there will be much fuss over two dead drunks. It was common knowledge that Creed once served seven months in jail for smashing a chair over Tom Caulk's head in Tee's Bar in Crisfield.

My regrets weren't for the deceased. They brought death on themselves as much as Beth or Elizabeth. Creed couldn't let go of the past, and a fool and his life are soon parted. Isn't that the way the old saying goes? If it doesn't, it should. I'm not sorry I killed him. I'm sorry I didn't act sooner. One little, two little, three little Indians. . . . And then there were none.

It has to be that way. I've been negligent in not cleaning up the remnants of that old mess a long time ago. If Creed couldn't be trusted to hold his tongue, the others can't either. And there are those who must be protected at any cost.

I dip my hand in the water and find it warmer than it was a week ago. I wonder if this will be another bad season for the watermen. Most people seem to think the old ways are dying, and I suppose they are . . . one by one.

All but self-preservation.

Daniel was absent at breakfast that morning as Emma, red-eyed from weeping, served Bailey pecan pancakes, hot coffee, extra-crisp bacon, and scrambled eggs. "Hardly enough of him left for a decent burial." She sniffed. "Ida's still not shown hide nor hair of herself. For my money, she died in that house along with poor Creed. No telling when the state will hand over what's left of him." She poured glasses of tomato juice for the two of them. "Unless you'd rather have apple?"

Bailey shook her head. "This is fine."

Emma glanced at the wall clock. "Lord, girl, it's quarter to eight. You'd best hurry or you'll be late for your first day of school."

"Ida may be there. I may not have to—"

"Sure, she will. And my hens will lay golden eggs. Get on down there, Bailey. Cathy and those kids need you."

At eight o'clock sharp that morning, Bailey arrived at the school to find that Ida was still missing and now presumed, by many on the island, to be the second body in Creed's house. Cathy and Amy were in the library, where a group of excited students were checking out books.

"Quiet! Quiet, everyone," Cathy ordered. "This is Miss Elliott. She's visiting our school this morning, and I'd like her to get a good impression. Well?"

"Good morning, Miss Elliott," came a weak response from a half dozen kids. "Good morning," echoed from three middle schoolers near the windows.

"Mornin', ma'am," said a handsome dark-skinned boy shyly.

"Hi!" Two identical towhead first graders wearing green shorts and orange T-shirts giggled and hid their faces in their hands.

A chubby boy about eight years old with a buzz cut stared at her so hard that he bumped into the twins and dropped the stack of library books he was carrying to the desk. The children around him laughed, but another boy helped gather up the books. An older girl whispered to a friend, and Bailey heard the name Tawes.

"Not even half of the kids came to class this morning," Cathy confided. With her hair pulled into a ponytail and no makeup, she reminded Bailey of a pregnant Reese Witherspoon. "And those that did," she continued, "are too upset to settle down. Someone's started a rumor that Creed and Ida were murdered and that a killer's running loose on the island. I think I'll give everyone reading assignments and send them home."

"That's probably best," Bailey agreed, "but I'll admit, I was looking forward to getting to know some of them."

Cathy motioned her aside and lowered her voice. "Poor Ida. She had a wicked tongue, she rarely told the truth about anything, and she was a malicious gossip, but she surely didn't deserve to go that way."

"If she had all those faults, why did Forest McCready employ her?"

"Because they were second cousins, and because Ida wouldn't have had enough to live on if it wasn't for her salary from his office."

"But she taught here on Tawes?"

Cathy shook her head. "Ida was an unpaid volunteer. She never got a penny for her work with the children, and she never lost her patience with them, especially with the kids who struggled academically." She held up her index finger and stepped between a gum-chewing girl in a denim skirt and a mischievous-looking red-haired boy, about eleven, who would have made a perfect Tom Sawyer in any theater production. "Jason? Let me see that book."

He tucked the oversize picture book behind his back. "Give!"

Jason sighed heavily and passed her the offending volume.

Cathy opened it and glanced at the contents. "I don't think so. This is a little too easy for you. If you'll wait a minute, I'll show you a book on sharks that just came in. Reading little kids' books won't help you score higher on your test."

She re-joined Bailey. "That's Jason Somers. Yes, some

relation to Creed, but not close enough to matter. He's an excellent student at math, but he's lazy when it comes to reading. Jason's a good kid, but full of it. You have to keep an eye on him. He's the one who put tadpoles in the library aquarium, live crabs in my desk drawer, and crazy glue in Ida's chair all in one day last week."

"Ouch, Poor Ida. Did she—"

"Yep, she did. Sat in it and glued her new black slacks to the chair. Of course, they were ruined. I had to run home and get her another pair so she could be seen in public."

"What did she do to Jason?"

"Talked to him. Told him he'd have to spend four hours weeding her garden, but she wouldn't let me punish him. And she didn't tell him that she only had two pairs of slacks to wear to school."

"I'm sorry I never got to meet her. Someone said she was at Emma's, but there were so many people. . . ."

"I know. And chances are she would have been hiding in the dark, sipping from a flask. She had an old tin one that had belonged to her father." Cathy shook her head. "I don't know what we'll do when I go out on maternity leave. Try to get someone over from the mainland, I suppose. There are other teachers when school starts in the fall, but Amy has the baby, and two others are working elsewhere for the summer."

"My classes start after Labor Day. And I have to be home in time to—"

"I realize that. Summer school only lasts—Billy, no pushing!—until the middle of August. Sorry. As I said, they're out of sorts today." She hugged her. "I can't tell you how much I appreciate this, Bailey. I feel so bad for Ida. She had a good heart, even if she was rough on the outside. She used to bake cakes for kids' birthdays, and every fall she organized a coat and boot trade for the school. She and Forest would contact manufacturers and get donations of outerwear seconds, so that every child on Tawes would be warm and dry walking to school. I guess Forest will be on his own this year."

"I wish the public schools would do more of that. Too many children don't have proper clothes and shoes. It doesn't seem right, in America."

"I know. I saw it all the time back on the Eastern Shore." Cathy smiled. "Tawes is a lot like Ida—rough around the edges, but with a good heart. We try to take care of all of our kids. They may not have the iPods and latest games for Xbox and PlayStation, but we provide free hot lunches, school supplies, and one of the best libraries around. Most of all, we like to think we treat them as we would our own family."

"It sounds good to me. And as happy as I'd be to have Daniel do my repairs, I probably could have been talked into helping without the bribe. I'm a sucker for a sob story that involves children."

"Good. That's what we need—innocents who know how to teach. Just be certain you check your chair before you sit down, and don't be surprised to find a live snake in your raincoat pocket. Jason's not the only jokester among us. And as a mainlander, I'm afraid you'll be fair game."

"You didn't warn me about that," Bailey teased.

"Ooops." Cathy giggled. "Oversight on my part. Now, if you'll excuse me, I have to see a young man about a shark."

"Tomorrow morning?"

"Absolutely. Be here or I'll send Jason looking for you."

Amy followed them out of the library. "I'd better be

getting home. Maria's watching Joel, and I told her that I'd only be gone an hour."

"Go ahead, you two," Cathy said. "I've got to close the windows in my classroom."

"See you tomorrow." Bailey smiled at her and caught up with Amy. "Are you coming back to teaching in the fall?"

"No, not until after Christmas. I want to stay with him a little longer. My mother-in-law and Maria will take turns babysitting, but it's still hard to leave."

"I'm in awe of working mothers."

Amy hesitated, then touched her arm. "I heard— never mind how—but I was told that you wanted to see your christening records at the church."

"Yes." Bailey waited. Apparently, everything she'd done or said since she'd gotten to Tawes was public knowledge. "I want to learn everything I can about Beth Tawes. It's funny: I've always thought of her as a woman. Now I'm twice as old as she was when she died."

"Sometimes . . ." Amy looked uncomfortable. She took a breath and blurted out, "Don't poke around into the past. You'll only be hurt, and you seem like a nice person."

"Why? How could I be hurt? Do you know something?"

Amy shrugged. "Only what I've heard, but . . ."

"You do know something about my mother. Do you know who my father is?"

"Forget it." Amy took a few steps away from her. "I'm sorry; it's none of my business, really. You can't believe gossip. People say all kinds of things."

"What do they say?"

"That you're . . . That Will Tawes is crazy. That there was some scandal with him and Beth. That—"

"Hey." Cathy pushed through the outer door and came out onto the step. "What am I missing? It looks serious."

"Nothing," Amy said. "See you tomorrow."

"What else?" Bailey demanded.

Amy shook her head. "I'm sorry. I never know when to keep my mouth shut." Giving Cathy a strange look, she hurried away.

"What was all that about?" Cathy asked.

"I'm not sure," Bailey said. "She said something about my mother and a scandal. Do you know anything about it?"

"If I did, I'd tell you. You forget, I'm a mainlander too. Don't let it upset you. Beth Tawes was a young girl who had a baby without having a husband. I guess that's all it took to make the gossip list back then. And dying tragically the way she did, I guess it just makes the gossip juicier."

Moisture gathered in Bailey's eyes, and she blinked it away. "Did you know . . . Do you know your grandparents?"

"Me?" Cathy's eyes narrowed. "Sure. They're all still alive. My Dad's parents, Mom-Mom and Pop-Pop Miller, live on a farm across the road from the house I grew up in. My mother's family lives in Federalsburg. Why?"

"I never had that. I had a good mother and father. But no one else. No brothers or sisters, cousins, no grandparents, aunts or uncles. At least none that anyone had ever told me about. I was always closer to Mom; then after she died, Dad remarried. . . ." She swallowed, trying to dissolve the constriction in her throat. "I just have this need to *know* about them. And here on Tawes, I haven't gotten the answers. I've only got more questions."

"You want to know about your mother—about Beth—even if what you find out isn't—"

"Knowing would be better than imagining the worst. Can you understand that?"

Cathy nodded. "Sure, I can. I had a beagle puppy when I was five. She got hit by a car and killed, but my parents didn't want to hurt me by telling me the truth, so they said she'd run away. I kept looking for her . . . calling her name. I used to pray every night that I'd wake up in the morning and find Cricket in the kitchen in her bed. Finally, Pop Allan, my mom's father, told me the truth, and he showed me where Cricket was buried behind the barn. I cried, but I put flowers on her grave, and I felt better. . . . Like you said . . . *knowing*."

"I thought if I could find some of the family records in the church rolls—birth dates . . . deaths—that might lead me somewhere."

"Right. So when do we start?"

"You'll help?"

"Why not? What are friends for?" She grinned mischievously. "After all, I'm an outsider too. Right?"

"Do you have time to go to the church with me now?"

"Sure. And I'm a member. Grace can't refuse me." She started to walk in the direction of the church. "Come on. I've got time."

Bailey hurried to keep up with her. "Grace didn't exactly—"

"I can imagine. You probably asked, and she probably made excuses why they—"

"Actually, it was Matthew. He said that his father, the last pastor, kept terrible records."

"Right. But Matthew doesn't sneeze . . ." Cathy stopped to wave at a woman painting her front step. "Hi, Ellen!"

The woman raised her paintbrush and smiled.

"Be sure Ryan is at school tomorrow. He still needs help on his fractions if he's going to pass that test."

"I will."

"She's nice," Cathy said. "Two kids, both boys. You'll have her oldest, Andrew, in your class. Very polite. Shy, but sweet." She rubbed the front of her shirt. "Settle down there, Tarzan. I think he's swinging from tree to tree this morning."

"Is it uncomfortable?" Bailey asked.

"No, just weird. Where was I? Oh, yes, I remember. Matthew's nose. He doesn't sneeze unless Grace gives him permission. She's devoted to him, fusses over him more like a mother than a wife. And she's done a lot of good for the town and for the church. I always thought she was a pastor wanabe. She's never stood up and given the sermon, but none of us would be surprised if she did."

They crossed the street to the graveyard and entered by the main gate. "I can't say that I particularly like Grace, but she has been kind enough to loan me her bike. And she invited me to lunch after Sunday services."

"Run. Run away. Avoid the parsonage lunches like the plague," Cathy whispered conspiratorially. "Grace is the mistress of bad cooking. She bakes her chicken for an hour and a half." Cathy pulled a pack of chewing gum from her pocket. "Gum?"

"No, thanks."

"It helps with the heartburn. Anyway, if Grace can't drive nails with the drumstick, she puts it back in for another half hour. Her Maryland beaten biscuits are like stone, and she boils her vegetables until they're limp and tasteless."

"Don't worry. I didn't intend to accept. Emma has

spoiled me beyond belief." They stopped at the rear of the church. "I don't know—"

"Not that door. That leads into the sanctuary. That one there. Ah, yes, perfect Emma. Even my husband tells me I should take cooking lessons from her. He would trade our firstborn son for her oyster fritters." A bell over the door rang as they stepped into an office area in a frame addition to the brick building. "The light switch is on the left."

Bailey flicked on the lights. The room contained a desk, a table with six chairs, a computer and printer and copier, and a row of filing cabinets.

"What we want should be in there," Cathy said. "Matthew may be unorganized, but Grace keeps everything shipshape around here. The older records would be at this end. So what we want is probably somewhere in—"

"Hello?" Footsteps sounded from an inner door. "Is someone—"

"Oh, Grace." Cathy smiled at her. "We didn't know you were in the church. I told Bailey that I would help her find—"

"Yes, she asked about her family records earlier." Grace entered the room and smiled graciously. "Matthew didn't forget you, dear, but he's taken poor Creed's horrible death so hard that I'm afraid he's made himself quite ill."

"I'm sorry," Bailey said. "If it's a bother, I can—"

"Nonsense. I already pulled some of them and copied down the information. Here, on the table. I was hoping you'd stop back. We can look at them here, or you're both welcome to come back to the parsonage for coffee. I just made a—"

"No, thank you," Cathy said quickly. "I have to get

home, but I know Bailey would love to see what you've found on her family, especially her mother."

"On Beth Tawes. Yes, yes, of course." Grace picked up a yellow legal pad from the table. "I'm quite concerned about Matthew. He and Creed Somers, Emery Parks, and Senator Marshall all went to school together, you know. They hunted together, fished, knew each other from the time they were babies. And now both Joe and Creed are gone. It's so difficult for him to understand . . . to accept God's will. Death is difficult, even for a man of the cloth." She handed Bailey the pad.

"I went to see my great-uncle," Bailey said. "But he doesn't want to talk to me. These records seem my only—"

"Will Tawes." Grace pursed her mouth. "Will Tawes is an ungodly man. Crazy as a coot. Lord forgive me if I'm being uncharitable, but you should stay clear of him, my dear. Nothing good will come of that man. Nothing ever has, and nothing ever shall. He's evil, if you ask me. A spawn of Satan."

"He may not be the most pleasant person I've ever met, but he didn't seem crazy to me," Bailey said. "And he didn't seem evil."

Grace frowned. "You're very young, my dear. You've not seen as much of the world as I have."

"That's true." Bailey forced a smile. "May I have this?"

"Certainly. The records are public. But no father is listed, if that's what you hoped for. I'm afraid Beth always was secretive. Especially when she'd done something . . . when she was hiding . . ."

"You knew her well enough to know that about her?" Bailey scanned the names and dates on the paper. Grace's handwriting was full of exaggerated loops and oversize capitals, but clear enough to easily read.

"I don't think anyone knew all Beth's little secrets. She was . . . troubled. I don't believe that she should have lived with Will Tawes, uncle or not. Elizabeth was the proper guardian for a young girl. There was always talk. . . ." Grace trailed off suggestively. "Not that Beth would have been responsible for the way she was raised. She was spoiled. Will Tawes is the one who—"

"What about Will?" Matthew stood in the doorway.

Bailey noticed that his eyes were bloodshot and his face swollen and pale. "I'm sorry, Matthew," she said. "I forgot all about the archeological dig."

"Canceled," Grace said. "Until next month. No one felt it was appropriate, under the circumstances. Unfortunately, you'll have left us by then."

"Unfortunately," Bailey said.

Matthew looked from his wife to the paper in Bailey's hand. "Is there something I can help with?"

"No, dear, it's all taken care of." She moved to stand alongside him. "Bailey attempted to contact Will Tawes. I told her that was unwise."

"Absolutely," Matthew agreed. "Leave him to his own pursuits. He's a lost soul, and the less contact you have with him, the better."

Cathy glanced at her watch. "Would you look at the time? I've got scads to do at home, and I forgot to take anything out of the freezer for dinner." She edged toward the door. "I hope you feel better, Matthew."

"Yes." He sighed and shook his head. "Thank you."

"Well, I'll be going too," Bailey said.

Grace brightened. "Maybe you'll be able to make lunch next Sunday."

"I can't promise. My friend said something about returning—"

"Bring Mr. Elliott too, dear. Always room for one more."

Outside, with the door to the office safely closed, Cathy giggled. "Always room for one more. Your ex isn't really coming back, is he?"

"How did you know he was my ex?" Bailey grimaced. "Right. It's a small island."

"Exactly." Cathy folded her arms over her belly and rubbed them. "I try to be pleasant to Grace, but she's such a . . ." She shook her head. "Poor Matthew. It can't be pleasant, living with her."

"I wouldn't think so." Bailey glanced back at the church. "I just hope that Grace isn't right about my great-uncle. That he isn't so bad."

"That's what my husband says. Daniel likes him, and . . ." She shrugged. "Daniel's word is gospel with Jim."

"But what if I *am* prying into things better left in the past?"

"I don't know," Cathy said. "But if it were me, I think I'd keep digging. The truth has to be easier to accept than all the crazy stuff you can imagine."

CHAPTER ELEVEN

"You don't look well, dear. Come back to the house and lie down." Now that Cathy and Bailey had left them alone in the church office, Grace's demeanor softened as she rubbed the knotted muscles at the back of her husband's neck.

"I really wanted to have some sort of prayer vigil for Creed this evening, but—"

"Never mind, Matthew. It will be fine. We'll have a memorial service for him once his remains have been released by the medical examiner's office. When I called, whoever answered the phone couldn't tell me just when it would be. She acted as though he wasn't a high priority."

"That's disgraceful."

She patted his cheek. "What can't be helped must be endured. And, it isn't as if Creed was a member of our congregation."

"He was my friend . . . drunk or not."

She folded her arms and gave him a stern look. "You mustn't trouble yourself about him anymore. We need to think of the living, who need to be protected from Will Tawes's spite."

He removed his glasses and wiped his eyes. "It could have been an accident. Will had nothing against Ida Love."

"Poor Ida. If she was in that house, she was a witness to his crime. He would have had to silence her as well."

Matthew replaced his glasses and peered down at her. "But you said—"

"I don't care what I said," she protested. "I'm scared. And you know I speak before I think. My tongue has always been too harsh, and I'm too quick to judge others, Lord forgive me."

"I know some think that, but I know how good-hearted you are."

"No, Matthew, I've never denied my faults. I'm an embittered woman. When I miscarried our babies, one after another, compassion died inside me. And try as I might, I can't find it again. It's a cruel joke, isn't it? My name is Grace, but I possess so little of it."

He embraced her. "That's not true."

"It is." She pulled away, her eyes full of moisture. "With all the infants born in this world to mothers who don't want them, why couldn't I have given you just one living child?"

Matthew clasped his hands together. "We should have adopted when we were younger, when my health was better."

She nodded. "And now it's too late, and you're stuck with a shrew of a wife instead of the caring one you deserve."

"No, I won't accept that. You're the most caring person I know. You're always doing for others." He glanced away absently. "Didn't you just go to the trouble of finding those dates for Bailey? I'd intended to look for the records today, but . . ."

She turned to the outer door leading to the churchyard. "Enough of my sniveling. I have some nice lentil soup and biscuits for your dinner, and I can fix a spinach salad, if you'd like." She kissed his cheek. "Oh, dear, you forgot to shave this morning."

He patted her shoulder. "You go ahead. I need a few minutes to pray for Creed and for the other poor soul who died with him."

"I'm going to heat up that soup. I'll give you ten minutes, and then if you aren't at the table, I'll come looking for you."

"Just a quick prayer. Ten minutes. You know I always find inner strength . . . forgiveness . . . in the sanctuary."

"You're human, Matthew. Isn't that what you always say—'the church is for sinners'?"

"Yes." He forced a thin smile. "I suppose I do."

"Whatever sins you may have committed in the past are long forgiven by an understanding God. You can't go on chastising yourself. You do His work every day."

"And I sin every day."

Grace sighed heavily. "Don't we all?" Nodding, she said, "Only ten minutes, and then Precious and I will expect you."

As his wife hurried out of the office door, Matthew's shoulders slumped and his chin sank almost to the knot of his tie. He knew that people on Tawes said Grace ruled his life. And perhaps she did. But life had been cruel to her. To him, she was a rock. When she wasn't with him, he sometimes felt he didn't have the strength to go on. How he wished he had Grace's energy. There was no doubt in his mind that she loved him, and he'd often worried that perhaps *he* wasn't good enough for *her*.

Blinking back tears, he smoothed the front of his white dress shirt, switched off the office light, and went back into the adjoining hall that led to the church proper. He pushed open the sanctuary door and went rigid. Someone or something was in here. A chill skittered over the surface of his skin. "Hello? Who's there?"

A bulky figure rose from a bench halfway down the aisle. "Matthew? It's me."

His knees went weak, and he reached out to steady himself against the back of the nearest pew. What had he expected? Creed's blackened corpse? Will Tawes come to add one more notch to his gun?

"Emma? What are you doing here?"

"Are you alone? Where's Grace?" She came toward him. "We need to talk."

"This is God's house. Be careful what you say within these walls."

"He's heard worse."

"Has He?"

"I can't put it behind me. I want to go to Will and settle it, once and for all."

"At what cost? How many more have to die to satisfy your conscience?"

"What about your conscience? Has your wife erased that completely?"

"Leave her out of this!"

"But you can't, can you? She's as much to blame as—"

"It's over and done with. Can't you let the past lie?"

Emma seized him by the tie and yanked his face down to hers. He was taller by nearly six inches, but she outweighed him, and her arms were corded with muscle earned by a lifetime of hard work. "She's the image of her mother! How can you look into her face and not remember?"

"Let me go!" He pushed at her shoulders. "You're hysterical. He doesn't know. He can't know, or we'd all be dead."

"Damn you for a fool." Emma shoved him away. "Go on telling yourself that Joe's death was an accident. And now Creed's. Keep saying it when you're staring down the barrel of Will's shotgun." She sank onto a pew and lowered her head into her cupped hands. "Maybe it would be best if he did end it. Maybe then I could sleep."

"Don't go to Will. Wait. She'll be leaving in a few days."

"That's Grace talking. You're wrong. Didn't you hear that Bailey is taking Ida's place at the school? She'll be here for weeks."

"Weeks, then. Not months. And who's taken the woman under her wing—treated her like family? You."

"I like her. None of this is her fault."

"I know that. I like her too, but Grace is right. We're both too soft. It's either keep quiet and wait for the inevitable, or stop Will before he gets the rest of us."

Emma raised her head.

Matthew could feel the intensity of her stare.

"You want me to commit murder?"

"No." Matthew's voice cracked. "No. I'd not damn you to hell by suggesting that you kill another human being."

"But you thought it, didn't you?"

"No, no, I didn't. I'm a minister of the church."

"You're more a hypocrite than I am if you can't admit the truth. I've thought of it. Believe me, I have, but the fact is, I'm as much of a coward as I always was."

"Please, Emma," Matthew bargained. "All I'm asking for is a little more time. What if Joe and Creed both just suffered tragic accidents? What if their deaths were just an awful coincidence? Why open Pandora's box?"

"It's what I keep telling myself. But I don't know how long my conscience will let me stay silent."

"And take the chance of putting three more of us in the grave? Do you really think mere words can undo the wrong that was done?"

"I don't know," Emma said. "Lord, help me. I don't know."

Back at Emma's, Bailey surprised herself by getting a signal on her cell long enough to make one call to her neighbor to ask her to water her plants and check the mail and another to Forest's office in Annapolis. Forest assured her that he was dealing with the last obstacles to getting a clear deed for the bequest and told her that he'd be speaking with her in person soon. When she tried to stretch her luck by calling Elliott, she suddenly lost the signal.

It was just as well, she supposed, as she tossed a load of laundry into Emma's washer. It was becoming harder and harder to overlook her ex's failings. She knew what he earned at the restaurant where he worked, and she knew what his monthly expenditures were. If Elliott had enough cash to pay a skipper two hundred and fifty dollars to transport him to Tawes, he'd been at the Dover slots. It was the same old story. He rarely won, and when he did, he considered his winnings "found money" and spent it without regard for his debts. Bit by bit their relationship had changed, until the man who had once been her lover now seemed like an irresponsible younger relative.

Ouch. She winced inwardly. She'd resented Elliott's attempts to advise her on what to do with her inheritance, and she'd been more than a little suspicious of his motives. The two of them shared a lot of memories, and she valued his friendship, but maybe she was being as immature as Elliott. Maybe it was time she grew up, admitted that her marriage was over, and moved on before it was too late to make a new life.

A life with whom? Daniel had been the first man in a long time to ignite her hormones, but he'd made it clear that his interest in her was purely platonic. Platonic? Bailey laughed. Where had that come from? Freshman Philosophy 101?

She nibbled at her lower lip. This inheritance gave her options she'd never had before. Maybe she should take some art classes. Or . . . She considered the possibility of taking a tour of Europe next summer. She didn't even have to remain in Newark. If she wanted, she could sell the condo and buy a house in Sussex County, enjoy the beach life, less traffic, and lower taxes. Surely they needed teachers in southern Delaware, and the schools there would be less stressful.

Teasing thoughts of a little vacation house on the corner of Elizabeth's property kept returning. She could almost imagine sitting at her cottage window and watching the seasons change. . . .

But not alone.

If she wanted to get married again—if she wanted children—she couldn't wait forever. Too bad she didn't spring from a culture that still arranged marriages, like her college roommate, Lila. Just last year her parents had come up with the perfect husband for Lila.

Making a snap decision, Bailey decided when she finished teaching the summer school classes here on

Tawes, she'd fly out to Oregon and visit Lila. She'd missed her friend terribly for the last two years, and all the phone calls in the world didn't make up for an all-night girls' session. Both she and her new husband, a plastic surgeon, had begged her to come and stay as long as she liked. Maybe, if she'd been Hindu, Lila's parents would have come up with a handsome bachelor for her too. If all else failed, maybe she should consider converting to Hinduism.

Unfortunately, she couldn't see herself marrying a man she'd never laid eyes on. It had been right for Lila, and she was happy for her friend. A little jealous, but happy. How was it that two people from opposite ends of the country shared so much culture and religion that they could find love and contentment in a marriage that had begun as a union of families?

What was it Lila had said to her the night she'd gotten the call from her father about the betrothal? "Old ways are best, Bailey. And who knows me better than my parents? They have picked a good man from a good family. We share the interests of medicine and books, and we both want children, so why wouldn't it be a successful match?"

"You don't know him," she'd protested.

"In my family, it is said that first comes respect between a husband and wife, and then love will grow."

"How can you marry a man someone else picked for you?"

Her friend had laughed. "You chose Elliott. You thought you knew what he was like when you married him. But you picked the wrong man, and the love and respect you felt for him vanished."

Lila was right. Elliott had destroyed the respect she felt for him with his irresponsible behavior . . . and with it the love, at least the love she'd felt toward him as a husband. And now maybe even their friendship was stretching thin.

She decided to write to Lila, ask about the baby, and tell her everything that had happened since she'd arrived on Tawes. Unlike Elliott, Lila had always urged her to investigate her birth family, to try to find her roots.

"They are your blood," she had insisted. "And blood always matters."

A series of late-afternoon thunderstorms rolled in from the west, crashing and booming overhead, sending torrents of rain down upon the island. It was still pouring when a pounding at the back door of the parsonage startled Grace. "Who's there?" The terrier leaped out of his basket and ran barking ahead of her.

Grace pulled aside the curtain and peeked out before opening the door. "What are you doing out in this storm?"

Emma pushed her way into the kitchen, shirt and overalls soaked through and dripping. "I need to talk to Matthew." She raised her voice to be heard over the yipping terrier.

"Shh, shhh, Precious. Get down. Matthew? He's not here."

Emma's face was pale, her eyes wide and frightened. "Where is he?"

"At the church." Grace gathered up the squirming dog. "Hush, Precious. Wait, I'll just get him a treat."

A puddle of water spread from Emma's high-top leather shoes. "No. Matthew's not at the church. I just came from there."

"Oh, dear." Grace retrieved a dog biscuit from the

cookie jar on the counter and handed Emma a tea towel decorated with lemon slices. "Dry your face," she said. "I hope he's not out in this. He's not well."

"Are you certain you don't know where he is?"

Grace shook her head. "I don't know. What's so important that you would come out in this storm? You could be struck by lightning." She motioned to a chair. "Sit down. You're shivering. Let me pour you some hot"—another clap of thunder shook the windows, and Grace put her hands over her ears—"coffee. Is it something I could help you with?"

"No. It's Matthew I need."

Grace reached for the coffeepot on the counter. "You're more than welcome to wait, but you know how he is. He could be anywhere."

Emma turned back toward the door and rested a hand on the knob. "Never mind. I'll find him."

"You can't go out in this downpour." Grace pursed her lips as Emma dashed back out into the rain. "What do you suppose that was about, Precious?" The little dog circled around her, hopping on his back feet. "That isn't like Emma, is it?" She slid the old-fashioned bolt home. "She worries me."

"Who was that?" Matthew called from the dining room. He was clad in pajamas, and his feet were bare. "I thought I heard voices." He looked at the wet floor. "Who—"

"Emma."

"Why didn't you call me?"

"So she could repeat the same nonsense she gave you earlier in the sanctuary?"

Matthew came into the kitchen and poured himself a cup of dark roast. "I knew I shouldn't have told you about that."

"And why not, dear? Doesn't everything that concerns you, concern me? I won't have Emma upsetting you again. Besides, you were sleeping. Even a minister is allowed time to rest. You give too much of yourself, my dear. You always have."

"Not always."

"Always. And if it takes telling a few little white lies to protect you, then I'm guilty. I'll always protect you, Matthew. You know that. As long as I live, you'll be safe with me."

Emma and Daniel still hadn't returned when full darkness fell, so Bailey went around the house and turned on the lights. She was at odds, too restless to read, and when she switched on the television in the den, she discovered that the thunderstorms interfered with Emma's satellite reception and she couldn't get a single station.

Realizing that she was hungry, Bailey went to the kitchen and opened the refrigerator door. Rain still pattered against the windows, and thunder boomed overhead, the sound echoing through the empty rooms, making the house feel big and empty.

She found the makings for a salad and was mixing olive oil and vinegar for a dressing when she heard the first notes of whistling from the yard. She was so startled that she dropped the vinegar, and the small cut-glass decanter shattered. The acrid scent of vinegar filled the air as liquid spread across Emma's spotless linoleum floor.

Gooseflesh prickled on Bailey's arms. She pushed aside a curtain and stared out, and when the next flash of lightning lit the sky, she thought she saw the outline of a figure standing beneath the oak tree. It was all she could do to stifle a cry. Then adrenaline surged through her, and she ran to fasten the door.

But the old door had no lock, not even a slide bolt.

Grabbing a kitchen chair, she wedged it under the knob, then ran to the side door. That one had a small lock built into the doorknob, but the top half of the door was made up of panes of glass. Anyone who wanted to break in could simply smash the glass, reach in, and turn the knob. Still, a small lock had to be better than nothing. If whoever was watching the house tried to get in, she'd hear the sound of breaking glass. The front door had a brass panel and a keyhole for an oversize key, but no key in sight. Determined, Bailey dragged a marble-topped table in front of the door, went upstairs, and retrieved the key-chain pepper spray Elliott had given her.

By the time she reached the kitchen again, the worst of her fear had drained away. She had heard the whistling outside her window before, but no one had ever tried to break in. Feeling foolish, she dropped the spray container on the table.

Maybe it was a prankster, or someone who wanted to frighten her into leaving the island without selling Elizabeth's property, she thought. Or . . . She smiled. Perhaps it was the ghost Emma had told her about.

But she didn't believe in ghosts.

More likely it was her imagination running away with her. She lifted the wall phone, intending to call Cathy, but there was no dial tone. When she hung the handset up, she couldn't help thinking of how alone she was. No one was coming to help her. If there was an intruder outside the door, it was up to her to protect herself or suffer the consequences. She picked up the spray again and tucked it into her jeans pocket.

Switching off the kitchen light so she wouldn't be a target, she went to the window over the sink, unlatched it, and pushed it up. "Who's there?" she demanded. Rain splattered against her face and throat. "Show yourself! If this is a game, it's not funny."

The whistler moved away from the tree, and her heart skipped a beat. This wasn't her imagination. Someone was out there, standing just a few feet from the back porch. She could just make him out, a tall, cloaked shadow with a wide-brimmed hat, standing in the rain.

"Go away!" She drew the pepper spray out of her pocket and then flipped open the top.

Wind whipped the brim of the specter's hat as it moved away toward the water.

"And stay away!" Bailey found her way to the light switch and turned it on. She closed and locked the window; then, knees suddenly weak, she sank onto a chair, still scared but triumphant.

The smell of vinegar lingered in the air. Putting the pepper spray on the table again, she got a broom and swept up the broken decanter, then used a mop to wipe up the vinegar. She was cleaning up the last of the spill from the linoleum when she heard a loud knock at the side door.

Dropping the mop handle, she snatched up the spray. "Who is it?" she called. "Emma? Is that you?"

The only answer was a repeated banging.

"Okay, cowardly lion, he's calling your bluff," she murmured. She couldn't decide if she should run for the front of the house or answer the door. Reason prevailed. Someone trying to break in would hardly knock.

"Bailey! For God's sake, unlock the door!"

"Daniel?"

CHAPTER TWELVE

Daniel turned the knob. "Bailey, will you please open the door? I'm soaking wet."

Hesitantly she flipped the lock. Without budging, she looked directly into his eyes. "Were you the one outside?"

"Is this some kind of a joke?"

She blinked. "What?" He shoved the door open, and she stepped aside to let him in. "I heard it again—I mean, I saw someone. Outside. In the rain, under the big oak. He was whistling. I thought . . ."

"It was me?" He gave a snort of amusement as he stripped off his wet denim jacket. His black Jimmy Buffett T-shirt was as soaked as his jeans. "Do you mind?" He motioned to his shirt. "Emma will kill me if I leave a trail of water from here to the laundry room."

It wasn't the first time she'd seen Daniel without a shirt, but tonight his hard-muscled chest and the thin scar that ran from one nipple down across his ribs seemed more ominous. "No." Bailey tried to make a joke of it as she attempted to slide the pepper spray into her pocket without being seen.

She failed.

"Were you planning to use that on me?"

She felt her cheeks flush. "No, I—"

"You're certain you saw someone? It wasn't just—"

"I'm not blind or stupid." Her words came out sharper than she'd intended, but tiny hairs still prickled at the nape of her neck. She couldn't decide if Daniel was innocent or a good actor. "It wasn't five minutes ago."

Something indefinable flickered in his eyes before his expression lost its sharp edge. "I didn't see anyone, and I didn't hear anything."

She gripped the back rail of a chair. "You don't believe me, do you?"

"I never said that." His lips curved into a smile, and he rolled the wet clothes into a bundle. "Emma would say it was the ghost."

"Don't tell me that you believe in ghosts?"

"Truthfully? Hell, I'm not sure what I believe in. I've never seen one, but I have seen a lot of weird stuff I couldn't explain. What *exactly* does this whistling sound like? Are you certain it isn't a willet or some other shorebird?" He walked into the kitchen and she followed him.

"Not unless it knows the tune to a nursery rhyme."

"Hmm." Daniel glanced back at her and grimaced. "Well, it sure as hell isn't me. I couldn't whistle my way out of a bucket. Matthew can—at least, he could when he was younger. He tried to teach me, but he said I was hopeless. He can sing, too. If he hadn't picked the church, he could have made a living with his voice."

Bailey went to the back door and removed the chair that she'd jammed under the knob. "No lock," she explained.

"Not much call for locks on Tawes."

"Somebody was out there."

"All right, I believe you. But just because someone was out there doesn't mean you were in any danger." He crossed the kitchen and pushed open the sliding door to the laundry room.

"The washer's empty," Bailey said from the doorway. "I did a load earlier." She handed him the detergent, and he set it on the counter beside the washer. She didn't think Daniel was the whistler, but neither was she going to put herself in a small space with only one way out.

He dropped the T-shirt into the washer, put his jacket in the dryer, and set the timer. "High heat or low?"

"From the looks of that jacket, I don't think that's an issue."

He grinned. "You're probably right." He pushed the button and the dryer began to spin. "And you've noticed that I go out a lot late at night."

"It's none of my business."

"No, but you've noticed." He set the washer on the low water level and threw in a small amount of detergent.

"Yes, I have."

"What's for supper? I take it Emma's not here." He came back into the kitchen and looked at the empty stovetop. "No chicken tonight."

"I was going to fix a salad. Would you like me to make extra?"

"Give me five minutes to jump in the shower and put on some dry clothes and I'll see what's in the refrigerator. I think I want something more substantial. What's your take on spicy stir-fry?"

"Good." If this was an act, she thought, he deserved an Oscar.

"All right. There's brown rice in the cupboard over the refrigerator. You start the rice, and I'll do the rest."

When Daniel returned in a clean shirt and khakis ten minutes later, Bailey had the rice cooking and the table set for two. "I found celery, garlic, onions, and green peppers," she offered.

"Wait." He motioned toward the back door, stepped out on the porch, and returned in seconds with two bottles of imported beer. He opened the first one and handed it to her. "Glass?"

She shook her head. "I'm a purist." She took a sip. The beer was cold, with a crisp tang. If she'd had the brand before, she didn't remember. "Good. Where did this come from?" She studied the label of the Dutch imported beer.

"I get off the island now and then. And Emma can be bribed."

Bailey laughed, beginning to feel embarrassed that she'd suspected Daniel of being the prowler. "Can I help cut the vegetables?"

"Dice the onion. They always make me cry," he said. "And see if you can find oyster sauce or duck sauce in the refrigerator. Might be Chinese cabbage in the bottom drawer."

"Pretty fancy ingredients for a 'plain country cook' to have around." Bailey smiled. "Isn't that what Emma says she is?"

Daniel rolled his eyes. "You can't always take what Emma says as gospel. Her mother is a plain country cook. Blind or not, Aunt Birdy still makes the best pies on this island. But Emma . . ." He shrugged. "Emma has her share of secrets. I'd put her up against the chefs at Four Seasons in Boston any day."

"You've eaten there?"

He nodded as he chopped celery on a wooden board. "I like good food and I like fine restaurants. It's my weakness." He laid down the cleaver and reached for the garlic.

She peeled an onion and rinsed it off in the sink. "I take it that you must get off the island a lot."

"Okay, so this is where I come clean, right? It's not exactly a state secret on Tawes, so you may as well hear it from me. I worked as an agent for the CIA for nine years."

She stared at him. "For real? Or is that a joke?"

Daniel picked up the cleaver and began to smash garlic cloves with the side of the blade. "Sometimes it felt like one."

"You're serious. You were some kind of James Bond, saving the free world from—"

"Nope. Nothing so romantic. The agency simply gathers information."

"Emma said you traveled a lot."

"Yes, Europe and the Far East."

"Collecting information?"

"Exactly. Just the facts, ma'am." He heaped the crushed garlic on one side of the cutting board.

"But you don't work for the CIA anymore?"

"Nope. Things got complicated, so I resigned."

"And that big government pension?"

He grinned. "Gone with the wind."

"And now you're a poor but humble carpenter?" Bailey sensed there was a lot more to the story than he was telling, but she was unwilling to pry further into his personal life.

"I think I've already given more than my name, rank, and serial number." He took an oversize cast-iron frying pan from a hook on the wall, added olive oil, and set it on the gas range. When the oil was hot, he began to add vegetables.

Bailey washed and chopped the Chinese cabbage. "Anything else I can do to help?"

"Finish your beer before it gets warm." He opened the refrigerator, rustled around inside, and came out with a package of raw shrimp, a few stalks of broccoli, and two large mushrooms. "I thought there were some of these in here." He took a drink from his bottle, retrieved some spices from another cupboard, and turned the rice down. "It should all be ready together."

The scent of pepper filled the kitchen as Daniel sprinkled it onto the vegetables. "How hot?"

"If you can stand it, I can."

"Okay, but don't say I didn't warn you."

Another five minutes, and Daniel scooped the stir-fry onto a bed of rice and placed it in front of her. "Chopsticks or forks?"

She laughed. "In for a penny . . ."

He went back to the porch for another two bottles of beer and joined her at the table. When she reached for her napkin, he raised his bottle toward her.

"What are we toasting?" she asked.

"Your farmhouse. Cathy tells me I'm being blackmailed into doing your repairs."

She touched her beer to his with a clink. "And you're all right with that?"

"I owe Jim a big favor. You're doing Cathy a favor by helping with summer classes at the school, so I'm trapped between a storm tide and the marsh." He flashed a crooked grin. "I'm not happy about it, but I'll do it, and I'll do it cheap and right. Island justice."

Bailey was still smiling as she walked to school in the morning. The evening before, which had started so frighteningly, ended on a much more pleasant note. After Daniel's delicious stir-fry, topped off with some of Emma's homemade strawberry ice cream, which they found in the freezer, they had sat on the porch swing and talked until Emma came home at midnight. Daniel hadn't touched her, but the night air had been charged by more than the storm's electricity.

Bailey couldn't remember when she'd enjoyed talking to someone more, or when the time had passed so quickly. With Daniel beside her, she'd felt safe in a way she could never remember experiencing. For the most part they'd chatted about silly things, movies, a used-book store in Newark, ethnic food, and bands from the eighties. They hadn't discussed her uncle Will or the inheritance or what she intended to do with Elizabeth's house, and Daniel had said nothing more about his travels with the CIA or why he'd quit.

Despite the casualness of the evening, Bailey couldn't deny an intense sexual attraction to Daniel, and if Emma hadn't returned to the house, she wondered if the evening might have ended differently. Daniel Catlin was an enigma, one who intrigued her. She definitely wanted to know more about him.

She'd intended on taking the bike to school, but the back tire was soft, so she'd changed into athletic shoes and capris and set off on foot. Forest stopped her on the street a short distance from his house.

"Good morning," the attorney said. "I was hoping to

catch you early. Could you stop by the office after class? I have some information to share with you."

"I'll be glad to."

Forest McCready appeared as dapper as ever in brown leather deck shoes, khaki trousers, and a white knit three-button henley with blue piping, but the lines around his mouth seemed more pronounced, and his eyes were red-rimmed. "I just can't get over what happened to poor Creed."

"I understand you were friends. I'm so sorry."

"Friends, yes, but cousins, too. In so many ways, his life was wasted, but we had some good times. Not to mention poor Ida."

"Is it definite that hers was the other . . . the other body?"

Forest shook his head. "No, nothing official. Reports on accidents like this can take weeks, sometimes longer. You come by as soon as you can. And don't worry about lunch. I'll have a loaf of wheat bread hot from the oven, some delicious crab bisque, and fresh strawberries and cream."

"Stop, you're making me hungry, and I just finished Emma's French toast. By the time I go home I'll be twice my size."

Forest chuckled. "I don't think we need to worry about that for some time. I hear you've contracted Daniel to do the repairs to the house."

"Already? Who told you that?"

"Never mind. It's fine. There's no question about your right to have the work done and to choose whomever you like to do it. There are no other heirs to contest the will. The house and land will be yours, once I have these bugs ironed out."

"I don't understand the problem," she said.

"That's why you have me to worry about it." He smiled again. "Don't let it give you a moment's trouble. It will be fine. I can fill you in on the details later, if you like."

"I would," Bailey said. "Have you found out anything else about my mother's death? That's what I—"

"Yes, I have." He lowered his voice. "She died of complications of her pregnancy, but this isn't the place to discuss it. I'll answer whatever I can this afternoon. I'll be looking forward to seeing you, and I'm so sorry to have put you through all these delays."

"Thank you—thank you for everything."

"It's my pleasure, Miss Elliott."

"Bailey, please."

"Very well, Miss Bailey Elliott. Then I insist you call me Forest. Everyone else in Tawes does."

The morning hours passed quickly. Bailey found her new pupils shy, but refreshingly uncomplicated and well behaved. For the past four years she'd been teaching in an overcrowded school with needy students. The Tawes children weren't all working up to grade level, but they displayed a warmth and innocence that surprised her. One girl, Rebecca Somers, had Down syndrome, and another boy, Roy Love, was mentally challenged, but both seemed completely accepted and protected by their classmates. One student or another was always at Rebecca's side, encouraging and praising her, and Roy received an equal amount of attention from his peers.

When Cathy came to tell the class that they'd worked fifteen minutes past dismissal, Bailey was as surprised as anyone else. Cathy invited her to share a picnic lunch with her and the children on the playground, but Bailey had to refuse.

"Mr. McCready asked me to stop by the office. I'm afraid that I've already accepted his offer for lunch," she explained.

"Tomorrow, then," Cathy urged. "I should have told you. Everyone brings a bag lunch, the teachers provide lemonade or iced tea, and we trade sacks. And some lucky person gets a free 'get out of trouble' pass to be used any day in the coming school year. Joshua has a standing offer to trade his best fishing rod for that pass, and every boy in my class and most of the girls want to win that fishing pole."

Bailey laughed. "I'll keep that in mind."

"I might as well tell you the rest," Cathy confided. "We have a school garden in the back. First we water all the vegetables and gather the ripe ones, and then we eat. So come dressed to crawl in the dirt tomorrow."

Forest's lunch was as delicious as Bailey had imagined. After the attorney had cleared away the dishes and poured them both tall glasses of sparkling water with slices of lemon, he took the big leather chair next to her. The dogs lay sprawled at his feet.

"Now, what can I tell you?" he asked.

"My mother. I want to know everything."

Forest took a sip of his sparkling water and set the glass on a coaster on the table between them. "I've obtained a copy of her medical records. Don't ask me how." He smiled as one of the dogs nuzzled his ankle. "We country lawyers have our ways," he said, as he leaned down and stroked the animal's head. "But I warn you, it isn't pleasant."

169

"Please tell me." She leaned forward in the chair.

"Beth hid her pregnancy from everyone. She went through the entire eight and a half months without any medical care. Apparently her guardian, your great-uncle Will, knew nothing about her condition. On the day before her death, an accident or a scuffle with a person or persons unknown caused her to go into premature labor. You were born in Elizabeth's house with only your great-aunt and -uncle present. Afterward, your uncle summoned medics from Crisfield. Sadly, Beth had lost so much blood that she slipped into a coma and died that day in the hospital without ever revealing how she came by her injuries or the identity of the father."

Bailey's eyes widened as the enormity of the truth sank in. "She never told anyone?"

"No." Forest shook his head. "Will was in a rage. He felt—and perhaps rightly so—that whoever fathered Beth's child had contributed to her death. He doted on her. The shame of her pregnancy and the loss of her life were almost too much for him to bear. But what came next was even worse."

"Worse?" Bailey felt light-headed. "How could it be worse? And everyone knows everything on Tawes. How could she have had a boyfriend without anyone being aware of it? Surely somebody must have known."

Forest leaned forward and patted her hand. "Your mother was just sixteen when she died. You would have been conceived when she was barely fifteen. Will would never have allowed her to have a boyfriend at that age. And if he'd found out who had seduced her and gotten her pregnant, the chances are he would have shot him."

"He's that violent?" Bailey thought back to the meeting on the wooded trail between his house and Elizabeth's, and the shock of seeing that ax in her uncle's hand. "Surely . . ."

Forest scoffed. "It's not a question of being violent or not. Tawes may seem old-fashioned to you now, but thirty-five years ago it might as well have been the seventeenth century. Beth was a Tawes, strictly off-limits. The Tawes women were always good women and good wives, honorable women."

"That sounds so archaic."

"Island justice."

"Daniel Catlin used that same phrase last night."

The attorney nodded. "It's true. It's been true for three hundred years, and that kind of habit doesn't die out easily. Will Tawes was a man whom few wanted to tangle with—still is, for all his years. I wouldn't want to. There are rules that islanders live by, and that Tawes women are off-limits is one of them."

"Somebody didn't follow those rules, because somebody got a fifteen-year-old girl pregnant and left her to bear the trauma and shame of her coming baby alone."

"It's the truth," Forest admitted. "And that truth has eaten at Will every day and night since."

"Do you know why I was placed for adoption?"

"You remained in Will's care for three months, until Elizabeth asked me to make arrangements for a private adoption. As I mentioned before, your parents—your adoptive parents—were distant cousins of hers with ties to the island. I'm not comfortable saying anything more. I was Will's friend and still am. I don't feel that I can give you any more details. If you want to know why you were put up for adoption, I think it's best that you ask Will."

Bailey rose. "But that's the problem, isn't it? My uncle doesn't want to tell me anything. He doesn't even want to talk to me. How do I get around that?"

Forest stood up, his eyes full of compassion. "That, my dear, is the nut of our dilemma. Because if there is anyone on earth who could help that man become part of the human race again, I think it's you."

CHAPTER THIRTEEN

As she entered Emma's front door, Bailey was still far more upset than she'd expected to be. A few words from Forest McCready had washed away the resentment she'd held all her life toward her birth mother. Instead, Bailey felt a deep sympathy for the girl, and now she wanted to question Emma, to learn anything more she could about Beth and her friends. Now, more than ever, leaving things as they were and accepting that she'd never know the identity of her biological father were unacceptable.

Bailey knew she needed to consider all the possibilities. Beth's lover might have been as young as she was—terrified to face the consequences of a few hours of reckless teenage passion—or she could have been seduced by an older boy. Without proof, Bailey couldn't assume the worst. Whatever the scenario, Bailey couldn't help wondering how the two had managed to evade both her uncle and the community long enough to conceive a child. Of course, Beth could have been assaulted, unwilling afterward to disclose her shame, a possibility Bailey didn't want to consider. Not yet, at least.

The sleigh bell hanging over the door jingled as Bailey stepped into the entranceway. "Emma! Are you—" She stopped midsentence when she heard Matthew's raised voice from the back of the house.

"Grace is worried," he said. "I—"

"Sorry," Bailey called. "I didn't know that you had company."

"Is that you, honey?" Emma shouted. "We're in the kitchen. I'm making strawberry jam."

Matthew said something, too low for Bailey to make out, but when she reached the kitchen doorway she guessed that she'd interrupted a heated discussion, because the pastor was as red-faced as Emma. Embarrassed, Bailey turned away, thinking to make a beeline for the staircase. "I was just headed upstairs to—"

"Nonsense," Emma interrupted, her joviality seeming forced. Her hair was pinned up in its customary knot on the back of her head, and she wore an oversize red-and-white-checked apron over a T-shirt and jeans. Her workworn hands were stained red to the wrists from the strawberry juice.

The steamy kitchen was thick with the sweet smell of boiling jam, but Bailey got the impression that it was more than the temperature of the berries that had put color in their cheeks.

"I hope your first full day with the children went well," Matthew said.

"It did, but—"

"You're a godsend to those kids," Emma said. "I can't tell you how much people here appreciate your help."

"Yes," the pastor agreed, glancing from Bailey to Emma and back to Bailey again. "The children are the heart of Tawes. Without them, there's no future for the island."

"The summer program can't be that vital to your entire school system," Bailey said.

"It is." Emma wiped her hands on a clean hand towel. "Believe me, it is. Are you hungry?"

"Stuffed." Bailey crossed to the refrigerator and removed a bottle of water. "I had a meeting with Forest McCready, and he insisted that I have lunch with him."

"Well, I must run," Matthew said, backing out of the kitchen. "The Lord's work is never done."

Emma followed him to the side door, and Bailey heard them murmuring. Then Emma came back into the kitchen. "Grab an apron, girl, and give me some help with this jam. It's only fair. You owe me. I fixed your bike tire this morning after you left."

"I know it was soft. I thought that putting air in it—"

"It had a leak, but it's right as rain now. I pumped up both tires."

"Thanks. I didn't mind walking to school, but I'd hoped to ride out into the country later this afternoon. It's such a beautiful day." It wasn't a lie. It was a pretty day, but she wasn't prepared to explain to Emma that she wanted to approach her uncle again. "I didn't mean to intrude on you and Matthew," she said as she unscrewed the cap on her bottle of water.

"Don't be silly. I want you to consider this your home while you're on Tawes. Matthew's just upset about Creed's death. We all are. Matthew's always taken things to heart. It's not easy losing a good friend." She rested her fists on her ample hips. "Maybe you'd better go upstairs and change into something you won't mind getting stained."

"It's all right." Bailey slipped the Mother Hubbard

apron over her head. She washed and dried her hands and turned back to Emma. "Now, what can I do?"

"You can start by capping those berries in that bowl. Aren't they lovely? Not Sure Crop. Those are Honey Eyes, the sweetest berry you'll ever taste. They don't keep worth a darn, so you won't find them at the supermarket, but they sure do taste good, and they make the best jam."

Bailey began washing the strawberries. There were a lot of questions she wanted to put to Emma, but she sensed that this wasn't the right time. Instead, she let the older woman chatter on about varieties of strawberries and tomatoes that her mother had grown a generation ago. Emma, thank the Lord, was never at a loss for words.

It was nearly five o'clock when Will returned to the house to find Bailey Elliott waiting on his porch. The dogs caught her scent before he even set foot on the dock. They leaped out of the boat and would have charged her, but he commanded them to stay.

The girl had courage; he'd give her that. When he'd come upon her on the path between his place and his sister's she'd gone white as a ghost. It was clear as new ice to him that she was terrified of dogs, yet she kept coming back.

He'd pondered half the night over the sketch she'd left for him to find. Her talent was raw and untrained, but it was strong. No denying whose child she was or that she possessed the grit of the Tawes women who'd come before her. Elizabeth had painted flowers in oil, filling her canvases with blooms and buds and every shape of leaf and stem. Beth had been proficient in her own medium. Now here was Beth's daughter, another artist, forcing herself into his life, not taking no for an answer, and threatening what little peace he'd carved out for himself these last few years.

Short of drowning her, he wasn't sure how to be rid of Bailey Elliott.

Scowling, Will stalked down the dock and up the bank toward the house. He motioned and the dogs followed. "What will it take to get you to mind your own business?"

"Answers," she flung back, bold as brass.

His stomach clenched. Bailey was more than twice the age Beth had been when they'd laid her to rest in the churchyard, but he would have known her in a crowd of hundreds. Her hair was a different color, but looking at her, he knew what a beauty his little Beth would have been if death hadn't claimed her too early.

She came toward him warily, eyes on the dogs. "I'm sorry if you think I'm rude," she said. "We started wrong, and it's gone wrong ever since. All I want is to get to know you and to learn something about my birth family . . . about Beth. You're the only—"

"You don't know what you're asking." He glared at her.

She glared back, and for an instant he had the sensation that he was looking at his sister, Elizabeth.

"Aren't you afraid of me?" he asked.

"Yes, a little."

Her eyes welled up with tears, and he felt a wave of compassion for her. "You don't know what you're getting into," Will grumbled. "Didn't anyone tell you that I was tried, convicted, and spent nine years in prison? That half the island believes I got Beth with child and murdered her rather than face the consequences of having her give birth to a babe conceived in incest?"

"No." Her eyes widened and tears suddenly glistened in the corners. She shook her head in disbelief. "No. No one told me anything of the sort. No one . . ." She drew in a ragged breath, turned, and fled into the woods.

"I tried to warn you," Will hollered after her as she tore through the underbrush, heedless of the wild grapevines that tore at her clothes. He stood there for a long time until the snapping of twigs and the sound of her distress faded. Then he signaled to the dogs and trudged slowly back to the boat to unload his catch.

Bailey was halfway to Elizabeth's beach, and she could see the shore of the bay through the trees when she dropped to her knees and vomited the remains of the lunch she'd shared with Forest McCready. Coughing, she wiped her mouth with the back of her hand and waited until the sick feeling passed. Then she made her way to the water's edge and washed her hands and face.

Everyone had warned her to stay away from Will Tawes, to leave the past buried, but she hadn't listened. As stubborn as always, she'd kept prying, not realizing until now that the islanders might not be hiding the truth, but attempting to shelter her from an ugly possibility. And now that she'd learned the secret, she wished she hadn't.

Daniel was coming around the corner of the farmhouse when she reached the edge of the lawn. "Bailey? What are you doing here? What's happened?"

She didn't want to see or talk to anyone, and most of all she didn't want to come face-to-face with Daniel Catlin when her breath reeked, her eyes were swollen from crying, and her hair was tangled with leaves. "I'm fine," she said, but Daniel was having none of it.

"Are you hurt?"

"No." She rubbed at a scratch on her elbow. "I went back to Will's and—"

Daniel's features hardened. "Did he—"

"No." She shook her head. "He didn't lay a hand on me. It was what he said. I just panicked and ran away."

"Come into the house. You're as white as Emma's sheets."

When arguing with him didn't work, Bailey allowed herself to be coerced inside into the bathroom. Surprisingly, someone had scrubbed it free of dust and mouse droppings and even laid out soap and fresh towels. She found toothpaste and a new toothbrush, still in its wrapper. When she came out, five minutes later, she felt much more in control.

Daniel was waiting for her with a thermos of hot tea. "Sit down," he ordered.

"Who called in Merry Maids?" She motioned to the bathroom and then glanced around the kitchen. This room, too, had been cleaned until the glass shone and the floor was spotless. "You?"

Daniel poured her a cup of tea. "I can't stand working in a mess, and I expect to be using these rooms while I'm working on the repairs." He handed the cup to her. "Careful, it's hot. Now, tell me exactly what happened at Will's."

She took the tea. It was strong and sweet, and she drank half the cup without answering. Then, having gathered what composure she had left, she was able to tell Daniel everything her uncle had said. "He didn't admit to sexually abusing Beth," she concluded, wiping back a stray tear, "or to beating her. But he didn't deny it either."

Daniel frowned. "I've heard the gossip, but that doesn't make it true. Will didn't go to jail for incest."

"No?"

"Hell, no! What made you assume that?"

"I don't know. He said . . . When he said . . ." She looked away. "I thought it sounded like a confession."

The tall case clock in another part of the house rang the hour in a clear tone, and Bailey noticed how the rays of sunlight coming through the windows illuminated the pattern of the grain in the tabletop.

Daniel refilled her cup and poured a mug of tea for himself. "The jury found Will guilty of beating Beth so badly that she went into early labor and then died."

"But Forest McCready said she died of blood loss the day after the baby was born. Surely she could have—"

"According to Aunt Birdy, Beth never regained consciousness after you were born. And her jaw had been broken. She might not have been able to talk, even if she was conscious."

She sipped at the tea, trying to make sense of it all. "But why would the jury find Will guilty if there wasn't proof?"

Daniel went to the sink and rinsed out the thermos and cap, then set them upside down to drain. "Let me start at the beginning. Back in the fifties, Beth's mother, Anne, was seeing Will before she broke off the relationship and married his brother, Owen."

"Forest told me that Owen Tawes was my grandfather. I didn't ask my grandmother's name. Anne. I like that," she said thoughtfully.

"Will was the firstborn, but he was something of a disappointment to his family. He had a reputation for being wild, even then. People said it was the Tawes Indian blood coming out. He spent his time roaming the marsh and woods, hunting, trapping. He liked to fish well enough, according to my mother, but Will wasn't a man for settling down to work from dawn to dusk on a crabbing boat or a farm."

"And Owen, I suppose, followed tradition?"

Daniel nodded. "Exactly. Owen was as solid as the church cornerstone. A real go-getter. He would milk cows before dawn, take the boat out, and be back in the fields plowing by noon. And the two brothers didn't get along too well either. According to custom, Will should have inherited the farm, but Owen was the man working it."

"Cain and Abel?"

"Aunt Birdy said Will was more fey than lazy. He was always whittling birds or painting pictures of otters on the walls of his father's barn when he should have been cutting hay or putting up fence. Will was the artistic type back when there was no such thing. I suppose the neighbors would have been hinting that he was gay if he hadn't been so popular with all the girls. Emma said she can remember him when he was handsome as the devil and just as ornery."

"So Beth's mother was his girlfriend?"

"Crazy-mad for him, according to Aunt Birdy."

Bailey drained her cup and set it on the table. "And did he seem to return her feelings?" She picked a twig out of her hair.

"Yes, but Anne's parents were against the match. They'd forbidden her to see Will, but nobody could stop him when he made up his mind to do something. Once Will came to church during services, and the next thing my father knew, the two of them had climbed out the Sunday-school window and ran off together. Anne didn't get home until almost dawn the following morning."

"But she didn't marry him. She chose his brother."

"They'd had a fight, as Aunt Birdy tells it, but Will thought he could soft-talk Anne out of being angry, the way he always had. And the next thing anyone knew, Anne and Owen were standing in front of the congregation taking wedding vows."

"What did Will think of it?"

Daniel returned to stand near her. "He didn't say, and no one had nerve enough to ask him. But years later, when his brother and Anne drowned in a storm, he took Beth to raise."

"And neither of the grandparents protested?"

"Will and Owen's parents were dead by then, and Anne's mother was an invalid. She and her husband had raised six daughters and didn't want to fight Will over Beth's custody."

"But if he had strong feelings for Anne . . . he might have seen the same thing in his niece." A chill passed through Bailey. "What if the gossip is true and the father I've been looking for was Beth's uncle?" She shivered, glancing away. "Not much of an incentive for me to have children, is there? No telling what interesting genes I have floating around in my genetic soup."

Daniel crouched down on his heels in front of her. "Look at me, Bailey. Please." He touched her chin with two fingers, gently tilting her face up. "I don't believe it. I've known Will all my life, and I think I'm a pretty good judge of people. I wouldn't have lasted long in my last job if I weren't."

"You didn't know my uncle then. You couldn't have been more than a kid yourself."

"No, that's true. I wasn't born until three years after he went to prison." He took her hands and gripped them. "But I've known him since I was six years old. He isn't the kind of man who would molest a child or beat one to death because she became pregnant."

"Then why did his sister believe it? She must have."

"I asked Matthew that once. He said that Elizabeth came to our father for counseling after Will was arrested, and that he overheard them talking in the sanctuary. As I said, Elizabeth wanted to keep you herself, but our father convinced her that you couldn't have a normal life here—that people would always whisper behind your back. I suppose she took his advice."

"So that was it. She sent me away to protect me from the rumors, not because she didn't want me."

Daniel stood and pulled her to her feet. "It's a nasty charge, but where's the proof? They didn't do DNA testing in those days."

She swallowed. "So now what do I do with all this?"

"First thing you do is come up to the attic with me. I was inspecting the underside of the roof, looking for leaks, and I found an old trunk." He offered his hand to her. "There are some things in it that you might want to see."

She looked into his eyes. "What kind of things?"

"A sketchbook, for one. It has Beth's name on it."

Although the cover was unstained, the pages inside were slightly damp, as though moisture in the air had seeped into the trunk. Holding the sketchbook, Bailey experienced such a surge of emotion that she began to weep all over again. She wasn't sure how long she sat there, crying like a baby, but when the storm passed she felt infinitely better.

Fortunately, she was alone in the attic. After Daniel had turned on the lights and led her upstairs to show her the location of the trunk, he'd made the excuse that he needed to get back to his repairs on an outside shutter. She'd guessed that it was his way of allowing her privacy as she went through her birth mother's belongings, and she was glad he'd thought to be so considerate.

She laid the sketchbook on the dusty floor beside her and looked to see what else was in the trunk. She carefully lifted out worn copies of *The Red Fairy Book*, *The Yellow Fairy Book*, and *The Blue Fairy Book,* and wedged under that she discovered a photo album. After carefully replacing the storybooks, she carried the sketchbook and the photo album downstairs and out onto the porch, where the light was better.

Daniel, true to his word, was mending the shutter— within sight, but far enough away not to intrude.

Beth's drawings were sketched and painted in the form of stylized cartoons. There were images of castles, kings and queens, unicorns and fairies. Beautiful costumes graced the pages, and she seemed to be developing a comic strip set in an imaginary kingdom, with a story line that gave evidence of a lively wit and a vivid imagination. The inscription in the front of the book showed that the sketchbook was a fourteenth-birthday gift from Elizabeth. From the dates beside the images, Beth had started her drawings soon afterward and continued on until a week before her death.

Bailey shed more tears as she looked through the pages. If her mother had lived, they would have found so much in common. The book was a tribute to a dreamy personality and a budding artist's passion for her craft. But there was something disturbing about the pictures as well. Most of the book was filled with bright colors, flags snapping in the wind from the top of castle walls, and dashing knights and beautiful ladies, but the last quarter of the pages grew steadily darker, with twisted trees, threatening ogres, and monstrous eyes staring from the forest.

Uncertain as to what the changes in Beth's style meant, Bailey set the sketchbook aside and began to thumb through the photo album. The black-and-white snapshots showed a laughing little girl who—except for the fifties clothing—looked strikingly similar to her own childhood pictures. There were images of Beth on a pony, Beth and an attractive young woman fishing off a dock, Beth dressed in what appeared to be a mermaid costume, and one photo of Beth and a much younger Will with a basket of puppies.

The pictures showed no trace of a strained relationship between Beth and her uncle, and they offered no obvious explanation for the dark drawings of stormy skies and twisted trees that filled the end of her sketchbook.

Puzzled, Bailey carried the album to Daniel. "Did you look at these?"

He shook his head. "No. As soon as I saw that there were pictures inside, I closed it. It belongs to you."

"I don't know what to think. She looks like a happy child . . . a child who went to bed knowing she was safe and loved, not a little girl haunted by a real monster. It makes no sense, unless the abuse didn't start until she was much older."

Daniel gave the screw a final turn, tucked the screwdriver into his tool belt, and moved the shutter experimentally back and forth. "There. That should hold for a few years."

"You do good work."

"No sense doing it if you don't do it right." He looked

at her. "There's more stuff up there, toys and clothing that must have belonged to Beth. Elizabeth went to some trouble to preserve them. I'd say Beth was certainly a much-loved child."

"I want to see them, but not now," she confided. "I need to decide whether I want to pursue questioning my uncle or not." Another tear spilled down her cheek, and she wiped it away. "I'm sorry. I'm not usually a basket case. It's just that—"

"Shhh, it's all right." He put his arms around her, gently pulled her against him, and squeezed her. She clung to him for long seconds, not wanting to let him go, but he kissed her gently on the forehead and stepped back. "I should have told you what to expect, but I didn't think you'd be so damned persistent."

"I thought I was prepared for anything," she whispered, "but not incest." She could still feel the heat of his body. It was a good feeling, and for an instant he made her feel that everything would be all right.

Daniel smiled at her. "Hey, don't take this to heart. If I learned anything from government service, it was never to take things at face value. I don't believe Will Tawes is the kind of man who would use violence against a child in his care, and neither does Forest. Just the opposite. Forest represented Will at his trial without charge, and no amount of money could have persuaded him to do that if he didn't think his client was innocent. Will Tawes wouldn't be the first man convicted unjustly."

"If that's true, if he is innocent, then why is everyone on this island afraid of him? They know him. Why aren't they convinced that he didn't do it?"

Daniel arched a dark eyebrow. "It's complicated."

She waited.

"Matt said that Will pleaded not-guilty to all the charges. They held the trial over in Easton, because the prosecutor couldn't find enough people on Tawes who weren't related to Will to make up a jury. To make a long story short, the Eastern Shore jurors found him guilty. Later, the jury foreman said he wasn't a hundred percent convinced, but there were no other suspects, and if there was all that smoke, there had to be fire."

"Circumstantial."

"Yes, something like that. But the charges were for beating Beth, not for getting her pregnant. The prosecutor kept repeating that Beth's pregnancy shamed Will and he'd lost his temper and started hitting her."

"But he never admitted it."

"No. Apparently when Will was sentenced he lost it, shouting that he was innocent, that whoever had fathered her child had attacked her. He threatened to find out who he was, hunt him down like a dog, and put a bullet through his head. He swore he wouldn't stop searching, not if it took the rest of his life."

Bailey sank down on the grass and cradled the sketchbook against her chest. "But that was so long ago, thirty-five years. It's not reasonable that he'd carry a grudge that long."

Daniel laughed. "You don't know Tawes as well as you think you do. The Chesapeake used to be a wild place. Blood feuds between families rivaled those of the Hatfields and the McCoys."

"You've got to be kidding me."

"Hardly. Just after the Civil War, three Catlin boys shot it out with two Tawes brothers. Only one Catlin survived, and he didn't live out the year. Folks claimed that it was one of the Tawes widows who did him in."

"Unbelievable."

"I can show you the headstones in the cemetery. You can still read their names." Daniel's expression hardened. "Call it vigilante justice if you want, but if the man who caused Beth's pregnancy and death is still alive, he has every reason to fear Will."

"You believe that?"

"I know it."

She sighed. "Okay."

"What do you intend to do?"

"I don't know yet."

He nodded.

Taking both the sketchbook and the photo album, Bailey went out to Elizabeth's dock and sat there for a long time, watching the tide and the birds and letting the peace of the early evening seep over her. Seeing Beth's artwork and the pictures of her as a child made Bailey all the more determined to discover who had wronged her. She knew what she had to do, but she wasn't certain she could summon the courage to do it.

If only her mother had confided in someone . . . if she'd gone to her aunt or told her secret to a friend, Bailey mused. But, as Emma would say, "If wishes were horses, beggars would ride."

If she was to learn anything about the final hours of Beth's life, there was only one place to start. Carrying both books, Bailey retraced her path down the beach and took the overgrown lane that led to her uncle Will's house. She'd gone no more than a few hundred feet into the woods when a rustling of brush brought her to a halt.

Heart thudding, Bailey watched as the boughs of a cedar parted and a doe stepped daintily onto the path. The graceful animal stared at her with huge eyes and, when Bailey didn't move, uttered a small grunt. Seconds later a spotted fawn leaped out of the tall ferns. The mother nuzzled the little one and then moved away into the trees on the far side of the lane. The fawn made two stiff-legged hops and darted after her.

A small bubble of joy rose in Bailey's chest, and she hurried forward to where the deer had crossed. A single hoofprint, hardly larger than her thumb, was pressed into the damp soil. For the space of a dozen heartbeats she stood there, wondering if she'd stumbled into paradise or a community so rife with secrets that it was rotten to the core.

CHAPTER FOURTEEN

Daniel stood at the corner of the house and watched as Bailey entered the woods. She was a lot tougher emotionally than he'd expected, and he had to admit that, despite his determination to avoid her, she'd gotten under his skin. His intuition told him that she was in no physical danger from Will, and whatever the two had to settle between them was personal. He didn't have the right to interfere, but if things went bad and he'd been mistaken in his assessment of Will's character, he might be forced to help pick up the pieces.

He was unstrapping his tool belt when his satellite cell phone, one of the few toys he'd retained from government service, rang. He was annoyed but not surprised when he recognized Lucas's voice on the other end.

"Daniel."

The tone was far too old-comrade-in-arms hearty. He'd worked with Lucas twice and didn't particularly like or trust him. "What can I do for you, buddy?"

"Just wondering how you were making out in the

wilds of Treasure Island." Lucas chuckled, a dry laugh that never came off as genuine. "Had a few drinks at Madigan's the other night with some of the boys from the office, and your name came up. Not much action on Tawes, is there? I heard they roll up the sidewalks at night."

He glanced around to be certain that he was alone, and that Bailey hadn't returned. "What do you want?"

"Daniel, Daniel, is that any way to talk to—"

"There's nothing you could tell me that I want to hear."

"What do you know about the senator's *accident?*"

"Marshall died of a shotgun blast to the chest, presumed accidental. I found the body in the marsh weeks later, but I'm sure you're already aware of that. Otherwise, no more than what I read in the papers."

"Right." This time the amusement in Lucas's voice was real.

"I'm a civilian."

"And I'm the next candidate for pope."

"Your point?" The silence drew out between them, and a faint static that shouldn't have been there told Daniel that someone was recording the call.

"We need to talk."

"Do I have a choice?"

Lucas gave a time and place. "I've got to catch a flight to Prague. Don't be late."

"Wouldn't think of it." If Lucas was telling him Prague, his destination was more likely Australia or Tokyo. One thing he wasn't was sloppy.

"Same old Daniel."

"No, not the same old Daniel. And this had better be worth my time, or—"

"Making threats?"

"Just a promise."

The call was terminated. Daniel gripped the phone and swore softly, wondering when it would be over. If ever . . .

As Bailey neared Will's house, the three dogs ran down the path toward her, barking wildly. She forced herself to pretend that she didn't see them and kept walking until she reached the clearing, where she discovered her great-uncle splitting wood.

Will tossed two sections of a log into a pile, turned, and scowled at her. "Don't you ever give up?"

"No."

"The trouble with you is, you're too damned much like your mother." He picked up his tools and leaned them against a pile of neatly stacked wood.

The dogs circled her as she approached him.

"There's no way I can discourage you?"

She shook her head. "I'm afraid not."

Something close to a smile passed over her uncle's chiseled face. "Then I suppose you'd best come inside and have some coffee." He waved the dogs back. "Go on now; you're worse than kids. She doesn't like you, and she doesn't have any bones in her pockets."

She followed Will to the porch, beginning to think that his bark was worse than his bite. He opened the wide door and stepped back to let her go in first. A combination kitchen and living area opened on the right. A comfortable couch and several easy chairs, all obviously dog-friendly, were arranged around an elaborate cast-iron woodstove raised on a brick foundation. Although the stove was not in use at this time of year, kindling and wood were stacked neatly beside it.

The galley kitchen area was neat, the wide maple

flooring free of dog hair and dust, although rope chews, several balls, and a ragged stuffed toy duck littered the rug. A partially painted carving of a bird of prey stood on newspapers on the table.

The cathedral ceiling over the main living area made for large expanses of white walls. These spaces were hung with wildlife paintings and photographs, a Navaho rug, and a faded patchwork quilt. Books lay on the tables, on the floor, on the chairs, and overflowed the shelves of a floor-to-ceiling bookcase. Bailey had expected the house to smell like dog, and it did, a little, but most of all, it smelled of wood shavings, pine oil, and fresh coffee.

Will waved her to a chair at the table and rummaged in a cupboard for an oversize cup. "Cream? I warn you, it's goat's milk. I don't keep a cow—too much work."

She sat and laid the photo album and the sketchbook beside her. "Black is fine." She inspected the carving on the table. Apparently her uncle was in the process of painting the wing feathers on one side of the piece. The head and shoulders of the life-size hawk were completed, and so real that she expected the eyes to blink. "Is it an osprey?" she asked.

"That's right." He nodded in approval. "There's honey on the table. I don't keep white sugar in the house. Any man who eats white sugar every day will be chewing with false teeth by the time he's sixty." He poured two cups of steaming coffee and carried them to the table. "This is good. Comes from Central America, and it's shade-grown. No pesticides, so it doesn't harm the birds."

She looked at him in surprise. Hadn't Daniel said that Will was a hunter and trapper? "Where do you buy it?"

"I have it all shipped in. Coffee's my weakness. I've

cut back to no more than six or seven cups a day, but . . ." He shrugged. "A man has to have at least one addiction or he starts to think of himself as a martyr."

She glanced back at the osprey, amazed by the intricate detail of the legs and claws. "This is fantastic."

"Should be, for the price I charge."

"How long have you been doing work of this caliber?"

"Since prison." He took a seat across from her, blew on his coffee, and took a drink. "Not this good, of course. But it's where I began to take my art seriously. I took a class in sculpture, clay. They didn't trust us with knives and chisels, but the concept is the same."

They talked about the carving and what kind of brushes Will liked to use, her first impression of the island, and Bailey's fourth graders before she summoned the nerve to mention the photo album and the sketchbook.

"Is this what you were looking for that day I met you in your sister's house?" she asked.

Will reached across the table, picked up the book, and reverently turned a few of the pages. His Adam's apple bobbed, and he averted his eyes. "This meant the world to her, but . . ." His voice cracked, and he had to clear his throat to go on. "I'll show you." He rose and motioned for her to follow.

Leaving the books on the table, she did, moving out of the two-story living area and passing the foot of a staircase before entering another room. Here, the walls were covered with yet more photographs of ducks and marsh birds. Over a desk hung a charcoal drawing of a woman on horseback. The picture was simple but moving. The shape of the horse's head and neck, the flawlessly proportioned legs, and the muscles of the animal's hindquarters were a perfect foil for the graceful lines of the spirited rider.

"Is this your work too?" Bailey asked.

"Beth did it for me as a birthday gift. It's Elizabeth and Dandy," he answered quietly. "Beth was only thirteen."

"She must have been very talented."

"She was." His eyes narrowed. "Are you brave or foolish to come into the fox's den, knowing that I could be a pervert or a madman?"

"Probably foolish," she admitted. "I'm not particularly courageous."

"That's what I wanted out of Elizabeth's house." He stared at the drawing. "It was mine, and my sister took it there for safekeeping while I was in prison. Never did give it back, and I was too proud to ask for it."

"You didn't speak to Elizabeth for years? It's what . . . what I heard."

Will scoffed. "From who? Emma?"

"No."

"Daniel then. He talks too much for his own good."

"But it's true?" Bailey asked. "Was it over Beth?"

"You cut right to the heart of things, don't you, girl? I need more coffee if you're going to open that nest of hornets."

They returned to the kitchen. Will poured them each another cup, and he removed a pie from the refrigerator with only one missing slice. "Have you got nerve enough to try my baking? Blueberry."

"You bake?" she asked.

"Bread, biscuits. This is one of those pie shells you can buy in the dairy section of the supermarket. I picked the blueberries myself last summer."

"And you froze them?"

"Sure didn't can them. My name's not Emma."

Bailey found herself laughing. "She's a marvel, isn't she? I don't think there's much she can't do. She puts me to shame in the kitchen."

Will frowned. "You've fallen under that one's spell too, have you?"

Bailey accepted a slice of the pie and a fork. "I like her. She's been wonderful to me since I've been on Tawes."

He poured them each more coffee and came back to the table with the two mugs and his serving of blueberry pie. "You know, Elizabeth never thought that I'd taken advantage of Beth, not in a foul way. She knew me better than that. But she knew I had a temper, and she knew how much store I put on the family honor."

"She thought you beat Beth when you found out she was having a baby?"

He nodded. "Went to her grave believing it, I suppose. She never had a child of her own, and she loved Beth with all the passion of a lonely woman. When Beth showed up at her house in that thunderstorm, her face smashed, one wrist broken, bruised and bleeding, Elizabeth thought she'd run from me. I don't know what she would have done if I hadn't come looking for Beth. By the time I got there, Bethie was bleeding worse and already in hard labor."

"With me." Bailey laid the fork down, her bite of pie untouched.

"With you. Later we found out that you'd come early, probably because of what had happened to her. She was just a little bit of a thing, like you, and too young to be a mother. Maybe the beating killed her, and maybe it was just bad luck that everything went wrong with the delivery and she lost so much blood."

"I don't understand. How could she have been so far along in the pregnancy without you noticing? Without someone—"

"Hell if I know," Will snapped. "You think I haven't asked myself that a thousand times?" He lowered his head and cupped his face with his hands. "I was stupid, I guess. I'd seen that she was putting on weight, but she wore loose clothes. It was cold weather, and when you were born, you didn't weigh as much as a five-pound sack of sugar."

Bailey leaned forward in her chair. "You didn't do it, did you?"

Her uncle straightened and looked directly into her eyes. "On all I hold sacred, girl, I never hurt her. Damnation, I only spanked her once in her whole life, and that was when I caught her and Grace Widdowson throwing stones at a blind mule."

He shook his head. "I never could abide cruelty to an animal, a woman, or a child, and I wouldn't tolerate that meanness in Beth."

Bailey pushed the photo album toward him. "Daniel found this in a trunk in Elizabeth's attic."

"That was hers. Elizabeth was always big on taking pictures. She had a talent for painting, but she always did oils of flowers. I never could get her to try seascapes or houses."

"All the snapshots are of Beth. I'd like to have the album, if it's all right with you, but I'd be glad to make copies for you."

Will tapped his head with one finger. "I've got her here, in my mind, from the first time I laid eyes on her until the last. I don't need photos of my Bethie."

She took a deep breath. "I can understand why you'd hold me responsible for her death, but—"

"You? Damn, girl, I thought you had better sense than that."

"I've got a name," she flared. "Bailey. I'm Bailey."

Will snorted. "You've got the Tawes temper; I'll give you that. And I know your name well enough. I gave it to you minutes after you were born. Elizabeth thought you wouldn't survive the night, so she sprinkled well water on your head, and I came up with the name. My grandmother on my mother's side was a Bailey, Mildred Bailey. She was always a favorite of mine." Mischief sparked in his eyes. "I'd hardly be doing you any favor if I'd named you Mildred, would I?"

"So I'm named for my great-grandmother?"

"Your great-great-grandmother. It's a family tradition with us."

"You really didn't do anything to cause Beth's death, did you?"

"It's what I told Elizabeth, and she didn't believe me. It's what I told the judge and jury, and you know how that went. Not much sense in repeating it, is there?"

"But if you didn't," Bailey said, "then who did?"

Will's hand tightened into a fist, and the eyes that had been full of amusement only a moment before became cold. "I'd give my right arm to know the answer to that riddle," he said softly.

Bailey suppressed a shiver. Suddenly, for the first time, she glimpsed the man whom the islanders feared. "It's been a long time," she offered. "Whoever it was may have moved away, or he could even be dead."

"Maybe, maybe not. But if I ever find him, he'll wish he were."

She pushed the remainder of the pie away. "Thank you for telling me," she said. "It means a lot. I know we're strangers . . . but you're the only real relative I have, other than my father. He's living in California, and I hardly ever see him."

"He was good to you?"

"Yes, he was a good father. He and my mother gave me a home, an education. I never lacked for anything." Anything but affection, she thought. "I loved them both, and I had a lot of respect for them as parents and as educators."

Will nodded. "That's as it should be. I always hoped you were with good people. None of what happened was your fault. I always figured Elizabeth would keep you, raise you as her own. But she thought it was better for you to be away from all this."

"But in the end, she brought me back here. When she left me the bequest, she must have known that I'd—"

"Blood is blood. And that's something that can't be changed by laws or courts or papers. You're Beth's girl, and no matter who fathered you, you're as much a Tawes as she was. And I know she'd be proud of that."

Bailey stood. "I've kept you from your work long enough. I'd better—"

"No." Will pointed toward the chair. "You sit. You wanted the truth, and I've given it to you. And so long as we're digging old turnips, there's more you need to know."

Bailey sank down in the chair again. What more could he possibly tell her? Surely . . .

"I want to share a secret I've carried since before Beth was born. There's nobody else alive who knows, and I think it's your right to be told. Beth wasn't my niece, like everybody thought. She was my daughter."

Bailey stared at him in disbelief. "What?"

"I know it sounds crazy, but it's true. I had a brother,

Owen, who was more what my mother and father expected in a son than I was. Owen and I rarely saw eye-to-eye, but for what's it worth, I loved him. The trouble was, we both cared for Anne."

"Beth's mother?"

He nodded. "My head was full of drawing and whittling. I would work thirty hours on a carving without stopping to eat or sleep, but I didn't give a tinker's damn for planting corn or hauling in oysters for market."

Will got up and walked to a window and looked out. And it seemed to Bailey that he was seeing not what was so much as what had been.

"I had it bad for Anne, and she was as wild as I was. I would have married her when I found out that she was in the family way, but she wouldn't have me." He pressed the palm of his hand against the windowsill. "She knew how Owen felt about her, and she went to him and told him straight out about the baby."

"And he married her," Bailey finished.

Will glanced back at her, his weathered face a mask of grief. "Owen knew that I'd put that child in her, but he didn't care. He wanted Anne, and he got her."

"But they never told anyone?"

"The Taweses protect their own."

The sound of a four-wheeler and the dogs' barking brought Bailey to her feet. "That's got to be—" she began.

"Daniel Catlin. I know who it is, but we've got to be straight on this, girl."

"Bailey," she insisted.

He nodded. "Bailey. Let me finish. Anne and Owen made a marriage, and they both stuck by their vows. They were good together, probably a hell of a lot better than Anne and I would have been. But when they drowned, I knew it was time for me to grow up and take my daughter to raise."

The engine stopped. "Bailey!" Daniel's voice. "Will? Is she inside?"

"You're not to tell—not him, not Emma, not anybody. I'll not have Anne shamed now. Am I making myself clear, girl?"

"Yes." She nodded. "I won't tell. But . . ." The implications of what he'd just said sank in. "If . . . you weren't Beth's uncle, then . . ."

"Then I'm your grandfather," he finished.

She stared at him, suddenly unable to find the right words.

Daniel banged at the door. "Bailey!"

She glanced at the door and then back at her grandfather. "What do I call you now?"

"Will's fine. Just Will."

CHAPTER FIFTEEN

"Why the hell are you knocking, boy? You walk in any other time you damn well please." Will winked at Bailey as he went to the door. "What'd you think? That I'd shot her and nailed her hide over my fireplace?"

Daniel came in, followed by all three dogs, one of which made a dive for the toy duck and carried it under the table. "I thought I smelled coffee." Daniel picked up the teakettle and filled it with water from the sink faucet. "I don't suppose you have any of that Gyokuro left?"

"Look in the back, behind the Russian Caravan blend. In that black tin." Will glanced at Bailey. "Man can't drink Ceylon or Earl Grey, like normal folks. No, he wants fancy foreign tea."

Daniel grinned. "It's all foreign tea, Will. And you like a cup as well as I do."

"Tea's for drinking alone. Coffee is for sharing."

"I hear you." Daniel put the water on to boil, got down a brick red teapot, and measured out the tea leaves.

Bailey glanced down at the large animal near her feet and edged her chair back a few inches.

"Stop fidgeting," Will said. "She's not going to take your leg off. Not unless you attack me with that fork, anyway." He crouched and whistled softly. The dog went to him, duck clamped in its mouth. "You think I want this old toy? Why would I want that mangy thing?" He patted the animal's head and it wagged its tail. "Why you scared of dogs, girl?"

"One attacked me when I was a child," Bailey said. "I had eight stitches in my left arm and two on my chin." She turned her hand so that he could see the scar near her elbow. "He bit my leg and my right hand too."

"I'm sorry for that, but you needn't worry about these three. They guard the place for me, but none of them has ever bitten anybody, so far as I know." He patted the shaggy tricolored dog again. "This one's Blue, and she's a mongrel and the smartest of the bunch. The male over there, the big Chesapeake, is Raven, and the bitch is Honey. She's the sweetest, and the hardest to keep out of my bed on a winter's night."

Daniel brought the teapot and his blue pottery mug to the table. As he sat down, he glanced around the room. "Where's your shotgun, Will? That old Fox double-barrel that belonged to your daddy? This is the first time I haven't seen it hanging over the kitchen door."

Will scowled. "Lost it hunting last winter."

"Lost it? How did you do that?"

"Fool dog. Raven was having some trouble climbing back into the boat, out on the far side of Freeman's Marsh. I laid the gun down to heave him in, and it slipped over the side before I could catch it."

"You couldn't retrieve it?"

"Water's twenty feet deep there, maybe more. Muck bottom."

"Bad luck. I know how much that shotgun meant to you." The two exchanged looks. "Funny, you never mentioned it before."

Will shook his head. "I put some store by that gun. It cost Daddy a whole winter's muskrat skins."

"I'm surprised that you hunt, being such an animal lover," Bailey said.

"Deer, waterfowl, an occasional squirrel or rabbit. More for meat than sport these days." He glanced at Daniel. "He don't, though. Used to when he was a young buck, was a pretty damn good shot."

"I ought to be," Daniel said. "You taught me to use a gun."

"Somebody had to." Will chuckled. "His granddaddy gave him a twenty-two rifle when he was ten, but none of them took the trouble to show him how to keep from killing himself or wiping out Nathan Love's milk cows."

"Pay no attention to him," Daniel said. "I only shot one cow."

Will folded his arms over his chest. "Took half its left horn off. Nathan was some put out, I can tell you."

"He chased me for the better part of a mile."

"Would have caught you too, if the snow hadn't been so deep." Will laughed. "Daniel didn't weigh as much as that dog over there. He could run on top of the snow crust like a fox, and Nathan kept sinking in with every step. But if he'd caught him, he'd had taken the hide off the boy's rear end, preacher's son or not."

"But you don't hunt anymore?" Bailey said. "Why?"

A shadow passed behind Daniel's eyes. "I suppose I saw enough bloodshed in Afghanistan."

"Pay no attention to him," Will teased. "If they ever

have an Angus hunting season, he'll be out before dawn. He likes his steaks rare, and he won't say no to venison stew either."

Daniel drank his tea, and Bailey listened as the two men made idle talk about fishing and the best place to dip for soft-shell crabs in the summer. "I should get back to work," Daniel said, glancing at her as he carried his cup to the sink. "I wouldn't want my employer to think I was slacking on the job."

"No need to hurry off." Will gestured at the chair Daniel had just left. "Work's not going anywhere. The two of you are more than welcome to stay to supper."

"Thanks," Daniel said, "but Emma's making crab cakes tonight."

"How about you?" Will looked at her.

"Perhaps another day, but I don't have to hurry off." Bailey didn't want to leave—not yet. She was still in shock from what Will had told her about actually being Beth's father, rather than her uncle. She didn't want to wear out her welcome, but she had so many more questions that she didn't know where to start.

"Suit yourself." Will stood. "I was planning on putting together a fish chowder and some corn bread. Nothing fancy."

"I'd like to get that back step fixed before one of us breaks his neck on it." Daniel opened the back door. "A shame about your daddy's gun."

"Yeah, it is. Not many of those Damascus-steel barrels left."

Will walked out on the back stoop. "Stop back tomorrow if you want some of that fish soup," he offered. "Either that, or I'll have to feed it to the dogs."

When Will came back inside, Bailey looked up at him expectantly. "Is it true? Are you really my grandfather?"

Will's mouth tightened into a thin line. "I don't lie. Ask anybody. No matter what they think of me, there's none who can say I ever have."

She sat there, numb, unable to think of what to say.

His expression softened. "Maybe you'd like to take a look at your mother's room."

Bailey felt a rush of excitement. "Could I?"

"Nothing left of hers up there, course. Elizabeth cleaned it all out while I was in prison."

"I see." She glanced toward the front entrance and the staircase. "I guess it's silly, but I'd still like . . ."

"Come on, then. We'll take the grand tour."

"I've always loved sketching and watercolors," she offered, as she followed him up the steps. "I wanted to study art in college, but—"

"But you went into teaching instead," Will finished.

"It was what my parents . . . what my father and mother thought was best for me. I probably didn't have enough talent—"

"Art is a gift you're born with, an eye for what's right. When I carve a snow goose or a chipmunk, I start with a piece of wood and start whittling. I just carve away what doesn't belong there."

He looked back over his shoulder, and she saw a flash of mischief in his eyes. "No magic to it. You can do the same thing with a brush or charcoal, if you have the patience and a mind to it. Important thing is, have a clear picture in your head of what you want to end with before you make the first mark. Start with a blank sheet and just work in reverse."

At the top landing, Will led the way past a bathroom, stopped in front of a closed door, and cleared his throat. "Look all you want," he said huskily. "I haven't set foot in there since I came home."

"Thirty-five years?"

"Yep. Nothing left for me in there."

He turned and went back downstairs, leaving her to turn the knob and gaze into the empty room. Faded pale yellow wallpaper with pink roses curled and peeled on three walls. On the fourth, two big windows, curtainless, opened onto the outside world from a fairy-tale forest mural complete with rainbows, waterfalls, unicorns, and dancing otters. The painted walls showed the decay of time, the braided rug was thick with dust, the ceiling laced with cobwebs, but amid the stark silence and the sorrow lingered a hint of laughter.

Bailey's throat constricted with emotion. She pulled the door shut with too much force and hurried back to the main floor. Will Tawes—her grandfather—stood in the adjoining room gazing at the charcoal of Elizabeth on horseback.

"I'm sorry I . . ." She took a deep breath and wiped her eyes. "I'm . . . I wish I'd known her. Aunt Elizabeth."

"She would have liked you. You two would have got on like peas in a pod. She was a teacher too, you know. Acorn doesn't fall far from the tree."

"I was so wrong about her," Bailey said. "I'd conjured this image in my head of a sick old woman."

"Elizabeth?" Will snorted in amusement. "Strong as an ox. Never needed a doctor in her life, except one time she fell out of the barn loft and broke her arm. She rode those horses of hers every day, rain, snow, or sleet. Never could figure how she fell down those steps."

"Is that how she died? An accident?"

He nodded. "She'd gone up and down that staircase every day of her life."

"It must have been a shock to you."

Grief etched his features. "It was. So long as Elizabeth drew breath, I thought there might come a time when we could mend fences between us. But then she was dead. And where I'm going, I don't expect to see her again."

"Where you're going?" she asked. "Are you planning on—"

"Going to hell, if there is one. I don't suppose I'll be too welcome anywhere else in the hereafter."

"Why would you say a thing like that?"

He scoffed. "I've done a lot to be ashamed of in my life, girl, but what I've done is between me and my Maker. If you're not staying to supper, you'd best get on back to Emma's."

"Can I come here again? Another day?"

He shrugged. "I don't suppose there's any way to keep you away, short of digging a moat and filling it with alligators."

"Thank you." She clasped his hand. For an instant he gripped her fingers.

"Mind you, keep a sharp eye on Daniel. He's a good man, but he's not for you. Daniel's carrying his own demons. There's things in his past that eat at him. You just remember, he's a Catlin and you're a Tawes. The two don't mix any better than matches and black powder."

Later that evening, Daniel borrowed Emma's boat on the pretense of doing some night fishing, took rods and bait, and crossed to Kent Island. Mooring the skiff at a dock, he went to the Jetty, ordered two beers and a half pound of steamed shrimp, and took a corner table under a burned-out Coors sign. At precisely ten o'clock Lucas, in faded jeans, a torn tee that read IN-

TERNATIONAL BROTHERHOOD OF ELECTRICAL WORKERS—LOCAL 18, and a dirty ball cap, walked into the bar with a tall, lanky ponytailed man whom Daniel had never seen before.

The two stopped and looked around, letting their eyes adjust to the dim lighting; then Lucas spied him and waved. "Hey, Bubba," he called. Anything bitin' but the black flies?" Lucas asked in a passable rendition of a Baltimore blue-collar accent as he and his companion joined Daniel at the table.

Lucas hadn't changed a bit. He was a man whom few people would notice in a crowd, and even fewer remember. His dark hair, regular features, and swarthy complexion were common enough that he could pass for a native anywhere but Scandinavia. It wasn't until you gazed into Lucas's small, dark eyes that you saw something exceptional, a cool intelligence and the ruthless expression of a feeding barracuda.

"A rock, but I had to throw the damned thing back," Daniel replied. He waved to a passing waitress. "Couple more Buds here."

Lucas slid into a chair next to Daniel. Ponytail sat directly across, his back to the bar. "You're on time, I see," Lucas said, and then, louder, "You know my old lady's brother, Al."

"Yeah. How's it hanging?" Daniel said.

Don't overdo it, Lucas, he thought. A little more local color, and he was apt to puke on Lucas's worn work boots. "Blend in" had been the cardinal rule for field agents. "Do nothing that would attract attention." He casually took Al's measure. Young, maybe thirty at most, and a little edgy for the role he was playing. The straggly ponytail was a good touch, but the jeans were new, and instead of Levi's, Daniel suspected they might be Polos. He wondered if Lucas was breaking in a new kid or if he'd brought Al here as a reinforcement.

The waitress returned with the beer. Lucas took a sip of his and grimaced. Al merely played with his glass.

"Thought all you good ol' boys drank Bud," Daniel remarked.

"Questions," Lucas said, once the waitress had moved on to other customers.

Daniel glanced at Al and then back to Lucas. "I agreed to talk to you. Alone." He stood and tossed a twenty-dollar bill on the table.

"No need to get testy." Lucas nodded to the younger man. "Wait in the truck."

Al glared at Daniel. "Are you going to be intimidated by this—"

"Make up your mind," Daniel said. "He goes or I do."

Lucas nodded. "Have it your way." He motioned toward the door. "Outside."

His partner pushed the beer back, rose, and walked out.

Daniel went the men's room, returned in two minutes, and sat down in the same seat again. "Are we recording?"

"No. Care to frisk me?"

"I'll pass," Daniel said. "What can I do for you?"

The waitress showed a couple to the table next to theirs, and Lucas lowered his voice. "Someone on Tawes had been blackmailing the senator for the past fifteen years."

Daniel tried not to show surprise. If what Lucas said was true, someone else might know about Marshall's connection to the drug trade. He almost laughed at his own stupidity. Of course the agency would know. And Marshall's associates in Washington, the ones who were equally guilty of betraying the American public and using their own power to line their pockets. But on the island? Lucas must be lying. Who on Tawes could possibly have that information? "You have proof?" he asked.

"We've learned that funds had been deposited regularly to a bank in the Caymans. We haven't been able to track down who the blackmailer is, but we will."

"What makes you think it wasn't another of Marshall's retirement nest eggs?"

"He did his private banking in Zurich. That's keeping the grieving widow in Prada."

"So what's this got to do with me?" The hair prickled on his arms as he took another drink of Bud. It was warm, but it gave him something to do. Did they think he'd killed Marshall? Did the agency care? Or was this meeting a trap? He wondered what his chances were of seeing Tawes again.

Lucas leaned forward. He smelled of breath mints. "Marshall was an important man. The opposition party had his name on the short list of possible vice presidential candidates in the coming election."

"Really? It was my impression that it was a done deal."

"You know a lot for a carpenter with shit on his shoes."

"A pity the senator didn't live long enough to run."

A man and a blond woman at the bar exchanged angry words. She snatched up her purse and walked toward the entrance. "Bitch!" he shouted.

She twisted around, smiled, and lifted three fingers. "Read between the lines, you limp dick!" A round of laughter from the crowd followed her out the door as the man called to the bartender for a double.

Lucas turned his attention back to Daniel. "The agency would be pleased if you'd check around, see who on Tawes is living beyond their means."

"Nobody comes to mind." Daniel rubbed his chin thoughtfully. "Money's tight for watermen and farmers."

"Not for you, apparently." Lucas smiled thinly.

"You suspect that the senator's death wasn't accidental."

"The supposition is that old Joe got tired of paying, went to the island to confront his blackmailer, and that unknown party shot him."

"Am I a suspect?"

Lucas shrugged. "You have to admit you had a grudge against him."

I hated his guts, Daniel thought, trying to hold back the sudden tide of mingled grief and rage that threatened to knock him off balance with Lucas.

"And word is, he wouldn't be your first."

"That was different."

"It always is."

The waitress, balancing a full tray, came toward the table. "Need a refill?"

Daniel shook his head. "Later, maybe."

She removed the basket of shrimp shells, the remainder of the cocktail sauce, and the crumpled napkins, and scooped up the twenty. "I'll be back with your change—"

"Keep it."

"We were talking about what happened in Afghanistan," Lucas said when the waitress was out of earshot.

Daniel stiffened. "No, we were talking about old Joe."

"I'm all ears."

"The man was a royal bastard. Whoever killed him should get a medal. What's your point?"

"Odd how you up and quit last fall." Lucas sipped at his beer and made a face. "How can you drink this stuff?"

"I don't, usually. I ordered it special for you."

"One of these days I'll return the favor."

"It wasn't me."

"I never said it was."

"Cut the bullshit," Daniel said. "I'm out of all this." But even as he said it, he didn't believe it. He might not know as many names as the agency suspected he did, but enough to get him killed—or to send a lot of rats scurrying for their holes when the dominoes started falling.

"Not unless we're satisfied that we have a clear picture of what happened and why." Lucas tapped two fingers on the tabletop impatiently.

"Joe wouldn't be the first hunter to be mistaken for a duck."

"No? Funny how bad luck settles over a place. You had another accident there a few days back, didn't you? A fire? Or was that a murder-suicide?" Lucas smiled. "And I understand you had the misfortune to discover those bodies as well."

"Creed Somers was a drunk who lived in a firetrap. It was bound to happen."

"Someone got axed. Not too common an occurrence, even for a backwater like Tawes."

"What reason would I have for killing Somers and his girlfriend?"

Lucas toyed with his napkin. "No need to jump to conclusions, buddy. Did I say you were a suspect?"

"Take this message back to the agency: I don't work for them anymore. I didn't have anything to do with Marshall's death or Somers's. And if they expect me to dig up evidence on the senator's shooting, they can wait until hell freezes over."

CHAPTER SIXTEEN

In the week that followed, Bailey fell into a routine of teaching in the morning, and spending afternoons with Will and evenings with Emma and Daniel. The work at the school was challenging, something she looked forward to. One by one she got to know her students, learning about their strengths and weaknesses, their siblings, and their extended families. And every day the friendship she and Cathy shared strengthened.

Twice Forest contacted her, once by phone and again by note from his Annapolis office to let her know that he'd made progress on securing the deed to Elizabeth's farm. Settling the estate would mean a lot for Bailey's future, but it was no longer the most important reason for her remaining on Tawes. Two men had somehow taken center stage in her life—Will Tawes and Daniel Catlin.

The time spent with her grandfather seemed a gift beyond anything an inheritance could buy. Neither of them wanted to risk opening completely to the other, but hour by hour she found the walls between them crumbling. Often she sat without speaking a word for an hour or more in his studio, watching him carve a fox from a section of seasoned cherry or paint the feathers of an osprey, one by one.

Once Will took her with him deep into the woods, where they lay motionless on a carpet of moss and watched as a mother fox and her kits came to a stream to drink. The vixen curled up in a patch of sunlight and dozed while the four little ones chased each other, tumbled, and played like puppies.

Will had brought a camera to take pictures of the wildlife, but he didn't snap a single shot, fearing that the sound would frighten them away. She sensed that here was a man who had shut himself off from the human world for decades and had turned all his attention to his art. With Bailey, Will was terse of speech but never distant. At his side she found a quiet sense of acceptance and belonging that had always been absent from her life.

As for Daniel, she found him both intriguing and perplexing. He acted as though he was as attracted to her as she was to him, but he'd made no step toward taking things further than friendship between them. Often, despite Will's warning to be wary of Daniel, Bailey would stop at the farm to see the progress he was making on the repairs. They'd talk and laugh together, but despite the look in his eye, he hadn't even tried to kiss her.

On her second visit to Elizabeth's after she'd made the breakthrough with Will, she'd summoned strength enough to return to the attic to search the trunk again. She was rewarded by the discovery of several more loose photos inside the pages of the storybooks. Two pictures were of Beth, but one was of a young man.

The picture had been taken in poor light, and the boy's face was in shadow. She'd taken the photo to her grandfather's the following day, but he hadn't been able to identify the boy.

Later that night, at Emma's, Bailey had shown the picture to the older woman, but she'd been as much at a loss as Will to name the youth. "It could be anyone," Emma said. "Maybe one of her classmates from school."

"This might be Beth's boyfriend," Bailey suggested. "Are you certain you don't recognize him?"

"Nope. Wish I could help." Emma handed the snapshot to Daniel. "Anyone you know?"

He shook his head. "I'm afraid not. Look at the date on the back. I was barely out of diapers when this was taken."

Emma removed a pork roast from the oven and set it on the stove to cool a little before slicing. "I hope you two are hungry. I think I got carried away and made enough for an army." She wiped her hands on her apron. "Have you decided what you're going to do about the horses?"

"Horses? What horses?" Bailey asked.

Daniel rolled his eyes. "I guess Will didn't tell you yet."

"Didn't tell me what?"

"Elizabeth's riding horses," Emma said as she carried a blue pottery bowl of coleslaw to the table. "Jim Tilghman's older brother is interested in one of them for his girl. I don't suppose it will be too hard to find a buyer for the other one, not if you don't ask too much for them."

"Forest didn't say anything about the horses," Bailey exclaimed. "Will either. I saw two horses in the pasture, but—"

"They come with the house," Daniel said with a shrug. "Will's been taking care of them since Elizabeth died. They were her pride and joy. She loved them like children. I guess Will wanted to take your measure before he told you that you'd inherited those as well."

I've let this go too far. Bailey is as stubborn as Beth, and as troublesome. She had her chance to leave the island, but instead she remained to pry into things that should have been left buried. I can't wait any longer. Tawes is already crawling with police and medical investigators. Sooner or later people will begin to pry into Elizabeth's death, as well.

She should have known better. I warned her not to leave her farm to Beth's brat, to let her live out her little life on the mainland, but Elizabeth was always obstinate. The house and land should have been mine. It all should have been mine.

I went to Elizabeth that night to reason with her, to make her see that what was she was about to do was wrong, that it would only cause more heartache. I never intended that she should die, but she brought it on herself when she slapped me and ordered me to get of the house. What did she expect? That I would allow her to abuse me without striking back?

I punched her with my fist, harder than I should have. She fell back, hitting her head against the corner of the kitchen table. The blow must have fractured her skull, but she tried to get up. I had to use the pewter candlestick on her. By then, I realized that I couldn't let her live to tell anyone what I'd done.

Dragging Elizabeth's unconscious body to the top of the staircase and throwing her down the steps was genius on my part. She tumbled all the way to the bottom, but she always was too stubborn. She didn't have sense enough to die. She moaned and thrashed until I finished her off with several whacks from an old flatiron.

The bitch. How was I to know that she'd already made her bequest to Beth's bastard? And now it's up to me to finish what I started a long time ago, to carve away every trace of Beth's shame and make it all right, once and for all.

Midmorning Friday, Bailey was going over a math concept on negative numbers that several of her students had difficulty understanding when Cathy opened the classroom door and called to her. "Excuse me, but there's someone here to see you. He says it's important."

"Who is it?" Bailey asked.

Cathy nodded. "Your Mr. Elliott. I asked him if it could wait until school was dismissed, but he insisted."

"All right." Bailey turned back to her kids. "We'll finish this Monday. In the meantime, please take out your library books and read quietly in your seats. Ashley, would you take charge for me? I'll just be a few minutes."

"He's waiting for you in the office." Cathy rolled her eyes. "Cute, but bossy. He said he was your husband. Didn't you tell me that you were divorced?"

"We have been. For years. I wonder what he wants." Bailey had given her stepmother Forest McCready's number for use in an emergency. Surely if Dad was ill, someone would have called the attorney's office. Tracking down Elliott's unlisted cell number would have been difficult at best.

She was halfway down the hall when Elliott saw her and came out of the office. "Is something wrong?" she called to him. "Is Dad—"

"Nothing like that, but we need to talk." He shoved a copy of a newspaper article at her. The headline read, "Jury Finds Tawes Island Man Guilty." "This is from the trial thirty-five years ago," Elliott said. "The great-uncle you're so anxious to talk to . . . At best he's an abuser, and at worst . . ."

Bailey felt her throat and cheeks flush. "This isn't the time or the place," she said, fast losing patience with him. "I have class for another forty-five minutes. Go back to Emma's and wait for me there." She tried to give him back the paper.

"Read it," he insisted.

"Later. I have fourteen children waiting for me."

"Do you have any idea what you've gotten yourself into?" Elliott demanded as he took hold of her shoulders. "This man was convicted of beating his pregnant niece to death."

Bailey stepped back away from him. "Will didn't do it," she said sharply. "He's innocent."

"And who told you that? Uncle Will?"

Cathy opened her classroom door. "Is everything all right?"

"Fine," Bailey said. "Go to Emma's, Elliott. I'll see you there in an hour."

"Be there, Bails, or I'll come looking for you."

The time between Elliott's abrupt arrival at the school and Bailey's return home did nothing for either's mood. He met her at Emma's gate. "I hope you told them that you're not coming back," he said. "I have a boat waiting for us at the dock. I'm taking you with me."

She stared at him as though he'd taken leave of his senses. "You can't come here and give me orders. You didn't have the right to do it when we were married, and you certainly don't now."

She walked past him into the house and stopped just inside the doorway. Her suitcase stood at the bottom of the steps. "Elliott, have you lost your mind? What would make you think that I'd leave Tawes now? I've promised to help out at the school until the end of summer session and—"

Elliott grabbed her arm. "I don't know what spell these people have put on you, but—"

"Let go of me!" She tried to pull free, but he held her fast. "Elliott!"

"The lady asked you to take your hands off her." Daniel appeared in the doorway, his tone low and deadly serious.

"Get lost. This is none of your business," Elliott said. "And for your information, this lady is my wife."

"His ex-wife." Bailey attempted to pry his hand off her arm. "And I don't need your help, Daniel. I can deal with this jerk on my own."

"I'm serious," Elliott insisted. "You're coming home with me."

"What you want doesn't matter," she said. "You gave up that right a long time ago."

Daniel advanced on them, anger contorting his face. "I'm asking you one more time," he said. "Let go of her or—"

"So that's the way it is?" Elliott shouted. "Fine, if you love these yokels so much, maybe this is where you belong!" He spun around, stalked out of the house, and slammed the door behind him.

She followed him out onto the porch. "You're wrong about Will," she called after him.

Elliott stopped and glanced back over his shoulder. "Am I? Read that newspaper article and call me if you get your senses back."

"Pleasant man," Daniel said, coming through the door to stand beside her.

"He's not usually like that," Bailey said. She rubbed the spot on her arm where Elliott's fingers had left a red mark. "He's never been like that. I think he's really afraid that I'm in danger here."

"Is that what your marriage was like?"

"No." She shook her head. "He never . . ." She hesitated. "Well, almost never. Once . . ." She shrugged. "We married young, and . . ." She looked up into his eyes. "Can we not talk about Elliott now? I appreciate your help, but . . . I think I'd like to be alone for a while."

"If that's what you want. I hoped you . . ." He took a breath and started again. "Friends of mine, Paul and Janice, are getting married tonight. Over on Smith Island. I thought you might like to go with me."

"Tonight?"

He nodded. "It's informal. On the beach. I think you'd have fun."

"You mean . . . like a date?"

"I think that's what they call it. It's an old island custom."

She couldn't keep from smiling. "Isn't this a little sudden?" He met her gaze, and she felt a flush run over her throat and up her cheeks.

"Sudden?"

She put her hand on the door. "What time?"

"I thought we'd leave here at four. We'll take Emma's boat."

"All right. I've never been to a wedding on a beach. It does sound like fun."

"I know you haven't been to a wedding like this one. Janice is due to deliver any day. They've been living together for four years."

"Obviously a man who takes his time popping the question," she said as she reentered the house and reached for the overnight bag that Elliott had brought downstairs.

"No, it was Janice who put the brakes on. She said she wanted to be certain this was the real thing." Daniel's hand covered hers. "I'll carry this back up for you." He grinned. "Wait until you taste the Deal Island Cake."

"Deal Island Cake? What makes it special?"

"You'll see. Another old island custom. Janice's mother is baking this one."

"I see." She stood there as the warmth of his strong fingers seeped into hers and her insides did a shivery dance. "Thanks. For before . . . with Elliott. I don't know what got into him."

"It's wrong, a man laying his hands on a woman in anger. You don't have to take that, Bailey, not from anyone."

"No, I know that. I mean . . ." She pulled away, breaking the spell. "It just surprised me. He's not the type."

"Any man can be the type under the right circumstances."

"I hope not."

"You still have feelings for him?"

Daniel was standing so close it made her giddy. She didn't know how to react. First she'd tried to defend Will to Elliott, and now her ex to Daniel. And no matter what she said, it sounded foolish. "Not in the way you think," she managed. "That was over between us a long time ago."

"He bullied you then?"

She uttered a small sound of amusement. "Elliott? Not really. I smacked his face once. I shouldn't have, but I was so angry. He ruined my credit rating. He was . . . is a gambler, and he ran up so many debts that it's taken me years to work my way free of them." She shook her head again. "Elliott and I are friends who used to be husband and wife. But the marriage was a mistake from the beginning, and I know it." She looked up at him through her lashes. "There's no chance in hell that it could ever be more than friendship again."

"Good." Daniel brushed her chin with the pad of his thumb. "Because you don't need friends like that."

"Is that all?"

"No, it isn't. . . ."

The moment stretched out between them, and then, slowly, he lowered his head, and his lips brushed hers in a tender kiss so quick that it was over almost before she realized what was happening. "Oh," she murmured.

"Four," he reminded her as he started up the steps. "Casual. Remember, it's on a beach."

"All right," she murmured. "Casual."

The wedding was fun. The bride and groom exchanged vows standing in the damp sand with a tight circle of friends and family around them. There was no minister or clerk. "They took care of the formalities in Elkton Wednesday night," Daniel whispered.

Janice wore pink shorts, a pink-and-white maternity top that barely stretched to cover her belly, and a wreath of honeysuckle. The groom came garbed in blue swim trunks and a flowered Hawaiian shirt. The bride's sister played the guitar, and the groom's nine-year-old son produced two shiny gold rings.

"Paul's divorced," Daniel explained. "He's a single dad."

The bride's face glowed as Paul slipped the ring on her finger. "Thank you," he said, "for giving me a happiness I never knew before."

Tears gathered in Bailey's eyes. Daniel caught her hand and squeezed it tightly. A feeling of warm giddiness filled her as they watched Janice pledge her love to Paul and promise to be a good mother to both their children.

When the ceremony was over, guests and the bridal party shared a picnic supper on blankets spread out under the trees. There was fried chicken, potato salad, crab cakes, and coleslaw, iced tea and beer. Later, the bride threw her wreath instead of a garter, and when the Deal Island Cake was brought out, Bailey discovered that it was a huge, multilayered dessert that was more fruitcake than iced confection.

"Bananas," Daniel whispered as he'd pulled her into the trees for a quick kiss. "Can't stand them, but you've got to eat a piece of the cake for luck."

His lips were warm and sweet, and Bailey caught her breath before murmuring, "Are you certain I should?"

"You have to," he teased. "If you don't eat the cake, the wedding guests will probably burn us both at the stake."

She giggled. "Heaven forbid."

They stayed, danced barefoot together on the beach, laughed and talked, and mingled with the wedding party. They didn't return to Emma's skiff for the return journey to Tawes until the sun began to go down.

It had been a magical evening for Bailey. She couldn't forget the feel of Daniel's mouth on hers or the way he hadn't taken his eyes off her. She didn't doubt for a moment that they would finally end up making love.

"Where do you want me to take you?" Daniel asked as the stars glowed around the boat when they were more than halfway home to the island. "Emma's or my cabin?"

"Your place." She couldn't imagine having to explain things to Emma in the morning. Right now, at this moment, she didn't want to think; she only wanted the evening to go on and on.

"You're certain?" he teased. "I don't want you to think I'm too easy."

She laughed. "I think that line's been used."

"But it still works?"

"It works with me." She smiled at him. "Your place."

A few more minutes and Daniel nudged the skiff against his dock in the darkness. "I can't see a thing," Bailey said. "How can you?"

He laughed. "I can't. I just know the way home." He caught her around the waist and swung her up onto a walkway of planks. "Trust me."

"Should I?"

He kissed her again, and this time tenderness flared to passion. He pulled her hard against him, molding her body to his. She reveled in his taste, his touch, as she ran her fingers through his soft hair and uttered soft moans of delight deep in her throat.

Daniel's clean scent filled her head as he kissed her again and again. When he slipped a hand under her blouse to cup her breast, urgent need surged through her.

"Are you absolutely, positively sure?" he asked her.

"Yes." She fumbled with the buttons of his shirt, wanting to feel his bare skin against hers.

"Positive?"

"Shut up and kiss me again."

Their lips met, and their tongues touched, deepening the kiss, fueling the fire that leaped between them.

"Yes. Yes. Yes."

He laughed as he gathered her up in his arms and carried her to the house. They made it just inside the front door, where they sank to the floor in a tangle of limbs and exploring hands. Bailey slid her jeans down over her hips and opened for him.

Neither spoke, but each seemed to know instinctively what would give the other pleasure. Their lovemaking was hot and fierce, and Daniel barely had time to get a condom on before they passed the point of no return. Her climax, when it came, was shattering, and when she felt him drive deep inside her one last time and give a shudder of release, her joy exploded into a rainbow of colors and sweet, sweet ecstasy. Exhausted, breathless, laughing, they stripped off the remainder of their clothing, ran back to the beach, and dove into the warm waters of the bay.

He held her and she lay back in his arms, floating between earth and sky, enchanted by this man and this night. Later, when they had dried off and retreated to a comfortable air mattress in the cabin, they made love a second time. And while Bailey slept wrapped in his arms, she was free of nightmares or haunting melodies.

She woke slowly to the delicious smell of almond tea.

"Not much to offer you for breakfast," Daniel said, handing her a steaming mug as he approached the mattress. "I could catch you a fish and grill it. Or see if I could knock a squirrel out of a tree with a rock and—"

"I'll pass." She laughed sleepily. "Do you think Emma will notice that we didn't come home last night?"

"Have you ever known Emma to miss anything?"

She sat up and pulled the sheet around her. "Mmm, good," she said as she took a sip of the tea. "Honey?"

He kissed her playfully on the mouth. "Sweets for the sweet."

She groaned. "That's awful."

"You're something, Bailey Tawes. Do you know just how *something* you are?"

He was barefooted, wearing nothing but his jeans. His hair was damp, as though he'd just come out of the water. And he looked good enough to eat. She averted her eyes, not wanting him to read her thoughts.

"Too bad you didn't get the coin last night," he said, sitting cross-legged on the rug beside the mattress.

"What coin?"

"The wedding cake," he explained. "It's a tradition that goes back centuries, some say to Cornwall. Only a few families still hold to it. A silver coin is baked into the cake, and whoever finds it is supposed to be the next one married."

"I'm glad I didn't get a slice with money in it. I probably would have choked to death."

"Three hundred years, and I don't think they've ever lost a guest yet. I suppose there could be a first time." His gaze lingered on her face. "Do you ever want to get married again?"

"I don't know," she answered. "I suppose it would depend on the man. I've always wanted to be a mother, but I'm not certain I want to actually carry a child and give birth to it."

"Cathy says you're wonderful with the kids. I think you'd make a good mother."

"Really?" She smiled at him. "It's sweet of you to say so."

"I mean it," he said. He reached out and cupped her cheek in his hand. "Stay on awhile, Bailey. Not just for the school, but for me."

She looked away. "Do you say that to all your girls?"

"No, I don't. And there's only been one other serious relationship."

"And?"

"It's over."

"Really over?"

"She's dead. Been dead for a long time."

"I'm sorry."

He exhaled softly between his teeth. "I think you're the one, Bailey, but I have a few things I need to iron out. I can't promise you anything solid yet . . . but . . . it was good between us last night, wasn't it?"

She nodded shyly. "Yes, it was. More . . . more than good." She suddenly realized that although she'd told things to Daniel that she rarely spoke to anyone about, she still didn't know very much about him. Had he ever been married? She didn't think so. She was certain he would have told her if he had—someone on Tawes would have told her. And she didn't think he had ever had children. But she wanted to know exactly what he'd done for the government.

"There's one thing I wanted to ask you." Curiosity tugged at her. "What did you do at the CIA?"

He grinned. "I could tell you, but—"

"I know," she said. "Then you'd have to . . ."

He chuckled. "Afraid so."

"One more question?"

"Not about the agency."

"Cross my heart and hope to die." She drew a ragged cross in the air over her breasts. "Those beautiful horses—are they really mine?"

He laughed. "Yes, or they will be, once all the legal stuff is cleared up."

"So I could . . . we could . . . Could we go riding sometime? That is, if you ride. Horses." She felt herself flush, and they laughed together.

"I do, and we can. I had a horse when I was a kid. Will kept it for me. He bought it from a farmer who was about to shoot it because of a leg injury. An infected hoof. Will nursed that animal for months until it was sound, and he gave it to me as a birthday present."

"Wow, some gift."

"I told you he was a special man. My father didn't want me to have it, said it cost too much to feed a horse, but Will always found a way to let me work off the cost of the grain. We cut the hay ourselves, by hand, and stacked it in the barn. Duke was twenty years old, had a big head and a rough gait, but he meant a lot to me."

"What color was he?"

"Piebald, with one white eye. Ugliest horse on the island." Daniel laughed. "I rode him bareback for years until I saved up enough to buy a saddle by trapping muskrats one winter. But in answer to your question, I'd like to go riding with you. And I can show you places you'd never get to on foot."

"It's a deal," she said. "And I'll hold you to it."

"Absolutely," he said, kissing her on the tip of her nose. "I'm a man who always keeps his word."

Small talk and laughter eased the awkwardness as they dressed and boarded the boat for the trip back to

Emma's. By daylight, Bailey could see the beauty of the cabin nestled against a grove of old hardwoods. "It's lovely," she said, as he started the motor and slowly backed out of the slip.

Daniel smiled. "I like it. It's quiet out here on the point. Gives me a chance to think."

The morning air was brisk with the promise of a clear, bright day, and the incoming tide was rushing in fast so that foamy whitecaps formed on the waves. They passed a crabbing boat and two fishing skiffs before they rounded the island and followed a natural channel close to a high, wooded rise. A great blue heron rose out of the trees to soar over the boat.

"Oh, isn't he beautiful!" Bailey cried. "Look at how he stretches his legs out behind—"

A crack sounded from the shore, and Bailey let out a cry of pain as a splinter of wood suddenly tore a furrow across the top of her arm.

"Get down!" Daniel shouted, shoving her facedown onto the deck.

"What happened?" She clutched her bleeding arm and looked at the ragged hole in the side of the boat.

Daniel crouched beside her, staring at the wooded bank. "Are you all right?"

"Yes, I think so." Her heart was pounding so hard that it was difficult to think. "It's not deep, just a scratch, but what—"

Daniel fingered the hole in the skiff. "A bullet," he said. "I think someone just took a shot at us."

CHAPTER SEVENTEEN

"Shot at us?" Bailey attempted to push herself up from the bottom of the boat.

"Stay down!" Fear made Daniel's grip hard enough to bruise her arm—fear that the nightmare he'd left behind in Afghanistan had followed him to the one place in the world where he'd felt safe, fear that this woman who'd given him a reason to embrace life again could have been cut down by a careless assassin's bullet.

Leaning low, Daniel let go of Bailey long enough to shove the throttle forward, pushing the engine to top speed. He held his breath and cut the wheel hard. The boat tipped dangerously to starboard, but Daniel knew he had to get them around the wooded point before the shooter got off a second round, and he had to do it without running the skiff aground on Tilghman's Sandbar. Spray splashed over the side, drenching them, but the engine purred without a sputter and they cut through the water at a good forty knots.

"All right," Daniel said, once a solid stand of oak and cedar stood between them and whoever had fired at him. Cold sweat trickled down the back of his neck. "I think it's safe for you to sit up now."

Shaken, eyes wide, Bailey unfolded herself from the deck and stared at him. "Why would anybody—"

"Probably some fool kid shooting squirrels," he said, cutting her off. Anger made it hard for him to keep his tone normal so that Bailey wouldn't know he was lying. There was no way in hell the bullet that had ripped a hole through the hull was an accident. He'd given up believing in fairy tales a long time ago. Someone wanted to kill him. Whether it was for what they suspected he'd done—killing Marshall—or for what they thought he was possible of telling about people still very much alive, he wasn't certain.

"A child with a gun?" Bailey said. "It's not even hunting season, is it?"

All the color had drained from her face, stripping away the veneer of resilience, exposing a naked vulnerability, filling Daniel with the overwhelming need to protect her.

"No, it's not," he answered, "but hungry people hunt year-round on Tawes." Lucas or another professional shooter should have been too good to have missed. Or . . .

Daniel tried to remember. Had he turned the wheel just before the shot in an effort to follow the natural channel? A rocking skiff didn't make the best target. If he had altered course, his action might have saved them. So the bullet could have been an attempt to scare him, or it could have been a genuine attempt to silence him once and for all. The powers that be would never let him live long enough to testify against them. There'd be no trials, no newspaper reporters asking questions that might embarrass the wrong people and

233

cause an international scandal. Homeland security covered a myriad of sins.

But Bailey was an innocent bystander. Whoever had fired that rifle had broken an unwritten rule against harming civilians, and Daniel vowed to extract a price for that transgression. "I'll make inquiries," he said. "See what I can find out. Kids on Tawes should know better."

"Their parents should know better than to let them walk around with guns."

He frowned. "It isn't like the mainland. Suburbia may be opposed to hunting and firearms in general, but it's different here. Our boys and girls grow up respecting—"

"By taking potshots at passing boats?" Bailey had lost her terror and was fast becoming angry. Pink crept back into her cheeks, and her eyes glittered in the sunlight. "One of us could have been killed. If that's teaching your children responsibility, then I'm glad that I grew up in Newark."

He wondered how he ever could have dismissed her as cute. Right now, mad as hell, with her hair in disarray and dirt on her face, she looked like the most beautiful woman on earth. He eased back on the throttle, slowing the skiff to a more reasonable speed. "You know, it might be better if you remained in town for a few days, until I find out who the shooter was. I don't want any more near misses."

"Me either. I guess I'm not cut out for that much excitement."

Images of Bailey ripped apart, of her broken body lying in a puddle of gore, sent a chill through him. "It was a shock. Maybe you should take a long weekend, go home for a few days."

Bailey stiffened. "And leave my class in the middle of

summer school?" Her eyes narrowed in that steely gaze that he'd seen from Will Tawes.

Daniel swallowed the lump in his throat as memories he thought he'd put behind him rose like haunting specters. "It might make a good break."

She arched an eyebrow, and he read the hurt in her eyes. "Is this a polite brushoff?"

"Hell, no, Bailey. Where did you get that idea?"

"We just climbed out from under the same blanket an hour ago, and already you're trying to send me home?"

"I don't want to see you hurt."

"And I don't want to get hurt. I see your point in staying out of the woods for a few days, but . . ." She took a breath. "I don't expect a lifelong commitment after one—"

"Bailey . . . it's not like that."

She folded her arms protectively over her breasts, but the stubborn pose did nothing to hide her trembling. Whether it was anger or fear, he didn't know, but he wanted to cradle her against him, to feel the rise and fall of her chest as she breathed, and the warmth of her skin against his again.

Her bottom lip quivered. "Did last night mean anything to you besides a good lay?"

"More than you could ever know."

"So we're friends?" she asked suspiciously.

"No games between us. You know that we're more than that. A lot more."

She took a deep breath. "If you're my friend, even if you're my boink buddy, then help me. You said that your job in the agency was gathering information. Who better to help me unravel what really happened here with my family?"

He cut the engine and let the boat drift with the tide. "You could be opening a bigger can of worms here than you know. Tawes is a small community. Any man on the island over fifty could be your father. Even Emma or Creed."

"What?" She stared at him as if he'd taken leave of his senses. "Emma?

What are you talking about? Emma or Creed? How could Emma—"

"Yes, Emma. Sweet Lord, Bailey, for a thirty-five-year-old woman, you're such an innocent."

Her eyes widened in confusion. "But how . . ."

"You didn't know? Didn't even guess?"

"Know what?"

"That Emma Parks is biologically a man."

"What?"

Daniel raked a hand through his hair. "Emma Parks was born Emery Parks. A boy. He grew up buddies with Matthew and Creed. Apparently there were always rumors that he was . . . well, sensitive . . . but he didn't start living as a woman until he was twenty or so."

"I don't believe it! Not Emma. She's—"

He shrugged. "You're telling me that you didn't have a clue?"

"I thought she was . . . plain. Homely, even. Until I got to know her, and then . . . But you're saying she's a homosexual?"

"Nope. Just herself. One of a kind. What's the matter? You're not homophobic, are you?"

"No." Bailey shook her head. "You're putting me on. She couldn't be. Especially not on an island like Tawes. How could . . . how could she do such a thing and have people accept her so completely?"

He turned the wheel to port to avoid a floating log.

236

The skiff responded like a dream. "Tawes guards its own," he said. "If the islanders are tough, they have big hearts. And they appreciate individualism. Why would anyone object to how Emma wants to live her life when she's obviously made such a success of it?"

Bailey stared at him for long seconds before scoffing. "This is your idea of a joke, isn't it?"

"Walk in on her in the shower and you'll see for yourself how much of a joke it is. Emma has all the standard male parts, and she's pretty well-endowed."

Color streaked across her cheekbones. "That's more than I needed to know." She thought for a second. "If it's true, why tell me now?"

He shrugged again. "To make a point. Things aren't always as simple as they seem. When you pull a single nail loose, you risk bringing down the wall, maybe even the house."

"I don't care." She brushed a few grains of loose sand off her chin. "I have to find out what everyone seems to be hiding from me, what even Uncle Will's not telling me. I want your help, Daniel, but if you won't help me, at least don't get in my way."

"Suit yourself. But don't say I didn't warn you." He started the engine again. "And, please, no bike rides until I find out what kid got a new rifle for his birthday, and I put a stop to the target shooting."

"Deal."

They rode in silence the rest of the way back to Emma's dock. When the boat was secure, he took her arm to help her out of the skiff. She winced, and he noticed that the marks his fingers had made were plainly visible on her fair skin. "I'm sorry about that," he said.

"Don't be silly. Better that than a bullet through my brain."

Together they walked back toward the house. "Best not to say anything at the school about the gunshot."

"Why not? I'd hate to think that any of my students could be hurt because I didn't warn them."

"Whoever did it will be scared. He'll probably put the rifle back in the house and not touch it for weeks. But if people are talking about the incident, it will make it harder for me to learn the shooter's identity." He pulled her close and hugged her hard.

She looked up into his face, and her mouth quivered. "Will you help me, Daniel? Please. You can't know how much it would mean to me." Her eyes glistened with moisture, and for a second he was afraid she'd burst into tears.

Reluctantly, he nodded. "If you want me to. Just be prepared for anything. Secrets buried that deep may have a lingering stink about them." He took hold of her shoulders and kissed her. "Trust me, Bailey."

"I think I do," she admitted.

"You'd better." He brushed her lips with his again. "I may not be back for the evening meal. There are some things that are best taken care of alone. Ask Emma to look at the cut on your arm."

"I don't know if I can look her . . . him in the face and—"

"Sure, you can. She's your friend. And she's a damn good nurse."

They reached the house, and he held open the back door for her. "Emma?" he called. "Emma, are you here?"

"In the pantry," Emma answered. "How was the wedding? Must have been quite the party if the two of you are just getting in!"

"Bailey will tell you all about it." He pressed a finger

against his closed lips. "Not a word about the damage to the boat," he whispered. "I'll break that to her later."

Leaving the two women in the kitchen, Daniel hurried up the stairs to his room and retrieved a semiautomatic pistol from a safe recessed into the back wall of his closet. Minutes later, after removing the safety lock and loading the handgun, he descended the front steps and left the house without another word to either woman.

Rage clamps a fist around my chest. Disappointment, sharp as honed steel, tears through my vitals. How could I have missed that shot? I'm so mad that I want to bash my rifle against the nearest tree, fall on my knees, and rip up the grass in handfuls.

They say I get my temper from my father, so it may not be my fault. People should know better than to cross me. But I hang on to my gun. I maintain my control and bite down on the inside of my lip until I taste blood. The pain is good. I need it to clear my head.

I suck in jagged gulps of air, allowing myself some measure of release. I missed a shot. So what? It could happen to anyone. It should have ended here, but it didn't, and I just have to make things right. I can't give in to weakness. Every minute longer that I remain here makes me more vulnerable to discovery.

It bothers me that I missed my target. This rifle has never failed me before. True, my vision isn't what it once was, and the water is rough today, but I've never missed a shot that easy.

Since the day I was born I've had streaks of bad luck. I've always been cursed by people who try to rob me of what is my rightful due. Fortunately, I've learned how to take back what's mine, and I've had experience covering my tracks.

Once I cross into the deeper woods, no one will know what direction I take. And in a few days or weeks, once I finish what I started, all this will be forgotten. Life will go on here on Tawes as it always has, exactly as I want it to.

"Had some time for yourselves, I suppose," Emma said, coming from the pantry with both hands full. "I was thinking of making a pineapple upside-down cake." She glanced at Bailey in amusement. "Unless you two didn't come *straight* home from the—" Emma's face fell. "Ohh." She grimaced as she let out a deflating sigh. "Somebody outed me, didn't they?"

"No, it's . . ." Bailey's face took on the hue of ripe plums.

Emma dropped her ingredients on the round kitchen table. "You're a terrible liar. Don't ever take up working for a carnival."

"I . . . I wasn't planning on it."

"I did once." She grimaced and rested her fists on her hips. "Ran away and spent a whole summer traveling from the Eastern Shore to Delaware, New Jersey, New York, and then back south through Ohio and the Appalachians. It wasn't what I expected it would be. When I finally hitched a ride home I didn't have a cent in my pockets, and I'd lost fifteen pounds, my good boots, and a jacket. And I had the worst case of head lice my mother had ever seen."

Bailey looked like a scared child who didn't know whether to cut and run or come clean, Emma thought as she motioned to the table. "Sit down. I won't bite. I promise. At least, not today. What you need is strong coffee and plenty of it." Her insides churned. Why did the girl have to be the spitting image of her dead mother?

Guilt enveloped Emma like cracker crumbs on a crab cake. God, but she'd give both arms to go back and change that one day . . . one cursed hour.

"I'm sorry," Bailey said. "I didn't . . . I mean . . ."

Emma placed a large mug of black coffee on the clean tablecloth in front of the young woman and took the seat opposite. "Nothing for you to be sorry about. I am what I am—whatever that is. I started out one way, but, like a hand-me-down pair of shoes, the Emery part never seemed to fit. I tried. I didn't want to let my mother down, but it got too hard. It's better this way."

Emma took a big sip. The coffee was too hot, but she swallowed anyway. When the hot liquid burned her throat, she didn't feel the gnawing guilt in the pit of her stomach so badly. "Most people around here take me in stride. I figured you guessed that I was one of a kind, and it didn't matter to you."

Bailey nibbled at her bottom lip. Her eyes were huge and sparkled with tears. "Daniel told me. He said that it was possible . . . that you might be my . . . my biological father."

"Sweet Jesus! Is that why you're trembling like a willow in a blow?" She shook her head. "I'm not, hon. I swear to you, there's no chance." *But there could have been*, an accusing voice echoed in her head. *Another beer, a little more nerve* . . . "No, I never was with your mother, not in the biblical sense. I knew her, but not that way."

"Then who is?" Bailey demanded. "You must have some idea."

Emma drew in a ragged breath as a tear ran down

her nose and dropped into her coffee. More tears followed the first one. "If I had to put money on it," she managed, "I'd guess it was either Joe Marshall or Creed. Maybe even Matthew."

"Matthew Catlin?" Bailey swallowed hard. "It could have been Daniel's brother that got my mother pregnant?"

Emma pushed her coffee back so quickly that some sloshed onto the oilcloth. She folded her arms on the table and buried her head in them while she fought to control her emotions. So much hurt after so long. It would never be over. She'd never sleep without waking to find Beth's lipstick-smeared face seared into her mind.

"Tell me," Bailey urged. "What do you know?"

Emma raised her head and dashed away the tears. "I know you need to get off Tawes before something terrible happens."

"Why do you say that? What's going to happen?"

"You'll think me a superstitious fool, but there was an owl hooting in the tree outside the back porch this morning. An owl in broad daylight. They hunt at night, not when the sun's up. It's an omen; that's what it is. An omen. And it's a bad one. It means somebody's going to die. You get out today, before it's too late."

"That's nonsense. I'm not leaving now. Not when this whole ball of twine is starting to unwind. Was Joe Marshall Beth's boyfriend? Was Creed or Matthew?"

"I'll say no more on it. I've said too much already."

Bailey's fair complexion turned the color of lye soap. "It's true, then, what Grace hinted at? My mother . . . Beth . . . was promiscuous?"

The girl looked as if she might faint, and Emma worried that she'd made things worse by giving any answer at all. She got to her feet heavily, retrieved a sponge from the back of the sink, and began to mop up the spilled coffee. "I'll say no more, not if you sewed me into a sack of roosters and dropped me into the bay." She dropped the sponge into the sink. "The tide's right for crabbing. I've promised crab cakes for the church supper. I was just waiting for you two to get back with the boat." She put her hand on the doorknob. "God knows I think the world of you, Bailey. But you go. You go today, while you can. And don't come back." She rushed out the back door and slammed it behind her. *Never come back*, she thought. *Because whoever that owl is hooting for, I don't want it to be you.*

Daniel barged into Will's studio and found the older man gluing glass eyes into the life-size image of a great blue heron. The dogs leaped up and greeted him with wagging tails and lolling tongues. Will laid the tweezers and an eye on the counter and regarded him with an enigmatic gaze. "What's got your shorts on fire, boy? Hope you're not packing that pistol for me."

"Somebody took a shot at me off Tilghman's Sandbar."

Will uttered a sound of disgust, picked up the tweezers again, and pressed the glass eye into the heron's head once more. "Wasn't me."

"I suspect it has something to do with the senator's accident."

Will glanced over his shoulder at him, all the while keeping pressure on the glass eye. The carved and painted heron was magnificent, so lifelike that Daniel half expected it to unfold those enormous wings and take flight. "Have to do this before the glue sets," Will said. "Makes a mess of the job otherwise." After another minute he stepped away and selected a second eye from a saucer.

"If it was you, I'd be dead." Daniel exhaled softly, wondering how much he could trust Will and if he should tell Will that Bailey had been with him. He couldn't stop the shame from washing over him, shame that he could doubt the one man who'd been more father to him than his own father.

"You're right about that. I don't miss too often, and if I do, my second shot takes down whatever I'm aiming at." He turned the artwork and fitted the eye into the blank hole for size. "Perfect fit. Hand me that glue, will you, Daniel?"

He passed the tube over. "Seen any strangers on the island?"

"Detectives nosing around, asking questions about Creed and Ida."

"No, not the state police and not the coroner's office. I got a call from someone I used to know. The agency is investigating Marshall's death."

"CIA?" Will's features twisted into a skeptical mask. "This neck of the woods is more the FBI's briar patch, isn't it? Didn't know the agency went poking around inside the U.S. of A."

"It's an unofficial investigation. I can't tell you any more."

Something close to a smile tugged at the corners of Will's mouth. "No need to risk your neck over me. They stay off my land, I don't give a flying damn what they do."

"Joe Marshall was into some stuff overseas where I was stationed."

"Something he shouldn't have been doing? There's a

surprise. Anybody whose fortunes rose as quick as Joe's had to be doing something crooked."

"I didn't say that."

"Didn't have to. Question is, what was Joe selling?" The amusement vanished, and steel flickered behind the older man's eyes. "Somebody tried to poison my dogs last night. I found a chunk of store-bought meat on the trail that leads to Elizabeth's place. Not far away lay a dead raccoon. It died quick, and it died hurting. Lucky for Blue and the rest, they've been trained not to take food from strangers."

"Bailey was with me in the boat. The bullet passed between us. She could have been killed."

Will shook his head. "She should have stayed away. She'll only break her heart on Tawes."

"I don't think wild horses could drag her away now. She's determined to find out what happened to her mother, and why."

Will applied the glue sparingly to the back of the second glass eye. "This piece is going to Tokyo. Can you believe that? Something of mine on display in Japan. Man paid top dollar too. Not that I met him face-to-face. His agent contacted me just after the Boston show two years ago."

"Bailey's your flesh and blood. She's as much a Tawes as your sister was. Don't you care that she came so close to harm?"

"Funny, isn't it, that McCready's taking so long to work the kinks out of that deed to the farm? It's been in the family since the eighteen hundreds," he mused. He pulled several dog biscuits from his jean pocket and tossed them to the dogs. "I don't see what anybody could find wrong with the title."

245

"I told her that it didn't matter to you that Elizabeth left the place to her."

"That much is true." He rubbed his hands on his pant legs. "I got as much here as I need. I've got a lot of faults, but greed isn't one of them." He gathered up his tools. "Don't let me keep you from whatever you were hunting."

"Will. Damn it, Will. This has got to tie in with how the senator died."

"It just might. Or it might be something altogether different. Can't tell until it plays itself out. One thing for sure—anybody poking around here after dark had best be careful. These dogs mean a lot to me, and I'll not stand by and see them—"

"More than Bailey?"

"Don't put words into my mouth, boy."

"I'm going to find out the truth one way or another."

"Hope you do." Will ran a finger over one wing of the carving, almost as if he were smoothing a feather into place. "There's nothing lower than a dog poisoner, nothing lower under the sun."

CHAPTER EIGHTEEN

It took Daniel nearly an hour to reach the high ground overlooking Tilghman's Sandbar. Once there he proceeded to map out an imaginary grid over the two acres of woodland, picturing where a sniper could have stood and waited for Emma's boat to pass by. He walked back and forth, searching the ground for any trace of the shooter.

When he was a boy, this had been farmland. Cows and horses had grazed here; now it was overgrown with a mixture of cedar, pine, and maple, wild rose and sassafras. Once there had been a house and outbuildings, but lightning had taken the house and wild grapevines, and time had left the barn and sheds in ruin.

As long as he'd been back on Tawes, Daniel hadn't gotten over the sheer joy of smelling home . . . of the salt bay air, the earthy scent of the freshly turned soil, or the sweet odor of clover crushed under his feet. It was so familiar and comforting on a primal level, so different from the high country of Afghanistan and the Far East as to be another planet. He'd known instinctively that if there were anywhere on earth where he could become whole again, it would be here on this island. And day by day he'd felt himself healing . . . until cracks began to open in the fragile eggshell of security and the horror began to seep in, drop by drop.

He had closed the door on Mallalai, sealing her grave, burying it beneath a mountain of regret and grief. He wouldn't allow himself to dwell on the memory of her small hand in his, her soft voice, or the brush of her lips against his skin. She was dead, and she'd stay dead, because once he allowed the stones to crumble beneath the onslaught of why and what-if, he'd begin to relive the senselessness of the ensuing carnage.

The breeze was coming off the water, and not a single mosquito buzzed around his head. It would have been a good place for a man to think, to make plans for his future. At least, it would have been a perfect spot if he weren't hunting a would-be assassin.

If he hadn't come close to losing the second woman he'd let inside his heart . . .

He could almost hear the groans and cries of the dying, smell the splattered mud and spilled coffee . . . taste death in the air. There'd been little left of Mallalai to identify as human, let alone recognize. He might not have believed the body was hers if it weren't for the gold bracelet he'd bought her in the bazaar only days before. One hand remained, small, slender, and bloodless, and on the macabre wrist, his last and only gift, now twisted and blood-soaked.

He couldn't think about Mallalai now. It was Bailey he had to think about, Bailey he had to protect at any cost.

It took the better part of two hours of careful searching before Daniel found the place where the shooter had stood, and less than five minutes to pick the spent shell out of the undergrowth. He swore as he grasped the brass between thumb and forefinger. This was no .22-caliber, no careless kid out squirreling. The shooting had been deliberate.

Unconsciously Daniel clenched his jaw as he turned the casing to catch the last rays of the setting sun. The head stamp on the shell was plain enough: Remington .308. Not military issue, as he'd expected, but civilian, a weapon used primarily for hunting, and it should be easy enough to match bullet to rifle. Trouble was, there were probably a hundred Winchesters on Tawes that could have fired this bullet.

"Clever bastard." Leaving the brass where it could be found had been sloppy, but so had the attempt on his life. For the first time he wondered if maybe the shooter hadn't meant to kill him, but to frighten him. If so, the plan had worked . . . maybe too well.

Still cradling the shell casing in his hand, Daniel hunched down in the grass. He had a clear view of Tilghman's Sandbar from this spot. Not that he could see how shallow the water was, but the eddies around it showed him the sandbar as plainly as if it had been outlined in fluorescent orange paint.

Daniel knew what damage a .308 could do to a two hundred-pound buck. The bullet would enter, leaving a small, neat entrance hole, then continue, exploding through muscle, bone, and vitals to exit in a gaping wound of total devastation. He could easily imagine how close Bailey had come to dying. He hadn't thought the agency—if it was the agency that had done this—would go so far. His carelessness had nearly cost her life. Or his . . . He couldn't afford a second mistake in judgment, not after Mallalai.

* * *

Emma eased back on the throttle and slowed the engine to fifteen knots. Downing the last drops of the McCallan, she dropped the empty bottle into the bait well. She'd never been a particularly brave person, and she hoped that the Scotch had given her enough courage to do what had to be done. She was through running, through hiding secrets that should have been exposed decades before. Better dead than living scared night after night, jumping at every footstep, and lying awake these last few weeks listening to the haunting refrain outside her bedroom window.

Emma slowed the skiff and prepared to nose up against Will Tawes's dock. Her heart was leaping in her chest, and her hands felt numb. She expected that Will would kill her once he heard what she had to say, and it was no more than she deserved. Thirty-six years, and she'd never found the stones to tell the truth for Beth, but now, for Bailey, it had to come out and be finished.

Emma cut the engine, and the boat glided almost soundlessly into the slip. She knew there'd be no reprieve this time. She looped a mooring rope around a post and climbed up onto the dock. By the time she had the skiff secured, Will's dogs were running toward her in full cry. Behind, tall and menacing, she saw him striding to the dock.

"You're not welcome here. And well you know it, Emma Parks."

She stood her ground, knotting her hands into fists to keep them from trembling. "Few are, from what I hear."

"With good reason, I'd say."

The dogs rushed at her, and she had the sudden urge to empty her bladder. The big male Chesapeake hesitated, hackles raised, teeth bared, while the female circled and the shaggy shepherd snarled a warning. Will dropped them to earth with a single command.

"What do you want?"

Emma's throat tightened. "I need to tell you something I should have said a long time ago," she said in a strangled croak. "About your Beth . . . about what happened to her."

Will was on her before she had the chance to defend herself. A big hand closed on her shirtfront. A kick drove her legs out from under her. She slammed hard onto the ground. Stunned, gasping for breath, she lay prone with Will's knee pressing into her chest and his fist inches from her face.

"Say your piece while you still can draw breath!"

Once more they were trying to send her away from the island. Why? And had the shooting been an accident, as Daniel had said? Was his explanation as simple as a foolish boy playing with a gun, or was it something more? And why had Emma rushed out of the house as through her hair were on fire? His hair?

Bailey shook her head. It was all a maze of maybes, and she needed to think things out for herself. Could she trust Daniel? Should she? Running might help clear her head, but so would any kind of hard physical labor. Hadn't the weeds in the garden behind the school been getting out of hand since the shower the other night? Weeding was as good a way to distract herself as any.

She raced upstairs, changed into her oldest pair of shorts and shoes, and pedaled the bike through town to the summer-school garden. She had the rows of vegetables to herself, and for the next few hours she crawled up and down, making neat piles of the weeds and watering the pepper and tomato plants. Already, green tomatoes were starting to turn color, and with any luck, in a week or two they'd get to taste the results of all their work.

Finally, when her back was aching and the worst of her agitation had worn off, Bailey gathered the lettuce, green beans, and radishes she'd salvaged and carried them to Emma's mother's house. The elderly woman wasn't at home, but Bailey left them in the basket attached to the windowsill beside the front door and returned to Emma's. She still hadn't found answers to any of her questions, but she knew what she wanted to do next: get clean.

At the house—Emma's house—Bailey undressed and got into the shower. She turned the water hot enough to steam up the bathroom and leaned her head against one wall of the stall as doubts rushed back to plague her. Why hadn't she listened to reason? she thought as she used a long-handled brush to scrub every inch of her body. Why hadn't she left when everyone warned her to? Why hadn't she been content with childish fantasies about the tragic death of her beautiful young mother? Will had warned her; Emma had warned her.

Daniel had warned her: "Are you certain you want to know?"

Now she was sorry she had persisted. What if Matthew Catlin was her biological father? Daniel's brother. She felt as though she needed to vomit. The thought was too disgusting to imagine. If Matthew had fathered her, then she'd just fallen hard for her own uncle. Worse, she'd committed incest.

She rubbed shampoo through her hair, scrubbing at her scalp with her fingertips. She'd lost her mind, going to pieces because of a wild guess on Emma's part. Emma or Emery, or whoever she was. Someone had told her that, too—nothing was ever as simple on Tawes as it seemed. She turned off the hot and shivered in the hard stream of icy water.

Stepping out, she dried herself and wrapped a clean towel around her wet hair. The blotchy face that stared back at her might have belonged to a deranged woman. She was as crazy as all the rest of them on this godforsaken island. Or as inbred. By morning she'd probably be walking on all fours and devouring raw squirrels.

She returned to the bedroom, suddenly aware that she hadn't had enough sleep in the last twenty-four hours to think clearly. Crawling between the sheets, she laid her head on the pillow, intending to rest for just a few minutes. She woke nearly three hours later feeling like a new woman.

Impulsively, she ran a comb through her hair and pulled on a clean T-shirt and matching shorts. She felt empty inside, numb as if she'd been injected with massive doses of Novocain. But she had to know whether she was panicking over an unsubstantiated rumor or if she'd committed the worst mistake of her life when she slept with Daniel Catlin. She had to find Matthew and demand that he tell her the truth.

The hushed street was strangely empty as Bailey hurried past the store in the shadowy twilight. No one, not even a dog, was in sight. She went first to the parsonage, but her repeated knocking went unanswered and she saw no lights on inside. After a few minutes she gave up and crossed through the cemetery to the church office. There was no sign of anyone there either, but she called Matthew's name several times before circling the building to the sanctuary. The interior was as dark and silent as the graveyard.

She didn't want to go back to Emma's without getting answers, and the only other person she could think to ask was Forest. As Bailey approached his house, she saw someone on the porch speaking to the attorney. The two golden retrievers sat by the men, but readily abandoned their master and came to greet her.

Forest broke off his conversation with the stranger. "Bailey. What a pleasant surprise."

His companion abruptly descended the front steps and strode past her without replying to her "Good evening."

Forest came to the edge of the porch. "What a coincidence," Forest said. "I was just going to call you. Come in, please. I was about to have some tea."

"No, thanks. I need to talk to you. It's"—she glanced over her shoulder to make certain they were alone— "urgent and confidential."

Some of her agitation must have been evident in her voice, because his normal cheerfulness vanished and he appeared concerned. "Is something wrong?" he asked as he ushered her inside. "Something I can help with? If it's the bequest, I'm afraid we've hit another snag. I'm embarrassed to say that the delay may drag on for weeks. You might want to think of going home to Delaware and returning when—"

"No, I don't want to go home." She shook her head. "Why does everyone seem to want me to leave Tawes? I'm sorry." She let out an exasperated sigh. "At least, I don't think I want to go." She sank into a chair near Forest's desk.

"Wait. You need something stronger than Earl Grey. A glass of merlot?"

She nodded. "Yes. That sounds good."

"I have some nice roast beef and onion rolls. Would you care to share my—"

"No, thank you. I couldn't eat anything." She couldn't remember having lunch, but she wasn't hungry. "The wine would be wonderful, though."

"Certainly. I hate to drink alone." He went to a cupboard built into the wall beside the fireplace and removed a bottle and two crystal glasses. "There's nothing wrong at Emma's, I hope? Daniel hasn't taken a header off the roof?"

She fixed him with an accusing gaze. "You mean Emery's roof?"

Forest inclined his head slightly, a courtly gesture that would have been accepted gentlemanly behavior when the house was built two hundred years earlier. "Ah, so you've ferreted out another of our small secrets."

"I just found out what everyone else seems to know about my hostess."

"You really didn't guess, did you?" he said kindly. "Please don't be offended. I didn't mean it as a criticism. We've grown accustomed to Emma's ways. It didn't occur to us that you might feel deceived. And no one could tell you without violating Emma's privacy."

She sipped the merlot. It was dry but rich and fruity. She liked it.

"Now, what's really troubling you? It certainly isn't Emma." The attorney sat on the corner of the desk with the dogs sprawled contentedly at his feet.

"Daniel Catlin and I . . ." She stopped, uncertain as to what to say. What were they exactly? Dating? Lovers?

Instead she blurted, "Is there any chance that Matthew is my natural father?"

"Good God, who told you that?"

"Is it possible?"

The color drained from Forest's face.

"Tell me!" she insisted.

"All right." He nodded. "There were rumors that Beth and Matthew were—"

"Sleeping together?"

"No." Closing his eyes, Forest rubbed his temple. "I never thought that you and Daniel . . ." He swallowed. "It's possible, yes. I used to see Beth and Matthew . . . coming out of choir practice laughing and whispering, but . . ."

"But what? Was Matthew her boyfriend, or was she the kind of girl who—"

"No. It's not what you're insinuating. She was shy, sweet, the kind of girl any father would want for a daughter. That's why the pregnancy came as such a shock to everyone. There were other young ladies on the island that . . . Well, your mother wasn't one of them. Matthew's father was the pastor here then, and he was strict, every bit as strict as Will Tawes. The Catlins had plans for Matthew, and they didn't include his becoming serious with a local island girl his freshman year of college." His mouth tightened. "Or any other year, for that matter. They wanted more for him."

"Matthew was already attending college then?"

Forest nodded. He rose and refilled his wineglass, then offered her more. "Would you like—"

"No, just answers, Mr. McCready. Just the answers no one seems to want to give me."

"I hadn't seriously considered that the father might be Matthew. In his own way, he was just as shy as she

256

was. Never had a serious girlfriend until he and Grace . . . No, it couldn't be Matthew. He was a good-looking boy, but he was terrified of disappointing his parents. I can't imagine him involved in premarital sex, certainly not with Will Tawes's niece."

"If not Matthew Catlin, then who? You don't believe that Uncle Will did—"

"Not for a minute. He loved that girl as if she were his own. He'd have cut his own throat before he'd have done anything to hurt her. There's been plenty of scandal on the island, but not by the Tawes men. And I don't believe he beat Beth the night that you were born. Or any other night. Will was a hard man—is a hard man—but he's never used his fists on a woman. I would never have defended him if I believed that."

She rose. "Thank you. I appreciate your honesty. I still intend to ask Matthew. If there's the slightest chance . . ."

"I understand."

"There didn't seem to be anyone at the parsonage when I came by, but perhaps now . . ."

"You're upset, Bailey. I'd be happy to come with you, if you'd like."

"No, thank you. I'll be fine. I need to do this alone." She set the wineglass down on a coaster. "If I do decide to leave the island, I'll let you know. But unless Matthew confirms my worst fears, I have every intention of remaining here, at least until summer school is out."

He followed her to the door. "I'm so sorry about the additional delays with the will. I feel as though I've let you down. You must think me a terrible example of my profession."

"No, not at all," she said. "You've been very kind."

"I feel like the worst kind of host. At least let me walk you back to Emma's."

"No." She forced a smile. "It's not as though I'm going to get lost. All I have to do is follow the street back to the house."

Head throbbing, hurting from a half dozen blows, Emma pushed herself up on her hands and knees and spit dirt and blood from her mouth. A tooth felt loose, and something wet and sticky trickled down her chin as she staggered to her feet. The sound of Will's curses coming from the house drove her back toward the dock. She swayed on her feet as she found the edge of the wooden walkway. She could see the boat, but the distance seemed more like miles than yards.

One eye was fast swelling shut, and she thought her cheekbone and at least two ribs must be cracked. Faster, she had to move faster. Once she reached the boat, she jerked loose the mooring lines with stiff hands and climbed in. Scrambling across the deck, ignoring the pain of bone grating against bone, she frantically turned the key. The engine clicked once and roared to life as a cursing Will burst from the house, gun in hand.

Emma put the boat in reverse, shot backward, and then cried out in fear as the engine stalled. Will came across the yard, jamming a shell into his shotgun as he ran. The moon was rising over the water, making its surface nearly as bright as day. Another minute and she would be as dead as Creed and Joe Marshall.

Emma shoved the throttle into neutral and prayed harder than she'd ever prayed before. The engine caught, sputtered, and throbbed to life. She threw the throttle forward and the boat leaped ahead in a cloud of spray. Will's shotgun blasted from the dock, but the skiff was already moving away at a good twenty-five knots, and the pellets rained around her head and pinged against the transom like hail.

Emma headed out into the bay. Her hands were shaking so hard that she could hardly feel the wheel, and she ached from belly to temple. Cautiously she tested the loose tooth with her tongue. She'd be lucky if her jaw wasn't broken.

No, she reasoned, as her heartbeat slowed to somewhere near normal. She'd be lucky if Will didn't follow her out onto the bay and kill her. She should have felt better now that the truth was out after so long, but she felt only empty dread. Maybe it would have been better if she'd just waited for Will to get the gun from the house and finish her off.

When she was a good mile out, Emma slowed the boat and switched on her running lights. She knew the bay waters like she knew her own house . . . the channels, the tides, and where the sandbars were exposed or covered just enough to be dangerous. But when the engine noise changed to a shrill whine and then cut off, she realized that her panicked flight had caused her to run straight into a line of crab pots. Rope had tangled around the propeller, disabling it and bringing the boat to a halt as surely as if she were anchored to a concrete wall.

"Damn it! Damn it." She groaned. She needed medical attention, but if she couldn't free the propeller or repair it, she'd be here until the first commercial boat or sport fisherman came along in the morning. She wondered if she was in any shape to strip and dive down to check out the damage firsthand. If there was net or line she could cut loose, maybe the engine would run well enough to get to Smith or even the Eastern Shore. Hell, the way she felt, she'd probably drown and save Will the trouble of shooting her.

For perhaps fifteen minutes she sat there, not knowing what to do. Her head was pounding, and the pain in her side was sharp enough to draw tears with every breath. She wondered which was worse; waiting all night in agony or forcing herself into the water to try to set things right. A cloud of bloodsucking mosquitoes forced her decision. She pulled off her shoes just as she became aware of the sound of another boat engine.

"No," Emma stammered. "No, Will, don't. Please." The boat was coming fast, and she was trapped like a duck in a barrel. "Sweet Jesus."

A single shot rang out. Emma gasped as pain knifed through her. She clutched at her belly and toppled backward over the side. The warm bay waters closed over her head, and she felt herself sinking down and down into peaceful oblivion.

Hours later, in the blackness before the first faint fingers of dawn, Daniel Catlin grasped the edge of the swim platform on the stern of a thirty-six-foot Bayliner and heaved himself up out of the Chesapeake. Once he was on the boat, it was a small matter to climb over the transom and cross the deck to the louvered hatch. It was locked from the inside, but it took only a few seconds for him to overcome that barrier. He pushed open the hatch and stepped in, guided though the cabin darkness by a small night-light and the sound of Lucas's snoring.

The galley smelled of wine, onions, and liverwurst.

The door to the head stood ajar. Daniel moved past that to the sleeping area in the bow and slipped a knife from the sheath at his waist. He leaned close to Lucas, pressed the blade against his throat, and whispered in his ear, "Careless agents don't live to collect their pensions."

"You're crazy, Catlin. You can't get away with—"

"Shh." He pressed harder so that the point penetrated slightly. "If I'm not sane, it wouldn't do to push me over the edge, would it? A slip of the knife and you'd bleed to death before I could summon the EMTs."

"Your prints are all over this boat."

"Are they? Are you certain? I'm wearing gloves. And a wet suit."

"Why?"

"That's what I wanted to ask you, Lucas. Why do the powers that be want me dead?" It was hot inside the suit, and Daniel didn't feel good about this.

"You aren't dead," Lucas rasped. "I warned you. A professional courtesy."

"A courtesy that almost killed an innocent woman."

"I don't know what you're talking about."

He arched Lucas's head back farther. "Keep it up. My patience is fast running out. What's this about?"

"You know as well as I do."

"I wasn't blackmailing Marshall."

"Who else . . . on that shithole of an island would know about . . . the senator's windfall?" Lucas swore softly. "Let me go! You've made your . . . point."

"Drug money, Lucas. Say it. Senator Joe Marshall, the golden boy—heir to the White House—made his fortune off the international drug trade."

"That's what . . . makes people nervous." Lucas's harsh voice echoed through the cabin. "You say . . . what's best . . . left unsaid."

"I didn't kill Marshall, and I don't know who did."

"You blamed him . . . for the bomb."

"Shouldn't I?"

"Zahir's work—not Marshall's."

"Was it? I was the target." A narrow ribbon of blood trickled down Lucas's neck.

"You think . . . too much."

"And you don't?" Daniel asked.

"Nope. I follow orders."

"And you can sleep at night."

"Like a baby."

"I couldn't. Not anymore."

"You shouldn't have left. Inside . . . you were . . . one of us. Outside . . ." Lucas trailed off.

"I'm a liability."

"A big one."

"And Bailey Elliott? Is she a liability?"

"Maybe."

Daniel steeled himself. "I can see this may take longer than I thought." He released Lucas's hair and slammed a knotted fist into the base of the agent's skull. Lucas collapsed like a ruptured pig's bladder. "Sweet dreams," Daniel murmured.

CHAPTER NINETEEN

Bailey had returned home from Forest's to find the house empty and dark, and so far as she knew, neither Emma nor Daniel had returned in the hours before dawn. Her own sleep was erratic, disturbed by periods of wakefulness and by nightmares. Sometime after two, when exhaustion finally claimed her, she dreamed that a ghost dressed like a Civil War soldier was standing at the foot of her bed whistling a nursery tune. She opened her mouth to scream, but nothing came out. And when she tried to move, she found herself paralyzed. She woke at half past nine on Sunday morning with the nursery tune running over and over in her mind.

> *. . . and if that diamond ring don't shine,*
> *Papa's going to buy you a coach and nine.*
> *And if that coach and nine won't pull,*
> *Papa's going to buy you a baby bull . . .*

It was annoying and frightening at the same time, and she wondered again if Daniel was right, if she should consider going home to Newark for a few days. She couldn't imagine what had kept him or Emma away all night, especially since neither had mentioned they would be away. Truthfully, she was more concerned about Daniel. What if he'd found the careless shooter and the boy had shot him? She'd given Daniel her cell number, but she realized this morning that he hadn't given her his. She had no way to contact him. All she could do was to wait.

She had to do something positive, something normal. Going to the deck in the hallway, she removed a yellow legal pad, went into the kitchen, and began her week's lesson plans. She already had a full schedule, but she'd learned during student teaching never to enter a class unprepared. It wasn't fair to the kids, and she'd figured out long ago that it was better to have too much to finish in the allotted time than too little.

But it was difficult to concentrate on the schoolwork. She kept reliving the night she'd spent with Daniel at the cabin. She couldn't help fearing that she might have unconsciously committed incest.

The possibility that an act so beautiful could be so wrong sickened her, but she refused to accept it until she had proof. If someone other than Matthew had fathered her, then she would be free to be with Daniel, not just for a night of fun and games, but for more. Not that she was thinking of marriage—she wasn't ready to make that leap of faith so soon. She'd made one mistake in that department with Elliott, and she wasn't about to make a second try with a man she'd known only weeks. She'd made such a bad choice in Elliott that it was difficult to trust her judgment.

Truthfully, she didn't know what she wanted, other than a repeat of the giving and taking that those hours with Daniel had brought. She had felt more desirable, more alive than ever before. She'd never known anyone, before or after Elliott, who had that effect on her. When Daniel walked into a room, it lit up. Colors seemed brighter and more vivid, scents stronger. She might be a foolish romantic, but she wasn't willing to walk away from him if there was any chance they could have a life together.

Reason told her that she was a stranger on Tawes— she didn't belong here—but something deeper whispered that she did. This was exactly where she should be, and these were her people. What was the phrase Emma and Will used? Blood kin? Was it possible that the ties of family were stronger than culture, education, or the influences of the rest of society?

Thoughts of Daniel didn't make her forget the scare of the stray bullet the previous day; nor did they curb her need to know her biological father's identity. Why hadn't he stood with her mother when she'd become pregnant? Had he been responsible for Beth's beating and, ultimately, her death? Surely Matthew knew more than he'd told her. She was still going to try to get him alone and question him further, but she knew that he'd be busy conducting services at church until after noon.

When her lesson plans were in order, she tried her adoptive father's number in California. For once the connection went through, and she managed to reach him on the second ring. They chatted briefly, mostly about his recent medical checkup and about her stepmother's vacation plans for the month of August. They exchanged pleasantries and hung up without her mentioning Daniel or her near accident the day before. Her father had never been a person to confide in, and he would have been as uncomfortable as she if she'd tried. Their conversation was civilized, as usual. They were both cheerful and courteous; they said all the right things, but nothing could fill the gap of emotional detachment that had always yawned between them.

Once, when Bailey was young, before her mother had contracted the illness that killed her, she'd overheard a heated discussion between her parents. It wasn't an argument. They'd never argued or become emotional on any subject other than debating the best methods to curb illiteracy and to cut the burgeoning birth rates in third-world countries. In this instance her father had considered a change in mutual funds, and he'd reminded her mother that they would have been in a better position to save for retirement if they didn't have a daughter to educate. Her mother's reply had been, "Charity begins at home," and that he could hardly profess a concern for people in South Asia if he wasn't willing to provide for one motherless child here in his own house.

The words and the guilt she felt while eavesdropping had hurt, and she'd run to her secret spot in the attic where she kept her favorite books and an old blanket that had been designated for the Goodwill box. She hadn't cried, but she'd wanted to. It was the first time she could remember feeling that adoption was somehow shameful, and the thought remained to haunt her for all the years that followed. ". . . Charity . . . motherless child . . ." Even now, the memory made her ache inside.

By midafternoon, when Emma and Daniel still hadn't shown up, Bailey returned to the parsonage. A red-eyed and disheveled Grace opened the door. "Oh, child, you're a godsend. I'm so glad you came. Please."

She waved her inside, and Bailey was instantly struck by the smell of Lysol and furniture polish. Obviously the older woman had found someone to do her heavy cleaning, because the banister and front entrance hall gleamed.

"I've been so distraught," Grace said. "Matthew's ill, you know. Harry Tilghman—our senior deacon—had to stand in for him at church this morning."

Bailey followed her into the dining room. "I'm sorry. I didn't know. I wouldn't have come if—" The terrier came yipping out of the kitchen and leaped up on its hind legs, scratching at Bailey's bare shins.

"Hush, hush, baby," Grace soothed, scooping the dog up. "Naughty. You'll wake Daddy. Excuse me." She rushed to the back door and dropped the dog on the step. The animal continued barking and digging at the screen, but Grace ignored it and returned to the dining room. When she returned, she handed Bailey a large mug of coffee. "Have some of this. It's a French roast that Matthew particularly likes."

"No, thank you, I—"

"Please. You know the old saying: 'Waste not, want not.'"

Giving her a half smile, Bailey took a sip. The coffee was strong, but good. Grace had apparently added sugar, but it seemed impolite to complain, so she sat and drank the coffee. "It was wrong of me to come without calling first," Bailey said, "but I wanted—"

"Don't apologize. I was just getting ready to come in search of you."

Bailey's legs stung, and when she glanced down she noticed a thin line of blood on her left ankle from the dog's sharp claws. "I wanted to talk to Matthew, but I'll come back in a day or two when he's feeling better. I don't want to disturb him if he's sleeping."

"Nonsense." Grace brushed a stray lock of hair away from her face. "If that noisy rascal doesn't rouse him with his incessant barking, we certainly won't. I'm afraid Matthew picked up a stomach bug when we were in Crisfield shopping for groceries. The checker at the market looked positively green. She told us, after our order was half rung up, that she was going home because she was sick."

Bailey wished she hadn't come. Once again she found herself trapped by Grace and her ceaseless chatter. "You must have your hands full," she said apologetically. "I'll come—"

"No, you must . . ." Grace dug a tissue out of her apron pocket and blew her nose. She looked as if she were about to burst into tears. "I've wronged you, dear. . . ." She clapped a hand over her mouth, smothering whatever she was attempting to say. Moisture glistened in her eyes. "Please listen to me."

It was the first time Bailey had seen Grace without makeup. Now she realized why the woman wore such thick foundation. Old acne scars pitted her cheeks. Despite her disfigurement, with her hair pulled back into a knot Grace looked years younger and much more human.

"If there's something I can do . . ." Bailey offered.

"I don't know which was worse, poor Matthew's embarrassment at throwing up all over the upstairs hall on a dash for the bathroom or missing services this morning. My husband takes his duties as pastor seriously, but I told him straight out—'Matthew,' I said, 'it would be a disservice to your flock if you passed this upset to any of your congregation.'"

"You said you had something to tell me," Bailey reminded her.

"It's Daniel." Grace reached out and patted her hand. "I know I haven't been as welcoming as I should have, but please know that I've never meant to cause you any distress." She wrung her hands nervously. "It just my way to speak my mind before considering how my words may sound."

"I don't understand." In spite of the perfectly manicured nails and several expensive rings, Grace's large hands were neither feminine in appearance nor attractive. The knuckles on her long fingers were red and swollen with arthritis.

"Daniel called here just a little while ago. He found something at Elizabeth's farm, something you must see. He wanted me and Matthew to bring you out by boat right away. It's the quickest way to get there, but when I told him Matthew was ill, he—"

"You spoke with Daniel this morning? Is he all right?"

"Daniel, why, yes. He's fine." Grace peered at her over glasses that had slid down on her thin nose. "Is there some reason why—"

"No. Why didn't he call me? He has my number."

"He said he tried, but you know our phone service on Tawes is hit-or-miss. I think it's worse out past the grocery."

"It must be, because Emma's phone was working this morning. I called my father in California."

"There you go, then." Grace nodded.

"Did Daniel tell you what he'd found?"

Grace shrugged. "I got the idea it was a message or a letter, but he was adamant that you must come to the farm as soon as you could. He said it would answer all your questions." She untied her apron. "Just let me change into something more suitable for the boat, and we can go now."

"But Matthew—"

"He's miserable, but not dying. He barely had a fever, and I left a pitcher of ice water on the nightstand, where he can reach it." She pushed her glasses up with one crooked finger. "I assumed you'd want to go right away. Of course, if you'd prefer to bike out to the farm . . ."

"No, no," Bailey said hastily. "If you're sure you don't mind, I'd appreciate it if you'd take me in your boat."

"Fine. That's settled then. Give me five minutes, and I'll be ready. Would you like to borrow a windbreaker or a scarf, dear? It can be breezy on the water."

Bailey shook her head. She couldn't imagine what Daniel had found, or why he wanted his brother and sister-in-law to accompany her to the farm instead of simply bringing his discovery back to Emma's. The fact that he'd included his brother sent a chill up Bailey's spine.

"All right, then," Grace said cheerfully, reentering the room minutes later. "We'll hop into the boat, run around to Elizabeth's, and see what Daniel's being so mysterious about. I just hope he hasn't gotten your hopes up for nothing. Daniel's been a nervous wreck ever since he returned from overseas. He witnessed a terrible tragedy over there, you know. A young woman he wanted to marry died in one of those awful terrorist bombings. Blown into so many bits they had to identify her by fingerprints and a piece of jewelry."

"How awful."

"It never would have worked out," Grace continued as they boarded the Boston Whaler tied to the dock at the back of the parsonage. "Can you imagine a woman like that fitting in on Tawes? Lord knows what they eat. Cats and goat heads, for all I know. They're better with their own kind. Not that I wouldn't have welcomed her into the family. I try to do what's right, regardless of others, and I do try to bear my share of Matthew's ministry."

"Daniel never told me he'd lost someone he cared about overseas," Bailey shouted over the sound of the motor.

"All I know is what he told Matthew. Daniel certainly doesn't confide in me."

"It must have hurt him deeply."

"It's what comes of becoming involved with foreigners." Grace turned the wheel to guide the boat around a buoy. "She fancied herself some sort of militia soldier." She glanced at Bailey.

The younger woman held on to the gunnel and stared out at the receding shoreline. The wind had whipped her hair loose, and she looked more like her mother than ever. An older version, of course, Grace thought, Beth Tawes having passed away so young. But so much likeness she almost found it disturbing. Both Beth and Bailey were small women, and they shared those delicate features that so many men seemed to prefer. Lucky for them that they'd been born into fortunate situations, spoiled, some might say. Neither would have survived a week in her stepfather's house.

" 'Live by the sword, die by the sword'," Grace murmured, "According to the Good Book. I wouldn't know anything firsthand about bombs, other than what I've seen on the news, but Matthew reads a great deal. He said he didn't suppose there was enough left of his brother's fancy woman to fill a dishpan."

Once they'd left the town behind, Grace cut the engine and let the Boston Whaler drift. "Don't be alarmed, dear," she said. "I just thought we needed to have a few minutes before we find out what Daniel has to show us."

Bailey tilted her head and gave Grace a curious look.

Grace made no attempt to hide the tears welling in her eyes. "I must admit I haven't been completely forthcoming with you, and I think you need to be prepared. As I said before, I'm plainspoken. I've even been called rude, but I don't mean to be. I call a spade a spade. And if you want the honest truth, Beth Tawes wasn't the girl she pretended to be."

Bailey's wondered what Grace was getting at. "How so?"

Grace shrugged. "Times were so different then. More difficult, in some ways. Life was hard, but the rules were more straightforward. There were good girls, and then there were the other kind."

"I don't understand."

"Beth was terrified of her uncle—of Will, and with good reason, as it turns out. I suspected she was hiding some secret. We were girlfriends, but she never confided in me, not the way I did in her. And she changed so much that summer."

"In what way?"

Grace steepled her hands and averted her eyes. "In those days . . . there were things that went on . . . things that the better sort of people didn't talk about. Alcohol abuse. Mischief of a . . . of a carnal nature."

"Are you saying my mother was—"

"There were rumors. There always are. Some said Beth let the boys take liberties. . . ."

"Sexually?"

"Frankly, my dear, Beth was known among our

crowd as being . . . rather loose. But I never believed it. I think I would have known. Oh, she might have done things she shouldn't, but . . ." She held up an open palm. "Wait, I have something for you." She dug into the pocket of her nylon windbreaker and handed Beth a silver locket. "Open it."

Bailey fumbled with the snap. Her fingers seemed clumsier than usual, and she was developing a fierce headache. Her stomach was none too steady either, but she attributed that to the motion of the boat.

Inside the locket were photos of a dark-haired young man and a girl. "This was your mother's. It meant the world to her. They're your parents. Her parents, I meant to say. Your grandparents, Owen and Anne Tawes. Owen was Will's twin brother, you know."

Bailey stared at the black-and-white images. "But why did she give it to you?"

Grace sighed. "She said her uncle was jealous. He'd destroyed all the pictures of her parents. Rumor has it that Will went with Anne before she left him for his twin brother. Beth cherished this necklace, and she was afraid he'd find it. I think you should have it."

"Thank you. Thank you so much." She swallowed the lump in her throat. "You can't know how much this means to me."

"But there's more you should know, dear. That summer Beth stopped coming to church. When I did see her, she always looked as though she'd been crying. Twice I saw ugly bruises on her arms and face."

Bailey leaned forward, clutching the locket tightly with both hands. "Did you ask her what was wrong?"

"She wouldn't say. I begged her to go to her Aunt Elizabeth or to our pastor, Matthew's father. I suspected that her uncle was mistreating her. She'd always been slim, but she put on a lot of weight that summer. Her clothes were baggy, but I never suspected that she might be pregnant." Her face grew red. "I was raised strictly, and I was an innocent in those days. Not worldly. Beth was always the pretty one, the one all the boys wanted to flirt with, but as I said . . . it all changed that summer. She changed."

"Do you know if she had a boyfriend?"

"Other people thought she did."

"Someone in particular?"

Grace rubbed her nose. "Honestly, dear, any of a half dozen young bucks could have fathered you. Beth wasn't a bad girl—I'll never believe that—but she was too free with her affections. And with Will Tawes's temper, if he found out, he would have killed her."

"Is it possible . . . it isn't right to ask you this, but . . . could Matthew have—"

"Sweet Lord in heaven! No!" Grace laughed. "Creed Somers, maybe. Joseph. Or even that Forest McCready. He's always been one for the ladies. But not my Matthew. He was already studying for the ministry, and he never looked at any woman but me in his life."

"So you think she had a secret boyfriend. That one of them . . ."

Grace frowned. "I didn't say that." She lowered her voice. "You have to know the history of the family to know what I thought Beth was hiding."

"What history?"

"It's not something decent women should speak of, but . . ." Grace sighed again. "Will had been in love with Beth's mother. Before she married his brother."

Bailey nodded. "Daniel told me something about that."

"Maybe Beth reawoke old memories . . . old desires."

"That's disgusting."

"I'm so sorry, child, so sorry to have to burden you with that." Graced pursed her lips. "But Daniel may have found proof of sexual abuse, and I thought you should be prepared."

"No. You're wrong. Not Uncle Will. He would never do such a thing."

"If he was so innocent, why would his own sister disown him?"

"I don't know," Bailey said.

"Something wasn't right there," Grace insisted. "Something was evil in that house, and Elizabeth knew about it."

"I won't believe that."

"Maybe once you see what Daniel has found, you'll stop defending Will Tawes."

"No," Bailey insisted. "It isn't true. It can't be."

Grace sniffed. "You don't know how things are on this island. No matter what Elizabeth knew about her brother, she was a Tawes. She wouldn't have gone to the law. And in the end, keeping that dirty secret is probably what caused your mother's death."

CHAPTER TWENTY

"Matt! Grace!" Daniel banged on the parsonage door before opening it. "Anybody home?" He stepped inside, carefully avoiding the hyperactive antics of the barking terrier despite his inclination to give the nasty little dog a swift kick in the butt. "Matt?"

"Up here!" His brother's slurred voice came from the second floor.

Daniel took the steps two at a time with Precious nipping at his heels. Matthew leaned against a doorjamb halfway down the upstairs hall. He was unshaven, his eyes bloodshot, and his long face was as drained of blood as if he were a butchered sheep. "Good God, what's wrong with you?" Daniel demanded.

"Sick." Matthew staggered, barely caught himself, and began to choke. "Bathroom. Help . . . me."

Daniel slipped an arm around his brother's shoulder and half supported, half carried him into the bathroom, where he barely reached the toilet in time to throw up. Matt smelled of vomit but no alcohol. Not drunk then, but as sick as Daniel had ever seen him. "You need a doctor."

"No . . . no time." He clutched the bowl and spewed a trail of gray slime.

"Where's Grace? Has she called a doctor? When did this start?" Daniel asked him. "You look as if you should be in a hospital."

"Damn the hospital." Matthew motioned toward the old fashioned sink. "A wet . . . wet cloth." He folded his arms and leaned forward.

Daniel snatched a hand towel off the bar, soaked it in cold water, and wrung it out. He wiped his brother's face, noting his sweat-soaked hair and Matt's ragged breathing. "Do you have any chest pains? Pain running down your arm?"

Matthew shook his head. "No. This is . . ." He suffered another choking spasm and, when he could speak again, rasped, "Not my heart. I think . . . I think Grace put something . . . in my coffee."

"Something? What do you mean? She drugged you?"

Matt cleared his throat. "Water." Daniel handed him a glass. Matthew took a mouthful and rinsed his mouth.

Daniel felt his head for fever, but he was cold, not hot. "You need medical help, and you need it now!"

"No, wait . . . Need you to see something . . . You can't blame her. She's ill."

"You're the one who's ill."

"No, her mind. She's . . ." He gasped for breath. "She's never been strong, not in that way."

"Your wife is as strong as a horse."

Matt shook his head. "Please. In our bedroom. On the floor. I dropped it . . . next to the bed. A paper. Get it."

"Later. You need—"

"Now, Daniel!"

The terrier, still barking, followed him into the master bedroom, bared his sharp little teeth, and leaped into the center of the bed. Daniel hadn't been in this chamber since his mother had died and been laid out here. When his mother ruled the parsonage, the room had been sparsely furnished, always bright, and smelled of lemon oil. Now heavy red velvet drapes blocked out the sunshine, and too many tables, dressers, chairs, and arrangements of artificial flowers made the space look crowded. His parents' twin beds had been replaced by a queen-sized one with a rose satin canopy over the headboard. The aroma of furniture polish was long gone, replaced now by the artificial roses and the stench of vomit.

Nothing in the room seemed out of place except the rumpled sheets and the thrown-back coverlet, a man's stray slipper, and a sheet of wrinkled paper on the braided rug. Daniel bent and retrieved the paper. It had been folded and refolded until it wasn't much larger than a deck of cards.

Daniel unfolded it and scanned the letterhead, a series of numbers, and the total at the bottom.

"What does it look like to you?" Matthew stood panting in the doorway. "A bank statement? Because that what it looks like to me."

Daniel wasn't familiar with the financial institution, but the address was George Town on Grand Cayman, an area known for offshore banking. There were no names on the statement, and the numbers were obviously in code. If his quick calculations were accurate and the Cayman–dollar rate of exchange remained steady, the balance came to something around eight hundred thousand American.

"I don't understand," Daniel said, but he had the sinking feeling that he did. He had a strong suspicion that what his brother had revealed was directly connected with the tale Lucas had related about money being extorted from the deceased senator. He glared at Matt. "How did you come by this?"

"I found it this morning in the pocket of Grace's bathrobe when I was doing laundry. When I confronted her, she flared up, rambled something about this being her due."

"And you left it at that?"

"No. I asked what she was talking about and tried to question her further, but she became hysterical." Groaning, Matthew staggered to the bed and sank onto it. "All this time I've wondered how she managed so well . . . on a poor parson's pittance. But that was Grace's domain. It was the only thing she was good at in school. You know she took accounting courses after we were married—when I was finishing up my divinity—"

"Grace attended college?"

"She didn't get a degree, but she attended for several years, mostly business courses. She majored in accounting."

"And all this time she's handled all your personal finances?"

"Yes. I had no head for it. And I never—"

"It never occurred to you to ask how you could buy all these things on a minister's salary?" He gestured at the knickknacks and Victorian furniture.

Matthew grabbed tissues from a box on the end

table and wiped his mouth. The dog ripped one out of his hand and dashed to the far end of the bed with it. "Precious, stop it. You know—"

"Never mind the damned dog! You're telling me that you never realized you had more money than you—"

"I've been such a fool," Matt said, cutting him off. "She said there were large donations . . . once a bequest from some relative I'd never heard of." He raised teary eyes to meet Daniel's gaze. "All I wanted to do was keep her happy. And when I got too demanding . . ." He shrugged. "You know her temper . . . how excitable she can be."

Daniel stiffened. "You never actually saw any evidence of large amounts of money?"

He flushed. "Grace liked to go to Atlantic City on our anniversary. I never did. I couldn't bring myself to go into . . . where they have those slots. But she was lucky."

Daniel folded his arms across his chest. "So you thought that your wife was a lucky gambler?"

"It seemed a small sin. Hardly worth chiding her over. She always tithed ten percent of what she won to charity."

"And you didn't see anything else? No other cash or purchases you couldn't account for?"

"Bits of jewelry, furnishings she found at estate sales. Investments that paid off well for us. After you'd told us you were putting money into Apple computers, she said she'd borrow against a life insurance policy to buy some for us." He groaned. "The conferences, the trips . . . donations to Bible colleges. I thought we were living beyond our means . . . but never . . . Grace said the Lord would provide, and somehow . . . He always did."

"Are you certain?" Daniel demanded angrily. "Are you certain it was your wife? Not you?"

"I'm no thief, Daniel. You have to believe me. A fool maybe. Weak, but no thief." Matt was openly weeping now, his nose running. "Where would she get it? Where would Grace come into so much money?"

"Joe Marshall. Our esteemed late senator. Somebody on Tawes had been blackmailing him for years."

"Blackmail?" Matt made a choking sound of disbelief. "Not Grace." He shook his head. "You're wrong. She's always been high-strung . . . maybe even unstable at times. Her horrible childhood . . . the unspeakable conditions in that house she grew up in. But not blackmail. Not my Grace. I'd know. I'd know if she could—"

"Maybe worse than blackmail. The agency believes Marshall was murdered."

Matt sank forward onto the mattress. "No, you can't come in here and accuse my wife of—"

Daniel seized his shoulders. "You say she drugged you, and you're defending her? Where is she? The whaler's not at the dock. If you're this sick, why would she leave you?"

"I don't know." Matt's white face took on a yellow shade, and he began to tremble violently. "You can't accuse her of murder. She'd have no reason. None."

"And this statement? An offshore account? Where did the money come from if not from blackmail?"

"There must be a reasonable explanation. . . ." Matt rubbed his head. "I have a splitting—"

Daniel swore. "Where is Grace?"

Matthew blinked. "Bailey? Have you seen Bailey?"

"Bailey?" Daniel yanked him upright and shook him. "Why? Why would Grace—"

"I . . . heard someone downstairs . . . after I became ill. I was all right until breakfast. We had French toast, and I drank two cups of coffee. There was a funny taste. Then . . . I started to feel dizzy, and Grace insisted I come back to bed."

"What about Bailey?"

Matt looked dazed. "Maybe I was dreaming, but after I came back up here, I thought I heard—"

"Bailey's voice?"

"It could have been. Precious barked, and I heard the front door open. It may not have been." Matthew began to tremble. "You have to find her, Daniel. You need to find Bailey before—"

"Before what? Is she in danger? Why would Grace want to harm her?"

"Beth." He swallowed and wiped his mouth with the back of his hand. "Bailey's Beth's girl. You know Grace was always jealous of Beth. Obsessed with her at times. Sometimes . . . No." He shook his head. "It's personal."

"Tell me," Daniel insisted.

Matthew flushed. "In our most intimate moments . . . when we were doing . . . having marital relations, she used to beg me to call her Beth. God help me . . . sometimes I did. It seemed to make her so happy."

Daniel was so angry, he could barely keep from smashing his fist into his brother's face. "And you never thought that was bizarre?"

"Odd, yes," he admitted, "but not completely crazy. She always thought I was still in love with Beth."

Daniel swore. "The woman's been dead for years. How could—"

"You don't understand. Beth and I . . . Before Grace and I became a couple, I was fond of Bailey's mother—maybe even thought I was in . . . I was nineteen, a freshman at a Bible college. What did I know about love at nineteen?"

"And Grace has brooded on that—been jealous all this time?"

Matt nodded. "She suspects that Bailey . . ."

"What? What does Grace suspect?"

"That Bailey . . . that's she's my natural daughter."

Daniel gripped his brother's shoulders until Matt winced with pain. "Why? Were you and Beth—"

"I don't know."

"You don't know?" Daniel had the urge to shake the answer out of his brother. "How can you not know? Did you have unprotected sex with Beth or not?"

"I don't remember. I was drunk . . . out of my head," he blubbered. "I never meant . . . I just wanted to be one of guys. You know how it was—being the minister's son, always being judged by our father. Just once I wanted the others to accept me. To be like—"

"What are you talking about?"

Matthew dropped his head into his hands. "Joe told me they were having a party . . . on the beach. At the island. Grace said I should bring Beth. Somebody had liquor and . . . I'd never drunk anything but beer before. I didn't think it would . . ." Sobs racked him. "It made it worse that Grace and I were never able to have children. Grace wanted a son . . . a boy to carry on . . . to be pastor after—"

"To hell with that." Daniel crouched in front of his brother. "How could you not know if you were intimate with Beth? Was she your—"

"My girlfriend, yes . . . before Grace. It was all so innocent."

"Innocent?" Daniel swore. "Somebody got Beth pregnant. She died having some man's child. Was it yours?"

He felt suddenly as though he wanted to make a run for the toilet his brother had just thrown up in. If Matt had fathered Bailey, then that made her his niece. He'd not only fallen in love with his niece; he'd just had sex with her.

Matt collapsed onto the mattress again like a puppet with cut strings. "Sleepy. Really sleepy."

"Not yet. You can't sleep yet! Is she dangerous? Could Grace hurt Bailey?"

"Dangerous." His brother's words slurred drunkenly. "Unpredictable. Nervous. She had such low self-esteem. Her doctors never thought she was an actual threat to anyone but herself."

"Nervous, hell. Is there a chance Grace would hurt Bailey?" He shook Matt. "Talk to me. Didn't she spend time in a mental hospital?"

"A few weeks, but that was years ago. Not a sanitarium, a church treatment center . . ."

"Why, Matt? Why was she committed?"

"We'd . . . she'd been so sure she was pregnant, and then she started her period. She cut her wrist with a razor blade. By the time I found her she'd lost so much blood. She wasn't rational . . . shouting that Beth had come back from the grave to kill her. Beth had been dead for years. I was afraid Grace might harm herself, so I hospitalized her."

"So she is capable of violence?"

"Not against anyone else. She threatened to kill herself—that's why I put her into the center. But she responded to treatment . . . got better."

"Better, hell! Someone took a shot at us yesterday! Could it have been Grace?"

"Shot at you?" Matt's eyes widened in shock. "No . . . not my Grace. She . . . I should have given her a child.

284

Prayed for one. We both did. She would have been all right if—"

"And you let Beth go through that alone?"

"No, I didn't know. I swear. No one did. We argued. After that one day . . . we argued. I never knew that Beth was pregnant."

"You knew it when she died! Why didn't you come forth then? Why didn't you testify at Will's trial? Tell what happened? Tell the jury that you and Beth were intimate?"

"I couldn't because I didn't know. It got out of hand. We were having fun on the beach. First Grace and Joe, and then Grace and Creed. I was cherry, Daniel. I'd never . . . I don't know how it happened, but things just escalated. The girls were as drunk as—"

"And you never told anyone that you and Beth—"

"No . . . Couldn't . . . couldn't . . . Can you imagine Father's shame?" Matthew groaned. "I couldn't put him and Mother through that. It would have destroyed his ministry and any chance I had of finishing college. And Will Tawes would have killed me if he thought—"

"If he thought you were the father of her child? And you let him take the blame? Let people think he—"

"Nobody thought Will would be found guilty."

"You stood back and let people accuse him of having sex with Beth?"

"No. They never charged Will with that. They said he beat her—not sexual assault. It wasn't the same thing."

"Wasn't it? Or were you such a coward it was easy to let the lies grow bigger and bigger?" He grabbed Matt, pulled him to his feet, and shook him as hard as the dog was shaking the tissue box. "How was it, then? Explain it to me, you sniveling coward!"

"You don't understand. . . . It was just a party. Joe

and Creed brought hard liquor. Emery was there too. You know I didn't drink. And Grace . . . you know how she was. . . ."

"How was she?"

"She'd been raised without structure . . . as wild as all the Widdowsons."

"She'd do it with anyone."

"No, that's not true."

"And Beth Tawes? Was she like that?"

Matthew shook his head. "She was so sweet . . . so young . . . just fifteen. Will never let her date. I didn't mean—"

Daniel shook him again. "Wake up. I have to know. What happened?"

"It got out of hand. . . . We did things. Grace said it was all right, that Beth was okay with it . . . that she . . . she wanted it. You know how it was. They said things about Grace . . . but they were a lie. Just because her sisters were loose didn't mean . . ." Matt sagged forward and Daniel caught him. "Her stepfather . . . her brother . . . But Grace wasn't like that . . . not her fault."

Daniel dragged his brother to his feet and back down the hall to push him, still in his pajamas, into the claw-footed tub. He turned on the cold water full force, and Matt cried out: "Turn it off! Turn it off! You're killing me."

"I'll kill you, you whining bastard, if you don't tell me what Grace is up to!" Then a terrible thought seized him. "Where does Grace keep her deer rifle?"

Matt sputtered. "Freezing. Let me out!"

"Where's the damn rifle? What caliber is it? Is it a three-oh-eight?"

Matt's teeth began to chatter. He tried to climb out of the tub.

"Where does she keep her gun?"

"Not deer season."

"Where's the damned rifle?"

"She has two, the Winchester and a Ruger ten-twenty-two. Ohh, I think I'm going to be sick—"

Daniel pulled his brother upright and handed him a towel. "The rifle, Matt?"

"Closet. Under the stairs."

Daniel raced down the steps and threw open the closet door. A gun rack with brackets for two weapons stretched across the back wall. Both gun racks were empty, but an open empty Remington .308 ammunition box lay on the floor beside a single .22 cartridge.

CHAPTER TWENTY-ONE

As Bailey and Grace neared Elizabeth's dock in the small, open Boston Whaler, Bailey couldn't imagine what Daniel could have found. She should have been excited, and she was, but she was also afraid that she was going to be seasick and throw up all over Grace's spotlessly clean deck.

The sun was bright, the sky a brilliant azure blue with racing white clouds, but the wind was strong off the bay, the seas rougher than usual, and the water dark. Between the creepy memory of having nearly been killed in a boat the day before and this afternoon's bouncing over the choppy waves, she wasn't certain she ever wanted to set foot in a boat again.

"Whatever Daniel has to show us, it had better be good," Bailey said between yawns. She couldn't imagine why she felt so lethargic. Anticipation and all the caffeine she'd consumed today should have supercharged her, but instead she found herself fighting to keep her eyes open.

Grace nodded vigorously as she pulled back on the throttle and slowed the engine. "He said it would be something you'll remember for the rest of your life." This was the first time Bailey had seen Daniel's sister-in-law in deck shoes, jeans, and a shirt. The tall, big-boned, usually prissy woman not only looked good, but she maneuvered the boat into the slip as easily as parking a car on a city street.

"You make this look so simple."

"It is simple if you've been doing it nearly fifty years, like I have. Never did come natural to Matthew, though. Of course, his mother's people were from the Eastern Shore. Kent County. What can you expect?" Grace chuckled. "You sit tight while I snug us to the post. I don't want to lose you overboard. The current runs pretty fast through this gut."

Something's going to run through my gut if I don't get on solid ground soon, Bailey thought. She'd never been seasick before, but she felt as though she was now.

"Give me your hand," Grace said.

Bailey regarded the ladder nailed against the side of the dock; it seemed to be moving up and down with the waves. "I'm not sure I can step—"

A pair of mallards were flushed from under the structure, startling Bailey as they flew up. She jerked back, nearly losing her balance, but Grace's long fingers gripped hers so tightly that one of Grace's rings cut into Bailey's hand. Grace gave a heave and Bailey found herself standing on the salt-treated walkway.

"Whoo," Bailey said. The muscles in her legs felt weak and wobbly. "I don't know what's come over me. I'm so tired."

"Being on the water does that to some people."

Grace scrambled back into the open boat, picked up a long, thin, fabric case that Bailey hadn't noticed earlier, and brought it up on the wooden planks.

Bailey's eyelids felt heavy as she watched Grace secure both bow and stern to the posts with heavy lines. Someone had cut and nailed sections of old tires, painted white, along the side of the dock to keep the force of the water from damaging vessels by banging them against the frame. Bailey had noticed the cushioning when she'd been here with Daniel, and it seemed a clever idea, especially with a boat as nice as Grace's. "I'm finished here. Come on," Grace said.

What was it Daniel had said? "Nothing on Tawes is as simple as it seems." That was certainly true. Bailey belonged to a gym in Newark and she worked out faithfully twice a week, but she'd never developed the muscle strength and agility that this fifty-something minister's wife seemed to come by naturally.

Grace led the way up the sloping lawn, and Bailey had a hard time keeping pace with her longer stride. Either the slight hill was steeper than it seemed or the ground was slippery, because Bailey felt as though she might make a misstep and fall on her butt if she weren't careful. She kept expecting to see Daniel open the front door or come around the house, but he didn't, so she assumed he must be inside. "Didn't he give you any hinc . . . *hint*"—she corrected herself—"of what he'd found?"

"No." Grace looked back at her and smiled.

The smile made Bailey uneasy. What was wrong with her? She swayed, but Grace caught her by the arm.

"Careful, honey. It's easy to turn an ankle on these old walks. See how some of the bricks are broken and crumbling?" Grace pointed down at the ground where grass sprouted in the cracks of the path. "Best have Daniel rip them all up and lay down new ones."

"I hope I'm not coming down with whatever Matthew has. I don't feel good at all."

"Something's going around," Grace agreed. "That's for certain. You never can tell. People traveling from one place to another by plane. They bring all kinds of germs into the country."

They entered by way of the oversize door to the wide front entrance hall, and Grace paused at the bottom of the steps. "Daniel! We're here!" she called, and then in a lower voice said, "Place certainly does look good. I believe he must have used ammonia on that old light fixture. That crystal hasn't shone so nice in years."

Bailey waited. Daniel didn't answer. Surely, she thought, he must have heard the boat motor. "Daniel!" Her voice came out more of a croak than a shout. She was getting sick. Funny, but her throat wasn't sore. Other than a little nausea, she was just sleepy.

"He must be in the attic," Grace said.

Bailey looked at the stairs. They seemed to go straight up, and all she wanted to do was sit on the bottom step, lean back, and wait for Daniel to bring his "find" to her. "I thought he was finished in the attic. He told me the next thing he had to do was replace a windowsill at the back of the house."

Grace tugged at her arm. "No, that's where he told me he found it. He probably can't hear us. We may as well go up."

Bailey noticed that the older woman still had the green case in her left hand and wondered what it was. The steps seemed terribly steep, taking all the energy she had to ascend them. She used the polished cherry banister for support.

"Daniel!" Grace called again. "Yes, he's up there," she said when she reached the second-floor hall. "I hear him nailing something."

Bailey listened. She didn't hear anything but the ragged sound of her own breathing and their footsteps on the wide maple boards. If anything, the house sounded empty.

"I swear, you city girls are weak as kittens," Grace said. "Wouldn't be if you'd had to work like I did. Up at five, milk two cows before breakfast, walk to school, and then—like as not—hoe weeds out of the corn until supper after walking home."

They walked past bedrooms and a bath in the upper hall. At the end of the passageway were two doors, smaller than the others, opposite each other. On the left, three narrow steps led to a board-and-batten door opening to the attic stairway. Grace pressed the hand-wrought brass thumb latch. "You don't see many of these. Elizabeth told me that one of those antique dealers was always after her to sell it to him. Can you imagine the nerve? Wanting to buy the hardware off your doors?" She motioned to Bailey. "You go on ahead of me."

"No, I think I'd better use the bathroom first. My stomach feels woozy." She glanced back down the hall. "I think I—"

Grace stepped back, unzipped the long case, and pulled out a rifle. "Do as you're told!"

Bailey's mouth gaped. She stared first at the weapon and then up at Grace's face. Her features were almost smooth, almost expressionless. Bailey shivered. "I don't . . . don't understand. . . ."

Grace lowered the muzzle of the rifle until it touched Bailey's midsection. "Up those stairs without another word, Beth Tawes, or I'll put a hole through you from here to Judgment Day."

"What?" Grace's voice seemed distorted. Had Bailey heard what she'd thought she'd heard? Had the pastor's wife called her by her dead mother's name? "What did you call me?"

Grace poked her hard with the barrel of the rifle. "No more backtalk out of you. I'd just as soon shoot you here and now."

"Shoot me? But . . . why?" The torpor that had gripped Bailey melted away. All she could see was the gun and the glint of hate in Grace's eyes.

"All right, Beth, have it your way." Her finger tightened on the trigger.

"No! No! I'm going!" Bailey half ran up the first steps. She stumbled, caught herself, and made her way up the narrow, winding staircase to the shadowy attic. "Daniel!" she cried, darting away and trying to take shelter behind an upright beam. "Daniel? Are you—"

"Shut up! He's not here, you little fool." She motioned toward the west end of the attic. "That way."

"Please . . . I don't understand. Why are you doing—"

Grace squeezed off a shot. The bullet whizzed past Bailey's head and tore through the shingles overhead. Bailey gasped.

"Why? Why?" Grace's voice mocked her. "You should have stayed away. I warned you. Everyone tried to warn you, but you wouldn't listen. Now, whatever happens, you've no one but yourself to blame." She came toward Bailey, the rifle raised so that the muzzle pointed toward the center of her chest.

"It was you." Bailey glanced frantically around for some way of escape. "You're the one who shot at us yesterday."

"A little late to figure that out now, isn't it?"

Step by step Grace backed her toward the last room, the place where Daniel had found her mother's big trunk. Everything seemed to be as it had been the first time Bailey had seen the attic, but the dust and cobwebs were gone. Daniel had swept the floors, polished the small windows at the ends of the house until they gleamed, and arranged the boxes and furniture neatly along the walls.

Sunshine streamed though the hand-blown panes of glass and illuminated the whitewashed walls and the honey-colored floorboards. People didn't die in attics that looked like this, Bailey thought crazily. Not on sunny afternoons. Not in a castle turret that any child with an imagination would love to make a secret playground. In every movie she'd ever seen, monsters lurked in the shadows and stalked their victims amid peals of thunder, downpours, and howling winds.

"Hurry up!" Grace ordered. "I don't have all day."

"Please," Bailey begged. "Why are you doing this? What did I ever do to you?"

"You know perfectly well what you did," Grace said quietly. "You tried to steal my life. My Matthew. You tried to make people believe nasty things about me—about my family—when it was always you."

Bailey nearly tripped over something on the floor. She glanced down and saw that it was *The Pink Fairy Book*. Books, papers, and photos were scattered around the trunk. The domed lid hung open.

"Get inside." Grace didn't shout. She didn't laugh. She might have been telling Bailey to pass her the salt, but the calm request was more frightening than any crazed cackling.

"In the trunk?" Bailey froze. Next to the window stood a can of gasoline. "What are you going to do to me?"

Grace smiled. "I'm going to make certain you don't cause any more trouble, dear. None at all. You're going to suffer a terrible accident."

Bailey shook her head. "I can't do it. I won't."

"You wanted this house so badly. I'll let you have it."

"No."

"I haven't the time for hissy fits. You're going into the trunk dead or alive, miss. It really doesn't matter." Grace smiled thinly. "And I'm going to burn this house down around you."

"You'll have to shoot me first. I won't let you put me in that trunk."

"Fine, have it your way. You always did." Grace glared at her. "Little Miss Perfect."

"I'm Bailey, not Beth. You don't know anything about me or my life."

"I know you well enough that I tried to bury you and that bitch of a mother of yours alive before you were born. Don't you remember? You must have heard her begging for your life."

Bailey raised her hands, palms out, and took several steps back. "Grace, please. You don't want to do this. Not really."

"Oh, but I do. I got the best of her. I smashed her over the head with a shovel and pushed her into one of those caved-in graves out in the old cemetery on Creed's road. There were still pieces of the coffin in the bottom. I didn't see any bones, but I'm sure they were there."

Bailey shook her head. "I don't believe you. You couldn't—"

Grace smiled. "Couldn't I? You should have heard her screams. I had to keep hitting her to make her stop, but she tricked me. She pretended to be unconscious. But when I turned my back on her, she crawled up out of that hole and hit me in the knee with a brick."

Pride surged through Bailey. Beth had fought to protect her.

"I limped for weeks afterward," Grace continued in a monotone. "Your mother was sneaky that way. Stubborn little whore—too stupid to die. She almost broke my—"

Bailey flung herself onto the floor and rolled behind the big camel-back trunk. Grace fired the gun and glass shattered. Bailey seized a book, hurled it at Grace's head, and scrambled to her feet to run.

There was a thud as the heavy volume of fairy tales struck the older woman on the left cheekbone. Grace staggered back, then lunged forward and swung the rifle at Bailey. The barrel struck her in the left shoulder and she nearly fell again, but she kept moving and dodged behind an oversize wing chair. The rifle cracked again. Chair stuffing flew.

Grace rushed forward. Bailey dove, not away, as Grace expected, but straight at her, under the gun. She grabbed Grace around the hips, knocking her to the floor. For seconds they struggled, wrestling, hitting, and kicking before Bailey smashed her balled fist into Grace's face. Grace hit her back just as hard, but Bailey was beyond pain. She caught a handful of hair and slammed Grace's head down against the floor.

Grace groaned. Bailey tried to snatch the rifle away, but Grace lay across it, pinning it down. Bailey turned and fled for the stairwell.

"Run! Run, you little fool! See if you can outrun this!" Grace shouted.

The gun boomed again, but Bailey didn't hesitate. She ran for all she was worth. She was halfway down the attic steps to the second floor when Grace fired from the top landing. This time Bailey felt a sharp sting in her upper left arm. One foot slipped and she fell, sliding down the remaining stairs to the hallway below. Grace pounded after her.

Stunned, Bailey clawed her way to her feet. Pain shot down her spine.

"I put you in the grave twice," Grace said. "This time you'll stay there!" She lowered the rifle again.

Bailey grabbed the barrel, pushed it to the side, and yanked, nearly pulling the weapon out of Grace's hands in the process. She twisted and rammed into Grace's knees, knocking her down again. Grace clung to the rifle, trying to strike her in the head with the stock. It glanced off her injured arm, and Bailey winced at the force of the blow.

Grace used the rifle as a brace to climb to her feet and tried to aim. Bailey wanted to run, but this time the big woman blocked the exit to the main staircase. If she tried to escape into the nearest bedroom, Grace would trap her before she could get a window open. Blood, hot and sticky, ran down Bailey's arm and dripped off her hand in a steady rivulet. Strangely enough, it didn't hurt. It felt numb. But she was suddenly tired again and wanted to sit down.

"Die, you slut!" Grace screamed.

Bailey ducked behind the attic door. Wood exploded, but the shot missed her. She snatched up a broken piece of the board and hurled it at Grace. It struck the woman full in the nose, and blood flew. Bailey whirled, tore open the door to the back servants' stairs, and fled down to the kitchen.

Cursing, Grace came after her. At the bottom of the twisting staircase, Bailey didn't bother with trying to find the latch in the semidarkness. She threw her good shoulder against the door and burst through into the kitchen to see Will running into the room.

"Run!" Bailey screamed. "She has a—"

Will leaped in front of Bailey as Grace came down the stairs and fired. Bailey recoiled in horror. She stared down at a small red stain growing on the front of his shirt.

"Go!" Will bellowed. "Get the hell out of here, Bailey!"

She darted toward the back door. When she looked over her shoulder she saw Grace still advancing toward them, leveling the rife, but Grace had to come through Will to get to her. He was upright, charging Grace, when she fired again. This time Will went down.

"I'll get you, you whoring bitch!" Grace called. "Don't think you can get away from me!"

Will grabbed Grace's ankle and jerked it. "Run!" he shouted.

Bailey flew out the back door and across the porch. The gunshot echoed through the house. Tears blinded Bailey as she bolted headlong toward the nearest outcropping of trees. Will was dead. She knew he was dead, but she kept running. It was all she could do.

"Come back here!" Grace screamed from the back step.

Bailey felt as though she were slogging though knee-deep mud. She was breathing hard, each step an effort, when abruptly the ground came up to hit her. She felt herself sinking down, down; the sleep that had threatened to overtake her finally . . .

* * *

"Get up! You're not dead yet. But you will be if you don't do as I say."

Bailey opened her eyes.

Grace stood over her, the muzzle of the rifle hovering only inches from the bitch's face. "Get on your feet."

She poked the girl hard in the forehead with the gun barrel. "Get up, or die there. I've no more time to mess with you." Just before she'd shot him for the last time, Will had said that Daniel was coming. He might have lied, but she couldn't take the chance. She had to get away as quickly as she could, but not without the girl.

She realized now why it had been so hard to be rid of Beth Tawes, why she hadn't lain quiet in her grave—why she'd haunted her all these years, and why her bastard had come back to spoil everything. It had to end where it started—at the cabin. She jabbed her again. "Get on your feet, and get down to the boat."

Bailey got up on her hands and knees and then climbed to her feet.

"I've got a full clip in here. Ten more shots. Don't make me waste any more than I have to on you." Grace motioned toward the dock. "Go on. We're going for a ride. Not far. Your last one."

Chapter Twenty-two

"Will! Will!" Daniel knelt on Elizabeth's dining room floor and pressed his fingertips against the older man's throat. A trail of blood had led Daniel from the bottom of the kitchen stairs to Will's prone body. He wasn't certain whether Will was dead or alive. He wasn't cold, but if Will was breathing, it was very shallowly.

The bullet holes were from a .22, not the deer gun. Daniel clung to that thought as he kept trying to find a pulse. He'd borrowed an eighteen-foot skiff belonging to Josh Thompson. It was an older boat, not as powerful as Emma's or Grace's, but it had gotten him to Will's, where he'd hoped his friend could advise him where to start looking for Grace and Bailey.

Daniel had been in Will's backyard when he'd heard the shots, and he'd run down the woods path to reach the farmhouse. He arrived in time to hear the sound of Grace's retreating motor, but not to see what direction she'd taken.

As Daniel lifted Will's head, the older man groaned and opened his eyes. "Daniel," he gasped.

"Who shot you?" Daniel asked, although he was certain he knew the answer as surely as he knew that Bailey was already dead or dying.

"Grace." The word came out so softly that it sounded like a death sigh. "Bailey . . . Did you . . ."

"Were they together? Is Bailey hurt?"

"Alive when Grace . . . shot . . . me. She's not . . . outside?"

"No. I heard Grace's Whaler, but got here too late to see who was in the boat."

"Send out . . . alarm," Will managed. Blood seeped from a hole in his chest, another from his shoulder, and a third from his midsection. "No time . . . Ring the bell. Watermen . . ." He grasped Daniel's hand with surprising strength. "Save Bailey for . . . me." Will choked and spit blood. "Save her . . . Daniel. Grace means to . . . to kill her."

Daniel pressed the palm of his hand against Will's chest in an effort to stop the bleeding, but Will shoved him away. "To hell with me. No time. Bailey. She's all I've got. . . ." His eyes rolled back in his head and he went limp.

Daniel shook him. "Will! Where would Grace take her?"

Will's breath rasped in and out, but he didn't open his eyes. Daniel took precious minutes to call the coast guard, gave his location, identified himself as retired agency personnel, and told them that Will needed immediate medical assistance for multiple gunshot wounds. He asked the dispatcher to notify the state police about Bailey's kidnapping, gave them a description of his sister-in-law, and told them that she was armed and dangerous.

When Daniel could turn his full attention to Will

again, he realized that he was still bleeding badly. Daniel looked around the room, ripped down a pair of white tieback curtains, folded half into a pad, and tied the other half to bandage the worst of Will's injuries.

Images of the carnage the bomb had wrought in the coffeehouse in Kabul flooded Daniel's mind and he pushed them back. If Bailey was still alive, there was hope he could get to her in time. And if Grace had blackmailed Joe Marshall—if she, rather than Lucas, had shot at them yesterday—then this was a different game altogether.

"Grace . . ." Will tossed his head and whispered urgently, "Grace told me . . . said . . . she killed . . . Beth. And Emma." His artist's fingers dug into Daniel's wrist. "Grace. It was always Grace."

"I know. I just came from Matt's. Grace has been blackmailing Marshall, and she may have murdered him too. But why?" Blood seeped through the pad, and Daniel tightened the makeshift bandage. "Don't die on me. Help's on the way."

"Go. Find Bailey. Emma's dead. You've got to stop . . ." He clutched at Daniel's wrist. "Ring the bell."

Daniel smelled smoke. Rising, he walked to the nearest window and saw that Elizabeth's boat and dock were in flames. Grace must have set them afire to keep anyone from following her. He returned to kneel beside Will. "I've got to go back and get your boat—it's the fastest—but help will be here soon."

"My pocket. Key. To the skiff." He drew in a long, rasping breath. "Never mind me. I've had my run. Find Bailey."

"A medevac helicopter is on the way. I hate to leave you, but—"

"Get the hell . . . out of . . . here. Wait. Get me Elizabeth's ship-to-shore radio. Under stairs. I can send . . . send out . . . distress call. Watermen."

Daniel ran to the closet and ripped open the door. Elizabeth's radio had been smashed. "Grace must have destroyed it. You hang on, Will." Daniel squeezed his friend's hand a last time. "Hang on until help arrives."

"The bell," Will insisted. "Don't . . . forget . . . bell."

Outside, Daniel paused long enough to pull the rope a dozen times. The two-hundred-year-old bronze bell rang out a distress signal, sending the wordless message across the island that there was dire trouble at Elizabeth's farm. Even in the sparsely populated countryside, the chances were that the sound of the great bell would alert neighbors. Daniel only hoped medical help would arrive in time to keep Will from bleeding to death.

Before the tolling of the bell had ceased to echo across the water and fields, Daniel was off and running back down the lane to Will's landing. He was halfway through the woods when he heard Will's dogs barking.

Gasping for breath, Daniel stopped and cut through the thick underbrush, cautiously coming out of the trees at a point just south of the house. To his surprise he saw someone on Will's skiff, bent over the ignition. Pulling the pistol from his belt, Daniel leaned low and approached the dock, taking advantage of whatever cover he could find until he recognized the crouching figure in the boat.

"Emma? Is that you?" Daniel exclaimed. "Will told me you were dead!"

She turned toward him. Her clothing was torn and bloodstained, her face a haggard mask. "Daniel?"

"Down! Down! Go on! Get back!" Daniel shouted at the dogs as he hurried toward the boat. "What the hell happened to you?"

Emma gasped and leaned against the gunnel. "I am dead," she said. "Gut-shot. Yesterday . . . last night. I thought it was Will come to finish me off," she managed as Daniel climbed into the boat. "But it was Grace. She shot me and set my boat adrift." She pointed toward the bay. "Out there. The shot knocked me into the water. I tried to get back . . . to the boat, but the tide caught it. I found a crab line float to hold on to and swam to shore."

"Grace has Bailey."

"Where's Will?" Emma sank down onto a seat and leaned against the headrest.

"Back at Elizabeth's. Grace shot him as well."

"What did he tell you? About what happened to Beth?"

"I guess that's what this is all about somehow. Will's hurt bad. He may already be dead."

Emma clutched at Daniel's shoulder. "Then you need to know that it was Grace who . . . who testified against Will . . . convinced the jury he was guilty. In the trial thirty-five years ago. She went to court and said that Beth was afraid of her uncle. Hinted that he fathered her child." Emma shook her head. Her damp hair hung in tangles, and she was shaking with cold or fever. "Grace's fault. Her part of it was all hushed up, hidden from the news, because of her age."

"Don't try to talk. The coast guard helicopter is already in the air. They'll get you and Will to the hospital and—"

"I don't need a damned doctor. I'm dying, Daniel. I told you—I took a bullet in the gut. I need you to listen . . . to listen good. There's nobody left but you—to set things right. To tell Bailey the truth. Beth came to a party with your brother, and she had too much to drink."

"Did she and Matthew have sex?"

Emma shrugged. "I don't know. If I was to be hanged, I couldn't say one way or another. Matt was pretty wasted, and they were in the cabin alone together." She gritted her teeth as pain etched grooves across her brows. "But afterward Joe and Creed took turns with her. Beth said no, but they did it anyway. I heard her crying."

"Why now, Emma? Why didn't you say something then? Why after all these years?"

She gripped her stomach. "I was tired of dreaming about it every night. Tired of hearing Will standing outside my window whistling."

"You heard it, knew it was Will."

"You heard it too, had to."

"I thought it might be him. I'd heard him whistling when I was a kid."

"He used to whistle like that for Beth, when she was little. It was a game between them. She always liked it. I hadn't heard it for years, not until after Bailey came to Tawes."

"Then it was his way of letting you know he was there, watching over Beth's girl."

"Me and anybody else who might want to hurt her?"

Daniel nodded. "Maybe, or maybe he thought Bailey's coming would make you crack, tell what he was certain you knew about what happened to Beth."

"It worked. I was scared he'd come to kill me. Or maybe I was just sick of waking up every morning and staring into the face of a coward."

"And you told Will that?"

"Some of it. He didn't kill me, but he came close. Beat the shit out of me and went for his gun."

"And you? Did you rape her too?"

Emma shook her head. "No. I didn't. I swear to you, I didn't. But I didn't have the balls to put a stop to it either. Joe and Creed were both older and bigger than me. Joe always had a mean streak in him. And Creed . . . Creed did just about anything Joe told him to do."

"And you just watched?"

"I told them to stop. They dared me to do something about it. I didn't. But I should've tried." Emma shook her head. "Afterward, Joe threatened to kill me if I told. God help me, I believed him."

"What about Matt? Beth was his responsibility. Why didn't he protect her?"

"He would have been just as scared of Joe and Creed as me. But by then he'd passed out dead drunk on the floor. I don't how much he knew about what they did. He never moved until morning."

Anger made it hard for Daniel to fit the key in the boat ignition. He and Matt had been too far apart in age and too different to be close when they were growing up. All these years, he'd considered his brother to be weak, but he'd never guessed Matt could stand back and let Will pay such a price for that weakness. "Stupid bastard," he muttered as he fired up the engine and pulled away from the dock.

He glanced at Emma. It was evident that the movement of the boat put her in agony, and in spite of himself he felt sorry for her. "Can you walk?" He couldn't look her in the face. Didn't want to. In a way, what Emma had done was every bit as bad as his brother's actions.

"Grace egged them on," Emma continued as if she hadn't heard him. "Thought it was funny. Lied about Beth. Told Joe that Beth done it with her uncle and with Forest McCready. But it wasn't true. Not about Will. Not about Forest. I saw blood on Beth's legs and on her clothes. She'd been a virgin until that night, Daniel. We killed her. Killed her as surely as if we'd put a gun to her head."

"Can you walk?" Daniel repeated.

"I made it this far, didn't I?" Emma rocked back and forth, holding her belly. "Burns like fire. Like crabs tearing at my gut."

"Let me see." Daniel pushed aside the ripped tee shirt that Emma had wrapped around her middle. "It's bad, but if you didn't die yet, you may survive. You should be in a hospital."

"Too late for doctors and hospitals. More important that Bailey know the truth. I think now that Grace might have been the one who beat Beth. She always wanted Matt, and she got him, didn't she? Once Beth was dead."

Daniel pushed the throttle forward, heading toward Elizabeth's dock again. Where the hell was that helicopter with the medics?

"I'm leaving you at the farm. If you can walk, you get up to the house. Do what you can for Will. Keep him awake. Keep him talking. And when help arrives, they can—"

Emma laughed. "Dead or alive, he'll strangle me with his bare hands."

Daniel shrugged. "So what have you got to lose?"

"True enough, boy."

He slowed the engine as he neared Elizabeth's beach. What was left of the dock poured black smoke and flames. "You'll have to jump out and wade ashore. Can you do it?"

"Didn't you hear what I said? I swam half the night to get back. I guess I can get twenty yards to shore if I have to do it on my hands and knees." Emma's voice cracked. "Matthew? Grace didn't . . ."

"Back at the house," Daniel answered. "Put something in his coffee. He's sick as a dog, but nothing he won't recover from."

"Probably those sleeping pills she takes." Emma took hold of the gunnel, pulled herself to her feet, and swung one leg over the side.

He put the engine into neutral. "Think, Emma. Where would Grace go?"

"Only one spot." She gave him a long, hard look. Her lips were cracked, her eyes bloodshot and red. "Black Oak Island. That old cabin. You know it?"

"Will used to take me duck hunting there."

"You go and get that girl. She's worth risking your life over. But you take care. Grace will kill you as quick as she did me. She's a crack shot with that .22. But I'd bet my mother's soul she'll be at that old cabin. It's where it all happened. And God damn me to a fiery hell, where my life should have ended a long time ago." With a groan, she eased over the side and splashed into the bay.

"You're no deader than I am, you mean son of a bitch," Emma said minutes later as she slipped a pillow under Will's head. "Just trying to heap more worry on that boy's head."

Will swore. "Shut up and get away from me, you damned hermaphrodite."

"No wonder nobody goes near you. You're nasty as a

constipated polecat. Can you drink water if I bring you some?"

"Are you deaf? Get out of this house. I'd die of thirst before I'd take a drop from your hands."

"That's what . . . what I figured you'd say." Emma dragged a tablecloth over Will. He was cold, too cold, and he'd lost more blood than Emma thought a man could lose and still draw breath. "But if you're bound on dying, you may as well listen to the rest of what I wanted to tell you yesterday."

Will raised his hand to strike at her, but he was too weak to move it more than a few inches. "Damn Grace always was a good shot."

"Shut up and listen to me."

"Find me a gun. Better yet, a butcher knife, so I can finish you off, you swivin' freak."

"Say what you want. No worse than I've said to myself all these years. But chances are, we'll both end up on the same rock in hell, so you may as well listen to what I've got to say."

"I'm dying. Have a little respect," Will rasped.

"Maybe you are . . . and maybe . . . you're not. Maybe you're too danged mean to die."

Emma staggered to the kitchen and returned with a cup of water. She eased onto the floor beside Will and lifted his head. "Try to drink some of this." She brought the mug to his lips with trembling hands. "It might keep you alive until the cavalry gets here."

Will knocked the cup away. "You think I'd take water from a man who raped my—"

"I never did, Will. I watched it." Tears rolled down her cheeks. "That's my sin. I watched Joe and Creed take turns with her . . . but I never laid a hand on her."

"Liar. Grace should have used the three-oh-eight on you."

"Probably so," Emma agreed. The pain in her belly was a constant grinding, but she'd come to terms with it. "But maybe the Lord had a hand in it. Or maybe she was too smart. Could be she killed Joe Marshall with that gun and throwed it in the bay to hide her tracks."

Will coughed up more blood. "You better hope I don't . . . live long enough to get to the hospital. If I can . . ." He swore softly. "If I live . . . long enough to get to the hospital, I'll get hold of a scalpel and skin you alive." Will closed his eyes and for a minute, Emma thought he'd quit breathing altogether, but then he opened his eyes again.

"Like I told you . . . we were all drinking."

"Liar. My Beth never—"

"She was human, Will. She drank. I saw her drink. . . . She wasn't used to it. It went to her head."

"A scalpel's too good for you." He groaned. "I'll cut your black heart out with a rusty spoon."

"Not if I die first." Emma laid her own head on the rug and curled into a fetal position as the pincers gnawed at her innards. "Maybe your girl and Matthew got up to mischief they shouldn't have that day. But she was only fifteen, and he wasn't much older. They were just kids, and kids do stupid things. As Mama always says, 'The little lambs will play.'"

"I don't want to hear . . . it."

"You're gonna hear it, Will Tawes. Beth was a Tawes, wasn't she? And God knows you sowed enough wild oats in your day."

"Go ahead, torture . . . a dying man. Add that to . . . your sins."

Emma was sorry Will had spilled the water. She wanted some badly, but the kitchen sink seemed a long way off, and she was tired, so tired. It was hard to string words together to make sense. "Matt cared about her. He never meant for anything bad to happen. Afterward . . . he was just scared. As scared as the rest of us. As scared as Beth must have been when she figured out that she had a baby growing in her and didn't know who the father was."

"Why didn't she come to me? Why didn't she trust me enough to tell me what—"

"I don't know. Maybe she was too ashamed of what she'd done. Maybe she thought you'd stop loving her if you knew."

"I never would have," Will sobbed. "I would have stood by her."

"I didn't know about the baby. I swear I didn't," Emma said. Her voice was nothing more than dried husks rattling in an empty corncrib. "I would have married her myself. Maybe I'm more woman than man, but I would have done that much for her. I would have given her my name."

"I loved her, Emma. More than anything in the world. I loved that child, and I couldn't save her. If I'd told her how much she meant to me—if I'd told her what she was to me, maybe—"

"Maybe it was her time, Will. The Good Book says we all have a time. Maybe it was meant to be. But it wasn't for nothing, was it?"

"How so?"

"Bailey. She left you Bailey. . . . And if you quit fighting so hard to die and quit hating so much . . . maybe you've got another chance to be for Bailey the man you couldn't be for Beth."

311

"You think that, or you . . . humoring a dying man . . . trying to save your own worthless skin?"

"Maybe both . . . Will. Maybe . . ." A whirring sound filled Emma's head. Birds? Angels? No angels for her. Helicopter. Maybe one of them would live to see a hospital. The noise grew louder.

Emma began to cough, and suddenly it was hard to stop. Blood was choking her nose and her throat. Vaguely she heard shouting and the pounding of boots. She tried to cry out . . . to tell them Will needed help . . . but she'd talked herself out. It was easier just to close her eyes and drift . . . just drift . . . and forget all about what she'd seen that afternoon . . . what she hadn't tried hard enough to end . . . the day she'd stopped calling herself a man.

Chapter Twenty-three

Daniel circled Black Oak Island in the skiff to approach from the south. The area was a maze of intersecting marsh and waterways, native reeds and phragmites, patches of woods, at least one freshwater pond, and two high, sandy areas where little would grow. There were also deceiving grassy flats that appeared firm enough to support a man's weight but wouldn't. The actual landmass was no more than a mile long by a half mile wide, although it had been a lot bigger when he was a kid.

Year by year the Chesapeake was nibbling at the islands. Like as not, Tawes, Deal, and Smith—the fields and forests, farms, and villages—would all vanish under the bay in a few centuries. But if Black Oak had ever been inhabited, other than by the foolish trapper who'd built the solitary cabin of virtually indestructible cypress timbers a century ago and died of swamp fever the same year, it had been by Indians, long before the first Englishman set foot on these shores.

Despite the hordes of mosquitoes and blackflies,

Black Oak was a hunter's paradise, so overrun by deer, foxes, otter, and smaller mammals that they were stunted in size. Waterfowl of every description flocked here, finding shelter from the winter winds and food enough to sustain them in every season. Any hunters tough enough to survive the environment and canny enough to find their way around the island without drowning or being sucked down by the bottomless muck were assured of all the game they could shoot.

The old cabin didn't stand on the bay; it was inland on a hillock above a creek barely wide enough to get Will's skiff up in low tide. Now the mud flats and sandbars were exposed, but the tide had already turned and was fast rising. If Grace was hiding here, there were a half dozen inlets where she could have hidden her small Boston Whaler and crossed to the cabin through the marsh. If she knew Black Oak as well as Will Tawes, she'd be hell for the authorities to find, let alone catch. And Daniel knew his sister-in-law could kill him and Bailey before he even caught sight of her.

If Grace had taken Bailey anywhere but Black Oak, he'd lost her. Daniel was betting everything that Emma's guess was right. But he had no intention of motoring up that narrow waterway to be shot from the cabin or the trees that surrounded it. Will had taught him far more than the agency ever had about moving stealthily in marsh and woodland, and he had the feeling he'd need every ounce of what he'd soaked up.

When Will had shown him the finer points of stalking game and hunting waterfowl, the old islander had never paid much attention to state game rules and regulations. Like other traditionalists who fed their families from the land and bay, they hunted and fished when they were hungry, and they had no intention of being stopped by game wardens or code enforcers.

Daniel cut the engine and dropped anchor near what appeared to be a collection of driftwood and tangled reeds. He wanted Will's skiff to be in plain view of any police helicopter that flew over. Using his satellite cell, he took the time to make a quick call to his cousin Jim Tilghman aboard the state conservation boat *Sweetwater*.

"Daniel! Where are you? The word's out. A full-scale search is on for Grace and the Boston Whaler."

"Could you send out some messages to watermen for me?" Daniel dug in a compartment for the waterproof bags he knew Will carried to protect his cameras and sketchbooks, and double-bagged his pistol and all the ammunition he had. Then he reached for the camouflage Will always kept in the skiff.

"Just told you, every boat is already hunting her. If she's on this bay someone will see her. We're headed your way ourselves, but we're on the far side of Deal."

"Do you know anything about Will and Emma?"

"They're on their way to shock trauma at Johns Hopkins. A copter picked them up a few minutes ago. Both alive, but rocky, from what I gather. Will's in a lot worse shape than Emma. I spoke to one of the dispatchers, Ernie Thompson, Cathy's cousin. He said Will's lost a lot of blood. Maybe more than a man his age can stand."

"I'm on Black Oak."

"Emma told the EMTs that's where you were going. I wouldn't be surprised if you had company real soon. Maybe you'd better wait for backup. Grace could be heavily armed."

"I can't wait, Jim. If anything happens—"

"I don't want to hear talk like that."

"I'm serious, Jim. Anything happens to me, my place and whatever's left goes into the wildlife preservation fund to protect Tawes from development."

"Be careful, cuz."

"Just pass on the news that I'm here. I don't want some trigger-happy vigilante mistaking me for Grace. I'll be the one in camouflage."

"Keep your head low. If anything happens to you, Cathy will find some way of putting the blame on me."

"Somebody's got to take the blame," he answered. "Got to go. And you remind those mainland lawmen that the women on Tawes usually hit what they shoot at."

"I'll do that."

Daniel pushed the disconnect button and set the phone to vibrate. No one except the agency had his number, but he didn't want any surprises. Quickly he removed a bottle of insect spray, stripped to his shorts, and rubbed it over every inch of his skin. He smeared black and green stain over his face and body, and lastly, strapped on his belt, waterproof holster, and sheath knife.

He slipped into the water and swam the twenty yards to the pile of debris. Underneath, just as he'd expected, he found Will's cypress dugout and a paddle. There was an old-fashioned sneak boat hidden in the reeds the next creek over, but it was slower and heavier, made to carry two men and their dogs. What he needed today was something that could float in six inches of water and move through the reeds as quietly as an otter.

Aided by the incoming tide, Daniel pushed his way into a narrow passage and began to paddle. In two minutes he lost of sight of Will's skiff, and in another three the phragmites closed in over his head, making him so much a natural part of the marsh that the three black ducks flying overhead took no notice of him at all.

Bailey didn't bother to struggle as Grace bound her wrists together and tied them to the post. She'd been bleeding on and off since Grace had shot her in the attic back at the farmhouse, and she knew she had to preserve whatever strength she had left for a fight she could win. She'd lost one shoe somewhere, and she'd already sunk almost to her knees once in the gooey mud.

Grace had tried to force pills into her mouth, but Bailey had spit them back out into the bay. "Suit yourself, Beth," Grace had said. "I was only trying to spare you the distress of your final minutes."

"Why?" Bailey had asked her for tenth time . . . or maybe the twentieth. "What did I ever do to you? What did my mother ever do to you that you hated her so?"

Grace gave the knot a solid tug and backed away. The black water came up to her waist and tugged at her clothing, but she didn't seem to notice. "How many times do I have to tell you?" she replied patiently. "You tried to steal everything that was mine. You took my life and tried to make it your own. People called me the town whore, when it should have been the other way around. I was the good girl. I was the one who could be the wife and helpmate Matthew needed, not you. You would have dragged him down to your own level."

"I'm not who you think I am," Bailey said, trying not to think of how fast the water seemed to be rising around the rotting dock. "I'm not Beth. She's dead and buried. She can't hurt you. You have Matthew."

Grace waded back toward the muddy shore and up

onto the sand. Behind her the door to a square log structure stood open. The rifle Grace had used to shoot both her and Will leaned against the door frame. "You should have died in that cemetery, both of you," Grace said. "I don't like this. I don't enjoy seeing people in pain. I'm not a monster, but I won't stand by and see what's mine be stolen." She slipped her bare feet into her Nikes and tied them.

Insects buzzed around Bailey's head. Something bit her in the center of the forehead. "I don't understand," Bailey said. "I don't hate you. I don't even know you, but I think you have a real faith in God. Is this what He would want you to do?"

"God helps those who help themselves," Grace intoned. "They thought I was ignorant, too stupid to do anything but work in a crab-picking plant or wait tables in a bar. But I showed them, and I showed Joe Marshall. I picked him as clean as a steamed blue claw at a Sunday picnic."

Something buzzed around Bailey's right ear. She fought panic and the weariness that made her want to give up. There had to be a way to reach Grace, to convince her that she didn't really want to do this. "If you'll let me go, I'll leave Tawes for good," she lied. "I'll never tell a soul what happened."

Grace laughed. "I guess you won't, at the rate the tide is coming in. You should have gotten in that trunk when I told you to, girl. If you're so religious, you'd already be knocking at those pearly gates. The smoke would have killed you long before the flames reached you. It would have been painless."

"Would it?"

"So I've read. I don't know for sure. But drowning probably isn't much worse. They say you should just breathe in the water. Don't fight it. Just let it fill your lungs. You'll go fast."

Bailey tried to free her ankles, but Grace had bound them just as tightly as her hands and tied them to the slimy post. It was only a few yards from what was left of this part of the dock and the muddy shoreline, but it might as well have been a mile for all the chance she had of reaching it. There was no way she could free herself before she drowned in the rising tide. She thought she should pray, ask forgiveness for her sins, but she couldn't remember anything she'd ever done to merit this end. And when she closed her eyes, it was Daniel's face she saw, Daniel's smile, and the twinkle in his eyes.

"Don't do that," Grace warned. "Stay awake. You'll sleep soon enough."

"You won't get away with this. People will find out. They'll know the truth. Matthew will know."

"He loves me. He always has. Even when you spread your legs for him . . . when you took in his seed that should have been mine, he didn't love you." Grace pointed back toward the cabin. "That's where it happened, where you seduced them. You remember, don't you? Where you played the whore for my Matthew, for Creed, and for Joe? Did you enjoy it? Having them all, one after another? Did it make you feel better than me?"

"It wasn't me, Grace. I wasn't even born then."

"But you were," she shouted. "You were conceived there, on that bed of sin. It wasn't supposed to be like that. You were supposed to be with Joe that day, not my Matthew. And you weren't supposed to quicken with his child. *She* wasn't," Grace corrected herself. "Beth wasn't. You're trying to trick me."

"I'm not. You're not well. You need help."

"Do I?" Grace smiled. "It doesn't look from here as though I'm the one who needs help. The water will be up to your breasts soon, and then your chin. And you know what happens after that."

Bailey swallowed her fear and sucked in a great gulp of air. There wasn't going to be a fairy-tale ending for her. She would die here, and it would be weeks, maybe months or years, before anyone found her. Would *things* eat her body? Crabs? Fish? Would just her bones remain here, tied to this damned post until the ropes rotted away? Suddenly anger filled her, pushing back the terror.

"Is Matthew my father, Grace? Is that why you hate me? Because Beth gave him a child when you couldn't?"

Grace picked up the rifle. "Don't say his name. I warn you, girl. You let his name come out of your filthy mouth again and I'll put a bullet between your eyes."

Bailey believed her, but there was no longer any need for caution. If she couldn't reason with the psychopath, maybe she could at least get answers. And what if she did die with a bullet through her head? Right now that seemed more appealing than slowly drowning. "You killed my aunt Elizabeth, didn't you? Why? What did she do to you?"

"She paid Forest McCready to find you. She wanted you to come back. She wanted to stir Will Tawes up again, to start up all the questions . . . the gossip. I tried to reason with her, remind her that you were a bastard nobody wanted. You had no business on our island, but she wouldn't listen."

"And so you killed her?" The water was colder than Bailey had expected. Something brushed against her ankle, and she flinched. A turtle? A snake? She shuddered and glanced down at the water. It was too muddy to see more than a few inches down. Were there poison snakes in the Chesapeake? She couldn't remember.

"I warned Elizabeth to let the past lie, just like I warned you. But no one can tell a Tawes anything. They think they're so smart, smarter than the Widdowsons, smarter than anyone. Well, you see who the smart one is now, don't you?" Grace used the corner of her shirt to wipe down the barrel of her rifle. "I should have thought to bring something to drink. There's a spring here somewhere, but it's probably polluted. It didn't used to be. We all drank from it that day, even Emery, and he was always afraid of his own shadow."

"Did he . . . was he with my mother too?" Bailey swallowed. *Say no*, she willed Grace. *For the love of God, say no. Leave me that much to hang on to.*

"That pansy? He couldn't get it up. Puked his guts out after a few swigs of moonshine. He always was odd, if you catch my meaning. A freak of nature. Not a man, not a woman. As far as anyone knows, he's never had a partner, male or female. It's not natural, if you ask me. God made two kinds of people, men and women. I don't know who made Emma."

A small ribbon of happiness curled in the pit of Bailey's belly. She was shivering now. Cold, despite the heat of the sun on her face. The water had risen to wash against her nipples. Flies bit her neck and face; swarms of mosquitoes threatened to invade her mouth, even her eyes; and she shook her head to keep them away.

"None of it was true about Uncle Will, was it, Grace?"

"It was true enough!" Grace flung back. "He used to

come into my room at night after my mother was asleep. I pretended I didn't know he was there when he touched me, when he put his hands between my legs, when he pushed his filthy fingers into my—"

"Stop!" Bailey cried. "Don't say that."

"I was little, too little to stop him. I tried to tell my mother, but she didn't believe me. She whipped me for telling lies. He didn't stop. It got worse until it wasn't his fingers, but his thing. The first time he rammed it into my mouth I wanted to choke, to bite it, but he said if I did he'd smother me with a pillow. He would have, too. Arney was mean. He beat my puppy to death with a bat because it peed on the rug. And he beat my mother all the time."

"Arney? Arney did?"

"My stepfather. At least, that was what he called himself. I don't think they ever got married. People said he had a wife on Chincoteague and they never divorced."

"You were a little girl. It wasn't your fault. There wasn't anything you could do."

"By the time I was ten he was doing it all. My stepbrother too. And what could I do? Once I tried to tell Matthew's mother. She was the minister's wife. She should have helped me, but she went to Ma, and Ma beat me worse than Arney for spreading filth about him. 'Keep what's in the family in the family'; that's what she said. 'Don't hang your dirty laundry out for everybody to see.'"

"But you got the best of them," Bailey said. "And even of Joe, a senator. You showed him."

"You got that right, girl. I showed him. I made him pay. Pay for what he did to me, pay to keep his dirty little secret. He wanted to be vice president, did you know that? Joe Marshall from Tawes, a storekeeper's son and a bully. No better than he should have been. But he paid for years, and he never knew which one of us he was paying to keep quiet."

"He didn't want anybody to know what he had done to my mother?"

"I told him that you were *his* bastard daughter. How would that have looked? Senator sleeps with town whore and produces a little by-blow that has to be given away like an unwanted kitten? Oh, he paid, gladly. And he could afford it. I wasn't greedy. I never took more than my rightful share. No more than was my due."

Water lapped against Bailey's throat, and she clenched her teeth to keep from crying out. She wouldn't give this madwoman that much. If she had to die, she'd do it with as much dignity as she could. She strained to raise her head. "It's not too late to stop this," she said. "Matthew loves you. He'll forgive you anything. He'll get you help, and he'll be there for you."

"Shut up!"

"But I might not be Matthew's child. I could be Creed—"

"What did I tell you?" Grace raised the rifle to her shoulder and took aim.

Bailey gasped as a night heron burst up out of the reeds to the left of the cabin in a flurry of wings, outstretched neck, and long legs. Grace whirled toward the spot where the bird had waded only seconds before. She squeezed off six shots, spraying the area with bullets before diving through the open cabin door.

Daniel cried out in pain and surprise as the bullets tore through him. One knee crumpled, but he forced himself to fire back, getting off two rounds before Grace vanished inside the solid wooden fortress and pulled the heavy door shut behind her.

Seconds later the tip of a rifle barrel appeared over the windowsill. "Are you still alive, Will Tawes? Because if you are, I have a surprise for you," Grace shouted. "You get to watch while the slut drowns. Unless you want to come out like a man and let me finish you off first!"

CHAPTER TWENTY-FOUR

Grace's rifle cracked two more times. Slowly circles of muddy water tinged with red spread wider and wider before being lost in the steadily rising tide. There was absolute silence from the cabin and the marsh, other than the annoying hum of insects and the rustle of a salt breeze through the interlaced phragmites.

Bailey's heart plummeted. She'd never wanted to harm another living soul, but she wanted to get her hands on Grace Catlin's throat and choke the life out of her. Bailey wanted to murder the demented sociopath who'd destroyed the lives of so many people to satisfy her own needs. She wanted to stake Grace to the muddy beach and let the mosquitoes, blackflies, and hermit crabs eat her alive, bite by bite, inflicting the most agony possible before they devoured her.

Every primal instinct Bailey possessed urged her to scream, but common sense told her that attempting to communicate with her would-be rescuer would lessen his chances of remaining alive—if he was still alive.

Just the thought that she wasn't alone anymore gave

her hope. And she knew her invisible ally couldn't be Will. He'd been badly wounded back at the house. Only one man could have come to rescue her—Daniel. She knew it was Daniel as surely as she knew he was still alive. He might be badly injured, but he wasn't dead. She could feel his presence, almost hear him whispering her name, telling her to hang on a few minutes longer until he could find a way to get through Grace's rain of bullets.

Bailey couldn't imagine how Daniel had known where to look for her, or how he'd found her in this morass of swamp and black water, but she would have bet her immortal soul that the person who'd fired off those shots at Grace was Daniel. She gritted her teeth to keep from calling to him, but nothing could keep her hands from going numb or the tears from streaming down her cheeks.

She yanked frantically at the rope binding her wrists together, but the water seemed to have welded the knots. The tide was still coming in, as Grace had told her it would. She could see the water creeping up the mud banks inch by inch, smell the subtle change in the humid air around her as stagnant pools filled with the incoming flow.

Minutes passed, and the restless waves lapped at the underside of Bailey's chin. She prayed with every fiber of her being for her own safety, and even more for Daniel's. A hundred questions tumbled through her fear and uncertainty, but nothing could dim her joy that he cared enough to risk his life for hers.

She had to do something. Will Tawes would have thought of something heroic. She couldn't imagine her aunt Elizabeth hanging helplessly on this damned post like a worm on a hook and drowning while Grace got off scot-free and maybe killed Daniel in the bargain. If she couldn't communicate with him, maybe she could distract Grace and give him a better chance to do whatever he was attempting.

Bailey opened her mouth to shout and was rewarded with a mouthful of muddy water. She choked, spit it out, and inched her way higher on the post with her bare foot, raising herself up out of the mud. She arched her neck back to keep her face as high as possible.

"Grace? Are you all right?" Bailey managed.

"I'm fine, you stupid slut. You're the one who needs help. Remember? Another five minutes and you'll be inhaling water. It's probably polluted, but that won't matter to you. What is the expression? Oh, yes, Cathy Tilghman's fond of it: 'That's a moot point.' Cathy loves to show off her education in front of the ignorant locals in our Ruth Circle. Fancies herself somewhat of an expert on the Bible."

"What will you tell—" Bailey caught herself before saying Matthew's name. "How will you explain this to him? We left the house together, and only you come back? He's bound to be suspicious."

Silence.

"Grace!"

"Shut up and drown, bitch!"

A green-headed insect the size of a horsefly flitted around Bailey's temple, lit on her cheekbone, and bit her fiercely. The sting brought tears of pain, and she felt a thin trickle of blood. She lowered her face into the water, trying to rid herself of her tormentor.

"What will he think?" she shouted when she came up again. "He doesn't know what you've done, does he? He loves you. He's always loved you. He's always seen the good in you that no one else has—"

Grace laughed. "Don't even try it. I know a little bit about psychology, college girl. My Matthew is a simple man, a good man, but easy to manipulate. Like all the rest, he sees the world in black and white. And all women know that it's really gray. It's all gray."

A hand clasped Bailey's ankle, and she bit her tongue to keep from screaming in panic. Scenes from every horror movie she'd ever watched flashed before her eyes. She opened her mouth, but then clamped it shut. She could have sworn her heart stopped before she realized that crabs didn't have hands. If there was someone under the water, it wasn't one of the walking dead or the Creature from the Black Lagoon. It could only be Daniel, come to free her from this waking nightmare.

She summoned her nerve and tried again. "What will he do when he gets up and finds you gone, Grace? How will he manage without you?"

Silence.

"Grace!" Now water was threatening Bailey's every breath when she attempted to speak, but the hand tugged at her calf and she felt what might have been a rope loosening on one ankle. She twisted, trying to take breaths between the tiny surges of incoming tide, waves too small and sluggish to be waves. She didn't look down. She kept her eyes on the cabin window, on the sunlight glinting off the barrel of Grace's rifle.

There was another loud crack, and a bullet pierced the surface of the water just to her left. Bailey's heart leaped, and she couldn't keep from gasping.

"Just wanted to remind you that I could put an end to it all quickly, if you'd like," Grace shouted. "To be merciful. As I said before, I'm not a monster."

Bailey strained against the ropes, pulling until she

felt as though she'd yank her arms from her sockets. "What do you want from me?" Her eye was beginning to swell just above the place where the giant fly had bitten her. The bump burned like a wasp sting, but one ankle came free, and joy surged in her chest.

A whisper rose from behind her. "Bailey, listen to me. Do exactly as I say."

She moaned, a sound she hoped would tell him that she'd heard—that she would do whatever he asked.

"How good an actress are you? You've got to pretend you're drowning. Take hold of the rope, under the water, where it's tied to the post. Can you do that?"

She coughed. She didn't have to act. The loss of blood from where Grace had shot her and the dull pain from the wound had sapped every ounce of strength from her body. Another minute and the water would be over her nose.

"Struggle. Turn to the right as far as you can and pretend to faint. Let your head fall forward into the water."

She coughed again.

"I'm going to cut the rope, and then I'll give you something to breathe through. Just like a straw. Can you do that?"

She groaned.

"Do just as I say, but when I start shooting, dive as deep as you can, and swim to the left and away from the cabin. The water's deepest there near the far bank. Stay under until you reach the reeds. Do you understand?" he murmured.

She let her head drop, just a little, just far enough that her nose and her mouth went under, but she could still hear. He was directly behind her, so that her body blocked Grace's view of him.

"Don't try to find your way out of here. Find a deep

spot in the marsh and hide. Don't make a sound until you hear me calling you or you see uniformed police. Help will come with search-and-rescue dogs. Do you understand me?"

She sighed and let her body go limp. She took a final breath of air, and the last thing she heard before the incoming tide rolled over her head was Daniel's reassuring voice.

"Trust me, babe. Go deep."

She grasped the rope, realized that she was no longer tied to the post, and pulled herself under. How long could she hold her breath? Not long. What would she do when—

Something shiny pierced the water in front of her. There was a muted *ping* but no pain. She did as Daniel had ordered. Panic clawed at her chest and throat. Blood drummed in her head.

His fingers touched her cheek. Gently Daniel inserted a reed between her lips, and instinctively she sucked. Sweet air filled her mouth and lungs. She grasped his arm, and squeezed it once.

Abruptly, silently, he was gone. She waited, mentally counting off the seconds as long as she could before taking hold of the reed with one hand and exhaling a second time.

Suddenly the water around her exploded in a burst of silver rain. A larger gun boomed off to the right. Clutching the precious reed in one hand, she dove for the mud bottom and kicked as hard as she could. Both ankles were free. She opened her eyes, but the water was too muddy to see more than a few inches in front of her, so she closed them again and swam for her life.

She struck something solid with her left hand, hard enough to hurt, grabbed it, and pushed herself off. She fought her way into the reeds, no longer able to swim, clawing, scrabbling until total exhaustion brought her to a halt, blocked by what seemed like an impossible barrier of foliage that towered over her.

Shots continued to ring out. The crack of the rifle— the louder boom of a larger-caliber weapon. She tried to pinpoint the location, but water and mud clogged her ears. She raised her head and gulped in mouthfuls of blessed air. Instantly mosquitoes and flies buzzed and circled, landing on her hair and exposed skin, but she paid them no heed.

Something croaked in the reeds—almost a coughing noise—and Bailey caught the flash of brown feathers as a bird nearly the size of a chicken scurried away into the morass. A duck quacked off to her left, and she realized that the shooting had stopped.

Bailey waited. Mosquitoes feasted on her cheeks and shoulders until she thought to scoop up handfuls of black mud and smear it over her skin. No-see-ums— tiny biting flies—crawled into the corners of her eyes. She clamped her lids shut and rubbed mud on them. She strained to hear another shot, Daniel's voice, anything but the *ribbit-ribbit* of frogs, the incessant drone of insects, and the honking of a vee of geese in the sky.

Nothing.

Bailey knotted her fingers around a handful of roots, rested her head on a handkerchief-sized patch of grass, and fell asleep. She didn't open her eyes again until she heard a helicopter hovering overhead.

There was a light. It seemed as bright as the moon. The searchlight swept through the marsh. Far off she heard barking. "Here! I'm here!" she cried, but her voice was lost in the whirl of helicopter blades. "Don't go!" she shouted. "Don't leave me here!"

The sound of the helicopter grew fainter. Gradually it faded.

"No." She sobbed. "No. Don't . . ."

She was alone once more. All around, the marsh seemed alive with the sighing of the wind, the gentle swish of water, the splash of fish, and the rustling of small creatures in the undergrowth. The mosquitoes renewed their assault, and she reapplied her mud armor, flexed her cramped fingers, and shivered in the cold.

Daniel hadn't come for her. Either Grace had killed him, or they'd killed each other. The truth was too bitter to face. She might as well have died there in the incoming tide as lie here and be nibbled to death, as she'd wished on Grace Catlin. If Daniel was alive, he would have found her by now.

Unless he needed her . . . Unless he lay somewhere, bleeding, perhaps looking up at the same stars and wondering why she hadn't come for him. Bailey struggled up out of the water, ripped off handfuls of leaves from the surrounding grasses, and rubbed her arms and legs until the worst of her shivering ceased.

She had to go back. The cabin was her point of reference. But she'd lost all sense of direction. How could she find her way if she didn't know north from south, or up-creek from down?

She strained to hear the sound of a boat motor, the bark of a dog. Daniel had promised dogs would find her, hadn't he? He wouldn't have lied to her. All she had to do was wait until morning, find her way back to the cabin and . . .

And what then? What if they'd given up the search? Moved on to another island without even—

"Bailey!"

Faint. So faint she might have imagined it. "Please,

God," she murmured, "let it be him. Let it be my Daniel."

A splash. Another fish? Was that what she'd heard? A deer swimming the creek? A wild dog? Were there wild dogs out here?

"Bailey! Where the hell are—"

"Daniel! Daniel!" she screamed. "I'm here. I'm here!"

She wiggled and squirmed through a clump of reeds, tripped and fell into water again. And when she splashed her way to the surface, she saw the most beautiful thing she'd ever seen in her life—Daniel Catlin illuminated in the moonlight, paddling toward her in some sort of tiny primitive boat.

She swam toward him. Every inch of her body ached; she was cold to the core of her bones, and she felt as though she were a hundred years old, but she'd never felt as strong or as lighthearted.

"Damn, babe, but you're a Tawes, all right. I've been hunting you for hours."

Then his arms were around her, and he was pulling her over the side into the wooden boat and covering her muddy face with kisses. "I thought I'd lost you, babe."

She squeezed him as tight as she could, heedless of the pain in her injured arm, no longer caring about the mud or the insect bites or the threat of Grace and her gun. She clung to Daniel, inhaling his earthy scent and savoring the feel of his warm body against hers. "You're not dead," she blubbered. "I thought you must be dead, or . . . or you would have found me."

"I told you to hide," he said between kisses, "not go Indian on me. Are you sure you're not a ghost, woman?"

She ran her hands over him, over his face and hair,

and felt him flinch. "You are hurt," she said. "Are you shot?"

"Nothing a few blood transfusions and a new heart won't fix."

"Daniel?"

"Shh, shh," he said, pulling her against him again. "I'm teasing you. I'll be fine. She hit me once in the left calf, grazed my head, and nicked my right upper arm in that first barrage. Damned bird. I thought I had the drop on her. I think I've got a bullet in my thigh too. Lucky for me she had the twenty-two and not the three-oh-eight."

"Grace . . . did you . . . Is she dead?"

"I hit her. I know I did. I found a blood trail. She's somewhere on this island, but I doubt if she's got enough left in her to come after us tonight. The police helicopters probably sent her into hiding."

"If she's alive."

He nodded. "If she's still alive." Gently he settled her in front of him on the bottom of the boat. "Careful. The dugout won't sink, even carrying two of us, but we don't want another dip tonight."

"Can you find your way out of here?" she asked, kissing his left arm and his bare chest.

"Out and home again, if some overanxious waterman doesn't shoot us before we reach Will's skiff. I talked to Cathy's husband, Jim. Every waterman on the bay is hunting for you, babe. And I don't doubt they've searched every inch of Tawes. By daybreak they'll be hunting the beach for our bodies."

"The authorities?"

"I imagine they're out, too. But it will be fishermen, crabbers, farmers, the people who know this place like the back of their hands who'll stand the best chance of finding us. Not just from Tawes, but from Deal, Crisfield, Smith, the Eastern Shore. We may have our own way of doing things, but we look after our own."

"I don't care if they do shoot me," she said, nestling against him. "All I want is to be warm and dry and . . ."

"And what?"

"Have you hold me."

"All you had to do was ask."

"Daniel?"

"Yes, babe."

"I'm asking."

The first rays of dawn were breaking over the trees when Daniel watched a medical technician wheel Bailey's limp body off the helicopter pad at Peninsula General in Salisbury and through the wide doors to the emergency room. He refused a wheelchair and followed them, clutching a wool blanket around his shoulders and ignoring the shouted questions of the TV reporter who'd appeared outside just as the helicopter was touching down.

"Can you verify that this is the kidnap victim?" the young black woman demanded. "What can you tell us about her injuries? Has the alleged perpetrator been apprehended?"

Two uniformed Maryland state troopers closed ranks behind Daniel. "There are questions we need to ask as soon as you . . ."

But Daniel's eyes remained fixed on the stretcher ahead of him, which was being wheeled through another set of double doors and into a curtained-off area. When he'd found her, Bailey had seemed in good shape, despite the bullet hole in her arm, but once they reached Will's skiff she'd collapsed. One minute he'd been stripping off her wet clothing to wrap her in a plastic tarp so she could warm up, and the next she'd seemed to go into shock. She'd slipped in and out of consciousness in the helicopter, and from what he could hear the medics saying, her vital signs weren't the best.

He could have felt better himself, but Bailey was all that mattered now, not finding Grace Catlin or seeing to his own injuries. Everything in the world centered on that one small woman behind the blue-striped curtain, and he didn't have the slightest intention of moving more than a few yards from her side until he was certain that she was in stable condition.

A dark-haired man in a white coat with a stethoscope hanging around his neck stepped from another cubicle. "Mr. Catlin?"

Daniel met the physician's gaze. "Go to hell, Lucas," he said quietly. "Get out of my way. Turn around and walk out, or I'll call that reporter in here and blow your cover so high you'll be spending the rest of your career counting counterfeit DVDs in Outer Mongolia."

"That's a bad attitude," Lucas answered, taking a step closer. "Not wise, not after what you—"

Daniel dropped the blanket and shoved the agent into the nearest open door, which fortunately led to a small toilet. He stepped inside and pulled the door shut behind them. "What the hell is going on? What are you doing here?"

"Tying up loose ends. You know how David hates loose ends."

"How many times do I have to tell you that I had nothing to do with Marshall's blackmail or his death?"

Lucas glared at him.

"I imagine that if you looked hard enough, you

could find a dozen people who wanted to be rid of him, including his own political party. If I found out about the drugs, who else knew?"

"Exactly. You're a loose cannon. What's to keep you from deciding to sully the senator's reputation, or to topple a house of cards and bring down—"

"To hell with them all," Daniel said. "Do you think I care about that now? I walked away from it, but I keep my word. Whatever I found out or didn't find out when I was part of the agency, it's buried as deep as Marshall."

"You keep going back to the senator, Danny. Why is that?"

"He made a deal with the devil, and his note came due. I didn't kill him."

"You took Marker's death to heart. And the woman's."

"Mallalai? Nobody forced her to strap a bomb to her waist and blow up that coffeehouse. I was wrong about her—about who she was and what side she was on. She was as much of a terrorist as Joe Marshall. The difference is, she did it for her 'holy war.' He did it for the money."

Lucas brushed aside the white lab coat, and Daniel caught a glimpse of the butt of a Glock tucked into his waistband. "Give me one reason why I shouldn't wrap this up here and now."

Daniel smiled. "Because I've left proof. Classified information. Names, dates. Pictures. Taped conversations. Members of Congress and other public servants who would be very unhappy if their dealings with the Afghani underworld became public. And they will. If anything happens to me—if I have heart attack, if I'm mugged by a crackhead on the street, if I go for a late-night swim and accidentally drown—it will all come out on the evening news. CNN, CNBC, FOX—"

"You're bluffing."

"Am I?" Daniel snatched the stethoscope off Lucas's neck and tossed it into the sink. "I'm no crusader. So long as no one pisses me off or decides to use Tawes for a missile base, your photo and biography stay out of the newspapers. Just make it clear that Bailey Elliott and my brother are strictly off-limits. Do we understand each other?"

A muscle twitched along Lucas's jawline. "I'll have to clear—"

"So, clear it. Make it all go away, Lucas. And you go with it. Because if I ever get the slightest notion that you're within a hundred miles of Tawes or of anyone I care about, you'll have your one moment of fame."

Lucas smiled with his mouth, but his eyes remained as expressionless as glass. "I told them that they were overreacting, that you could be reasoned with."

"It never was about Marshall's death, was it? It was always the coming election."

Lucas shrugged. "I wouldn't consider running for public office yourself, or writing a book. That would be . . . unwise."

"Nothing further from my mind. I'm just a country carpenter, a burned-out bureaucrat who saw a friend blown to bits and decided—"

"He didn't have the balls for this kind of work?"

"Let's just say I left for health reasons. I lost my appetite when I discovered that some of our most respected members of the U.S. Senate, and others within spitting distance of the Oval Office, are partners with some of the world's biggest drug-running warlords—"

Lucas touched his closed lips. "I think our conversation is over. We're satisfied that Marshall's death was accidental and that—"

"Was it true? Did he father Bailey Elliott?"

"There was a paternity blood test done several decades ago. Whatever else you might think of the senator, he wasn't stupid. He wouldn't have paid if he weren't the biological father."

"But Grace couldn't know that."

"No." Lucas smiled. "I'm certain she can't access the same information the agency does. It must have been a lucky guess on her part."

"And blackmailing Creed Somers or the other men involved wouldn't have been as lucrative."

"Exactly."

"Is your information accurate? Lab mistakes have been made before."

"Not those reinforced by DNA tests twenty months ago."

"How did . . . Never mind," Daniel said. "Our business is concluded, other than that small matter of Grace Catlin's eight-hundred-thousand-dollar bank account in the Caymans."

Lucas adjusted the hospital badge that identified him as John Lazzaro, MD. "The amount you mentioned is correct, but you're mistaken about the owner. That money's all in your name, Danny-boy."

"Drug money."

"It all spends the same, and as far as the agency is concerned, it doesn't exist."

"Why in my name?"

"Insurance that that conscience of yours doesn't cause us any more trouble."

"Blackmail?"

"Call it a severance package. You start talking, you're the first to go down. And you'll never live to see the inside of a federal prison."

"The money's mine? No strings?"

"All yours—with the agency's blessings."

Without another word, Daniel turned his back on Lucas and the agency and hurried back to take up his vigil outside the cubicle where Bailey's condition was being assessed. She was all that mattered now. He could sort out everything else later.

CHAPTER TWENTY-FIVE

"It's time we were getting you back to your bed, Mr. Catlin," the nurse said as she entered Bailey's hospital room.

Daniel glanced over his shoulder at her. "Give us a few more minutes."

"That's what you said thirty minutes ago. It's time for Ms. Elliott's blood work and . . ."

"Ten minutes." He flashed what he hoped was his most charming grin. "Please."

The nurse frowned and glanced at Bailey. "Ms. Elliott?"

"Five," Bailey bargained.

Daniel edged his wheelchair closer to Bailey's bed and took her free hand, the one not encumbered by the IV. Once they'd scheduled him for surgery late yesterday, he hadn't been able to convince a nurse that he had recovered enough to leave his room or that he needed to see Bailey more urgently than he needed another X-ray of his thigh.

The physician had cut a .22 from his calf and one from his arm. The bullet that had cut a furrow through his scalp wasn't a problem, and his surgeon decided that the safest course of action was to monitor his condition for another day before making a final decision on whether the last remaining bullet should be removed from his thigh.

It was nearly two o'clock in the afternoon, and Bailey was receiving pain medication as well as IV antibiotics for her bullet wound, the extensive insect bites, and the infection she'd picked up from swallowing so much marsh water. Her face, hands, and arms were swollen and bruised, and her hair was still a mess, but she looked beautiful to him.

"You scared the hell out of me," he said, picking up where they'd left off when the nurse had interrupted their conversation. "One minute you were joking with me, and the next I was trying to get a pulse. I was afraid you'd had a heart attack or you'd bled out on me."

"Sorry," she croaked. Her wan smile was genuine, but he could tell that she was in a lot of discomfort, despite her protests to the contrary. "I was cold. I'm still cold. I don't think I've ever been so cold."

"It must be the blood loss. You've got enough blankets on you for three people. You should have tried camping with me in midwinter in a tent in the mountains of Afghanistan. You'd have loved it."

" 'Just hide, Bailey,' " she teased in a hoarse whisper. " 'Hide until I come for you.' "

"I did, didn't I?"

"You damned well . . . took your time about it."

He stroked the back of her hand, then lifted it, turning it palm-up so that he could press his lips to the underside of her wrist. Her skin was fair, and the veins ran blue just below the surface. She seemed so small and fragile, so precious to him, that it was difficult to keep his own voice from cracking. "I told you, it was your fault that it took so long to find you. When I told you to hide from Grace, I didn't mean for you to hide so well that I couldn't find you."

Bailey closed her eyes and swallowed. "See if I can have some more ginger ale the next time Nazi nurse pops her head in. I'm so thirsty. I can't get the taste of mud out of my mouth."

"Most people don't try to eat it."

"Most people aren't tied to rotting posts to drown and be used for target practice." Her mood grew solemn. "She was frightening, Daniel. Grace wasn't just jealous of my mother. She wanted to be Beth—to steal her life. It was creepy."

"Not so creepy, if you consider what kind of family she came from. Sexual abuse, violence, alcohol. Her stepbrother's doing life in Virginia for stomping a man to death in Virginia Beach."

"She said things . . . awful things about her stepfather. Augie or Angie."

"Arney Murrain. He's dead, shot to death in an argument over possession of some stolen crab pots off Smith Island back when I was in college. Her mother froze to death in an alley outside a bar in Baltimore long before that."

"It's no excuse for killing all those people. It breaks my heart to hear of children being abused, but if they all became murderers . . ."

Daniel used a spoon to slip some ice chips between Bailey's swollen lips. "You're right. It's not an excuse." He grimaced. "But my brother will try to make it one. Matt's already hired an expensive criminal lawyer to defend her."

"When they find her."

"If they find her."

She swallowed a little of the melted ice. "Not Forest?"

"Matt asked. Forest turned him down flat. Said he wasn't qualified."

Bailey glanced at the ice pitcher. "More, please."

"As wily as Grace has proved herself, she might be getting a tan on some beach in the Caribbean by now."

"You don't think she'll get away with it, do you?" Bailey's eyes widened. "That she could come back to—"

"I highly doubt it. She's the chief suspect in Joseph Marshall's death, and that's not the kind of crime you walk away from. The world's not as big a place as it used to be."

"I thought his death was ruled an accident."

Daniel offered her a half smile. "That's the *official* version. In my experience, the authorities don't like loose ends when it comes to congressmen."

"Loose ends," she repeated softly. "Speaking of which, Elliott was here early this morning. He wanted to have me transferred to the hospital in Lewes to be closer to him. I thanked him for his concern and sent him packing."

"That's over, then?" he asked as lightly as he could manage.

She nodded. "I'm seriously considering having my legal name changed from Elliott."

"To?"

She smiled with her eyes. "I don't know yet. I was thinking about Tawes. It has a nice ring to it, don't you think?"

He kissed her wrist again. "Since you've brought up the subject, I don't think it's as good a choice for you as Catlin."

Bailey stiffened. "There are things we need to be absolutely certain of before—"

"I am certain of your biological father's identity."

Her lower lip quivered.

"I can tell you his name, and it isn't Catlin."

"Positively?"

"DNA confirmed. I just found out yesterday."

"How did you . . ." She pressed pale lips together. "Tell me."

"Your father was Senator Joseph Marshall, now deceased."

"And there can be no mistake about that?"

He shook his head. "The agency doesn't make mistakes of that sort."

She studied his face carefully for a moment. "I don't suppose you can tell me how you know this, or what the CIA has to do with my paternity? Why would they have cared or known in the first place?"

He put his finger to his lips. "Not here. Later. Just trust me. He was your father. Grace blackmailed him, but she never really knew the truth. He verified it years ago."

"But they haven't been doing DNA that long. How could he—"

"I can't give you all the details. Well, I could, but . . ."

"Oh . . ." She let out a long sigh. "But that means you and I aren't related."

"The Marshalls are relative newcomers to Tawes, no more than six generations. We can't be any closer than third cousins twice removed." He looked at her hand, stroking it, adding a playfulness to his voice. "So there's no reason why you and I can't—"

"One step at a time, all right? This has all been pretty sudden."

"Not for me, babe. I think I've been waiting all my life for you to come along."

Moisture sparkled in her bloodshot eyes. "But there was someone else, wasn't there? Someone in Afghanistan? A woman that you loved—"

"No." He shook his head. "Not loved. A woman that I was involved with . . . a woman that I might have come to love if we'd had the time to work on it. The Catlin boys may be a little slow to pick a wife, but when we marry, we do it for life. Mallalai, the girl I thought I could love . . ." His voice thickened. "She tried to lure me into a trap. A buddy of mine was going to meet us there, and something went wrong. A mechanical flaw in the wiring of the timer, I believe the report read."

"Daniel." She squeezed his hand. "You don't have to—"

"You have a right to know what happened. Mallalai and I were on different sides, and I didn't know it. If my taxi hadn't gotten stalled behind an overturned donkey cart, I'ves have been blown to bits along with George Marker, Mallalai, and a dozen or so innocent civilians. I'm not nursing a broken heart for her, Bailey. Regrets, maybe, but as Grace liked to say, it never could have worked out between us."

"And you think we might have a better chance? What about my being a mainlander?"

"You do come from good island stock. And if you're looking for work, I have friends in high places. Two cousins and an aunt on the Tawes school board. I just might be able to find you honest employment, if you'd like to stay on at—"

"You expect me to pick up my life, just like that, and move to an island in the Chesapeake?" She looked at him expectantly. "Live in that drafty old farmhouse on the water?"

"Someone has to feed and exercise Elizabeth's horses. It would be a shame to disrupt their lives. Horses are creatures of habit."

"And you're suggesting me? Or are you suggesting something more permanent between us?" she teased. "Are you asking me to move in with you? Or are you proposing marriage to me before you've discussed this with my great-uncle Will?"

Daniel groaned. "I was afraid you'd get around to that."

His cousin Jim Tilghman and Jim's wife, Cathy, had been at the hospital at nine o'clock sharp this morning to give them firsthand news from Johns Hopkins on Will and Emma. Apparently the two had already become celebrities at the shock trauma unit. Will had required several units of blood and survived a seven-hour surgery, with a second, less critical operation yet to come. Will's attending physician had told Jim that he wished he had the older man's heart and muscle tone, and he saw no reason why—with a few weeks of physical therapy—Will shouldn't make a full recovery. Emma remained in intensive care but was stable and sitting up, joking with nurses, and wanting to know when she would be discharged.

"I've been told that the Tawes men are devoted to the welfare of their women," Bailey said with a glint in her eye. "And Uncle Will does have the reputation of being someone you don't want as an enemy."

"True. He's a hard man, but a fair one. You do know that the Catlins and the Taweses have had a blood feud running for a couple hundred years? I might not be Will's first choice for a great-nephew-in-law."

Bailey chuckled. "And who's to say you'd be my first choice? I haven't agreed to anything . . . yet."

"Mr. Catlin." The nurse's stern tone brooked no more nonsense. "I really must insist."

Daniel made a shooing motion. "Just another minute."

"Please," Bailey said. "We were just getting to the good stuff, the part where Mr. Catlin explains exactly when he intends to finish the extensive repairs on my home."

"It might run a little past the time we first talked about," he said.

"And over budget?" Bailey laughed. "You contractors are all alike."

"Seriously," he told her. "I want you stay. With me."

"Uncle Will is going to need help for some time. And Emma can't possibly manage the shedding house alone for who knows how long. You couldn't run me off with a gunboat. And God knows, your sister-in-law tried."

The nurse took hold of Daniel's wheelchair and pulled him back toward the door. "Visiting hours are over for you, Mr. Catlin," she said firmly.

"I'm serious about that name change," Daniel said, as his fingertips slid from Bailey's. "You might consider Bailey Tawes Catlin. Officially."

"I might. Do you know a good lawyer I might consult about a prenup?"

"Not offhand," he said, as the nurse tugged him through the open doorway. "Give me time, and I might think of one."

"Time, Mr. Catlin," Bailey murmured, "unlike yesterday, is now something we both have."

* * *

Visiting hours were over for the public, and the evening shift change had taken place. Lights were dimmed on the surgical floor, and the only sounds Grace heard as she stepped off the elevator were the muted canned laughter of a late-night comedian's audience from a patient's TV and the buzz of a nurse's call bell at the far end of the hall.

Grace walked stiffly, the agony in her hip and shoulder dulled by the drugs she'd purchased from a Hispanic who offered third-world emergency surgery without questions for illegal immigrants in a trailer near Crisfield. He'd removed two bullets from her body with dirty hands and demanded far too much payment for his crude surgery and the prescription painkillers.

She'd given him exactly what he deserved and far more than he'd expected. She might be a pastor's wife and a genteel lady now, but she'd been Dot Widdowson's daughter, and she'd come up the hard way.

Grace had caught a glimpse of herself in a mirror, and she looked like hell. There was no polite way to put it. The cheap hair dye and overdone makeup did little to cover the effects of her ordeal, and white was not her color. Ivory, perhaps, but not white. The lab coat and loose blue trousers were stained, but the ID badge hanging around her neck would pass all but the most intense scrutiny, and the little container of vials, needles, and assorted items for patients' blood collection was real.

She slipped her hand gingerly into the roomy pocket of the elastic-waisted pants. The rude young man had told her that the barbiturate would put down a Great Dane, and that he'd seen the vet he worked for putting the medication into an IV. If it didn't work quickly enough, she'd removed the surgeon's pistol from a kitchen drawer on her way out of the trailer. He wouldn't need it again, and one way or another she intended to rid the world of Beth's brat and Daniel Catlin tonight. She'd have to find a way to deal with Will Tawes another day, but perhaps he was already dying and just hadn't had the good sense to get it over with yet.

She waited until the woman at the nursing station answered a phone call before walking briskly past, pausing to check her clipboard and read the information on the patient listing posted on the wall to find the correct room number. Elliott, yes—Elliott, B. And luck was with her tonight. There was only one name listed for that room.

Grace turned back toward Bailey's room. She'd reached the open doorway and was about to enter when the elevator bell sounded and the doors opened. A man in a wheelchair rolled out into the hall. She glanced at his face, and for a moment their eyes met.

Grace felt the shock of instant recognition.

"Stop! Help! Call security!" Daniel shouted as he leaped out of the wheelchair.

Grace dropped the little basket. Glass shattered on the tile, and blood splattered. She ran down the hall.

"Call the police!" Daniel yelled as he ran into Bailey's room.

Grace took the first turn to the left. Another bank of elevators marked STAFF ONLY caught her eye. She limped toward it, dragging a leg that didn't seem to want to support her. She hit a fire alarm on the wall before stepping into an open elevator that was surely provided by God, certain that in the ensuing panic she could make good her escape.

Only a few minutes later, trembling with pain, Grace snatched a walker from a first-floor storage closet and made her way out of the closest door. She'd left her stolen Jeep only a block away on a side street. Surely, masses of terrified patients and staff would be pouring from the hospital. She could already hear the wail of a fire siren in the distance. "Bitch!" she cried bitterly. "Rotten little slut of a whore!"

She was sweating heavily. The pain was excruciating as she forced herself off the curb and into the street. All she had to do was to keep moving. Lift the walker. Take a few steps at a time. Stop to rest. Take a few more steps. Out of the corner of her eye she could see the shadowy outline of a vehicle. Alarms were going off in the hospital behind her. People rushed past.

Horns blared. A woman cried out. Grace kept walking. A hundred feet more and she'd be safe. All she had to do was get to the green Jeep and—

Abruptly the roar of an engine broke through her concentration. She looked up to see a black Expedition accelerating down the street toward her. She threw her up her arms, waving to let the driver see her. She was wearing a white coat. It wasn't possible that he didn't see—

Grace's scream ended in a thud. Pain greater than anything she'd ever experienced radiated through her body. For an instant she felt herself flying, and then she slammed into the pavement. Agony. The grating of bone against bone. Excruciating. She tried to draw breath but a crushing weight bore down on her.

Tires screeched as the SUV squealed to a stop.

Grace tried to call for help. Blood poured in streams from her head and face, clogging her nose and mouth. She gasped for air. Tires screeched again. She forced one eye open, and through a curtain of blood saw the Expedition turning around in the street.

Help was coming. Someone would come to save her. Blood filled her throat, choking off her final scream as the Expedition drove over her sprawled body, crushing her head beneath the oversize tires.

From Bailey's window, Daniel watched the black vehicle bump over the remains of the walker, turn the corner, and speed away into the night with the lights off. He didn't need to ask who had been at the wheel. Hadn't Lucas told him he'd come to tie up loose ends? The agency couldn't risk the possibility that Grace would go to trial, that her connection to Joe Marshall and his drug money might come out.

"Grace? You're certain it was Grace?" Bailey called weakly.

Daniel stood and made his way unsteadily to her bed, sat on the edge, and drew her into his arms. "It's all right, Bailey," he murmured into her hair. "You don't have to worry about her anymore. I promise you. It's over."

"It's over? They caught her?"

"You're safe now. She'll never harm you or anyone else again." *In this world or the next*, he thought. "Never, never again."

Three weeks later, Daniel and Jim Tilghman lifted Will out of the wheelchair and into the big cushioned wicker chair on Emma's back porch. "Are you all right?"

"Hell, no, I'm not all right. Do I look all right? I've

been kidnapped, and I'm being held by a bunch of young fools," Will grumbled.

"Did you expect Bailey to run back and forth between her place and yours when she's still recovering herself?" Emma asked. "Use some common sense, Will Tawes. Think of somebody but yourself for a change."

"Shut up. I don't want to talk to you. I'm here. I'll pay whatever you charge for room and board for two days, and then I'm going the hell home. And anybody who doesn't like it can—"

Bailey kissed him on the forehead. "A week, Uncle Will. One week, and then you can either come out to the farmhouse with Daniel and me or go home."

"I don't suppose there's a decent cup of tea to be had in this den of iniquity," Will grumbled. "Something that doesn't come in a tea bag?"

"I'll think I can find some Earl Grey," Bailey offered.

"I'll see about that crab soup. If there's one thing we don't want, it's for that milk to come to a boil." Emma held the door open for Bailey. "Come on, honey. Your uncle will be fine out here with the men. He's only trying to save his pride by blustering like the old windbag he is."

"I'll get your tea," Bailey promised, "just the way you like it."

Daniel looked at her anxiously. "Are you sure you're not doing too much? You know the doctor said you were supposed to—"

"I'm fine, Daniel. I'll get you a cup, too. Jim?"

"No, thanks. Cathy's got supper on, and I'm late. She hates it when she goes to the trouble of making a hot meal and I don't show up on time. Of course, her meat loaf isn't the greatest, but it will have lots of peppers and onions. I'll stop by tomorrow to see if there's anything I can do for you, Will."

"Looking after my dogs and those horses, that's a godsend. Don't think I don't appreciate it."

Daniel eased painfully into the straight-backed chair next to Will, glanced at him, and then watched Jim stride around the house. Through the screen door Daniel could hear the two women clinking dishes inside.

"This was a bad idea," Will grumbled.

"It wasn't mine. It was Bailey's," Daniel reminded him. "And you know how she is."

"I'm beginning to see how she is, and I'm not sure I like it. Interfering with a man's life and livelihood. Pushing and prodding for me to make peace with that . . . that Emma after all these years. She doesn't deserve it. I almost killed her, you know. Should have. Cow-bellied parody of God-knows-what. We're never going to be friends. That's not going to happen. But I'm not going to hunt her down and shoot her, if that's what you're afraid of."

Daniel nodded. "I can see how you might feel that way. But Emma . . . If she hadn't told me where to look for Grace, we wouldn't have Bailey alive."

"There's another wrong that's eatin' at me. Has everybody lost their reason? Your brother bringing Grace Catlin's body back here to bury in the same churchyard as my Beth and the others after what she done?"

"She has to face a sterner judge," Daniel said quietly.

"Well, thanks be for that." Will leaned back in the chair and rested his head.

"While I've got a minute alone with you, there's something I've been wanting to ask you."

"You know I've always treated you more like a son

than a friend, but if you're asking me for permission to marry my Bailey, then you'd—"

"No." Daniel glanced in to see Bailey following Emma into the big pantry.

"It's got to be in there," Emma said. "Did you look behind the brown sugar canister?"

"No, that's not it," Daniel said, leaning close to Will. "It's something else, something that's been nagging at me. Joe."

Will scowled. "What about him? He's in hell, same as Grace, if there is a hell."

"Did you kill him?"

"What kind of question is that?"

"I can't help wondering how you could have lost your granddad's old shotgun. You thought so much of it. You knew Joe was Bailey's father, didn't you?"

Will nodded. "He said as much when he leveled that fancy gun of his on me. Said he wasn't paying anymore."

"He accused you of blackmailing you."

"Called me a thief to my face."

"Why didn't you tell Bailey who fathered her?"

Will sighed. "If I did, I'd have to say more, things you should never say to a woman. Better leave what's in the past in the past."

"That you shot her father?"

"Never said that, Daniel Catlin. Never did say it, never expect to."

"Did Joe take a shot at you?"

Will nodded. "Two barrels." He shook his head. "A man never should look for courage in a bottle. It makes his hands unsteady, makes him apt to miss what he fires at."

"You didn't think you could tell what happened, explain that it was self-defense?"

Will frowned. "You try it, if you're fool enough. A rich, powerful man like Joe Marshall—a U.S. by-God senator—and a man that's spent time in prison for a crime he didn't do. How much justice did I get from the courts before? And how much do you think I'd find tomorrow if I needed it?" He scowled. "You got a problem with that?"

"No problem. It's a shame about your grandfather's gun, though."

"It is. I put some store by that gun." The older man sighed. "But I put a sight more on what's fair, and I figured, in the end, it was a good trade. Granddaddy would approve. He might say, 'Will, you bought your own justice with that old shotgun.'"

"He might say that," Daniel agreed.

"Hot tea coming up," Bailey called.

"Let me give you a hand with those cups," Daniel said, rising to go to her. He stopped, met Will's gaze for an instant, and nodded. "I think you're right. Sometimes the old ways and old sayings are true. Island justice."

The Warrior

JUDITH E. FRENCH

In ancient times, tales were told of fierce warriors and the brave women who risked everything to love them. Alexander is one such man—the only son of Alexander the Great, he has a destiny to fulfill. But in the heat of the Egyptian desert, a beautiful slave girl named Kiara calls to his deepest desires. And for once, Alexander wants nothing more than to defy expectation and follow this willful beauty around the world.

But deception surrounds the lovers on all sides. From the great pyramids of Egypt to the misty hills of Ireland, history waits the one man brave enough to seize it. And the one woman bold enough to claim . . . *The Warrior*.

Judith E. French
AT RISK

He has a memento from each of them. Just little things to bring back memories of the shrieks, the blood. What will he take from the Professor, he wonders? She will be best of all, isolated in her old farmhouse by the edge of the swamp. She has no idea which of the men pursuing her she can trust—the handsome grad student, the bad-boy ex-boyfriend, the wheelchair-bound former police officer. She has no idea that while she fantasize about sultry nights and twisted sheets, very different plans are being made and studied in intimate detail. She has no idea she is at risk. But all that is about to change

CHARLOTTE MACLAY

MAKE NO PROMISES

Taylor Travini is used to roughing it. She and her brother are experienced travelers. But now Terry has vanished in Chile, and in searching for him Taylor has found a world of trouble. Offering to help is a stranger in a grungy Santiago bar.

Rafe Maguire has seen too much. His years with the Army Rangers hardened him, turned him mercenary. But though his hands are lethal weapons, Rafe can never snuff his instinct to protect.

An independent beauty and a war-weary veteran, both Taylor and Rafe have a lot to learn, including the discovery that life isn't worth living when you can...

MAKE NO PROMISES
